For Mum

My first fan

1

SATURDAY 27 JANUARY 2018

I've never been in trouble before. Not the sort of trouble that brought me here. Freshly painted, stark white walls surround me; their toxic scent lingers in the air. A fluorescent glow from strip lights so dazzling they must be there to desensitise the occupants. Everything is white or chrome, like I'm on the set of a futuristic movie. I swing my legs, which dangle over the edge of the bed, not quite reaching the floor. I do this for a minute to keep warm. Despite the blanket around my shoulders, I can't help but shiver. It's late and they didn't bring my jacket. I guess it's been taken away as evidence.

The woman in front of me is standing too close, hot breath on my arm. It makes me squirm and I fight the urge to yank my hand away from her grip. She's holding it like I'm a china doll, fragile and easily broken. I dislike the invasion of my personal space. It's something I've learnt to tolerate over the years. I was never a big fan of being touched, shrinking away if someone brushed past me or stood too close on public transport. I'm not a hugger either – no one was in the house where I grew up. After tonight, I can't imagine I'll let anyone touch me again.

Her name is Doctor Joyce Hargreaves, she told me as we entered the victim examination room. Her job, she said, was to collect evidence from me, which is why she was wearing a paper suit, so there wouldn't be any cross-contamination. She hasn't picked up on my anxiety, the tremor in my fingers; she's too busy. Brows furrowed, eyes focused as she peels the plastic bag away from my bloodied hand to collect scrapings from my skin and beneath my fingernails. The tool she uses makes me nervous.

'Is that a scalpel?' my voice barely a whisper.

'No, it's a scraper. Don't worry, it won't hurt. This is just so I can make sure we collect any skin cells that may be buried underneath the tips of your nails. I'm afraid I'll have to give them a trim in a minute too.' She wields the scraper with care and it's true, it doesn't hurt. Physically I'm okay, except my throat is on fire and the ringing in my ears is deafening, timed perfectly with the throbbing of my face. I have a feeling I might feel worse once the adrenaline leaves my system.

When she finishes with my hands, she pulls the fallen blanket back over my shoulders and offers a kind smile as she pushes her glasses up her nose. I can see strands of greying hair trying to escape by her ear, exposed beneath the coverall hat. She wears no jewellery and her face is free of make-up. Was she on duty or has she been called out of her bed to attend to me? Would we recognise each other in different circumstances? Probably not, I must be one of many people that pass through this room every day.

Joyce delicately inserts each of the specimens into small tubes before labelling them to be sent for analysis. I don't know why? I've told them what happened. Soon she'll want to examine me thoroughly. Internally. Until there are no more swabs left to be taken.

She glances at me, knowing what is coming, what she must ask me to do. Her eyes are full of pity. I must look a mess. Dried blood on my face and chest is beginning to flake away, like charred skin falling into my lap. My cheek is puffy and the vision poor on my left side. I wish I could stop shivering. They said it's shock and provided me with a mug of hot, sweet tea after the ambulance checked me over. They wanted to make sure the blood I am doused in isn't mine. It isn't.

2

SUNDAY 24 SEPTEMBER 2017

The attack lasted just seven life-changing minutes. The same amount of time it took the tattooist to ink my skin earlier this year or the minutes I've spent in a supercharged sunbed. It was strange how the same amount of time could feel so different. I was no longer someone who thought bad things happened to other people. How many times had I walked home from clubs alone in the early hours of the morning, still buzzing from the evening's events, oblivious to my surroundings. Too desperate to climb into bed to stand in line for a taxi. Those were the nights I made it to my destination unharmed. I never realised how lucky I was.

The plan was to catch the 8.55 a.m. train from Carshalton to London Victoria, which would get me in to meet my oldest friend, Jane, at 9.30 a.m., outside WH Smith's. We'd been to high school together, bonded over our mutual love of Eminem and stayed friends ever since. Work had been crazy for both of us and it had been a month since I'd seen her last. As a nurse she'd been doing loads of overtime at St George's hospital in Tooting, saving as much money as she could to go travelling next year.

We'd planned a joint birthday celebration, my twenty-fifth had passed in August and hers was coming up in mid-October. I'd booked tickets for the London Eye at half past ten, which is why we were keen to meet up early. It wasn't far to go: a tube up to Green Park and then back down to Waterloo. I'd been once before, with my ex-boyfriend, Dean, but it was Jane's first time. As soon as I'd told her about the amazing views across the city, she'd been desperate to book a 'flight'. We'd chosen to have lunch afterwards at the Rainforest Café at Piccadilly Circus, which looked exotic and fun. Choosing the restaurant took up most of our half-an-hour phone call as we discussed our plans for the day.

I'd been looking forward to our trip all week but had slept through my alarm so was in a rush to get to the station, a twenty minute walk away. It was becoming a bit of a habit, that I'd lie awake at night worrying about things, usually about how I was going to pay the bills. I'd end up watching the sun rise before passing out and waking in a panic. Thankfully, I'd chosen my outfit the night before, so after my five minute shower, I threw on a white and orange striped shirt with jeans and headed out of the door. It was going to be a beautiful day for our 'flight', there wasn't a cloud in the sky.

I cut through Grove Park, passing a dog walker on my way in. An old boy with a white and tan terrier who tipped his cap at me and smiled. They both seemed to be enjoying their early-morning stroll around the park. All was peaceful; the Sunday bustle didn't normally start until around half nine. It was usually my favourite time of day for a jog, before everyone else stirred from their lazy mornings.

Digging my headphones out of my bag, I selected a playlist on my phone and headed across the field. It was a large expanse of open space, where children's football matches were played on Saturday mornings. Two rusty goal-posts adorned each end of the pitch. Black crows gathered at the centre spot, feasting on what looked like a leftover kebab. To the left of the field stood a children's playground, fenced in, with brightly coloured swings and slides. On the right was a small yellow café with a mini crazy golf course at the front. The exit to the park was at the far end, two streets away from the station. Shaving around five minutes off my journey.

I felt buoyant, the sun shone overhead, and above the volume of Bastille's 'Pompeii', I could hear the birds chirping in the surrounding trees. As I neared the café, I could see its grey anti-vandalism shutters were down, covered in tags of local graffiti artists. A sign on the front indicated it didn't open until 10 a.m. I checked my watch. It was 8.35 a.m. Bugger, I'd hoped to grab a coffee for my journey as I'd missed breakfast.

Gravel underfoot shifted behind me, but before I could turn, I was slammed into the wall of the café. Stunned, I twisted my head and caught a glimpse of a black wool balaclava and a flash of ice blue eyes over my shoulder. Cold and emotionless. My breath caught in my throat and my limbs froze. I couldn't scream, I couldn't breathe. Pressed up against the yellow faded bricks, unable to move. The only sound I could hear was my heart beating in my ears.

A small, sharp penknife waved in front of my eyes, reflected the morning sun and blinded me momentarily.

'Scream and I'll cut you,' he whispered just behind my ear, his breath rippling strands of my hair. A sweet citrus smell mixed with coffee emanated from him. His voice was unnerving; soft and non-threatening, yet in complete control.

He gripped my shoulder and shoved me a few steps to the rear of the café. I resisted, legs rigid, stumbling over the contents of my bag which had spilled out onto the ground during the scuffle. The designer purse Jane bought me last birthday lay amongst the dirt. It registered with me that money wasn't what he'd come for and a feeling of dread seeped into my body. Behind the building was a narrow concrete walkway, hidden in the shadows and shielded from the view of the field and path ahead. The back door to the building was old, its green paint flaking off, a tiny padlock entrusted with keeping thieves out. Next to it was a large black lidded industrial bin, surrounded by cigarette ends. It smelt of chips and oil and attracted the flies.

Terrified to look back, but the fear of not knowing greater, I swivelled my head, getting another glimpse of his face. I couldn't see much, the majority covered with the balaclava, his lip turned up into a snarl. Hostile, close-set eyes stared at me with an emptiness that made my blood run cold. A flash of anger passed across them before he smashed my face back to the wall, scraping my cheek. I let out a whimper, a metallic taste pooled in my mouth.

He dragged me over to the bin, pressing his body against mine, using his weight to keep me still. His right hand resting on the lid, the knife on display. A silent warning to comply. I could hear him panting and felt the length of his erection pushed against me. Adrenaline and panic coursed through my system and the thud in my chest hammered my ribcage like it wanted out. My eyes began to well.

'Please. Don't,' I wailed, trying to work up the courage to

scream, but he pushed against me harder, enjoying the power.

'I know you want it.'

My legs crumpled like they no longer belonged to me. My eyes strayed to the ground; he wore plain black trainers and jogging bottoms, gathered at the ankle. I prayed someone would walk past or a dog would find us, sniff us out and raise the alarm.

My right arm was wrenched behind my back, almost pulling my shoulder out of its socket. Pushing his cock into my hand, he forced my fingers to wrap around it. My stomach plummeted to the floor and I fought the urge to urinate. His erection felt strange in my palm, not natural. Was he wearing a condom?

In a split second, I chose to be compliant. I was too frightened to scream or fight. I just wanted to live through whatever was happening to me. Tears ran down my cheeks as he groaned in satisfaction, moving my hand back and forth to pleasure himself until I'd got the rhythm. I could feel my throat closing up, the bile rising. Eyes focused on the brickwork, anywhere but my hand.

Suddenly he'd had enough foreplay and strong arms reached around my waist to the front of my jeans, where fingers fumbled to pull open my button and zip before he wrenched them down my thighs.

'Be a good girl,' he panted, the knife inches from my eye.

I swallowed hard and managed a strange squeak of submission. The cold realisation of what lay ahead dawning on me, powerless to stop it.

'No. Please.' I begged.

Grabbing my hair, he forced me down, over the top of the bin, the lid compressing my chest, and kicked my feet as far apart as my jeans would allow. I felt the rip of my knickers and tried to cry out, but no sound came. He groaned as his gloved hand thrust between my legs, exposing my vulva. He spat on his hand and wiped himself before roughly pushing his erection inside me, penetrating my core. The sudden burning sensation from below was excruciating, firing all my senses and nerves to red alert. Biting on my hand, I squeezed my eyes tight as warm urine dribbled down my legs. Violated in the worst possible way, I focused on the rhythmic shuffle of the bin across the concrete ground, inching forward with every thrust as my hip bones slammed remorselessly into it. The intensity of his rhythm grew. Each thrust getting harder and deeper, skin slapping against skin. My breath being sucked and pushed out of me. As his grunting pitched higher, he pulled on my hair, snapping my head back, and with one final thrust his body went rigid.

Finally, his body slackened with the release and then his weight lifted. My ribs felt crushed, I was sure the imprint of the bin would be visible on my chest. Seconds later, I heard the elastic of his waistband snap back into place. Leaning over, he used the thumb of his gloved hand, still wielding the knife, to stroke my cheek. My stomach heaved at the intimacy. He'd just violated me, yet he touched my face like we were a couple in love.

'You are perfect,' he whispered, his breathing laboured.

I tasted bile and fought hard not to vomit. I remained, splayed out over the bin, exposed to the elements like a rag doll, too distraught at what had just taken place to move. In that moment, I just wanted to curl up and die.

Seconds stretched out in front of me. I could hear no background noise at all. It was deathly quiet. I waited for something, a fist or a blade slicing my skin. Something to end my ordeal, but it never came. Was it over? A hollow silence filled the gap. I hesitated, unsure what to do.

After what seemed like the longest time my legs gave way and I slid to the floor; daring to turn around, to face what was coming. When I did, the space was empty. He was gone.

3

SUNDAY 28 JANUARY 2018

I've been moved to a cell. Names of former occupants and unimaginative insults have been scratched into the walls. It's a waiting room, a holding pen. There's a weird odour, a combination of piss and bleach, irritating my throat. I've been processed through the system and all evidence stripped from my body. Clothes were peeled away and dropped onto the sheet on which I stood to catch every fibre, every hair, every skin cell. Before moving to a shower, where they collected the diluted blood that ran off my skin. Photos were taken of my injuries, then fingerprints and a saliva swab before I got my phone call. The paper suit I have been given to replace my clothes does little to ward off the chill in the air. Although they let me keep the blanket. The suit crackles when I move, so I'm trying to remain still. I like the quiet.

Minutes feel like hours. The bench is hard, and my backside numb. I can add it to my list of complaints. My left eye is almost swollen shut now and my cheekbone feels like it's pulsating, a constant internal thud, like the bang of a drum.

I'm glad I took my contact lenses out before it got too painful to touch. I got rid of them before the ambulance arrived.

It's impossible to get comfortable, my neck hurts in every position I try, the bruised skin tender. I curl my legs against my chest, with my chin on my knees, trying to keep the warmth in. I'm being watched. There's a camera in the corner of the ceiling and I lower my head for a while, so my face is out of view. There's no chance of sleep, not with fluorescent lights flickering and the noise. Shouting radiates through the walls. The custody suite is busy tonight as I guess they are every weekend; the drunk and disorderly, the domestics and assaults. I hear the banging of metal on metal and the constant clicking of viewing hatches.

I need to stay calm; if I tell the truth I'll be fine. Part of the truth anyway. It must be about two in the morning by now, my eyes are stinging. Tears blur my vision, but I let them come. I am the victim here. They'll want to speak to me soon. Make me go through the events of tonight. I don't think they quite know what to do with me yet, but we'll see how switched on they are. I'm not going to make it easy for them. How long will it be before someone connects the dots?

* * *

Sunday 24 September 2017

I tried to stand, but my knees gave way and I hit the ground like a puppet whose strings had been cut. Pulling myself up on the handle of the back door of the café, I gingerly edged my jeans up my legs, repositioning my knickers that were almost torn in two. Legs damp with urine but not obvious on the dark denim. My striped shirt, dirty and torn at the shoulder. A couple of buttons had come undone and my fingers fumbled to do them up, covering my bra. I felt bruised and sore, the denim crotch grating my skin with each step. Everything moved in slow motion as I made my way around the side of the café to find my bag on the ground untouched. I gathered my purse, phone and other items, stuffing them inside before stumbling back across the field, the way I'd come no more than ten minutes before. My attacker nowhere to be seen. The park empty, the only noise the squawking of the crows still devouring their breakfast.

It was surreal, like I'd had too much to drink. In my head I wanted to run as fast as I could, get away, but my limbs wouldn't respond. They moved sluggishly across the field and back to the road. I drifted out onto the residential street. A couple of cars drove past and a woman across the road trotted along, she looked as though she'd been to the petrol station for milk. Her blue carrier bag swinging at her side. I stopped and stared at her. Hoping she would notice me, see the tears streaming down my cheeks, blurring my vision but she didn't even turn. Over my left shoulder, I caught a man with springer spaniel slipping into the park. He passed without so much as a second glance. I wanted to scream 'where the fuck were you when I needed you?' The injustice of it burned in the pit of my stomach. It was all so normal out here. I'd been violated, just feet away, and the world hadn't stopped. Everyone just carried on.

Clinging to a lamp post, I vomited bile on the kerb. I couldn't think straight. Where could I go? What should I do?

I stumbled towards home in a daze. The ten minute journey seemed to take forever, and no one stopped to ask if I was all right. I unlocked the door to my flat and fell across the threshold. The relief overwhelming. Pulling myself up to double-lock the door, I was finally safe. Across the hall was the bedroom of my lodger, Ben. I knocked on it. When he didn't answer straight away, I banged until the door flew open. He stood there in tattered football shorts, yawning.

'What the fuck, Eve?' Rubbing his eyes, he hitched up his waistband, sitting precariously low on his hips, before focusing on my face. 'Jesus Christ, what happened to you? Are you hurt? Your face!'

I couldn't speak of it. Not yet.

He looked me up and down, the front of my shirt blackened from the bin, a gaping hole at the shoulder. Face tear-stained and bloody; I must have looked a fright.

'Can I have a joint?' I mumbled.

Ben smoked pot occasionally – medicinally, according to him. He'd dislocated his knee a couple of years ago playing football and every now and then it would get inflamed. Apparently, it was better than any ibuprofen you could buy over the counter, for soothing the flare-ups.

He disappeared into his dark room, a musty smell emanated from within and I stepped back. My stomach threatened to heave, but then he was back at the door handing me a perfectly rolled joint. I was relieved, I wouldn't have had the first clue how to roll one.

'Can I get you anything? Do you want me to call someone?' he asked.

'I just need to be alone,' I mumbled, unable to look him in the eyes.

Ben nodded, his face full of concern as he watched me head into the bathroom.

I had to remove every trace of him from me. I filled the bath and double-checked the door was locked before peeling away my clothes, discarding the pile in the corner behind the washing basket. They weren't to be washed, they were to be burnt, forever tainted. Blood spotted the crotch of my jeans, and I sobbed, unable to tear my eyes away.

The water was as hot as I could stand it. Lowering into the heat, the stinging from below making me wince, I scrubbed until my skin was raw. Erasing every trace of him. But no matter how hard I scoured, the soiled feeling remained.

I flinched as water splashed my face. I'd forgotten about my cheek. Grabbing Ben's shaving mirror from the sink, I inspected the damage. My cheek was crusted with dried blood and dirt. Tinged yellow from the painted bricks. It hurt like hell but was only a graze. I dabbed at the wound with a flannel until it appeared cleaner and lay submerged as the water grew tepid. I could hear my phone ringing inside my bag; for the fourth time. It had to be Jane, wondering where I was, she would be waiting at the station for me, confused as to why I hadn't arrived. I needed to answer her.

I climbed out of the bath and took my bag into my bedroom. Leaving my towel on the floor, I shuffled into my pyjamas. The familiar smell of washing powder comforting. Unable to stop shivering, I wrapped my duvet around myself. Digging my phone out of my bag and brushing off the debris, I saw I had eight missed calls and two texts. All from Jane. I sent her a message.

`Have to cancel. Attacked on the way to the station. Can't talk now. Will ring later. x`

Twenty seconds later, my phone was ringing persistently again. Jane would have read that and be in a panic, but I couldn't talk about it, not yet.

I lit the joint Ben had given me and inhaled, coughing it

out. I never smoked pot, but I wanted to be out of it. I couldn't deal with what had happened. I held the smoke in, so the buzz came fast, and let myself drift into oblivion. I needed to feel numb. I smoked half, staring at my book collection in a jumble on the floor. Colours and titles blurred into each other. I must get some shelves. Who was I kidding? I barely knew one end of a drill from the other.

I lay down and switched off my phone. I wanted to drift away and forget it all. I knew I had to call the police, report there was a sexual predator on the loose, but it would have to wait.

The balaclava crept into my dream. His soulless eyes penetrated me, lip curled into a smirk, mocking my terror...

When I woke, there were a few blissful seconds of ignorance until my cheek throbbed and the memory of this morning crashed in. The room was dim. What time was it? Had I slept all day? My stomach groaned; I'd not eaten since yesterday. All was quiet, Ben must have already left for work. His job as a Security Manager involved working twelve hour shifts on rotation, often at the weekend.

I went into the kitchen, surprised to see the time on the oven, it was seven in the evening. I prayed there would be milk in the fridge. I badly needed a cup of tea; my lips were beginning to crack.

The smell of food hung in the air, making me salivate. Ben had cooked. I peeked in the microwave and saw he had left me a bowl inside with a note – 'Call me'. He was the best. Pesto pasta, a little congealed, but I was so hungry I'd eat anything. I wolfed it down and the hunger pains subsided. Normally I was the tidy one out of the two of us, but I left my plate in the sink. Ben wouldn't mind, not today. I scribbled 'THANKS' in large capital letters on the note before making tea and returning to the sanctuary of my room. Safe and warm in there, cocooned in my duvet, I smoked the rest of the joint, knowing it would help me sleep some more.

What would I do tomorrow? There was no way I was going into the office. I worked as an assistant in a small marketing department of a distribution company called Drive. It was my job to organise photo shoots and write press releases. I enjoyed it, especially the creativity it allowed, but the thought of going into work filled me with dread. I could ask Ben to ring in for me in the morning, but it would mean I'd have to tell him what had happened, and I wasn't sure I could. I knew I had to tell the police. If he attacked someone else, I'd never forgive myself.

4

SUNDAY 28 JANUARY 2018

When they come to take me to interview I've lost all sense of time. How long has it been since I was cautioned? A portly sergeant had stood at the front desk and held my forearm as he spoke. He had a lisp and spittle flew from his mouth as he struggled to enunciate each word. I averted my eyes to the clock behind the desk which read 1.05 a.m.

'Rose Harding, I am arresting you on suspicion of grievous bodily harm. You do not have to say anything. But it may harm your defence if you do not mention when questioned, something which you later rely on in court. Anything you do say may be given in evidence.' He looked me over, his mouth pulled into a grimace. My slight frame, my eye, the bruises. I know I look weak. It's going to be my advantage.

Before I was taken to the custody suite, I was offered legal representation and within twenty minutes a skinny man with wire-rimmed glasses and a bald head knocks on the heavy door. He's let in, introduces himself as Terry Deacon and asks me to run through the events of last night. As I tell him, he barely glances in my direction, there's no flicker of emotion as I explain what I've been through. No doubt he's heard it all before; I'm just another legal-aid case, a tick in the box. He flicks through a file of papers and advises me to respond 'no comment' to all questions.

We sit in the interview room and the detective switches the recorder on. He is heavy-set, I would guess in his late fifties, with unkempt ash blond hair, and looks like he has just rolled out of bed. Shirt crumpled, with a tie sat clumsily to the left. Someone should tell him; I'm surprised his colleague hasn't. A female detective sits beside him, she looks to be in her late thirties and in stark contrast is immaculately presented. Her crisp blouse collar, ice white and starched, is standing to attention. Chestnut hair pulled back into a tight bun, stiff with hairspray. I sense she has something to prove. She smiles at me and when she does her face softens as she slides the coffee I was offered across the table. I need it to stay awake now the adrenaline has left my system.

'Right, Rose, I think we're ready to start.' The male detective clears his throat and announces the date and time, occupants of the room – he is Detective Gary Hicks and she is Detective Sarah Becker – as well as stating the recording is taking place at Sutton police station.

'Call me Eve,' I say. No one calls me Rose now, not since my father died.

Hicks nods his head. 'Eve, I'm afraid there have been some developments since you were brought to the station. Unfortunately, Mr Shaw has died as a result of his injuries, so we have to re-arrest you on a different charge. Do you understand?'

I hang my head. I don't want my eyes to betray me, so I nod.

'For the purpose of the recording, Eve has nodded her

head,' Becker says. She lays a cold hand upon my wrist, I flinch but meet her gaze. Her eyes flash a glimpse of compassion and mine brim with tears on cue.

I'm read my rights for the second time.

'I'm arresting you on suspicion of murder...' And so, it begins.

* * *

Monday 25 September 2017

The police tapped so lightly on the front door, I didn't hear them at first. Floorboards creaking on the landing outside caught my attention, and my skin prickled. Opening the door a crack, I saw the uniform and my shoulders relaxed. It was early in the morning, around seven. I'd tossed and turned all night, images of him invading my thoughts. Was he getting ready to go out and find another victim? My conscience berated me for not reporting it yesterday. Eventually, I gave in and made the call to the police. They arrived within the hour and two female officers sat at the kitchen table drinking tea. One of the officers, a redhead with freckles, wore the uniform. The other, with blonde shoulder length hair, was higher ranking and wore a smart navy trouser suit. I sat opposite them, smoking one of Ben's cigarettes from a packet left on the kitchen table. Trembling hands betrayed my composure. I didn't want to relive it all over again but made sure my voice remained steady as I recalled the events of yesterday morning, explaining I had been raped on my way to the train station.

They both took notes, showing concern but maintaining their professionalism. The uniformed officer looked like she was trying to capture my words in their entirety. Her hand flew across the page like lightning, seizing every detail.

'Is there anyone we can call for you?'

I shook my head. I didn't want my mother to know. She wouldn't be any help, over a hundred miles away, and there was no point in upsetting her. She was in a fragile state most of the time when she was sober anyway. She and my father had moved to Norfolk to retire five years ago. Giving me the deposit for the flat and helping to arrange the mortgage before they left. I think they felt guilty, leaving me behind on my own, no siblings to rely on, but I didn't want to go with them. Leave my job and my friends to move to a new town and start all over again. They'd barely been there a year when my dad had a heart attack and died. Mum turned to alcohol to cope. I tried to get her to come back, to move in with me, but she didn't want to leave the home she shared with Dad, however briefly.

'Would you be able to give us the clothes you were wearing yesterday?' the uniformed officer asked; slipping on latex gloves and placing a clear plastic bag on the table.

I retrieved the clothes from the bathroom, where they remained untouched, and placed them inside the bag she held open.

'You've not washed them?'

I shook my head. It sickened me to touch them. The sight repulsed me, which was infuriating as they were my favourite pair of jeans. I could never wear them again.

'Great. Thank you. Now, would you be able to come into the station? We have an examination suite there. I can get a doctor to look you over, collect any evidence the perpetrator may have left behind. It can be vital when securing a conviction.'

'I've had a bath,' I admitted.

The blonde's face betrayed a flicker of disappointment.

'Well, it's worth a try. Do you think you would be able to show us where it took place?'

My chest tightened. I never wanted to go back there again.

The front door opened, and seconds later Ben walked into the kitchen. No doubt hearing unusual voices and wanting to investigate. He came to an abrupt halt in the doorway when he saw the uniform and blood drained from his face.

'My flatmate, Ben,' I said by way of an introduction.

They stood from the table and I followed.

'Eve, do you want to get your bag and coat?' the detective asked, and I obediently collected them from my room.

'She won't be long, just going to pop to the station.'

'Do you want me to pick you up?' Ben asked.

I looked first at him and then the detective.

'No, it's fine, we'll drop her back.'

'You look after her, Ben,' the uniformed officer continued, sizing him up. It was more of a command than a request.

'Of course,' Ben stammered and stood aside to let them pass, pulling on his ear.

They ushered me out of the door and down to the car.

I sat in the back, listening to the women discuss where to go first. It was decided the park and my stomach churned the closer we got.

Walking through the entrance and across the field made me feel sick, my entire body shook, the jacket I'd brought doing little to keep me warm. Every muscle tensed as I neared the spot; I wanted to run away. When we reached the café, it was business as usual. A group of children came bouncing out of the door, each clutching a Mr Whippy ice cream. Too innocent for this place. I looked around, searching every face. Was he here? Enjoying watching me relive the nightmare? I pointed to the rear of the building, not willing to go around the back and see where it had happened. It was already burnt into my memory. Images I would never erase.

Detective Sergeant Emmerson, who gave me her card whilst we were in the car, took notes on a pocket-sized pad and indicated for the uniformed officer to radio for the scenes of crime officers. Then she left me outside whilst she talked to the café owners about closing for the day. The look of horror on the face of the plump woman in an apron made my eyes well up and I had to turn away.

Within minutes, more officers arrived and were cordoning off the area. I was taken back to the car. The police station wasn't far. Inside the entrance was a short corridor with a thick metal door at the end. The front desk was to the right, cased in protective glass. It smelt stale and musty. As soon as we arrived, I was escorted into the 'rape suite'. A female doctor who looked too young to be practising explained that she would take samples of my saliva, urine, blood and pubic hair to keep as evidence and in the hope any DNA could be found. Her voice apologetic as she told me vaginal and rectal swabs would also need to be taken. As she moved through the process, I felt numb, only wincing when she got to the internal examination and collection.

'I'm so sorry. I know it's uncomfortable. I'll try and be as quick as I can,' she said gently as all my muscles tensed and I fought the urge to snap my legs shut. Unable to conceal the tears streaming down my cheeks, I looked away at the wall and bit the inside of my cheek until it bled. Once I was fully dressed, I sat at her desk as she wrote up my notes. The doctor gave me emergency contraception to take and advised me to get tested for STDs as soon as possible.

'I'm sure he wore a condom,' I mumbled.

'Better safe than sorry,' she replied. as she wrote up my notes.

Exhausted, I wanted to go home, but I had to give my statement first. I was escorted to an interview room where Detective Emmerson waited.

'Thank you for your time this morning, Eve. I imagine it's not been easy. Can I get you anything to drink before we start?'

'No, thank you.' I wrapped my arms around myself.

'Okay. Ready to start?' I nodded.

'How would you describe your attacker?'

'He was taller than me, around five seven, I think. I didn't see his face.'

'How old you do think he was?'

'I don't know, umm, mid to late twenties. Maybe even thirty. I can't be sure.'

'What colour was his skin?'

'White.'

'Hair colour?

'I don't know, I didn't see.'

'Did you see any hair at all, on his arm or legs? Eyebrows?'

'No. He had long sleeves, I'm not sure if it was a hoody or a sweatshirt and he wore jogging bottoms. He also had gloves and a balaclava on.'

'What colour were they? Any distinguishing marks or logos?'

My thoughts turned to those plain trainers.

'No, none that I could see. Everything was black.'

'Did you see his eyes? What colour were they?'

I recoiled. His eyes would haunt me forever. Ice blue, cold and empty, devoid of any emotion.

'They were blue.'

'Okay, tell me what he said to you, what did he sound like? Any accents?'

I told Emmerson about the soft voice, how it was more intimidating than if he had shouted.

'Fantastic, Eve, you're doing great. I know you've told me already this morning, but can you tell me again exactly what happened yesterday from when you stepped into the park.'

After reliving it again for the second time, Detective Emmerson dropped me back at home, walking me up to my front door and seeing me safely inside.

'Well done. I know it's been traumatic, and you've been incredibly brave. If you remember anything else, please don't hesitate to call, you have my card. I'll be in touch in a few days.'

I shut the door and my shoulders sagged, relieved it was over. I wanted a shower but contemplated going back to bed instead.

Hearing the front door, Ben came out of his room.

'Are you okay?'

I gave him a weak smile. 'I'm tired.'

'Tea?' he asked, and I nodded.

A few minutes later we both sat at the table, tea in one hand, cigarette in the other. An awkward silence between us. I hadn't smoked for a few years and I didn't want to start again now, but it was a slippery slope. I enjoyed the stress relief it brought and Ben was only too happy to share.

'Fuck!' I hadn't called in sick for work yet. It was half nine, they would be wondering where I was.

'What?' Ben said, alarmed at my sudden outburst.

'Nothing, I've got to ring the office and tell them I won't be in.'

'Do you want to tell me what happened?'

No, but I had to at some point. Perhaps if I said it fast it would be easier. Like ripping off a plaster. 'I was raped on the way to the station yesterday morning.'

Ben's mouth dropped open and the horrified expression on his face made my eyes fill with tears. He reached across the table and laid his hand on top of mine.

'I'm so sorry, Eve. That's fucking awful.'

I grimaced, yes it was.

'Hopefully they'll catch him quickly, they've got his DNA, right?'

I nodded, although I wasn't sure, now regretting the bath in the cold light of day. Hopefully there'd be some of him left on my clothes.

5

SUNDAY 28 JANUARY 2018

'But he attacked me! He tried to kill me,' I cry out, cradling my head in my hands. Tears pool on the desk beneath me and my legs tremble beneath the table.

Terry taps my arm and I flinch away. He ignores my reaction and leans in to whisper, 'I advised no comment'.

'Why can't I talk? I haven't done anything wrong,' I hiss back.

'Let's start with how you met Ian?' Hicks leans back in his seat, waiting for me to speak.

Relax. I can do this. I don't even have to lie, it's more bending the truth. I sip my coffee, use the seconds to gather my thoughts and wipe my eyes on the blanket. The stage is set.

'We met at the gym. Pulse, in town. I signed up a few months ago. It was an offer, ten months for the price of twelve.'

'Okay, so Ian attended the same gym?'

The continuous use of his name makes me twitch. It sounds so normal, not fitting for the monster he was.

'Yes. We went at similar times, so we'd smile and say hello. He was one of the regulars.'

'When did you first speak to each other?'

'I think it was about two months ago. He was waiting for a weights machine to come free and we chatted at the water fountain.'

I sniff, and Hicks pushes a tissue box towards me. I can't work out if he is being polite or just irritated by my sniffing. I hope it's the latter, but I take the tissue and blow my nose.

'What did he say, do you remember?' Becker leans forward in her seat, taking notes in a spiral-bound book. Hicks has his arms crossed, staring at me intently. I feel a flush rise in my neck.

'Just hello, he joked about the machines always being full, I think. He seemed friendly, normal.'

'Did you get the impression he liked you?' Hicks asks, his forehead wrinkling.

'I guess so. I didn't think much of it at the time. He used to watch me run, it made me feel embarrassed.'

Becker nods. 'Did you think he was creepy?'

'No, not then. Not at all really, not until last night.' I let out a sob and Hicks looks like he'd rather be anywhere else than here. 'He was clawing at my clothes. Like an animal.' I'm weeping again, and I know I'll have a headache before long.

The detectives glance at each other but I can't read them. Perplexed maybe? Sympathetic? I'm not sure yet.

'I just want to go home!' I wail.

It's true, I'm shattered and want a long bath. I want to hibernate for at least a week, but there is no way that is going to happen yet. I have to try and get out of here today.

* * *

Monday 25 September 2017

Ben headed off to bed and I stared at my phone. I couldn't face talking to my boss, Stuart. It was difficult enough to say and, ridiculously, I felt embarrassed having to say it to a man. I'd go direct to human resources. Debbie was the closest person to me at work. After a few rings, she answered, sounding puffed out with a cheery 'hello'. She must have ran to grab the phone.

'Hi Debbie, it's Eve,' I said, my voice already cracking. Tears erupted from nowhere and I had to stop myself hanging up. The kitchen walls seemed to shrink in around me. I'd never felt so drained.

'Eve, are you all right?'

Debbie and I had hit it off when I joined the company. Before I gave up smoking, we would congregate at the bus stop outside the office at least four times a day. She was nice, in her mid-thirties and married with kids, but too much of a gossip to be working in HR. As friendly as we were, I knew my story would be all over the building in minutes, but I had no choice.

'No, I'm not to be honest. I need a few days off.'

'What's happened?'

'I don't want to go into detail but...' I struggled to say it out loud. 'I was sexually assaulted yesterday. I've just got back from the police station and I don't feel up to coming in.' My voice wobbled as I tried to fight back the tears, sniffing loudly.

'Of course! Oh, my goodness, you poor girl. That's terrible. Don't even think about coming in. Take as long as you need. I'll have a discreet word with Stuart and you get in touch when you're ready to come back.' The genuine concern in her voice was comforting. Every time I said it out loud, to another person, made it more real. My limbs felt weak and all energy zapped. 'Is there anything at all we can do?'

'No, thank you, Debbie.'

'Okay, well we're here if you need us. Keep in touch.'

'Thanks, I better go,' I said, hanging up.

I put my head in my hands and wept.

The flat was quiet, I couldn't even hear Ben snoring. It made me feel uneasy, the silence, even though I knew I wasn't on my own. All the doors were locked, and no one could get in.

Just as I changed into my pyjamas to get into bed, a knock came at the front door. I wrapped myself up in my dressing gown and hesitated by Ben's door. Should I wake him up to answer it?

I tiptoed towards the door, but before I got to it, I heard Jane's voice.

'Eve, it's me.'

I flung open the door and began to sob as soon as I saw her face, overwhelmed by how glad I was to see my closest friend.

Jane had on denim dungarees, a neon cropped T-shirt beneath, allowing a glimpse of her tiny midriff, and plimsolls. Her golden hair, long and loose. She practically carried me to my room and we huddled on my bed.

'I've been so worried. You never called. I've been ringing and ringing.'

I glanced at my phone, redundant on my carpet. I'd set it to silent after I rang Debbie. Ignoring the notifications of texts and missed calls.

'I'm sorry.'

'Oh, Eve.'

I cried into her shoulder as she held my hand. She asked nothing of me and for that I was grateful. I fell asleep and woke up with my head in her lap as she gently stroked my hair. I sat up, wiping sleep from my eyes.

'Have you taken the day off work?' I asked.

'Called in sick.' Her eyes wide, a guilty grin.

I smiled. Jane always made me feel better.

'I'm sorry about the London Eye.'

'Don't be ridiculous. We'll do it another time. You're safe, that's all I care about.'

I told Jane some of what happened, snippets I could bear to talk about, as she looked on, disgusted at what I was telling her. Pausing to shake her head and pat my hand.

'Let me make you some tea,' I said, swinging my legs over the edge of the bed. Jane had been here hours and had had nothing to eat or drink.

'I'll make it!' Jane overtook me on the way to the kitchen.

She stayed until late, cooking dinner with what she found at the back of the freezer.

'You need to go shopping, or rather Ben does.' She laughed at her plate of chips, peas and fish fingers. I pushed mine around my plate as she tucked in. We talked about anything other than my attack, and she tried to keep me distracted, but I was relieved when she left to go home. I loved her, and was grateful for her visit, but I was desperate to be alone.

* * *

The next few days blurred into one. I spent my time sleeping, smoking, staring at the television and occasionally leaving my room to eat. Ben knocked on the door a few times to make sure I was still alive, offering me tea, cigarettes and on one occasion another joint, all of which were gratefully received.

We'd been flatmates for around two years. When I first had the flat, I coped on my own for a while, working full-time and supplementing my salary with bar work at the weekends. Then I had to renew my mortgage, the excellent rate I'd secured at first had gone up and so did my monthly repayments. I got a lodger, a girl called Vicky, but it was a mistake from the outset. I worked in the bar with her and everyone always came back to ours after closing time. It became a place for partying and there was always someone lying comatose on the living-room floor. One Sunday morning I woke up to find one of the customers she'd brought back fast asleep at the end of my bed and the rest of the flat wrecked.

When I advertised again, I knew what to avoid. Ben was polite and came across as chilled and easy-going. I didn't foresee him being any problem and thought I'd give living with a man a go this time. It was the best decision I ever made. He paid his rent on time and there were no parties; in fact, if he wasn't working or eating, he spent most of his time out or occasionally playing his Xbox. The bonus was that he worked nights, normally from around six in the evening until six in the morning. He once told me he was the regional manager for a group of large warehouses in the south-east that contained all sorts of items, from sports cars to designer stock for clothing stores. Items of value that had to be guarded twenty-four hours a day and he managed the night team on the ground and any movements of stock. I was impressed. It made my job seem boring. Although Debbie and I made sure we'd have a laugh most days, even when we were busy.

The day after I made the call to Debbie, I received a bunch of flowers from everyone at work. The delivery man knocked repeatedly, but I couldn't open the door. I felt paralysed by fear. Instead I hid, hunched in the corner of my room, terrified it was my attacker coming for more. A complete over reaction, I know. The courier left the flowers outside and Ben noticed them when he left for work in the afternoon. The card read 'thinking of you'. I was touched, but the thought of going into the office made me nauseous. I bet they were talking about me as well as thinking of me. I was doing everything I could not to think at all.

Jane kept in contact every day, checking in to see how I was doing. She sent me a beautiful gift of calming essential oils in pulse point roller balls and comfy pyjamas, knowing I hadn't got dressed in days. I answered the weekly call from my mother and told her I hadn't been well, I'd been laid up in bed with the flu. She sounded remarkably sober and gave me the recipe for her mum's chicken soup, which apparently was the best cure for flu. Her mood dipped as she told me she'd finally emptied Dad's wardrobe after all this time. I had no energy to talk her out of her melancholy. I felt selfish, as I would usually always try and lift her mood, but I was unable to see past my own darkness.

In four days, I hadn't left the flat. Ben was doing cigarette and shopping runs although I lived mostly on pasta, tea and toast. I had no desire to do anything.

6

FRIDAY 29 SEPTEMBER 2017

On Friday morning, Ben knocked on my bedroom door when he arrived home from work. It was an almighty effort to get out of bed to unlock it, but he was one of the few people I was not averse to seeing. He stood in the doorway, dressed in a shirt and tie, his top button undone. Dark circles sat beneath his eyes. His head almost touched the top of the door frame, but his body didn't fill the width of the space. Hair dark and unruly that he kept short probably for that reason. He yawned before he spoke. It must have been a long shift.

'Hey,' he said.

'Hey.'

'How are you doing?' He edged forward, over the threshold, and lowered himself down onto the end of the bed.

I shrugged, what could I say?

'Jesus Christ, it stinks in here,' he chided playfully, surveying the mess of my bedroom. He got up and threw open my curtains, bright sunlight blasting through the glass making me squint. He opened the window wide, letting fresh crisp air in before turning to face me, hands resting on his hips. 'Eve, we need to talk. I know what happened was dreadful, but this has to stop. You're letting him win if you carry on hiding in here.'

'Did you bring me cigarettes?' I asked flatly, holding out my hand, ready to receive.

Ben's eyes narrowed, and he clenched his jaw repeatedly. 'Fuck sake. No, I didn't.' He turned around, his frustration evident, and stomped into his bedroom, slamming the door behind him.

I tucked my knees up to my chest and cried. He was right, of course he was right. What the fuck was I doing? I hadn't washed or changed my clothes since Monday. The bedroom stank of sweat and smoke; the ashtray overflowing and mouldy cups littering the carpet. My reflection was grey and sallow. I resembled a junkie; thin, with sunken eyes and greasy hair.

I crept back out to Ben's door and tapped gently. A second later it opened, and he frowned at my puffy eyes.

'I'm sorry,' he said, stepping forward to give me a hug.

I scooted backwards, and he looked away. Mirroring my step with his own.

'I stink, you're right, I need a shower,' I said quickly. Relieved to see him laugh and the awkwardness dispelled. I didn't want to tell him I couldn't bear his touch. His kindness overwhelmed me, and I didn't know what I would have done without him. But he was still a man and I didn't want to be touched by one. 'I'm scared, Ben,' I whispered.

'I know.' He sighed, and I could see him teetering on the balls of his feet. Was he going to reach out for me again? Thankfully he decided against it and remained in the doorway. 'Go get dressed, have something to eat and once I've had a few hours' kip we are going out for a walk.' It sounded ambitious, but I would give it a go.

Three hours later, I'd showered, washed my hair and eaten a lunch of beans on toast. I'd filled my time waiting for Ben by tidying my room, which was now aired and smelling fresher. I examined my face in the mirror, as I pulled my mousy hair back into a ponytail. The graze on my cheek was almost gone, a yellowish bruise remained. I'd healed down below too, the pain I'd initially felt when going to the toilet had gone and the tenderness passed. Physical scars were always quicker to heal.

We stepped out of the door to our building onto the noisy street. Immediately my senses were overloaded. The sound of cars and chattering people was like a hammer to my skull. It made my head throb. Someone brushed past me and I fell against Ben, my whole body shaking. Sucking in fresh air like a marooned fish. It was too much.

A hand touched my shoulder and the world spun.

'It's okay, just breathe. Deep breaths, in and out. That's it.'

We stood for a minute, sheltered in the doorway, until the light-headedness passed and I was able to continue. It was slow progress, we walked towards the park initially, but then cut off towards the high street and found a bench in the square. School children zoomed past on bikes and scooters in their uniforms, pursued by parents struggling to keep up.

'You all right?' Ben asked, breaking the silence.

Warmth hit my cheeks and I stared at my trainers.

'I think so. There's so many people here.' My voice was shaky. I was looking at all the faces in the crowd. Could he be there? Amongst them? Looking right at me? Would I recognise him at all?

'The weather brings them out. You, on the other hand,

look like a vampire.' It was true, I did, with my pasty complexion, although Ben didn't have much more colour.

We sat for a few minutes and watched the people bustling. The square was always busy, rows of shops either side and in the centre the council had built a water fountain. I watched the spray shoot up into the sky and rain down into the stone surround.

'Next thing we need to do is feed you up. You look starved. Shall we get a kebab on the way home?'

I wrinkled my nose; kebabs weren't on the top of my junk food list.

'What about something from the bakers?' I said instead. Hot sausage rolls or Cornish pasties followed by carrot cake made my stomach growl appreciatively.

'Okay, good idea. And if you aren't planning on being a hermit tonight perhaps we could order a pizza and watch a movie. I've got a night off. What do you reckon?'

I hesitated, hoping Ben didn't assume this was leading to something. We'd been living together for around two years but had never hung out before. This was new territory for both of us.

'Sure. Thanks for being a good mate.' I cringed as the last word left my lips, but Ben didn't seem to notice, or if he did, he didn't take any offence.

'Well, if anything happens to you, I have nowhere to live so got to keep you alive at least!' he said, bumping his shoulder into mine. I tried my best not to flinch.

On the way back, we took a detour to visit the bakery. Clutching our spoils, we approached Blackwater Lane on our left, which was where the other entrance to the park was. The one I never made it to. My whole body tensed when the road came into view and a wave of nausea washed over me. I couldn't see the entrance to the park, but knowing it was there was enough. Facing forward, I marched on, speeding up until out of the corner of my eye, a glimpse of yellow caught my attention.

I stopped dead in my tracks, staring. There was a bright yellow rectangular police sign on the entrance to Blackwater Lane.

INCIDENT HERE printed in black letters and scrawled underneath in black marker.

INDECENT ASSAULT

Grove Park 24/09/2017 @ 8:30 a.m.

Witnesses please contact Crimestoppers

0800 555 111

Ben prised my fingers from his arm, tiny half-moon indentations left on his skin. He sensed my distress and carried on walking, propelling me forward.

I couldn't tear my eyes away, a cold sweat developed in the small of my back. I was mortified. As though the sign had announced my name. We hurried back to the refuge of the flat. I'd had enough fresh air for one day.

Later, when Ben was out picking up the pizza, I had a call from Detective Emmerson. She asked me how I was holding up and said she wanted to get in touch to give me an update. She was pleasant, but I couldn't miss the detached tone of business in her voice. She informed me that during the initial search of the area, no condom was found. If he'd used one, then he'd likely taken it with him, but they had searched all the bins in the vicinity of the park and were sifting through the rubbish. They'd retrieved CCTV from some residents in the surrounding streets, at both entrances to the park, and were looking through those images. My clothes were at the lab being tested, but no results were available yet.

'We're looking at historic cases to see if there's any links. Also, I need to ask you to look through some identity photos of potential suspects in the next few days, if you wouldn't mind coming back to the station?'

'Sure,' I replied. I was positive that even though I barely saw him I'd be able to pick those eyes out anywhere. She said she would call back to arrange a date, before going on to recommend the charity Victim Support, who were great in cases like mine. I took down their contact details, saying I would check them out.

Our conversation left a bad taste in my mouth. Emmerson didn't say it, but I was certain she thought he'd attacked before. As did I. He knew what he was doing; he was too calm, completely in control of the situation. I couldn't believe it was his first time. They would catch him, wouldn't they? Surely with his DNA, which must be on some of my clothing, he would be found. If only I hadn't taken that bath, they might have had more and been able to find him in the system. Assuming he was in the system at all. It hadn't crossed my mind he wouldn't be. Unless he'd never been caught?

7

HIM

She smelt like blossom. The scent of her shampoo drifting upwards as I yanked her hair and felt her quiver beneath me. I'm sure she enjoyed it although she barely made a sound. I can still smell her on my gloves. How I wish I could feel her again, this time skin on skin. So small, cowering like a mouse. It made me harder than I'd ever been.

I got lucky, I hadn't intended to walk that way, cautious to change my route. It was a last minute decision which turned out to be a fortunate one, for me anyway. She was crossing the road as I came round the corner. I held my breath, waiting to see if she would enter the park. I thought she must have been a sign. Sent just for me. Her ponytail bounced as she walked, petite hips swaying back and forth. She had me captivated and I couldn't resist.

She's been the finest, of all of them. I was reluctant to let her go, but I must be careful. I can't leave anything behind. Desire makes you stupid, clouds your vision and I need to be one step ahead, but one thing is for sure, I can't wait to see her again.

8

SUNDAY 28 JANUARY 2018

'Did you become friends?'

'It didn't happen overnight. We just started speaking to each other whenever we were at the gym. He knew the manager, everyone seemed to like him. I liked him.'

'What sort of person would you say he is? Sorry, I mean was,' Becker asks, stumbling over the last word and fiddling with her sleeve.

I ignore the mishap, but Hicks gives the slightest roll of the eyes.

'Nice, friendly. Genuine. Loved his workouts, bit of a fitness freak. Just normal, you know.' I rub my eyes. I don't have to pretend to be tired. I'm exhausted. Must stay focused.

'When was the first time you saw him outside the gym?'

'I've only seen him outside the gym a few times. The first time there was a group of us; we went for a drink on a Friday after a session. He asked me to come along and I thought it might be fun. I just went for one, but it was nice to get to know the people I'd been training alongside. At least to know their names.'

'Do you remember the date?' Becker is primed, notebook in hand.

'Sure, it was before Christmas, around the eighth, I think. I know it was a Friday and we went to the Half Moon,' she nods as I speak, scribbling.

'Who was there?'

'There was me, Ian, Charlie, Sam, Laura, James, Beth and the manager, Ahmed. I think that was everyone.' It's easy to reel off a list of names. They go out regularly and I would often see them all leave together, but it was the first time I'd been invited. I'd finally managed to infiltrate the group.

Now they will check the CCTV. I'll be sat in the corner, clutching my Diet Coke. I was only there for an hour and it was okay. A lot of dull exercise talk. A discussion on the benefits of protein shakes and the best trainers for long distance. A pre-Christmas celebration, which I believe went on until late. They'll be able to see Ian sit beside me, the two of us engaged in animated conversation. When I leave, they'll see him follow me outside to say goodbye and give me a kiss on the cheek. They'll see him staring after me for a touch too long as I walk away into the night.

Saturday 30 September 2017

Over the weekend, I made myself leave the flat. Ben and I went food shopping, larking around the aisles like kids. I felt safe with Ben, but I couldn't stop myself from looking over my shoulder. I felt *he* was with me everywhere I went. We bought mostly convenience food, resigned that we were living as students anyway. Students with a little more money and better kitchen equipment. I was putting more and more on my credit card, living beyond my means and burying my head in the sand. I would sort it out soon, once I was back to myself. I made a couple of trips to the newsagents by myself for cigarettes. I was still smoking like a trooper, and I'd forgotten how expensive it was. I promised myself I would quit.

On Saturday I ventured out to the library on my own; it was somewhere I felt safe. Quiet, with a few people milling around and no crowds. Getting there was fine. The anxiety lessening with each trip out. I got lost in the books and picked up some light reading, immersing myself. Dusk crept up on me, apparent from the switching on of the library lights. God, how could I have been so stupid? Looking out at the darkness descending like a blanket made me shiver. I felt trapped. I could ring Ben to come and meet me? No, that was ridiculous. I was an adult and able to walk home in the dark like everyone else. I repeated the mantra in my head until the sliding doors closed behind me. Shutting me out of the warmth and safety of the building.

I stood alone on the pavement. Outside noises filtered in, revving engines and car horns distracted me as I hurried along. It was hard to shake the feeling I was being followed. The sound of my feet slapping the pavement echoed every time there was a break in the traffic. My pace was fast, heart pounding with each stride, but the journey stretched on. Seeming far longer than on the way there. *Everything's fine, just keep going. He's not behind you.* Was he though? How I could I tell? Had he picked me specifically or had I been in the wrong place at the wrong time?

I balled my hands into fists, power walking, legs pumping as I marched along. My anger propelling me home. What had I become? That bastard. My faceless attacker. I hated him more than I'd ever hated anyone. I didn't know who I was any more. Everything had changed; everything I'd taken for granted. The freedom to walk down the street without a care in the world. I hated being so weak. He'd turned me into a prisoner of my own anxiety and I wasn't safe anywhere except inside my own four walls. I'd been stripped of my liberty, my confidence crumbled. He'd made me a victim.

When I got home, I was a panting, sweaty mess. I shut myself in my room. I wasn't making progress at all, if anything, I was going backwards.

* * *

'Why don't you book a doctor's appointment?' Jane said, when I spoke to her on Sunday and told her about my disastrous visit to the library.

'I don't know. I not sure I want to talk about it with anyone else.'

'I think you're being a little hard on yourself, Eve. You've been through a lot and maybe you need a little intervention. Something for the anxiety.'

'Maybe,' I replied, half-heartedly. I heard Jane sigh down the phone.

'I wish I could come over.' I knew she was working. She had the stamina of a racehorse, her plans to travel around Asia and America spurring her on. Sometimes I thought about going with her, being part of her adventure. I wasn't sure I was that brave, especially not now.

'I think I'm going to try and go back to work tomorrow. Perhaps some normality will do me good. Back to the old routine, so I don't think about it so much.'

Jane thought it would be a good idea The line crackled and I could hear the booming tannoy overhead.

'I've got to go, hon, they're calling for me.'

We said our goodbyes and I hung up. Dread washing over me at the thought of going back outside tomorrow and making that journey to work. At least it would be daylight, but I knew I'd be looking for him in the faces of the commuters. Seeing him around every corner, in every window.

9

MONDAY 1 OCTOBER 2017

When my alarm went off on Monday morning, I woke with a knot already formed in my stomach. It sat like a brick, refusing to move. I couldn't eat anything, instead relying on a cup of coffee to energise me. Would I be stared at by the staff? No doubt, pretending they weren't. Would they whisper about me? I'd be poor, broken, Eve. Well, fuck that.

Riffling through my wardrobe, I put on my smartest outfit – a grey trouser suit with a cream pussy-bow blouse. Pulled my hair into a chignon and put on some make-up, a first in over a week. A professional and confident woman stared back at me from the mirror, but it was a fabrication of how I felt on the inside.

Thankfully, the office was a short walk from home. Public transport would have been out of the question. Lots of people were on their morning commute, hurrying to start their day. Workers in fluorescent tabards were digging up a portion of the pavement to get to the water pipes beneath. Hemmed in by barriers, a sea of people swarmed towards me like an army marching on the enemy. I had to duck into a urine stained doorway to avoid being swept up in the crowd. I waited for them to pass, the back of my neck prickling with trepidation. I could do this.

I pushed forward and made a path for myself, veering off the main drag and around the corner where the office was situated. It was just before nine, but there were people I recognised at the bus stop smoking already. No matter what time of day, someone from our office would be there. Whispering travelled on the breeze as I passed. 'Is that her?' It was just as I had feared.

My phone buzzed, vibrating my handbag. A text notification popped up on the display and I was surprised to see it was from Ben. We'd swapped numbers when he had moved in, I was his landlady after all, but he'd never texted me until today.

`Good luck, you'll be desperate to come home by lunchtime!`

His message made me smile. I didn't realise, when I picked him out of the other applicants, he'd be such a godsend.

I resisted the urge to have another cigarette before entering the building. I was just putting off the inevitable. The fluttering in my stomach seemed to be a constant feeling and I wasn't getting more than a few hours of sleep a night. I saw him everywhere, imagining his face, trying to fill in the parts of it that I didn't see. I shook the thoughts from my head. I had to focus on work and get my life back to some sort of normality.

I hurried through reception, scanning my badge to gain access to the lifts. Inside, I stood at the back, waiting for the door to close, and rummaged in my handbag for a mirror. My hot flush so intense, I was concerned my make-up was sliding off my face. I was sure sweat patches would be visible under the arms of my blouse.

Someone slipped in just before the doors closed. A man stood with his back to me. Black trousers, black shoes; my gaze drifted upwards. The back of his head was sheathed in black fabric. Was he wearing a balaclava? I froze, holding my breath. My attacker had followed me to work. I had to get out.

Stretching my arm to reach for the panel, it was too far away, and I was worried the movement would cause him to turn round. The lift jerked into action, throwing me off balance, then slowly ascending. I had to find a weapon, something to protect myself with, but I couldn't move. I pressed myself to the back wall, not daring to make a sound. Waiting for him to turn. How did he find me?

Seconds later, the lift came to a halt with another jolt. My lungs screamed for air, heart hammering. I stared at the back of his head, the need to urinate becoming more urgent by the second. The doors slid open and he turned back to look at me.

'Oh, hey Eve, didn't see you there,' Gurpreet said, stepping out of the lift.

I coughed as I inhaled, filling my lungs up. It wasn't a balaclava. *Fuck's sake, Eve.* Gurpreet always wore a black turban. Idiot. I was losing my mind.

I hurried to the sanctuary of the toilets, relief turning my muscles to mush. I had to get my shit together.

After I'd spent five minutes in the toilets calming down, I skulked to my desk. It was spotless, like I'd never existed. Everything had been tidied into drawers. It took three attempts before I logged on to my computer, having forgotten the password. Eventually Outlook opened to reveal around fifty emails sitting in my inbox. Gathering from some of them that I had missed a major company announcement, I scrolled through to find it. Tapping my mouse, an email from our CEO filled the screen. We were being merged with another distribution company. Thank God I wasn't here for all the drama last week. There would have been tears and panic; not to mention a large amount of arse kissing from those worried about their jobs.

I rolled my eyes. I couldn't muster up any enthusiasm. Nothing seemed important any more. Work was trivial.

'You're back! How are you?' Stuart, my boss, appeared at my desk, his lips pressed into a hard line.

'Okay, thank you.'

He fidgeted with his tie, neither of us knowing what to say next. His eyes wandered and came to rest on my screen, displaying the announcement.

'Big changes coming, I'm afraid. Looks like we might all have to re-apply for our jobs. Well, that's the rumour. It was a bit of a shock last week.'

'Is the company in trouble?' I asked, feigning interest.

'No, the one we've rescued is, but now for every job there's two people vying for it.'

I frowned, trying to look concerned but unsure if I was pulling it off.

'Anyway, I'll let you catch up. If you need anything, let me know. If it's all a bit too soon and you want to take a few more days, then by all means do.' He strode into his office, closing his door.

I sighed, glad the awkward exchange was over. The call of my bed was loud. I wanted to be in my comfy pyjamas, enjoying the sanctuary my bedroom had become. If only

Stuart hadn't planted the seed. It was tempting, but if I went home, I would never come back.

Work dragged. I only left my desk twice, the first time to use the ladies'. The feeling of eyes on me as I passed made me jittery and I couldn't wait to get back to my desk. The second time, I joined Debbie for a cigarette outside. She wouldn't take no for an answer, insisting I accompanied her.

'How are you doing?' she asked, her voice shrill. It grated on me and I struggled to hide it.

'Okay. Don't want to be here. You know.' I shrugged.

'I can imagine,' she droned, sucking on her cigarette so hard her lips puckered. Her mouth resembling a cat's backside.

Can you, Debbie? Can you really? Do you know what the fuck it's like to have a knife put to your throat? My head screamed with it. Little flashes of rage came without warning.

The pause stretched out and eventually Debbie changed the subject to update me about the company restructure. She knew the HR girl from the other company whom she would now be up against and was confident she would stay. That didn't surprise me, Debbie knew everyone. I cringed inwardly, I wasn't being fair, my head was in a bad place.

'Thank you for the flowers. They were lovely.' I placed my hand on Debbie's arm and awarded her my best smile. Her spongy flesh beneath my fingertips. She beamed, lighting up like a Christmas tree.

'I'm glad. I chose them myself. We wanted to show you we cared. The whole office was in shock when they heard.'

You mean when you told them, Debbie? What was wrong with me? I liked Debbie, but everyone was irritating me. It was an effort to be pleasant or polite. I didn't know who I was any more.

I smiled as best I could, lips pursed, hiding my gritted teeth. I wanted to leave so flicked my cigarette into the bin and turned on my heels. She did the same, quickening her stride to keep pace.

'Ah look, the dog walker has brought Molly back.' Debbie stared at her phone as we waited for the lift. Over her shoulder, I could see a fluffy white dog bouncing around a kitchen on the screen.

'What is that?' I asked, more to fill the silence than because I was interested.

'It's a PetCam, got it on eBay. They're brilliant, plugs into your Wi-Fi and you can watch through an app on your phone. I can even talk to Molly if I want to.' Debbie made embarrassing baby noises into the phone. The dog, at the sound of her voice, barked and ran around in circles. I had to admit, pets didn't really interest me. It was just something else to look after. Eventually, we parted company and I was free, back to the solitude of my desk. My socialising quota had been fulfilled.

By the end the day, I had dealt with all the emails from the previous week and was up to date. I avoided speaking to anyone other than Debbie and Stuart, which, under the circumstances, was an achievement. The journey home was much calmer, less people on the streets, and I no longer had the worry of the day ahead. I was looking forward to winding down after a long Monday, like every other person making their way home.

The flat was empty when I arrived, Ben had already left for work. I tried to call Jane, but her phone was switched off; she must be on the ward. I left a message asking her to call me back. I wanted to hear a friendly voice. The flat felt like it was shrouded in a blanket of silence. The air was thick with it and even the television didn't fill the void. I stared at the screen, not absorbing the cookery programme I'd put on. It was something to fill the time before bed. I'd missed lunch at work so indulged in a big bowl of pasta, leaving some leftovers for Ben when he got in. It was nice to return the favour.

My phone rang, and I scooped it up, hoping it was Jane. Unknown number flashed on the caller display. Normally I wouldn't answer, but if someone wanted to waste their time trying to sell me double glazing, it was fine by me.

'Hello?'

'Hi, is that Eve?'

I replied it was and Detective Emmerson announced herself.

'I'm in the area. Are you home? Do you mind if I pop in and give you an update?' I agreed, eager for news and company.

Fifteen minutes later she arrived, and I set about making tea. We clutched our mugs and I sensed from her downcast expression, her day had not been a good one.

'I wish I came with better news, but I'm afraid we've hit a stumbling block.'

I frowned. How was that possible? I remained silent, willing her to continue.

'Your clothes came back negative for any DNA. I'll return them to you when the lab sends them back.'

I shook my head. 'Please get rid of them. I don't want them back.'

Emmerson nodded. 'Of course. We've managed to locate some footage from a resident's CCTV. The image is grainy, and we cannot identify him from it, but I'd like you to view it at the station when we run through some suspect photos, just to confirm it's the same man.'

'I'm sorry I washed him off me,' I said, my voice cracking and tears erupting from my eyes.

'It's okay, Eve. I completely understand the compulsion to get clean after what you went through.'

I hung my head, shame eating me up from the inside out. Emmerson squeezed my hand for a second, but she looked defeated, her expression grave. How could I have been so stupid? I gave away their only chance to find him.

'Has anyone come forward from the incident boards? I saw one at the entrance to the park.'

'No, I'm afraid not; no information that has given us any leads.'

'So, we have nothing?' It sounded more like a dead end than a stumbling block.

'We have the tape, but it doesn't help to identify him currently.'

'You need him to do it again?' I asked.

Emmerson hesitated, pushing her blonde hair back behind her ear, before nodding. 'Well, it would give us more to go on. We've got a team calling in on all known local sex offenders; cross-referencing those against the physical description you gave us and determining their whereabouts at the time. It might lead to something.' She looked tired and a fleeting flash of pity hit me before the anger burned brighter. It wasn't fair. He was going to get away with it and there was nothing anyone could do.

'Do you think he's done it before?'

She sighed and leaned back in her chair, as if anticipating my question.

'I can't discuss other ongoing cases, Eve.'

'But do you?' I pushed, knowing I was on to something.

Emmerson folded her arms tightly across her chest. 'Yes. We think so. But he leaves very little evidence behind.'

I felt sick. If only I'd gone straight to the police, we could have had his DNA. They could have been out searching for him immediately. Now, even if they caught him, it was his word against mine.

Lowering my face, I continued to cry. Emmerson reached across the table and rested her hand on my arm, the skin prickled beneath.

'We'll keep trying.' She sounded genuine, but I knew it was bullshit. I was being placated. The case would go cold, no leads to follow and they would move on to something else. Anger bubbled inside, filling me up. I entwined my fingers in my hair and pulled at the scalp.

'I'd like to be alone please.' It was as polite as I could manage.

'Of course. Can you come in around two tomorrow afternoon to look at the photos?' Emmerson asked, as she stood.

I nodded. I just wanted to get her out of the flat.

When I heard the front door click shut, I slammed my fists onto the wooden table top. Pummelling them into the flat surface as it shook. I howled like a wild animal and threw my chair to the ground, again and again until the wood split. Red-faced and sweating, I returned to my room to sob into my pillow. Everything had gone to shit.

10

SUNDAY 28 JANUARY 2018

I need to use the bathroom and the interview is paused while I am escorted to the ladies'. The custody officer waits outside for my return. There is little privacy when you are a suspect. I wash my hands in the sink and try to ignore the reflection looming large. It doesn't look like me. Bruises on my neck are starting to appear, purple blotches in the shape of his fingers. I can't bear to touch my face; one side is unrecognisable. I look away from the mirror. It won't do to get emotional now.

When I return, Becker and Hicks stop mid-conversation as the door opens. They look at me and then each other. Are they apprehensive? Perhaps worried I had overheard? Someone has turned the heating up as the room is warm now or perhaps it's because I've moved. I put the blanket over the back of the chair and sit, ensuring my body language is open. No crossing of legs or arms, no barriers of any kind. The interview has been routine so far. No questions have been asked that I haven't anticipated.

'Can you describe the next time you saw Ian?' Hicks asks,

once he's pressed the recorder to start again and continue from where we left off.

'I saw him a few more times at the gym.' I know this isn't what they want, but I can't resist being obtrusive. I don't want to make things too easy for them.

'Sorry, I meant outside of the gym. Just the two of you,' Hicks clarifies, without a hint of irritation.

I nod like I've just understood. 'Oh yes, of course. It was in the New Year. I didn't see him over Christmas. When we saw each other at the gym, he asked if I wanted to go for a drink.'

'Where did you go?' Becker asks.

'Mangos, the wine bar on the corner of the high street. We had a few drinks in there. I didn't want a late night as I was getting up early the next day and when we left at about half ten there were no cabs.' It was freezing outside, but the lack of transport turned out to be a stroke of luck. 'He said he only lived around the corner and we could wait in the warm whilst he called an Uber,' I continue.

'So, you went to his house. Do you remember the date?' Hicks asks.

'Not exactly. It was two weeks ago, the second Friday in January.'

Hicks taps his smartphone, appearing to struggle with the buttons. Sighing, he hands the phone to Becker, who finds the calendar and scrolls through.

'Twelfth of January?' she asks, directing the screen towards me.

'Yes.'

'You felt safe with him, at that point?' Hicks's tone is laced with something. Not sarcasm, perhaps judgement? I'm not sure.

'Yes, I had no reason to fear him. It wasn't like we'd just met.'

Becker coughs and shoots a furtive glance at Hicks. It may be a reprimand. These two are difficult to read. Not like Ian. He was easy, he was transparent.

* * *

Tuesday 2 October 2017

'Scream and I'll cut you,' he hissed, pulling my jeans to my hips and shoving me to the ground.

I sat up on my elbows, scrabbling backwards in the dirt, but he pulled me back by the ankles. My shirt rode up, and gravel scraped into the flesh on my back.

'Where do you think you're going?' he said as he began undoing the button of his fly.

'Eve. Eve!' Ben's face was above mine and I thrashed in my duvet. 'Wake up.' I could hear screaming, but it took a few seconds to realise the noise was coming from me.

I slumped back onto my pillow panting. Ben sat on the edge of the bed holding his cheek.

'It was a nightmare.'

He threw me an incredulous look. 'I guessed! Jesus, you've got a good right hook,' he grumbled and disappeared out of the room.

My T-shirt was damp and cold, hair slicked flat to my head. It was freezing, and I reached for my dressing gown, still half asleep. It was the third nightmare I'd had in a week. Every time I tried to sleep, I saw his cold eyes drilling into me.

Ben reappeared in the doorway with a bag of oven chips

pressed against the side of his face. It would have been funny if I wasn't so broken.

'How did you get in?' I asked, scratching my head.

He pointed to the bolt lock that was swinging from the wall, two of its four screws in Ben's hand. He'd forced entry to my room? My mouth went dry. Ben wouldn't hurt me though? Would he?

'I'll make some tea,' he offered.

It was before seven, my alarm wasn't due to go off for another half an hour. Ben must have just got home. Seeing him in various stages of undress had become normal, but when I entered the kitchen he was fully clothed in jeans and a hoody. Had he been to work? He placed a cup of tea and a bowl of cereal in front of me.

'What happened to the chair?' Ben asked, nodding towards the broken pieces of wood stacked in the corner of the kitchen.

I rolled my eyes and continued to push cereal around my bowl. I was still reeling about the lack of progression on my case, much of it down to my own stupidity, but I didn't want to talk to Ben about it now. I didn't want to go to work either, but I had to. Everything was so unfair.

'We had a falling-out.'

Ben didn't respond. Perhaps, ascertaining from my tone, it would be wise to leave it there.

'Maybe you should go and see your doctor? About the nightmares, I mean. Maybe you've got post-traumatic stress disorder. You could get some meds for that.' The idea sounded tempting, floating around all day, away with the fairies. Although I wasn't sure that's exactly what Ben, or Jane, meant when they suggested I go and see a doctor.

'I might do,' I replied, and Ben seemed pleased he'd

mentioned it. He sat on the kitchen counter to eat his cereal. 'I'll replace the chair today,' I added.

Ben shrugged; he wasn't bothered.

Later that morning, I sat in the small office of Doctor Sola, wringing my hands. Thank goodness there was a cancellation. Normally it took two weeks before an appointment would become available. What were you supposed to do if you were actually sick? In that time whatever ailment you needed to see a doctor for would have cured itself, or you'd have died waiting. The journey here had been uneventful, but I was still uneasy being surrounded by lots of people during rush hour. I'd left a message on Stuart's answerphone to let him know I would be coming in to the office late and quickly called my mum. She sounded pleased to hear from me, although I said I couldn't talk long, letting slip I was on my way to the doctors.

'Are you still poorly?' Mum had sounded concerned.

'No, Mum, not really. Something happened that I need to tell you about, but I can't talk now. I just wanted to make sure you were all right?' I heard her hiccup and gritted my teeth. That's why she was in a good mood, she'd had a drink.

'Yes, I'm fine, love. In fact, I have something I need to talk to you about, too.'

'Okay, I'll ring you later,' I'd said before hanging up. I had to sort out my own problems first before I tried to fix her.

Doctor Sola was a small Indian woman who had an excellent bedside manner. She put me at ease as I stumbled through my rehearsed and edited version of what had brought me to the surgery.

'Well, I believe you're suffering with PTSD. The side effects of an event like this are psychological as well as physical. I'm happy to give you something to help your anxiety, but I believe you should consider seeing a counsellor too.'

I nodded in all the right places and took the card she gave me of a local psychiatrist who saw NHS patients. I still had the details for Victim Support but couldn't bring myself to get in touch.

'I'll refer you and you should receive an appointment automatically, but if you don't then please don't hesitate to come back.' She gave me a prescription for some diazepam, 5mg dose, and advised me to take one, three times a day. She had only prescribed sixty-three pills. Enough for three weeks at the recommended dose. Did she think I might be a suicide risk? The thought had crossed my mind in the past week but only for a split second. It would never be something I'd seriously consider. Did I look suicidal? I had a few days of floating around in a cloud to look forward to. 'How are you coping at work?' she asked.

'I've only been back one day, but it's overwhelming. I'm struggling with panic attacks.' I was happy to exaggerate, if it kept the prescriptions coming.

Doctor Sola nodded and tapped her keyboard. 'I'll sign you off for the rest of this week. Just to help you get back on your feet.'

The chemist next door always took an age, the staff behind the counter moving at their usual glacial pace. My reflection in the make-up display scared me. I no longer looked like myself. Pale, sunken eyes, sallow skin and flat lifeless hair. My cheeks were hollow too; I'd been ignoring the extra room in my waistbands and ribs were starting to show. I wasn't vain, but I did take pride in my appearance. Wearing make-up most days, hair done and always clean. Now I was modelling the heroin-chic look from the nineties.

Blinking back tears, I accepted the small paper bag the lady behind the counter handed me and tapped my card against the reader. A loud beep and an error message told me my debit card had been declined. The queue behind me was growing as I quickly fumbled for another card in my purse, paid for the drugs and left. Clutching them close, I hurried back to the flat.

The phone call to Stuart was awkward and I used the emotion in my voice to my advantage. He said he understood and was worried coming back this week may have been too soon. I wondered if I would I lose my job? I couldn't worry about it now. I had to get to the police station.

On arrival, I approached the front desk, the protective glass covered in fingerprints.

'I'm here to see Detective Emmerson, it's Eve Harding,' I told the police officer behind the glass and was advised to take a seat. After perusing the noticeboard which displayed posters advertising FRANK, where you could find honest information about drugs, and a guide to preventing bike theft, I sat in one of the orange plastic seats that were bolted to the wall. This part of the station was cold and uninviting, the walls had scuff marks and obscenities were scratched into the black metal chair legs. The whole place looked tired and dirty. Thankfully I didn't have long to wait. The detective burst through the door, her cheeks flushed, and ushered me through the metal door and into an interview room.

'Patrol picked up a man yesterday afternoon who reportedly exposed himself to some teenage girls in a park. He will be charged with indecent exposure, but I was keen to see if you recognised him.' She paused and motioned for me to take a seat, but I was too jittery. 'He's of similar height and build to that you described, and I've got a feeling he's into more than flashing.' She didn't wait for me to answer, just nodded as though we had agreed on something and disappeared out of the room.

I backed against the wall, sweat manifesting on the nape of my neck. She wasn't going to bring him in here, was she? Force him through the door by the scruff of the neck for me to see? No, surely not. I didn't want to face him. I couldn't face him. God no. My legs buckled, and I leant against the desk in the centre of the room. Willing myself to keep calm, I listened to the drum of my pulse quickening in my ears. My head whirled. *Fuck's sake, Eve, you need to pull yourself together.* I lowered my head to my knees, trying to stop the room from spinning.

'Eve, are you okay?' Detective Emmerson was back in the room, her hand resting on my shoulder. When did she return?

'Yeah.' I sat, pressing my ice like palms against my steaming face. The room eased back into focus. Although relieved she was alone, there was a possibility I would be sick on the floor.

'Let me get you some water.' Off she went, and the room was empty again.

I balled my hands into fists and banged them against my thighs. Furious I had shown weakness. He was going to pay for what he'd reduced me to. I blinked away hot tears which threatened to spill.

The door opened, and Emmerson returned with a plastic cup of water, which I drank in one go. The way she observed me, her face full of concern, amplified the heat in my scarlet cheeks.

'I'm sorry, I didn't think. Are you okay? Do you feel able to continue?'

Continue what? We hadn't even started.

Her palm rested across a pile of blank sheets of paper on the table.

'I have six photos here of potential suspects. I've included the man arrested for indecent exposure and a still from the CCTV I told you about from the day of the attack. When you're ready, I'll turn them over,' she said, as if I were a child.

A photo, I could handle a photo, couldn't I? Exhaling the breath I'd been holding, I gave her a quick nod and she flipped the pages over one at time. The first was the CCTV image and I couldn't tear my eyes away from it. My attacker was striding past someone's driveway, dressed in black, his hood pulled up and face hidden. I could see what Emmerson meant, there was almost nothing to go on, but it was definitely him.

'You think it's him?' Emmerson asked as I tapped the image of the CCTV.

'Yes.' My voice was quiet, like a mouse.

After a minute, I looked at the other photos. Men aged between twenty and forty, some dark, some blond, all with white skin. One had a kind of tribal tattoo on his face. I looked at them in turn, waited for an emotion, any kind of emotion, but nothing came. I was numb. I searched for blue eyes, but none were his. These were the eyes of other people's nightmares, not mine. They didn't fill me with a sense of dread and they weren't the ones I saw every time I closed my eyes, as if he stood right in front of me. My attacker's eyes were bright blue, the colour of topaz. On anyone else they would have been a handsome feature, I was sure. But his were blank and lifeless, they looked straight through you.

'I'm sorry. It's none of them.'

'Are you sure?' she asked, still hoping for a positive identification.

'I'm sure.'

I walked home from the police station in a daze, unable to shake the feeling I was being watched. I kept hearing footsteps behind me that weren't there, turning around every few steps. Perhaps I'd been spooked by seeing a picture of him. My stomach felt tied up in knots and I couldn't wait to get back to the safety of the flat. There was only one thing I wanted to do and that was to block him out of my mind.

Twenty minutes later, armed with a mug of tea, I headed to my room and popped the small white pill out of the blister packaging. The spaced-out feeling crept up on me slowly. It was like slipping into a warm bath with no worries or cares. My mind wandered, never settling on anything. Time slowed and I with it. When it wore off at around seven, I took another, intending to keep going until I'd run out.

11

FRIDAY 6 OCTOBER 2017

On day three, Ben staged an intervention. The whole thing was ridiculous, and we argued. I didn't have the energy for confrontation, my mind dulled by medication, but I made my point. How was it different from him getting stoned in his room every time his knee twinged? I knew I wasn't being fair, but I felt under attack.

'The rest of the time I'm still living, Eve. I'm in the fucking world, not shut away.'

I pushed him out of my room, but he sat outside my door for a while, refusing to move. He was stubborn.

'Talk to me. It might help if you talk to me.'

So, I told him, I spat the words angrily at first, through a haze of tears. Told him how I was brutalised over a bin, discarded like I was a piece of rubbish. How I could barely look myself in the mirror knowing I'd hindered the investigation. How I worried about the other women he may have hurt. He listened through the door. I could hear his gasps of shock and sighs of frustration, but he let me talk without interruption until I had nothing left to say.

'If you carry on living like this, he's won.'

I couldn't answer him.

'Come and see me when you're ready. I've got some ideas,' Ben said, before I heard his door click shut and the sound of the Xbox firing up.

I lay on my bed staring at the ceiling as my anger subsided. Ben was just trying to help. I tried to imagine what it must look like to him, seeing his flatmate retreat from life altogether.

My phone rang, muffled by the duvet. Was it Mum again? I'd missed two calls over the past couple of days, not wanting to speak to her whilst I was out of it. I'd missed one from Stuart too, yesterday and when I finally found the phone, I saw it was him calling.

'Hi Stuart,' I answered, my voice shaky.

'Hi Eve. How are you doing?' he sounded relieved I'd answered.

'I'm doing okay.'

'That's great. Listen, don't worry, I'm not calling about your return to work. I wanted to check in and see how you were doing but I also wanted to let you know what's happening here.'

'Okay,' I said.

He paused for a second and I sensed bad news was coming.

'Debbie wanted to call you, but I wanted to speak to you first. As a result of the merger, they've put a large group of us at risk. Some will be able to request voluntary redundancy. If we don't want to take voluntary, then it's likely we may have to reapply for our positions.' His voice was sombre, he was clearly unhappy about the development. 'There's going to be a consultation meeting on Monday, it's the first step in the collective process. You do not have to attend if you don't want to, but I think it would be in your interest.'

There was a long pause and I could hear Stuart's rapid breathing at the other end. I wasn't sure what he wanted me to say.

'There'll also be one-to-one consultations where you'll be able to ask any questions and I've been told it's not an immediate thing. By law they have to give us thirty days for the process. Mike in Operations is going to be one of the employee representatives.'

'Okay,' I said slowly, trying to take it all in. My stomach churned.

'I think Debbie has sent you an email with the initial announcement, so you can take a look. Listen, don't worry. Come in on Monday to the meeting and we can talk it through afterwards.' Stuart rang off, having to go as he had his wife on the other line. Probably pacing her lounge waiting to find out if her husband was going to lose his job.

My heart raced at the thought of the bills stuffed underneath my wardrobe, some unopened. How was I going to pay them now? I had to face it, sit down and work out exactly what I owed. I knew my overdraft was maxed out and my credit card was slowly rising. It wasn't a massive amount of money, a few thousand pounds, but looking around, I had nothing much to show for it. Some clothes, a laptop, a few nights out, but before I knew it, it had snowballed. I'd cut back at home, cancelling the satellite TV, limiting the amount of food I bought. Ben always commented there was nothing in the fridge, but he thought I was just busy, not skint. I knew I had a large council tax bill coming too. Maybe a lump sum of redundancy could solve my financial problems? I could get another job and start again with a clean slate.

Before seeking out Ben, I took a much-needed shower, but I could no longer bring myself to eat anything. My stomach was in knots with indecision. When he came out of his room to find me, he looked pleased with himself.

'Right. Operation Let's Get Eve's Shit Together commences.'

I rolled my eyes.

'You got any gym gear?' he asked. I nodded; I had some leggings and a couple of T-shirts I'd bought for a yoga class stuffed at the back of a drawer.

'My mate runs a boxing club. He does Boxercise too, but I told him it might be a step too far. We're going there tonight, and you can have a few rounds with a punchbag. Get out that residual anger. What do you think?'

'I think it's ridiculous.' I sat with my arms crossed, there was no way I was going. Boxing? I barely had any muscle strength at all. My limbs were stringy at best.

'I'm going to come with you. I've taken the night off work. It's Friday night, so it'll be quiet, I promise.'

I sighed, resigned to the fact there would be no getting out of it; Ben would be like a dog with a bone.

When we walked in to the boxing club, half an hour later, it smelt of sweat and cleaning products combined. I was expecting an old brick building, like in the Rocky films. This one was modern, housed in a warehouse on an industrial estate. There were a few men inside; two were pounding punchbags and one was skipping so fast you couldn't see the rope. It was mesmerising, like a permanent arc of light.

I shrank behind Ben as soon as we walked through the door, using him as a shield. A tall, heavyset, mixed-race man, with short black hair in tight curls, came out of the office and gave him a slap him on the back before noticing me.

''Ello mate, how you doing?' He was bouncy, with a slight cockney accent, and wore one of those ridiculous muscle vests. Although he had the physique to carry it off. They shook hands, the man pumping Ben's arm so hard I thought it might fall off.

'Not too bad, I see you got your lockers fitted?'

'Delivered yesterday.'

I looked around. Everything gleamed. New equipment, modern silver lockers and specific zoned areas for each activity. The ring in the centre was enormous, with glaring spotlights overhead. Not at all what I was expecting.

'It's coming along. So, who is this young lady?'

They both turned their attention to me and fire rose in my cheeks. I was under the microscope.

'This is Eve. My flatmate. Sorry, Eve, this is my good friend, Jason. We used to work together a few years ago.'

I held out my hand, ready to have my arm pumped, but Jason was much gentler with me. His dark eyes glinted, looking at me and then Ben. I wondered if Ben had mentioned me to him before?

'Eve would like to learn a bit about boxing, using the bags and some technique perhaps?'

I glared at Ben, but if Jason noticed he didn't comment. Five minutes later I had my hands wrapped in tape and shoved in gloves which were so big, it was comical. I looked like a clown.

Jason took his time explaining the correct way to punch, the movement coming from my shoulder, and how to pivot on my feet. It was a lot to take in and I'd never been a fan of boxing before, but it was fascinating. He gave Ben some pads and I punched them whilst we circled each other on the mats. At first, we were trying not to laugh, but it wasn't long before I was sweating. My shoulders screaming at me to stop. I was so unfit.

'You're a natural,' Ben said, laughing as he absorbed a blow, teetering on the heels of his feet before regaining his balance.

'This is so hard,' I whimpered, letting my arms drop to my sides. It felt like I'd been carrying a bag of bricks. Ben grinned like a Cheshire cat, pleased with himself.

'What's your goal then? Do you want to start boxing?' Jason asked. He took the pads off Ben and danced around me. I raised my arms once more, my energy almost gone, and tried to strike out.

'I'm not sure. I mean, I'd like to build myself up a bit, get fitter, but I'm not sure about fighting,' I wheezed. I used to think three minutes in a ring was no time at all, but the physical exertion was immense. I staggered and sat on the mat, catching my breath. I was done. Ben sat down beside me, his skin glistened. He was slim but broad in the shoulders and I hadn't really noticed the size of his biceps before now. Warmth flooded my face and I looked away.

'Well, I reckon you could do with some weights. Get some protein in you and start lifting and you should see results quite quickly. Feel free to come and use the equipment here.' Jason grinned, and I was waiting for him to ask me to sign on the dotted line. Twelve months of gym membership I couldn't afford, but he didn't. Instead, he carefully removed the gloves and placed an ice pack on my swollen knuckles. The cold a welcome relief.

We had tea in his office and a couple of younger guys came in to train whilst we were there. I watched them through the glass, amazed by how fast they could move and the power behind their punches. When they began sparring in the ring, I was captivated. Ben and Jason chatted about old times, a few years previous, when they had both worked as weekend nightclub bouncers for a bit of extra cash.

'Do you remember Pacino?' Jason asked, nudging Ben's shoulder. The actor's name caught my attention and I turned back to the conversation.

'God yeah, he liked a good scrap, didn't he.' Ben chuckled.

Jason caught sight of my confused expression and elaborated. 'This guy, I forget his real name, he loved action movies, the more violent, the better. His favourite actor was Al Pacino. We had a row one night, making conversation, you know, when the door was quiet. I said Tom Hanks was the best actor of our generation and he went into one. From then on, he was known as Pacino. Loved getting stuck in to a fight – and he did all right with the ladies too.'

'I think that was why he worked on the door,' Ben added.

'It was why we all did,' Jason winked at Ben and continued to reminisce about the women from those days.

By the sounds of it, Jason was a bit of a ladies' man and teased Ben about trailing behind in bedpost notches. I was pleased. I had no claim on Ben, or any intention of our relationship moving beyond platonic, but it was nice to learn he wasn't a player.

12

SATURDAY 7 OCTOBER 2017

I'd had a nice evening at the gym, it was a laugh listening to the banter between Ben and Jason. It made me realise how little I knew him, his friends, his family. As I tried to sleep, I kept picturing his sweaty face beaming at me from the mats, watching me try to skip and having no rhythm whatsoever. His perfectly shaped teeth dazzling under the spotlights and the touch of his fingers wrapped around mine as he helped me up when I fell. It felt weird to think of Ben that way. Almost as though I hadn't looked at him properly before.

I booted up my laptop early Saturday morning, after another fitful night. I had forgotten to check the email Debbie had sent yesterday and wanted to find out what had gone on at work. She'd written that they were missing me in the office and hoped I was feeling better. Not to rush back before I was ready but to let her know when I was up for having visitors as she would love to pop in for a tea. It was sweet of her and I found it easier to interact when not face to face. I typed a quick response back, letting her know I would see her on Monday for the meeting.

The email Stuart was talking about was a communication that had been distributed to everyone involved; I found it further down my inbox. It explained the reason behind the decision for redundancies, that being the newly acquired company Drive had bought. The amalgamation would lead to a necessary restructuring of personnel. It laid out the terms of thirty days for consultations, one-to-one sessions with human resources and alternative proposals where possible to avoid losing staff. It added that voluntary redundancy options could be available for some candidates.

I'd have to go in on Monday, but I still didn't know what to do. Should I opt for the voluntary redundancy? I owed money that I didn't have, unless I got a loan out to consolidate my debt or, worse, ask my mum to release money from her house. The idea didn't bear thinking about and I didn't mention it when she rang that morning, annoyed I hadn't returned her call. Since my chat with Ben, I'd reverted to taking my medication at the prescribed dose so was back in the real world, more alert and better prepared to deal with her if she was drunk.

'How are you doing, love?' Her words slurred even though it was barely ten o'clock.

'Mum, you need to stop drinking. We talked about this, remember? We talked about going to that group, the AA. There's one in Norwich, your doctor suggested it.'

'What do I need to go to that for?'

It was pointless talking to her in this state. She wouldn't listen to reason. Other than go up there and lock her away, I wasn't sure what else I could do. There was too much going on down here to deal with.

'Mum, I was raped,' I said, hoping to shock her out of her stupor.

'What?'

'I got attacked two weeks ago. It's why I wasn't feeling well. A man, he...' I began to cry. It was always so difficult to say it out loud. To say what he'd done. Stripping my dignity, claiming my body.

I heard a shuffle, like she'd dropped the phone and then a man's voice, the country twang of his accent.

'Come on, Liz, the Nelson will be open in a bit.' Then the line went dead.

I threw the phone across my room, it crashed into the wardrobe and bounced on the carpet. Fuck it, if she didn't care, then why should I. Let her drink herself to death. The voice in my head said that it wouldn't have been what Dad would have wanted. I knew that, of course I did, but what could I do? The weight of everything sat upon my shoulders. I needed a distraction, to take my mind off things and I knew just the person to help with that.

Jane came down for the afternoon. She had suggested I come to her, to get out, but could hear my reluctance. She lived in Balham, in a flat-share with three other nurses. It was cramped and too busy, plus I didn't want to get on a train yet, not by myself. Train stations were always packed and lots of people made my anxiety spike. I feared I'd pass out on the platform, easy-pickings for the unsavoury. Ben joined us for lunch; awkwardly just after I'd told Jane that I might be developing feelings for him. Her excitement was palpable at a possible love interest and her eyes glistened devilishly. I knew she wouldn't say anything, but my mouth dried up, so getting through my sandwich was a challenge.

Ben was oblivious to Jane's background checks. Before I could get a word in, she'd found out most of his history. Born in Croydon, he was the eldest, with a younger sister. His parents moved to Spain when he was twenty-five, so he had had to find somewhere to live. Moved in with his sister for a while, then rented two other flats before he moved in with me. Apparently, he'd had similar problems with flatmates that I'd had. He turned twenty-eight in April and was saving up a deposit to buy his own place, then he wanted to open his own security firm.

'Any girlfriends?'

Ben's ears grew pink, and I squirmed in my seat.

'Jane!' I countered.

'Two serious, a few not particularly serious. Nothing at the minute.'

My pulse quickened, and I took a bite of my sandwich as Jane lifted her eyebrows at me.

'Eve's the same. One at high school, one from work and her ex, Dean, but you and him were only together for about six months, weren't you?' Jane pointed her crisp at me and I began to cough, choking on a slice of ham I'd swallowed too quickly. Ben had to pat me on the back to dislodge it.

'Thanks for the chairs,' I said to Ben when I could speak again, hoping to change the subject. He bought a set of four matching ones to replace the three mismatched ones left after my outburst.

'Chairs?' Jane screwed up her face and Ben began to laugh.

'She broke one,' he said, nudging my elbow with his. I rolled my eyes.

Later, when Ben had left to go out, Jane voiced her approval. She thought Ben was perfect, but I told her I hadn't even decided whether I liked him yet. In return, she threw me a knowing look, but I shrugged it off. I was able to offload my worries about Mum and her drinking, on top of the redundancies at work. I didn't tell her about my debt, some things were too embarrassing to talk about.

Jane told me she'd started seeing a doctor in neurology. He was tall with wavy blond hair and I could see from her face she was already smitten. She said he was toying with the idea of coming travelling with her next year and she'd set a date of the first of February. She thought that would give her enough time to save up the rest of her travelling money. I was excited for her but couldn't help feeling sad she would be leaving me, probably for a year.

* * *

Monday 9 October 2017

I scrolled down the page, trying to find what I wanted. It amazed me what could be bought online, delivered anonymously to an address with no repercussions. What would you have to buy for red flags to be raised? What purchases would result in a knock on the door from the police?

There, I found what I was looking for. A rape alarm to carry with me. Yesterday I went back to the boxing club with Ben, used the weight machines and the punchbag. I'd caught the bug and was keen to return. He'd offered me the use of his car during the day, when he would be sleeping, but the club was less than a mile away and I decided I would try to jog there and back. A tick in the box on the cardio front.

I checked out, my credit card details saved on the website from the numerous purchases I'd made already.

I had a few hours spare before I had to be at work for the redundancy meeting in the afternoon and I was itching to go back to the boxing club. I rang and told Stuart I would be taking another week, and that I was still anxious about going out, but I would endeavour to make the redundancy meeting. I didn't want to forget to hand in my doctor's certificate, which had run out on Friday. I intended to self-certify this week. What with us potentially losing our jobs, I wasn't in a rush to return.

I started slow, a minute's jog, then a minute's walk. Enjoying the fresh air. I didn't need music to propel me, anger carried me along. I only had to picture his face, the one I'd conjured from the shape of the balaclava, to boil my blood. His mouth, smirking, was what I visualised as my trainers pounded the pavement. I needed new ones, proper ones for running.

Jason was impressed when I arrived and gave me a quick circuit training session, moving from the bag, to the weights and then the speedball.

'Listen, you're not going to make any money letting me train here for free,' I said, as he helped me out of my gloves.

'You're my best mate's girl. I can't charge you.'

I snorted. What had Ben been telling him?

'Honestly, let me pay. Give me a half-price discount if you feel guilty,' I suggested cheekily.

'All right, if you insist.' We shook hands and went into the office, so I could fill in the direct debit form. I felt sick signing it, more money coming out when I didn't have enough going in, but at least I wouldn't feel like I was taking advantage.

I really had to push myself to jog home, only speeding up when it started to rain. As I rounded the corner, my flat in sight, I collided with a man, bouncing off him and falling awkwardly back onto the pavement, winded with a bruised backside.

The man towered over me, a looming monster in shadow.

He wore desert boots and jogging bottoms covered in dust. 'You all right, lass?' he said. Leaning down, he wrapped an arm around my back. His hand stuck underneath my armpit, pulling me up with ease.

Who the fuck did he think he was? The shock of the collision and him touching me uninvited made me erupt. Shoving his hands away, I screamed obscenities in his face. His eyes widened, and he stepped back. My face twisted in fury, teeth bared like an animal.

'Crazy bitch,' he muttered and pushed past me to carry on in the direction I had run from.

I felt invigorated. More alive than I had in ages. The veins in my neck and forehead stood proud, the rush of adrenaline immense. I could do this. I could get my life back. I could work at becoming better, stronger and faster. I had a purpose.

The group meeting at work was uncomfortable. Debbie tried to be professional, but even she welled up in parts, obviously not as confident as she first thought about staying. We stood together at the back as other members of staff chipped in their two pennies' worth. They'd riled themselves up and Mike, the Operations Manager, was having a hard time controlling the room. A booming voice from the human resources director talked over everyone. But there wasn't much more information than Debbie had forwarded on Friday.

At the end of the group meeting, Stuart and I met in his office with a man I'd never seen before. He was Russian, with a name I knew I wouldn't be able to pronounce as soon as he introduced himself. He was a HR consultant who'd been brought on board to streamline the merging of the two companies. The office was too hot, and I felt my underarms dampen the blouse I'd put on for my visit.

'Thank you for coming in, Eve. I understand this been a very difficult couple of weeks for you. I'm sorry to hear of your incident.'

Incident? That got my back up. It wasn't a car accident.

'I see you were in attendance at the meeting just now. Do you have any questions currently? Or if you'd feel more comfortable I could ask Mike, the employee representative, to get in touch with you if you'd rather go through him?'

'I'm considering voluntary redundancy if it would be an option for me?' I admitted, glancing guiltily at Stuart, who grimaced but remained silent.

'Okay, I'll discuss the possibility of this in more detail with Stuart and potentially get some figures together for you.'

I pushed my doctor's certificate across the table to Stuart and stood to leave.

'Is there anything else?' I asked, keen to get out of there.

'No, not at the moment. We'll be in touch.'

I felt sick as I walked out of the office. I couldn't find Debbie anywhere, and she wasn't at the bus stop. I'd make sure to text her later and see how she was. I debated with myself all the way home. Why would I give up a perfectly good job when I was knee deep in debt? What if I couldn't get another one? The voice in my head counselled, *You're just getting your figures, you don't have to accept whatever package they offer*. But my stomach somersaulted all the way home.

13

SUNDAY 28 JANUARY 2018

Hicks steps outside the room with Becker for a minute, my solicitor hot on their heels, while I remain, sat at the table. A custody officer guards the door, looking anywhere but at me. I stare at my hands which still have remnants of blood in the creases of my knuckles. I ache for a proper shower, so I can have a wash, with soap this time. I want to remove every trace of Ian from my skin. I need to sleep soon too. The ringing in my ears has developed into a pounding headache, like a woodpecker at my temple. What are they doing? Looking at CCTV? Surely the lab results wouldn't be back this soon? Perhaps they are trying to corroborate what I have told them so far? It shouldn't be hard. Maybe they are trying to unnerve me? It's working. I must stick as close to the truth as possible. I'm not lying, it all happened, and most of it in the way I'm going to describe.

I don't like sitting alone, the room seems to be shrinking and I drum my fingers on the desk. It could be that my name in the system has brought back a result and they are reading my file. It's going to happen eventually for sure, unless I'm really lucky.

Five minutes go by and Becker waltzes back in.

'We're going to finish this for tonight and pick it up again in the morning. Jamie will take you back to your cell.' It's not 'tonight' any more, closer to three or four. My eyelids are heavy and I'm glad for the respite. She gestures towards the young officer standing beside her at the door. I catch her try to stifle a yawn. Her pristine exterior is beginning to crack.

'What time is it?' I ask.

Becker glances at her watch. It's a plain, leather strap no-frills, design.

'Half past three. Can I get you anything? Tea? Something to eat?'

'No, thank you, I just want to sleep.'

I yawn, hiding my amusement as I watch Becker turn away to do the same.

Once inside the cell, I put on grey jogging bottoms and a sweatshirt that's been left for me, to replace the paper suit. Glad not to have the irritating crackle every time I move. Wrapped in my blanket, I huddle down on the bench. Fully intending to go over answers to questions I know I will be asked in a few hours, but within minutes my eyes are closing, exhaustion wins, and I drift off to sleep. For the first time in months I don't dream at all.

* * *

Tuesday 10 October 2017

The following day, I roped Ben into taking me to the supermarket, where I stocked up on meat, so I could get the protein I was lacking.

'I bet you didn't know I could cook,' I said to Ben, putting some diced pork into the trolley. The aisle was freezing, and my jumper wasn't doing much to stave off the cold. Outside, the temperature had dropped, the Indian summer we'd been blessed with had gone and autumn was on its way. The supermarket was already filling its shelves with pumpkins and sweets for trick or treat.

'Are you going to cook for me then?' Ben's eyes sparkled.

'I might. What do you like?'

Ben put two sirloin steaks into the trolley and raised his eyebrows at me expectantly. I swallowed hard but smiled. I hoped he was paying?

'Okay, you're on. I'll cook you a steak tonight. How do you have it?'

'Medium is fine. Anything as long as it's not bleeding.'

'Me too.' I chuckled.

'I've got to pop out this afternoon though,' he said.

'Table will be laid for seven. If you're late it's going in the dog.'

'We don't have a dog.'

I had a productive afternoon cleaning the flat, putting on washing and even fitted in a workout at lunchtime. Jason had been there and humoured me with some light sparring in the ring. I looked like an idiot, wearing the helmet and mouth-guard, but we danced around, and he was kind enough to let me land a few punches. My groin ached from yesterday's jog, so I walked most of the way there and back, not wanting to push myself too much too soon.

When I got home, I showered and put on jeans and a top, something fitted opposed to the baggy clothes I'd been wearing recently. When I looked at my reflection, the girl I used to be stared back. I wore my mousy hair down after smoothing with the straighteners. It felt odd as I hadn't worn it loose since the attack. Remembering him yank my hair sent a shudder through me. I applied a touch of make-up but still something was missing. I couldn't quite put my finger on it.

At six Ben still wasn't home. I laid the table, setting out the napkins and wine glasses. I found them in the back of the cupboard; we didn't usually drink wine. I lit a candle in the middle of the two settings, then blew it out again. Was it too intimate? Was I sending out the wrong message? What message did I want to send? I hadn't been out with anyone since Dean, a year ago, but things felt different with Ben. I'd never cooked for Dean, but we had gone out for dinner a few times before things fizzled out. A relationship wasn't at the top of either of our priorities at the time; I'd wanted to concentrate on building my career in marketing. Now the enthusiasm for that had dwindled too. I'd been changed by the assault, life had been turned on its head. Things that used to matter so much to me were irrelevant, and stuff which would previously go over my head infuriated me now. I wasn't sure who I was any more. I was still waiting for the pills to level me out.

At quarter to seven, I pan fried the steaks, turning them over and browning each side. They sizzled, filling the kitchen with a delicious aroma. I had made potato wedges and a salad to go with the steak and bought a cheesecake for dessert. It wasn't until I was taking the wedges out of the oven that I heard Ben's key in the door. My mouth dropped open in surprise, oven glove in hand, as he entered the kitchen. He'd been to the hairdressers and his shaggy dark hair had been transformed into a short back and sides. He wore a blue and red checked shirt tucked into dark denim jeans. I had never seen him look so smart out of his work clothes. He plonked a bottle of wine on the table and grinned at my open mouth.

'Wine? It's chilled,' he asked as he grabbed a corkscrew out of the drawer and opened the bottle.

'Wow. Look at you!' I turned my back on him and busied myself dishing up to hide the blush creeping up my neck. 'Sit,' I ordered and delivered the plates to the table as he poured. 'I didn't think you were coming,' I admitted.

'Like I'd stand you up. My life wouldn't be worth living. I've been on the end of one of your punches remember.'

The strange atmosphere between us, charged from when he'd entered the room, dispersed. Ben cut through his steak, blushing pink in the middle but thankfully no blood, popped it in his mouth and chewed. His eyes rolling in delight.

'Amazing,' he said. His pupils were dilated, but I couldn't work out if it was the steak or me.

We chatted about his afternoon, he went out to the barbers and then the shops before stopping in to see Jason on the way home.

'Did he tell you I was there earlier?'

'Yep. He's quite impressed, you know, thinks you have talent.'

I scoffed at that. 'Unlikely.'

We moved on to talk about his work, the issues he was having onboarding a company who wanted to store antique furniture. The conversation flowed effortlessly; Ben was easy to talk to and I enjoyed his company. Plus, he made me laugh.

'I have some news,' I said, taking a sip of my second glass of wine. My head swam. Wine wasn't my best drink and the alcohol was already starting to take effect, even with a stomach full of steak. Ben removed the empty plates in front of us, putting them on the side. He came back to the table and lit us both a cigarette. I didn't have the heart to tell him I was quitting.

'Go on.' The intensity of his stare made my stomach flip.

'I think I'm being made redundant.'

Ben frowned, taking in my announcement. 'Fuck, Eve. I'm sorry. God why do all these things come at once!'

'No, no, it's voluntary.' I wasn't sure why I was telling Ben, maybe because I'd decided to go for it, take the money, clear my debts and start again.

'Why?' Ben was still frowning. Why was he frowning?

'Because I need a change.' I crossed my arms, annoyed he wasn't looking at it positively. His concern mirrored my own and made me agitated, shifting in my seat. 'Anyway, forget it. Let's talk about something else,' I said, trying to change the subject.

'Okay, it's your decision. I just don't understand why, but I guess it's up to you.'

'Yes, it is, and I could do without your negativity.' Regretting it as soon as it was out.

Ben spluttered, almost spitting his mouthful of wine all over the table. 'Yeah, my negativity. Of course. That's a fucking laugh that is. I'm the negative one?'

'What's that supposed to mean?' I hadn't meant to raise my voice, it just happened. I stubbed my cigarette out in the ashtray.

'It's him, isn't it. You're throwing your life away because of him.'

'This has nothing to do with him.'

'Yeah, sure.' Ben's eye's darkened and he sneered.

'I'm taking control, Ben. I need a change, a fresh start somewhere new. I'll always be a victim there.'

'They'll forget in time.'

'I won't.' I replied.

Ben looked away, taking a large gulp of wine. I had to make sure that I was going to be more than what had happened to me. I was a grown woman and it was time I took control of my life and decided where I wanted it to go. A new career could be the positive outcome in all this. Perhaps one in fitness? I could train to be an instructor. I was enjoying the exercise and working out with Jason. The idea swam around in my mind, beginning to take shape. It gave me something to think about for the future at least.

14

TUESDAY 10 OCTOBER 2017

I couldn't tell Ben that, to a certain extent, he was right. Everything I did now was because of *him*. A knee-jerk reaction. My nameless attacker, who'd left me scarred, not physically, but in other ways. On the inside – scars that didn't show. Ones that didn't heal. I couldn't tell Ben about the rage that boiled inside, threatening to escape all the time. I didn't mention the man whose face I screamed into for no reason, except being in the wrong place at the wrong time. The emotion was alien to me and I had no idea how to control it. The only way I felt better was pounding the punchbag or the pavement. When my muscles screamed, the anger was channelled.

Before, I was so chilled out. Now a part of me was broken and I wasn't sure if it could be fixed. I didn't feel as scared as I had, not when I was outside. But the nightmares persisted, each one different; all with the same ending. My body, beaten and bloody, naked and exposed, left in the dirt.

My train of thought was interrupted by Ben reaching

across the table and placing his hand on top of mine. I stared at it, not wanting to meet his gaze. It felt warm and safe.

'I'm sorry. It's none of my business.'

I pulled my hand away and got up, retrieving the cheesecake I was no longer interested in eating from the fridge.

'It's fine. Priorities change, that's all. I'm going to take some time out, carry on with my training. Maybe do something else. I don't know.'

Ben nodded but didn't speak and we ate our dessert in silence. I struggled to swallow the cloggy sweet mixture. The evening had been spoilt and I wasn't sure I could pull it back.

'You're going to be rolling in the money then, eh? Steak every night?' Ben's tone changed, and the mood lifted, the atmosphere dispelled. If only it were true. If I was lucky, the redundancy would cover most of my debt but wouldn't be enough to live on for long.

'I'm not cooking for you every night. Get yourself a wife if you want that,' I retorted, grateful the banter had resumed.

'Well, I'm on the lookout. In fact, I'm inundated, as you can imagine.' It was as if a cross word hadn't passed between us.

Ben helped me to wash up even though I protested and then we finished the bottle of wine, watching the shadows the candle created flicker around the room.

'Thanks for dinner, it was lovely. You cook a mean steak.' Ben's brown eyes twinkled, his eyelashes long and dark. Ones women would kill for. My chest fluttered, I'd seen something different in Ben.

It may have been the clothes, or his hair, or even the wine, but when we said goodnight I didn't protest when Ben leaned in to kiss my lips. He stared at me afterwards, as if surprised by his actions. There was no awkwardness and we giggled, unsure how to proceed. He stepped closer again, over the threshold into my room. It wasn't until Ben placed his hand on my cheek as we kissed that *he* appeared. I was back there, behind the café, his gloved hand stroking my face. My throat tightened, and I pushed Ben's arm away, the moment gone.

'I'm sorry,' he said, retreating into the hallway. Did he think I was a tease? If only he could see inside my messed-up head.

'It's me, sorry. It's just he did that.' I raised my hand to my face, tears springing from my eyes. On tiptoes I gave Ben a quick kiss on the cheek and slipped inside my bedroom, closing the door on the exchange in the hallway. I was an idiot. Could Ben and I be more than friends? I was paralysed, unable to move forward. It was ridiculous, but how could I change it? Maybe it would take time?

Perhaps if the police had taken more of an interest. If they'd found him and I knew he wasn't still out there; probably wandering the streets and hurting other women, I'd be able to get over it. Maybe he wasn't looking for other women. What if he had only been looking for me? No, surely not. He was a predator, an opportunist. I was sure it was a case of being in the wrong place at the wrong time. It couldn't have been targeted, could it? Had I been followed?

With my mind whirring, the sleep that followed was broken. As it was every night since it had happened. Nightmares continued to plague my subconscious. I'd have to go back to the doctors', perhaps I could get some sleeping pills? In the most recent nightmare it was Ben chasing me through the streets, but when he caught me, his face morphed into my assailant. His grip was so strong, I couldn't get away.

* * *

I rose early on Wednesday morning, pleased to see my period had arrived. It confirmed I wasn't pregnant although I doubted I would have been anyway. I was sure my attacker had used protection to ensure evidence hadn't been left behind. I took an intermittent jog to the boxing club around eight o'clock. The sky was a threatening grey and fog lingered low to the ground. The rape alarm would be delivered this week, then I could carry it with me. I knew I would feel safer.

When I arrived at the gym, there were no cars outside. I was alone. Jason had given me the key code to open the thick metal door. Inside, it was pitch-black and I panicked, sliding my hand over the wall to find the lights. My heart jumped into my mouth as I fumbled around. Where was the damn switch? Finally, I made contact with the plastic panel and the fluorescent strips flickered, then powered on. Their intensity stinging my eyes. The silence was eerie, such a big open space with only me inside. Every sound I made echoed.

Trying to ignore the feeling I wasn't alone, I skipped for a minute or so as fast as I could, listening to the rope smack the mat over and over again. Blood pumped around my body and I put on the gloves Jason had loaned me. They were difficult to fasten by yourself. I danced around the bag, imagining his face every time I struck it. Punching until my knuckles were tender. My shoulders and arms were already looking defined and I was lifting more than when I started. I was stronger and more capable than ever. Grateful to Ben for introducing me to this outlet and Jason for being my unofficial trainer.

When I finished my workout, I left the club the same way I found it as no one else had arrived. Despite being sweaty, I detoured past the sports shop on the high street and purchased a new pair of running trainers. They set me back over a hundred pounds, but I was pleased. They were an investment and it was good to learn my credit card was still working.

When I got home, Ben had left the post on the kitchen table. No demand letters thankfully, but my redundancy offer was there, along with another bearing the NHS logo, which was most likely my psychiatrist's appointment. I tore open the letter from work, hoping to find a sum that would solve all my problems. My heart sank at the figure, it was only just enough to cover my debts. They'd offered me £3,956 and that included an enhanced figure of £2000 because it was voluntary. I could argue for more, but it was unlikely I'd get anywhere.

I typed a text to Debbie.

`Hi, how are you? How are things there? Can you let Stuart know I'm going to come in tomorrow please? If you've got time we'll grab a coffee. Xxx`

I left the kitchen and went for a shower, standing under the hot water for a long time. Trying to figure out what to do. I'd have to ask Mum for a loan, but before I did, I needed to add up exactly what I owed.

In my dressing gown, with a towel on my head, I started to pull the envelopes out from underneath the wardrobe. I looked first at the pile of unopened mail, then to the brand-new trainers I'd thrown on my bed. I tore open the first letter. It was time to pull my head out of the sand.

15

HIM

The itching has started again. It crawls over my skin like a swarm of ants. I tried to stretch her out a bit longer, make her last. But it's never enough. I try to relive it. The look of terror was so arousing, her green eyes like emerald pools as they met mine. Every time it's the same, the shock etched on their faces. Their bodies betray the panic they try to hide. Hearts race, veins throb, skin as cold as ice. Their fear is invigorating, but the time in between leaves me impotent and longing. Each one is different, but they all comply.

She was special. I consumed her. Stirring in my groin builds until I get the release I crave. I hope she'll be easy to find again. I considered following her as she staggered across the park, but I'm not stupid. I'm sure the police are following my trail and I must not make any mistakes.

I need more. No amount of violence can quell my urges. No amount of sex can satisfy my needs. In time I could surprise her, just when she thought I was a distant nightmare. If I had the chance again with her, I would take my time. I would make her last a lifetime

16

THURSDAY 12 OCTOBER 2017

I didn't see Ben on Thursday. When I got up his door was shut, and I assumed he was asleep. When I got home from the boxing club, his door was ajar, and his car gone. I hoped he wasn't avoiding me? I didn't want things to be uncomfortable between us. As much as my feelings had grown towards Ben, in the cold light of day, getting involved with someone you lived with would likely end in tears and I didn't want to look for another flatmate.

I put on my usual work staple of black trousers, teamed with a polka dot shirt, it looked a tad baggy but would have to do. After I added up exactly what I owed, sat on the carpet with my calculator, the future seemed a little clearer. The redundancy would cover all of my credit card debt and I could get a small loan from my mum for the council tax bill that I knew was coming. I'd change my electric and council tax bills to a manageable monthly direct debit in the hope I could turn things around. I had no phone contract, only a pay-as-you-go, so I only used what I could afford. As long as I stopped overspending, I should be fine. The weight of debt had been hanging over me for a while, the load getting heavier week by week, but for the first time in months, I felt positive about what lay ahead.

The rain drizzled, making my hair frizz, and I wrapped my coat around myself, missing the sunshine which now seemed a distant memory. I should have brought my umbrella. A black sky loomed overhead, threatening heavier showers to come. On my way to the office, I perused agency windows to see what job prospects were out there. Not much by the looks of it, but I wasn't going to let it ruin my mood. When I arrived, Debbie was outside at the bus stop, puffing away. She didn't seem her bubbly self.

'It's horrible in there, everyone is so down. It's like we're being pitted against each other. I'm worried I'm going to be pushed out in favour of her, yet I have more experience. Darren is worried, his company hasn't been making a profit for a while. It's just a blip, but we rely on my wage.'

I rubbed her arm, creating static to her satin sleeve, and pulled two cigarettes from my pack, handing her one. She sighed and took it, her eyes red-rimmed.

'Do you want to get a coffee later?' I sensed she needed to offload.

'No, I can't, hon, she's in today and I've got to show her how to access the personnel data.' That sounded ominous. 'Anyway, there's me moaning on. How are you?'

'I think I'm doing a bit better actually. I'm going to go for the redundancy.'

'Oh really! That's a shame, although I think they'll jump at that, hardly anyone has. I think they were hoping for more of a take-up, so choosing who stays wouldn't be as messy.'

Inside the office, Stuart called the Russian HR manager to ask him to come down when he was available. The news of the redundancy situation had affected Stuart, he looked as though his zest for the job had gone. I was glad I hadn't been in to witness it. He said he didn't know what he was going to do yet.

When the Russian came down, we sat down around the table in Stuart's office.

'I'd like to accept the voluntary redundancy package that was sent through please.'

'Okay, Stuart, what sort of handover period do you think Eve will need to provide.'

'I should imagine a few days, a week at most. However, Eve is currently on sick leave.'

'Yes, of course. Eve, do you think you would be up to coming in next week to show Jessica the ropes?'

I nodded. So, my replacement was called Jessica? I hadn't heard her name before. A twinge of jealousy hit my side. Why wasn't Stuart fighting for me to stay? Was she the better one out of the two of us?

'I believe once the handover is completed, we can pay you in lieu of your notice, which will begin on Friday the twentieth of October, for four weeks. On top of your redundancy package, which you will receive in a lump sum.'

'I won't have to come in once the handover is complete?' That was a result.

'No, it's not necessary. I understand you've recently had a traumatic time. Drive will always ensure its employees are treated compassionately, and given your extenuating circumstances, I don't think it's in anyone's best interest to make you work your notice.' He pushed the offer in writing, across the desk. Placing a pen on top. 'Now, if you'll just sign here and here, we can get this tied up today.'

Thirty minutes later, I left the office, a weird feeling

bubbling inside me. Positive and excited for change, but also nervous and worried for the future. What if I couldn't get a job as quickly as I needed to? What if I couldn't find one that paid as well?

My phone rang, it was Mum. I hadn't spoken to her since she'd cut me off.

'Hi, Mum.'

'I've been trying to get hold of you? I've rung every day. Are you okay? If you hadn't answered, I was going to drive down.' I wouldn't put it past her to just turn up. She'd done it before. I hadn't missed any calls though, so she couldn't have been trying that hard to get in touch.

'I'm fine.'

'You said you were raped?'

'I don't want to talk about it now, Mum.' That ship had sailed.

'I want to let you know I'm here if you need me.'

I rolled my eyes, sure she was.

'Who's Patrick?' I asked.

'Patrick? He's my friend. His son owns the off-licence.'

I snorted. That made perfect sense. At least she was sober this morning, or not yet drunk enough to slur her words.

'I need to have some company up here, Eve. It's lonely.'

'So, come home, Mum, back to Sutton.' I didn't want to be her carer, but if she was here I could support her recovery.

'I can't. You know I can't.'

We didn't speak for a few seconds, the silence stretching out between us.

'Mum, do you think you would be able to send me some money, please?'

'How much?'

'Five hundred pounds.'

'What for?'

'Council tax.'

'Of course. I'll write a cheque and put it in the post today, is that okay?'

I agreed and thanked her. Did people even use cheques any more? I wasn't going to moan. I hated borrowing money, especially from her. When she got drunk, she would likely throw it back in my face. It was a double-edged sword, but it was the only option I had.

Back at the flat, I cleaned and hoovered, resisting the urge to go in to Ben's room. It took all my willpower not to have a look around. I sat at the table dipping a digestive into my tea and pondering what to have for dinner when Detective Emmerson rang. I'd turned the volume up loud on my phone and when it went off, I almost hit the ceiling, spilling tea all over the kitchen table.

'Hello Eve, it's Detective Emmerson,' she said, her voice already sounding grave.

I sank back into the chair, staring at the puddle of tea, awaiting the bad news. 'Hello.'

'I wanted to check in, see how you were doing?'

'I'm okay. Have you any news?' I wasn't interested in niceties.

'No, I'm afraid not, nothing new. We've visited all known local sex offenders, however none match the physical description you gave us. The ones we spoke to, their movements were all accounted for that morning. So, we've hit a bit of a dead end.'

'Right.' I wasn't intending on make this call any easier for her or engaging in small talk. The silence grew between us until she spoke.

'Statistics show that around eighty-five per cent of victims of sexual assault are known to their attackers. Looking at that, is there anyone you can think of we could talk to. Anyone at work?'

An icy feeling zigzagged its way across my back and I sat up straight. I didn't know of anyone, did I? I thought of the men at Drive. Acquaintances, friends of friends.

'No, I don't think so.'

'Okay, please don't hesitate to get in touch if someone comes to mind. We will of course keep the inquiry active and I believe someone so bold as to do what he did in broad daylight, it's only a matter of time before he attacks again. I will keep in touch.'

We said our goodbyes and I launched my foot at the chair opposite me, sending it skidding across the kitchen floor. What was the point? They couldn't protect me. No one could. Even the police were counting on him doing it again. They were out of leads and I was on my own. Lack of resources, lack of enthusiasm; I could do a better job of finding him.

My skin tingled, and goosebumps appeared on my arms as the idea trickled through me. Could I find him? If I managed to, I could follow him, tell them where he lived. They'd have to arrest him. He'd be off the streets. But what if he saw me? My heart pounded at the thought. It was crazy. My palms began to sweat. *You can do this. Fuck, yes, you can do this. You can get the bastard and make him pay for what he did.* The voice in my head continued to campaign for me to take control. My father, who was the wisest man I'd ever known, had warned me when I was having trouble with friends at school that the only person you could rely on was yourself. He was right. The police were useless.

Riffling through my cupboard, I pulled out black clothes easily, it had always been my colour of choice. I tied my hair into a bun and tucked it under a baseball cap. My reflection resembled that of a pre-pubescent boy. It wasn't the look I was going for, but if it disguised who I was, I was happy. I just wanted to blend into the background, to watch and wait. He'd have to show up eventually and then I'd have him.

Walking back to where it happened in the late afternoon drizzle brought me back to reality. What was I thinking? The idea was stupid. Someone would end up getting hurt. *I* could get hurt again. I might not walk away this time. What was I, a vigilante? No, it was reconnaissance, there would be no interaction at all.

As I reached the entrance to the park, the one I'd used that morning, I paused to read the yellow police incident sign. There must be one at both entrances. The date and the time of the worst moment of my life recorded for everyone to see. It was surreal.

I didn't go up to the café. I couldn't bring myself to go to the exact spot, but I knew he must have followed me, as he came from behind. I sat on a damp bench, close to the entrance, staring into the distance. Hoping he would walk past but I knew my chances were slim.

Almost two hours and five cigarettes later, I was cold and damp from the rain, my backside numb. It was starting to get dark and I was getting jittery, wanting to make sure I was safely back home before the sun set fully. The only people to come past were: a group of three teenagers, a father and his two kids on bikes and two elderly women. What was I doing? What were the chances he'd come back here, return to the scene of the crime? I had this all wrong. I sneezed into my hands, and headed home.

17

SUNDAY 28 JANUARY 2018

The sun streams through the small oblong window near the ceiling, illuminating a rectangle of concrete on the floor as though it is a sign from a higher power. My back creaks as I move to sit, muscles stiff from the bench. Thankfully the headache has gone, but my entire body hurts. I feel sore everywhere after last night's struggle. I brush my fingers over my eye, feeling the puffy lid and socket. My cheekbone, once prominent, is hidden under swollen tender flesh. I feel like I've been run over. I have no idea of the time, but I can hear movement beyond the cell walls. I was hoping to wake in my bed this morning, but that was too optimistic.

The viewing hatch shoots up, the slicing noise making me jump, and a pair of brown eyes encased in pale creased skin stare through.

'Tea?' he asks in a cheerful voice and I smile and nod gratefully.

It's a while before he returns with a polystyrene cup, which I clasp my hands around. He's in his late fifties and I have a flash of concern that he's exposed to violent criminals daily down here. He doesn't look like he'd be too handy. But then, neither do I.

'Bacon or egg?' He holds up a cellophane wrapped breakfast roll. I guess I'd be screwed if I was vegan.

'Bacon please.'

'I guessed right.' He passes the roll to me and I tear off the wrapping and bite into it hungrily, disappointed that it's cold. What did I expect?

'Could you tell me the time please?' I say, my hand covering my still full mouth.

'It's eight thirty, miss.' He smiles at me and his eyes carry no judgement. 'Did you want five minutes in the yard once you've had that, to get some fresh air?'

'Please.'

The yard is tiny, but it's in the full sun and I face the sky to bathe in it. I feel like I haven't been outside for a week. The temperature is freezing, but I don't care. The air is clean and fresh, and I take in as much as I can. They have until around midnight to charge or release me unless they apply for an extension. Everything rides on my interview today. The enormity of the situation threatens to spill out, but I try to keep it contained. I must not panic. I can do this.

* * *

Sunday 15 October 2017

I sat in the chair, the lamp above my head had glowing red cylinders, reminding me of the film, *War of the Worlds*. The warmth was pleasant though, like being on a sunbed. My scalp burned, but I'd been told to expect that. I was dying to scratch my head and gnawed at my fingernails to stave off the urge. Finally, when it was washed off and I returned to the mirror, the change was shocking.

'It's a dramatic transformation.' I could tell she was nervous that I was going to cry. She had tried to talk me out of it in the beginning. I smiled to show I wasn't upset, and she began combing the hair before cutting.

Forty minutes later, the floor was covered in a layer of bleached hair, so blonde it was almost white. I'd gone from having shoulder length mousy brown hair to an ice-blonde graduated bob that stopped at my chin, making my features look more angular.

'I love it, it's so striking.' The hairdresser's fiery red curls bouncing from all the jiggling she was doing. Perhaps she needed the toilet?

'Thanks very much, it's perfect,' I said. It would take time to get used to. It would make me stand out for sure, which I wasn't sure I wanted, but it was the new me. As different as I could look for under a hundred pounds. I wouldn't be mistaken for Eve the victim any more.

I paid and dutifully rebooked in six weeks to have my roots done, although I wasn't sure I'd be back. Perhaps I could do it at home and save the nightmarish interaction I just wasn't any good at. Not to mention the price tag a cut and colour cost these days.

'Wow.' Was Ben's first word when he caught sight of me, his head snapping back as we passed in the kitchen doorway.

'Tea?' I asked, stifling a smile. What was it with men and blondes?

'Yes, please. I can't believe how different you look.' He sat at the table, still staring, open mouthed.

'Fancied a change.'

'Big change.'

I hadn't seen him all week, since the night I'd cooked dinner. He'd obviously been avoiding me, and this proved a good distraction from how the evening had ended.

'How are you?' I asked.

'Good. You?'

I nodded and placed the tea in front of him.

'It's the same colour as that bird off *Game of Thrones*.' It was then I remembered he had a thing for her. As long as he didn't think I'd done it for his benefit. My cheeks flushed. Maybe subconsciously I had?

I changed the subject and we talked about going to the cinema. There was a horror film he wanted to see on the big screen. It sounded fun. I hadn't been to the cinema in ages.

'You not opened this yet?' He tapped the letter propped against the empty fruit bowl which had turned into a deposit for junk. It was my psychiatrist's appointment and I'd forgotten to open it when it first arrived. I ripped open the envelope, the appointment was booked for a week Tuesday. I rolled my eyes. 'Not going then?' Ben's tone was disapproving, and he frowned at me.

'I'm not sure. What if they lock me up?' I tried to joke, but Ben's smile didn't reach his eyes. He looked concerned for me and I wanted to hand him my heart for safekeeping, but there was too much going on. Too many things I couldn't tell him. How could I open up and let everything out? I was barely keeping my shit together as it was. But I knew I could trust him and right now he was the closest friend I had. I reached over and squeezed his hand.

'What's that for?' he asked.

'I don't know, just for being you. I appreciate all you've done for me, I really do. It means a lot.' It was Ben's turn to blush.

'Have you seen Jason?' Ben asked, his voice strained.

'No, not for a few days, why?'

'He asked me if we were a thing, said he was thinking about asking you out. I just wasn't sure you were in the right place for that.'

'You didn't tell him?' I interrupted. I didn't want Jason looking at me in the same way everyone else did that knew.

'No, of course not, I just said you had a lot going on and you weren't looking for anything right now.'

I moved away from the table, rinsing my empty cup at the sink.

'I'm not.'

I turned round to face Ben and saw him heave a silent sigh.

'He's not my type anyway,' I added.

'Just be careful. He's a player.'

I nodded, I'd gathered that already.

'He probably won't even recognise me,' I said. I couldn't decide if I liked the blonde but different was good. Different was safe.

18

DC BECKER

I sit at traffic lights, five minutes from home, the image of Eve's battered face etched in my mind. I hate these kinds of cases, they hit a nerve. There are too many monsters out there. I wish I could catch them all, but even if I could, they'd get chewed up in the justice system. Spat out, apparently reformed after a pitiful sentence, only to offend again. We do the best we can with the resources we've got but it never feels like enough.

The car behind beeps its horn, signalling me to move. Lights are now green, and I pull away slowly. It's a taxi, the driver overtaking me as soon as he's able to. I don't care, I shouldn't even be behind the wheel. I'm exhausted. Only a couple more minutes and I'll be home. Then I can slip in beside Steve and grab a few hours' sleep. Recharge my batteries. Hicks will probably sleep in the rec room at the station, but you wouldn't catch me on that mouldy old sofa.

At least Eve's talking. I'm sure her solicitor will have advised her not to comment. So why is she willing to tell us what's happened? Is it because she believes she's done nothing wrong? Clearly, she's going to claim self-defence and by the state of her, I don't doubt it was.

I need to squeeze my husband tight, kiss my daughter's head in her cot and only then will I be able to sleep. I can worry about putting the pieces together later. Then I will find out who Eve Harding is, and how she got herself caught up in such a serious crime.

19

MONDAY 16 OCTOBER 2017

I rose early the next morning, feeling motivated. It was good to have a purpose. I had missed the routine of work. As much as I didn't want to go back, it was a reason to get out of bed which I no longer had. I'd planned to fill my days with training and exercise, but there was only so much my body could take. I hadn't anticipated how much rest my muscles would need in between workouts and I was getting bored of aching all the time. No amount of bathing in Epsom salts seemed to make a difference. Jason kept trying to get me to drink protein shakes, but the one he'd offered me tasted awful. Green tea and something? Perhaps I needed to try a different flavour?

Meeting Jessica at the office was interesting. She seemed nice, in her forties, dressed in floaty florals with thick black tights and a cardigan. If anything, she seemed more nervous of me than the other way around. She had already moved herself into my desk, my belongings stacked neatly in a box to one side. I could see she felt a bit awkward. She jumped up as soon as I walked in, offering me a limp handshake and saying she'd heard a lot of good things about me. Everyone in the office stared at my hair. Stuart said he liked it, but I wasn't sure I believed him.

He was happy for me to do a few hours a day, stretched out over the week and, to be honest, I thought that might be dragging it out. I wasn't going to complain, I was being paid for the entire four week notice period, so I was getting off lightly. There really wasn't much to hand over, especially as Jessica had been doing pretty much the same job for a competitor. It was hardly as if she needed showing the ropes. We started looking at the photo library where all the stock images were held, and I showed her how Stuart liked them to be filed. We put in a request to IT to give her access to the shared drive, so she would be able to see past press releases and the templates for all internal and external communications. That was enough for one day.

When I got back home, Ben was still asleep and I was pleased I didn't have to lie to him about where I was going. I gathered my things – the rape alarm which had arrived whilst I was out was the first thing to go in my bag. I couldn't decide whether to take a book, it risked my full attention not being where it should, but it was a good cover. Who would notice a girl sat on a bench reading?

I'd had a change of heart about the stakeout. I wasn't going to let one disappointment put me off. It was foolish of me to believe it would be so easy. That I'd spend a few hours in the same place and he'd just stroll on by. Imagine if he did? Anticipation made my skin tingle. What would I do if I actually saw him? I hadn't thought about anything else since the idea occurred to me. Where did he live? How did he live? Did he work full-time? Could he be married with a family? The idea sickened me. I couldn't bear to entertain the notion that he had a wife at home. One who was oblivious to his vile behaviour. Before, I hadn't wanted to think about him at all, but now I seemed to spend every waking moment contemplating what he was doing.

I wrapped up in thick leggings, trainers instead of boots, just in case I had to run, and a heavy coat. It was sunny, but the wind had a chill. I added extra layers, knowing I would probably get cold quite quickly. I pulled my cap down low on my head as I made my way towards the park, covering as much of my hair as possible. It was so bright it might attract attention and that wasn't the plan. How I looked was unimportant. As long as I was unrecognisable, I didn't care. He hadn't seen much of me. Not of my face, I was sure.

I arrived at the park, a mounting feeling of trepidation as I sat on a bench and watched the pre-school children and their parents in the playground. Squeals of delight rang out as they whizzed down the slides. It was reasonably busy, people making the most of the sunshine even though the temperature was only twelve degrees. All too soon it would be too cold for days spent in the park.

I strained my eyes to catch the faces of men in the vicinity. Only a handful came past whilst I was there. Two dog walkers, a jogger and one clutching his briefcase as he scurried along. None were him.

It was a needle in a haystack; I didn't even know if he lived or worked in the area. For all I knew, he could have walked or driven a couple of miles before chancing on me. But the park was all I had to go on. It occurred to me the best time to come back would be on a Sunday morning. It was a weekend when he was here, not during the week. Would he come back though? It would be stupid of him, an unnecessary risk, especially with the incident boards still out. But what choice did I have? If I left it up to the police then another girl would have to go through the pain and humiliation I felt. They wanted to wait until he struck again, hoping he'd make a mistake, but I couldn't let that happen.

I stayed a couple of hours, but my stomach was churning, and I needed food. Of all the things I'd brought in my small rucksack, snacks weren't among them. Next time, I'd know better.

Ben was up when I returned. I nearly bumped into him as he left the bathroom, he was fresh out of the shower, wearing only his towel. My face turned scarlet, confronted with his naked torso. Water droplets cascading down his chest. He apologised, before whisking past me into his room, his ears turning pink.

'Want to come spar with me later?' I called after him.

'Maybe,' he called back as the door closed.

I made myself beans on toast and sat down to eat, waiting for Ben to come back out, but he was taking his time. I hoped he'd come to the club with me and we could have a laugh. Get back to the way things were before the kiss. I hated the atmosphere being so awkward and was desperate to clear the air.

Opening my laptop, I checked my emails and banking online, running through the list of direct debits to see where I might be able to switch providers or change to monthly payments. I spent less than an hour feeding my details into a comparison site and saved over a hundred pounds a month by changing my electricity provider as well as buildings and contents insurance. I was terrible at shopping around, too lazy to waste time searching for a better deal, but now I had no excuse. With more time on my hands and the need to dig myself out of my financial pit, it was imperative I took more interest in what I was spending. Ben's rent had gone in, but it hadn't made much of a dent. I was still in my overdraft, although away from the limit. Mum's cheque and my quarterly council tax bill had both arrived in the post whilst I was out. I had to make sure I paid the cheque in today, then that would be one bill I'd be able to cross off my list.

Instead of waiting for Ben, I grabbed my bag and headed out of the door. It was Jane's birthday on Friday and I hadn't bought her anything yet. I could go to the bank and then look around the shops for something to get her whilst I was there.

When I got to the bank, the queue was long, and I was the youngest one in it. Eventually I got to the desk and paid in the cheque, the teller informing me it would take around four to five days to clear.

I found a lovely photo frame in the window of a quaint gift shop. They sold all sorts of decorative items for the home as well as gifts and trinkets. The frame was cream with two cartoon sloths hanging upside down from a line. The slogan 'I love hanging out with you' across the bottom. Jane loved sloths, she thought they were unbelievably cute. It was the reason her travels would extend to South America, she wanted to see one in the wild.

I picked up some posh hand cream for her too; she always complained how dry and cracked her hands were from the antibacterial gel she had to smother them in numerous times a day. I loved shopping trips where you were able to get everything you needed in one go.

It wasn't until I began my journey home that I thought I saw him, just ahead of me, across the pedestrianised area. Something about the way he walked. I pictured the image of him on the CCTV Detective Emmerson had shown me. The similarity in size and shape was striking. My heart pounded as I followed him up the road, away from home, towards the end of the high street where the bars and restaurants were located.

He slipped inside a betting shop and I paused, not knowing what to do. I'd never been in a betting shop before. I couldn't follow him in. Instead, I hung around outside, a safe distance across the way. Staring into an estate agent's window opposite, not looking at the properties but rather the reflection of the betting shop across the street. When he came out, he stood pushing a wodge of money or slips into his wallet. I turned to face him, and our eyes met briefly before he turned and walked away. I thought I might be sick and sucked in air to avoid bringing up my lunch. It wasn't him, even from this distance I could see his eyes were wrong. They weren't flat and lifeless, and the wrong colour too. My blood fizzed, rushing around my body, heart pumping at speed. I'd never felt so terrified.

20

TUESDAY 24 OCTOBER 2017

A week later I was still struggling with mistaking the man in the street. Now unsure of my plan to find him; the idea scared me. Despite being terrified of the moment we would come face to face, I continued to wait out in the park at various times during the daylight hours, wrapped up on the same bench, pretending to read. Even on Sunday morning too. It was eerie being there the same time it happened, but he didn't appear. Searching for him gave me a purpose. I was clinging on to the fact I would find him, and things could go back to the way they were. I would feel safer once he was off the streets.

Jessica and I had finished our handover on Friday and I was now officially free. She was a smart cookie and Stuart, if he stayed, would be lucky to have her. I was going to look into getting some temp work lined up once my notice period finished to keep the money coming in. I'd had a last look around the Drive offices before sneaking out. I hated goodbyes and was happy to slip away anonymously. Stuart offered to take me out for lunch, but I'd declined. No one was in a celebratory mood with the redundancy process still ongoing for some. I did meet Debbie for a final cigarette before I left. We would keep in touch. I needed all the friends I had.

I could tell Ben was avoiding me. We weren't often in the flat at the same time and days had passed without us holding a conversation that consisted of more than a few words. He wasn't spending much time at home either. The fridge was too full, the steaks I'd bought, just in case, were running towards their use-by date. Now relegated to the confines of the freezer. There were no cereal bowls left on the side, no sugar spilt over the worktop near the kettle and the teabag cannister was still full. I must have upset him, but he was never around long enough for me to clear the air. Yesterday I'd sent him a text asking if he was all right, and did he want to go for a drink? He took an hour to respond, apologising, he'd been busy with work and maybe we could next week. He didn't sound like his normal self, the text seemed stiff and unnatural.

I desperately missed him being around, the flat was lifeless and empty, mirroring my hollow insides. Maybe he thought I was a lost cause, or I wasn't interested in helping myself? Perhaps me pulling away from him ruined any chance of friendship between us?

I continued to go to the boxing club for self-imposed training and jogged there and back without the need to slow down and walk. The trainers had made a real difference and I bought some chocolate flavoured protein powder from the health food shop. The intention was to have one for breakfast every morning. My fitness levels had improved and for fun I'd screwed a chin-up bar in the door frame of the lounge. Chuffed I'd manage to fit it myself. Lifting your own body weight was difficult to do, but so far, I'd managed five in a row.

Jason hadn't been around for a while. I trained in the afternoons and I think he did the mornings and evenings. He didn't ask me out, which saved an awkward conversation. Was Ben telling the truth about that? Instead, we'd chatted about the exercises I was doing, and he commented on the definition already showing in my shoulders and arms. He offered to dig me out the books he'd studied whilst he completed his personal training qualification. He was cagey when it came to talking about Ben, which gave me the feeling he'd confided in his mate about what went on between us.

The psychiatrist's appointment was at three in the afternoon. Initially I had been determined to cancel, stewing over it all week. I couldn't see how it was going to benefit me. Ben had been the one to change my mind about going, although not by anything he'd said. If I went to the appointment it would show him I was trying.

I sat in a bright orange comfy chair across from the doctor, who was a tall dark-haired Mediterranean looking woman wearing a tight fitting shift dress. She perched, what looked like uncomfortably, on the edge of her chair. Her legs angled, knees pressed together with a notepad resting on her lap. My first impression was that she looked high maintenance.

The room was small but welcoming, decorated in warm autumnal colours. In between us was a coffee table, a glass dish of yellow boiled sweets and the obligatory box of tissues on top. I was determined not to use them.

'Eve, it's a pleasure to meet you. I'm Doctor Almara.' She leant forward and offered me her hand to shake. I grudgingly obliged.

'How can I help?'

I shrugged like a sulky teenager and crossed my arms. She didn't react, her smile remained fixed, waiting for me to answer until the silence became uncomfortable.

'I don't know,' I said eventually.

'Why don't we start with why you visited the doctors? What preceded the referral to me?' She must have known why. Doctors exchanged information, didn't they?

'I was struggling with anxiety, having trouble sleeping,' I said, unable to meet her gaze.

'Why do you think you were experiencing anxiety and problems sleeping?' Maybe she didn't know?

'I was raped.' It came out like a whisper and my eyes welled. I concentrated on my nails, picking at the skin surrounding them. Determined not to cry.

'I'm very sorry to hear that, Eve. When did this happen?'

'A few weeks ago.'

'Okay, do you feel able to talk about the attack itself?'

I sniffed, blinking away my tears as the image of being forced over the bin flashed into my mind.

'No.' I coughed.

'I understand. How have you been feeling since the attack?' Did she really ask me that?

'Terrified, revolted, unclean, I feel sick to my stomach when I think about what he did to me,' I snapped. This was a waste of time.

'It's completely normal to have all of those feelings after such a violation. I see Doctor Sola prescribed you a low dose of diazepam, has that helped?'

'Not really. I have mood swings. One day I think I'm fine, but then I feel so fucking angry all the time,' I blurted.

'Angry at whom?'

'At him, at the police, at myself.'

'Why at yourself?'

I could feel the flush creep up from my chest, my neck turning blotchy. Unable to hide my emotion.

'Because I didn't fight back. I was too scared, because he had a knife.'

'It sounds like you were in self-preservation mode, Eve. You were assessing the situation and doing what you could to save your own life.' I hadn't thought of it like that. 'Are you experiencing any other emotions?'

I didn't want to talk about it, but I had to try. I needed to try for Ben.

'Shame. Guilt. Disgust,' I sobbed. She'd broken me with a few words and a gentle push. It had all spilled out. I reached for a tissue.

'Tell me where the shame comes from?'

'I don't know, perhaps shame is the wrong word, but I feel tainted. I don't know how I'll manage, I mean, when someone touches me.'

'Someone you want to touch you?' she clarified.

Yes. Ben, when Ben touches me I want to be okay with it.

'Yes,' I replied.

'I think that will take time and when you choose to let it happen you must feel ready. It must be your decision. It would help if this person knew why intimacy could be an issue.'

I blew my nose. The sound echoed around the room. Her face was a mask and I couldn't tell what she was thinking.

'Is there a partner at home?' she probed.

I shook my head.

'Okay, tell me about the guilt,' she continued.

I sighed, not wanting to get into it.

'There's elements of the case I feel guilty about. Things I could have done to help the police.'

'It's their job to catch him. The responsibility doesn't lie with you.'

I nodded. Still the weight of it remained upon my shoulders.

'Has anyone spoken to you about Victim Support, they run groups and workshops in the area where you can meet with people who have been through similar experiences.'

'The detective on my case mentioned it.'

She slid a red leaflet out of her notebook and handed it to me. I held it in my lap. I had no intention of joining any kind of support group. Sitting around in a circle, telling complete strangers what I'd been through? It wasn't for me. I was not going to allow myself to be his victim.

'Who have you got at home? Do you live with your parents or on your own?'

'No, I have a flatmate, Ben.'

'Are you close?'

'Close-ish.'

'Have you told him what happened to you?'

'Yes, he knows.'

'What about other friends. Do you have a support network you can turn to when you need it?'

'My best friend, Jane, isn't too far away, but my mum lives in Norfolk.'

Dr Almara stood and turned to a cabinet in the corner of the room. 'Would you like some water?'

'Please.'

She poured two glasses and brought them back to the coffee table.

'How would you like me to try and help you, Eve?'

'I want to get rid of the rage,' I admitted.

'Okay, let's focus on that for this session. We could work on some relaxation techniques? Tell me, are you exercising at the moment?'

'Yes, I run and box most days.'

'That's good. How about keeping a diary or journal? I think it would be beneficial to have a creative outlet. Music, writing, painting, these enable you to focus your energy in a positive way and allow the expression of anger without harming yourself or others.'

'I could try, I used to draw a lot when I was younger.'

Maybe Ben was right. At the end of my session, I was lighter and couldn't wait to tell him the news. I had another appointment with Dr Almara in two weeks and she hoped I may be able to talk more about the event. Talking about trauma was the first step in helping to heal, she said.

I floated home, feeling positive, until I passed the park and saw my sign had been removed. Did this mean my case had been closed? It seemed like it'd been ages since I heard from Detective Emmerson. Had they just given up? Become reliant on him striking again, hoping he'd leave something behind? I couldn't wait for that.

As I put my key in the front door, I heard noises in the hallway. I shoved it open, locking eyes with Ben, who was coming out of his room. I smiled, wanting to tell him where I'd been; how I was taking my first steps in the healing process. His eyes widened and then he looked away.

'Hi Ben,' I said, suddenly unsure of myself. Then I saw what he was holding in his hand. He was pulling along a suitcase.

21

TUESDAY 24 OCTOBER 2017

'Where are you going?' My voice was more of a whimper and I hated myself for it. I sounded weak and needy.

'I've got a training course at work. It's to renew my SIA card. It's a security thing, a licence. It's only five days in Manchester. I'll be back on Sunday,' Ben grimaced.

'Okay. When you get back can we talk?' I sighed inwardly, grateful he wasn't leaving for good.

'Sure.' He walked past me, dragging his case, head bowed.

'I'll miss you. It feels like I haven't seen you in ages. Not properly.'

He whipped around, irritation flashing across his face. I took a step back, my body reacting on instinct.

'My head is all over the place, Eve. I don't know what you want from me?' His annoyance dissipated, features softened.

'I'm sorry. I went to see the shrink today,' I blurted, as if that was going to make it all better.

'That's great, Eve, it'll do you good. We'll talk when I get back. I've got to go, I've got a train to catch.'

'Okay.' I watched Ben walk past me and out of the door,

heard the key turn in the lock before crumpling in a heap on the floor.

This had to stop. My life had been messed with enough, I had to take back control. I was going to find him. Now.

I spent eight hours over the course of the next three days sat in in the same spot, in the park, waiting for him to appear. No one that resembled his height, build or swagger came past. The weather had taken a turn for the worst and I rarely saw anyone other than dog walkers. No one else wanted to come out in the rain. I took to running laps of the park to relieve the frustration and at the club I punched the bag until one of my knuckles split, but it didn't make me feel any better.

I'd hoped to spend the weekend with Jane for her birthday. I called her on Friday wishing her happy birthday. Thinking that perhaps I'd be brave enough to make the trip to Balham. To get away and go out for drinks to celebrate. When I caught her, she'd just finished work and was on her way home to pack. Apprehensive to tell me her doctor friend had booked a weekend away to Bath and she was leaving in a couple of hours. Could we postpone birthday drinks until next weekend? I was happy for her, it was about time someone treated her well. But I couldn't help feeling disappointed not to see her.

* * *

Saturday 28 October 2017

On Saturday morning, I decided attempting a three mile run would make more difference to my mental health than being sat on a park bench, freezing cold, for another pointless stake-out. As I pounded the pavement, every time my feet made contact, my shoulders loosened a little more. I would run until my legs stopped working. Some of the houses I passed already had Halloween decorations in their windows or carved pumpkins outside. I loved their ghoulish designs.

Without paying much attention to my route, I jogged down the road which ran parallel to the park; intending to do a loop of the town. My muscles ached, but the pain was addictive. It made me push harder and run faster. I was thrilled with the level of fitness I'd achieved in such a short space of time. Running was addictive. I sucked in air like fuel, panting hard, focusing on the horizon. I was in the zone, my arms pumping to a steady rhythm.

A hundred yards ahead, in the distance, a man was walking along the same stretch of pavement. I slowed as I watched him. A stitch stabbing at my side. There was something about the way he moved that seemed vaguely familiar. He kept stopping and starting, like he was waiting to run a race and had gone before the gun fired.

The back of my neck prickled, and my legs came to such an abrupt stop, but momentum carried me forward and I smacked onto the pavement. My chin hit the concrete, but my hands saved the rest of my face from the same fate. Despite my collision with the ground, I kept the man in view. He glanced around, not appearing to notice me flat on the pavement.

I stood up, looking into the horizon, he was walking again. Who was that ahead of him? Was he following someone? I shuddered and shook my head, my vision blurring. Was I really seeing this? He stopped, and I flattened myself to the side of a Range Rover, watching him look up and down the street numerous times. What was he searching for? He raised his arms and slipped on a hat before stepping into the road, out of sight.

My breathing quickened. I had to move. Was it him? Palpitations rippled through my chest. Scrambling to my feet, I strained my eyes and stood on tiptoes, searching for him above the line of parked cars in the distance, sparks shooting around my legs. He'd disappeared. I ran, making strides to catch up to where I saw him cross the road. A couple of cars passed as I approached, and I slowed to a walk, creeping along the side of parked cars.

I wiped the sweat from my eyes with trembling fingers. I could see him again. He was standing in front of something crouched on the ground. Or was it someone? Cornered against a fence? Brown timber ran along the side of a driveway, a vehicle sized gap in between the houses, the grassy trail leading to the garages of the properties on the right-hand side. A perfect spot not to be noticed. I stood, frozen, yards away. He had his back to me. Not as tall as I remembered, five foot six, maybe seven, but he was stocky. Was it him? His head turned slightly. It wasn't a hat at all, but the balaclava. Fuck! It was him. I'd found him. Who else was there?

I fought the urge to run and crouched down on the ground. I had no way to disguise myself. What if he recognised me? Another car went past. Oblivious to what was going on just out of sight of the road. I didn't have my cap, but I was wearing a hoody. I pulled it over my head, tucking in my hair.

Peeking around the car, I saw a flash of blonde hair as he pulled someone up to stand, bright against his dark clothes. Holy shit, there was a girl. He was going to do it again. Adrenaline charged around my system, nerves firing. I had to do something, but I couldn't move, my head swimming. If I called the police, they wouldn't get here in time. I had to stop him now. I had to stop him doing to her what he did to me.

Cold sweat trickled down my back, pooling at the waistband of my leggings. The waistband. I always ran with my rape alarm. Ducking behind the car, shielding myself from view, I pulled the compact alarm out from my trousers and pushed the button as hard as I could. Nothing happened. My hands were slippery with sweat and it was stiff, not wanting to give. After a few failed attempts, I felt it go. An intense shrill siren filled the air. The sound was deafening, and I dropped the alarm under the car to cover my ears.

I peeked over the bonnet, but the man was already running down the street; spooked by the wailing. I saw him pull his balaclava off as he went. Then I caught sight of the girl, huddled on the ground, but there was no time. I couldn't lose him now.

Pushing myself away from the car, I gave chase, as fast as I could move without my footsteps giving me away. He pelted along the opposite side of the road, putting some distance between us, but then he turned into a side road and immediately slowed to a brisk walk, running his hand through his dark hair and pulling out his phone. To anyone else, he would have looked normal, not someone who was escaping the scene of a crime. I hadn't seen his face, only glimpses of his profile. He didn't turn around to see if he was being followed. Was his heart pounding as loud as mine? The sound of it was all I could hear.

A few minutes later, he turned right into another residential street, which narrowed to a single lane winding underneath a railway bridge. I quickened my pace, assuming he would walk under the bridge; but he turned right again, and I lost sight of him. Shit. Where did he go?

I sped up, reaching the spot where I saw him last; and followed the path to a newly built block of apartments. There looked to be around eight from the number of floors, although I couldn't be sure. The outside was sandstone with white brick detailing around large sash windows. All the balconies had seagrass surrounds, allowing the residents privacy.

I loitered for a few moments before continuing to the door at the base of the building. It was a secure entry system with a key code; six apartments in total, but no names on the buzzers, only numbers. The reception of the building was awash with white marble, lockers for bikes at the far end and beneath, in the basement, was where owners parked their cars. It looked expensive. He couldn't have gone anywhere else, I would have seen. He must live there.

I retreated, jogging back in the direction I had come from. When I reached the driveway, the blonde girl was nowhere to be seen. I wasn't sure what I was expecting, maybe sirens and flashing lights, but all I could hear was the rape alarm still going. I retrieved it from under the car and switched the alarm off, my ears ringing. No one had come out of their houses to see what was going on. Perhaps they assumed it was just another car alarm, more of an irritation than something that had to be acted upon.

I went over and looked around the grassy floor where he had been, for anything he might have left behind. But there was nothing other than leaves and stones; no evidence an altercation had even taken place.

Nervous energy buzzed around my system and I was unsure what to do next. Should I call the police? Would the girl have reported the attack? I didn't see what happened, so maybe they wouldn't believe me if she hadn't. Was she okay?

My head whirled, I needed time to decide what to do next. There was one thing I was sure of. Knowing where he lived gave me the upper hand.

22

HIM

Fuck! That was close. Too close. She was blonde, just like my mother. Peroxide blonde, dirty yellow hair like straw, her roots still dark. She turned my head. A fine catch at this time of the morning. Dangerous so close to home but I have to take these opportunities when they present themselves.

I wanted to look her in the eyes as I took her, hold her by the throat. I hear my father's voice behind the bathroom door, the screaming and sloshing of water. The mourners telling me how awful her tragic accident was, how dangerous it is to fall asleep in the bath.

The girl and I were interrupted before we'd even started. Before I'd had time to touch her. Almost before she'd realised what was happening. I glimpsed her terror, wide-eyed, lips parted. A car alarm? No, too loud. At first, I thought it was sirens. They'd finally found me.

Still the itching continues, a constant clawing at my skin. I know I must seek out another. If only I could find my angel from the park.

23

SUNDAY 28 JANUARY 2018

From the yard, I am taken straight to the toilets so I can wash my hands and face. My skin is crawling. The smell of incarceration lingers, turning my stomach. Thinking about the bath I will have at home motivates me. I must leave here today.

When done, I am delivered to the interview room, where Terry, my solicitor and Detectives Hicks and Becker wait. It's surreal, everything looks the same as the day before except for Becker's outfit. Yesterday she wore a crisp white shirt, today it's blue. Hicks has returned in last night's clothes, I'm sure of it. It must be him I can smell.

The atmosphere is charged with something and I sense I'm in trouble, which is laughable considering I've been arrested for murder. How much worse can it get? Despite this, I resort to chewing my nails.

'Your full name is Rose Evelyn Harding, yes?'

I nod. I try my best to look oblivious, but I'm very much aware of what they've found.

'But you go by Eve?' Hicks raises an eyebrow and pauses

for effect before continuing. 'Last September you were indecently assaulted in Grove park. When you gave the police a statement, you did so under the name Eve Harding. Why was that?'

'I go by Eve, I have done for years, since high school; I told you that when we started.'

'Are you trying to be difficult? Is there something you're withholding from us?' Becker's tone is laced with cynicism.

I shake my head vehemently. 'No, no of course not,' I say.

'Then why, when asked for your details last night, did you tell us you were Rose Harding?'

'They asked me for my full name and I gave them the one I was christened with. I was in shock, it didn't occur to me it would make any difference. I don't have a criminal record.'

Hicks sighs and rubs his forehead, unable to hide the frustration on his face.

So now they know who I am, it took them long enough to connect the dots. I watch them exchange looks and catch the slightest shake of Becker's head. She shuffles some papers and slips them under her notepad. Pen poised, she continues.

'Let's go back to the first time you visited Ian's house; where we left off last night.'

* * *

Saturday 28 October 2017

Back home, I sat at the table chain-smoking and scribbling notes on the back of the psychiatrist's appointment letter. My hands shook, making my writing barely legible. Possibilities spun around my head. I needed to calm down and think practically, but the adrenaline hadn't left my system yet. My legs bounced under the table, unable to keep still.

I'd found him. I'd found him by myself, without any help from the police. Every fibre in my being told me he was the man who raped me. My body reacted before I was even sure, the memory of him on my skin still fresh. I knew where he lived, where he hunted, and it wouldn't be long before I knew his name. The feeling of empowerment was like nothing I'd ever experienced. I felt more alive than ever, my achievement was tangible. All my senses were heightened, like a lion stalking its prey. A tingling sensation ran over my flesh. I knew I was right about him. I knew he'd attack again.

I boiled with fury. What gave him the right, the audacity, to take what he wanted? Terrorising women in our town, how had this not been stopped? He was a predator; stalking women, cornering and overpowering them. A menace to society. Why were we not warned? Emmerson knew he was a possible suspect for past cases. I could see it written all over her face. Was he too clever for them?

If I contacted the police and passed over the information, they might not have enough evidence to arrest him. Perhaps not even enough to be granted a search warrant? I bet his apartment concealed plenty of dirty secrets. Would they follow him like I had? If they messed it up and he got wind he was being tailed, he could bolt. I'd lose him forever. No, he was mine. He was going to pay. There would be justice. He had to be stopped.

I needed to think of a plan, something that couldn't be traced back to me. I got up and paced the kitchen, unable to sit still. I wanted him to know who I was. I flicked the switch to boil the kettle, catching my reflection magnified in the chrome. I looked so different; thinner and pale, forever changed. Hair a different colour. What if I could change my eyes too? Would he even recognise me now? How much of me had he seen, not much of my face? We were strangers.

Forgetting the tea, I grabbed the pen again and scrawled an idea until the page resembled a spider's web. My spider's web and I was going to catch a fly. Taking the letter to the sink, I set it alight, watching shards of the page float to the floor before disintegrating to black dust. There had to be no trace. I didn't need it to be written down. The plan was cemented in my mind. It was crazy, but perhaps I was a little crazy now.

For the first time, I was glad Ben wasn't here to witness the manic high. After weeks of feeling low, I'd finally had a breakthrough.

I treated myself to snacks and wine from the convenience store downstairs, going outside for the first time at dusk, my confidence brimming. Then I settled on the sofa for the night to celebrate. I wanted to ring Jane, but I couldn't disturb her weekend away, it wouldn't be fair. And I knew she'd talk me out of it. Any sane person would. I'd have to keep it to myself.

I couldn't concentrate on the movie I'd chosen; my mind was on him. What was he doing? I imagined him angry, smashing through his flat in frustration at his attack being foiled. Had he gone straight back out to find someone else? Surely it would have been too risky? He had to assume she'd gone to the police.

Many crimes of this type were not reported, and I knew why. What was the point if you had no confidence in the police finding the perpetrator? A flawed justice system where the witness is cross-examined, their character smeared, allowing the offender to walk free. If I gave them his name and address, it would still be his word against mine. No witnesses, no DNA, no decent CCTV. The case wouldn't even make it to court, and even if by some miracle it did, what jury would convict based solely on my circumstantial evidence? To be guilty, it had to be beyond reasonable doubt and I couldn't give the police that.

I knew it was him, but it wasn't enough. He would never be convicted. It was the reason I had to step in. Make sure he got exactly what he deserved...

* * *

Sunday 29 October 2017

Awaking with a jolt, the room pitch-black; I was convinced I'd heard a noise outside. From the kitchen, there was a narrow black iron balcony with spiral stairs to the ground below. A fire escape, which every apartment above the parade of shops had. The sound I was sure I'd heard was metal creaking. The balcony made that sound when someone was on it. Groaning under the strain of any weight. Ben and I barely used it, convinced it was a death trap.

My eyes adjusted to the darkness. The television had gone into standby and I remained still, my head tipped to one side, ear raised to the air. Had he found me? What if he had seen me nosing around the entrance to his building and followed me home. Fuck, why hadn't I been more careful?

There it was again, the sound reminiscent of a gate blowing in the wind, the creaking of rusty metal. Someone was on the balcony.

My heart pounded so fast, it sounded like one continuous hum. I could feel my muscles pinging; my body entering fight or flight mode. I grabbed my phone ready to dial 999 and pressed the screen accidentally. The home screen flashed up, the light so bright it stung my eyes. I smothered the phone. Shit, would he have seen it? Did he know I was home? It must be him. Who else could it be? Ben would always use the front door. No one ever came around the back of these flats unless they were delivering groceries to the store or collecting rubbish.

I heard a shuffling sound as I stood, my bones cracking, and tiptoed across the hallway, pausing to look at the front door. Should I just run? Escape while I still could? I'd had enough of being afraid. Plus, it couldn't really be him, could it? I crept into the kitchen, easing open the cutlery drawer and grabbing the first knife I came across. I couldn't make anything out through the glass, not even a shape. If I turned the light on it would only make myself easier to see, not anything outside.

I crept towards the back door, ignoring the moan from my bladder. Gripping the handle, I violently shook the door, yanking the lever up and down. The door wouldn't open as it was locked, but I hoped it would scare the intruder away. I heard a crash and a squeal which didn't sound human. My heart stopped. Turning the key and opening the door, a rush of crisp air surged in, propelling me back. Outside, bright amber eyes glared at me, teeth bared, ready to pounce. I let out a scream, and the fox scurried away down the stairs. It had been going through the rubbish which was strewn all over the balcony. The darkness seemed threatening, so I didn't linger, instead curling up into my cold bed to hide under the covers until dawn came.

24

SUNDAY 28 JANUARY 2018

'On Friday the twelfth of January at approximately twenty-two thirty hours you left Mangos Bar, but there were no available taxis. Ian offered for you to wait for one at his apartment. Is that correct?' Detective Hicks looks back over the notes from our last interview.

'Yes, that's correct. It was cold.'

'Tell us what happened when you got back to his place.'

'We walked for about ten minutes to get there. It was nice, modern, he told me he'd bought it when the development was built. Quite posh. We had a coffee and he rang for a taxi.'

'What time did the taxi arrive?' Becker asks.

'Around quarter past eleven. Something like that. I remember being home by half past.' My stomach turns as I try to behave normally. Thinking about it makes me shudder.

'Did you notice anything strange about his apartment? Anything unusual?' Hicks asks, his stomach straining the buttons holding his shirt together. They are like a tag team today. Becker doesn't look quite as together as she did yesterday. Overnight, the dark circles under her eyes haven't completely receded.

'No, nothing. It was tidy, I remember that, but otherwise nothing out of the ordinary.' It was spotless, clinical even. Minimalist design with everything in its proper place. I was frightened to touch anything. I had to though, there was one reason I'd agreed to go back with him. It wasn't for more of his charming conversation or to get out of the cold.

'Okay, you spent twenty minutes there. Did Ian make a pass at you at all, did you feel uncomfortable?'

I almost laugh then, uncomfortable? How about revolted. I thought he could see straight through me. The way he looked at me I was sure he knew, but the conversation flowed, and it wasn't until the taxi arrived that he attempted any physical contact.

'We had a kiss goodbye when the taxi arrived, but that was it. He walked me downstairs and opened the car door for me.' When Ian leaned in to kiss me, I shut my eyes tight, hoping my pounding chest would be mistaken for excitement and not panic. His tongue darted between my lips like a snake and I had to fight the urge to shrink away from him. Thankfully the kiss was short-lived.

'When did you hear from him after the date?' Becker asks, interrupting my thoughts.

* * *

Sunday 29 October 2017

I jumped out of bed, unable to understand why bright sunlight shone through my window when it should have only just been starting to get light. It wasn't until I checked my phone that I realised I'd completely missed the clocks going back. It was eight thirty and, worried I was going to miss him, I skipped the shower and threw on yesterday's running clothes.

Jogging towards the railway bridge my knee twinged, so I took it slowly, keeping my eyes peeled for him. The streets were quiet, everyone else enjoying their extra hour in bed. Yesterday I found out where he lived, today I aimed to find out his name.

I took a gamble and waited at the entrance to his road, the opposite end to the bridge, and did some stretches. There was a possibility he might not come out at all. I had visions of watching him walk out of the apartment, a woman by his side pushing a pram. I prayed that wouldn't be the case. He'd ruined enough innocent lives.

As I waited, occasionally jogging up and down the road when I got cold, my thoughts turned to the girl from yesterday. I hoped she was okay and that I'd stopped him before he caused any unrepairable damage.

It was after ten o'clock before he showed; he was the first person I'd seen from his apartment building, sporting jogging bottoms and a green hooded top, with a duffel bag slung over his shoulder. I crouched down behind a green junction box and held my breath, glad he was on the other side of the road. Too engrossed in his phone as he walked past to notice anything. Where was he going? What was in the bag? I had an image of sawn-off limbs.

I watched him walk around the corner and waited for a minute before getting to my feet. He was fifty or so yard s in front, walking with purpose towards the main road into town. I followed him for ten minutes, all the time worrying he was going to turn around and see me. We walked past the library and through a small skate park, then I lost him. Standing where I last saw him, I spun round, but there was only one place he could be.

A new twenty-four-hour gym had opened in the summer. I remembered getting a leaflet through the door about it a month ago. These gyms were a new concept. During the day they were staffed, but at night, they were managed by security off site, who controlled the cameras. There was a key code and card entry to get in and the idea had become popular with those who worked shifts. So, he had gone to train.

I turned to walk back to the apartments. He wouldn't be home for a while. I jogged back to his street and sat on the kerb at the top of the road; unsure what to do next. I needed to know his name and which number he lived at, but how to go about it? Googling the address brought up details of the building company. No information on the residents. I could press all the buzzers and see if anyone would let me inside? It was the best plan I could think of at short notice.

Crossing the road to the block, I swung my keys around my finger like a cowboy spinning a gun. A well dressed lady in her fifties with long, flowing dyed locks emerged from the entrance. She carried a burgundy handbag, the handle tucked into the crook of her arm. It looked expensive, a designer brand.

If only I'd moved faster, I could have slipped inside before the door shut, but that would have been too obvious. I heard the click of the lock. Damn it.

'Excuse me, sorry to bother you,' I said in my poshest lilt.

She turned and smiled at me, taking in my sporting attire.

'Hello, how can I help you?' she asked.

'I saw a man come out of this building, heading that way. I was jogging and have been round the block since, but I've just come across this bunch of keys over there.' I turned and pointed towards the main road before continuing. 'Do you think they could be his?'

'Oh. I'm not sure. What did he look like?'

To say a monster would have been an exaggeration, to a stranger at least.

'About five seven, dark hair. Looked like he was going to the gym.'

'That'll be Ian. He's at number six. Do you want me to take them for you?' She reached out to take the keys, her fingertips brushing the swinging bottle opener.

I snatched my hand back. Her lips parted as though she was going to speak, but no sound came out.

'No. Thank you, but no. Just in case they aren't his. Perhaps I'll head over to the gym and if I can't find him, I'll hand them in to the police.'

'Yes. I think that's best,' she said as she backed up, away from me. Her mouth formed into a tight smile.

'Thanks for your help.' I waved as she retreated, desperate to get away from the mad woman on her doorstep.

I pocketed my keys and began my walk home. I had what I came for.

My attacker's name was Ian. A perfectly normal name, too normal for the animal I knew him to be. Now his apartment number had been confirmed, I used my phone to type his full address into the search engine. No results. I did the same again, this time using his first name and full address. Still nothing. Fuck. Everyone had a digital footprint, didn't they? He might be on Facebook, but typing in Ian followed by Sutton didn't bring up anyone who looked like him either. At a loss, I tucked my phone into my pocket and carried on home.

Ben would be back today, and I wanted to be waiting for him when he arrived. I was a little too late though, as I opened the front door I heard voices from the kitchen. Ben's distinctive laughter carried through to the hallway, followed by a girly giggle. My heart sank. This was a first. *Don't look, just go straight to your room and close the door*. I couldn't, it would be rude, plus I had to see who she was. I popped my head into the kitchen, plastering the broadest smile I could muster across my face.

'Hi.' Ben looked pleased to see me and my heart lifted a little. The girl, sat across the table in my chair, didn't look quite so pleased. She corrected her expression into one more friendly when Ben glanced at her. 'Eve, this is Amy. She's been on this course with me in Manchester.'

'Ah, the landlady. I've heard a lot about you,' she said.

I've heard absolutely nothing about you.

'That's me,' I replied, resisting the urge to throw her off my chair. She was attractive, in a horsey way, but she knew it. Unfortunately for her, she had the worst case of resting bitch face I'd ever seen. 'I'll leave you to it.'

Ben looked up at me and I returned his stare with a quick raise of the eyebrows and left the room to have a shower.

I wished I could share my news of finding Ian. I'd gone from elation to deflation in the space of an hour. Ben had never brought a girl back before, in all the time we'd lived together. I wasn't sure I liked it although there was no rule to say he couldn't. I wanted to share my progress. I knew Ben would think I was crazy for getting involved and not handing the information over to the police. Was I crazy? I needed evidence to get him off the streets, and I couldn't rely on the police to find it. The idea of going undercover made me twitchy and I paced around my room in my towel. I didn't want to dwell on the fact I would be face to face with Ian. His name bounced around my head like a pinball machine and I struggled to connect the horrific attack with such an ordinary name.

This was the only way. There was a sexual predator on the loose, in a place where I used to feel safe. I had to do something about it. I had to protect the women of this community if the police couldn't. I wouldn't risk handing him over to Emmerson and her finding nothing at his apartment and him being released from suspicion. I had to be sure, without a doubt, that they had enough to put him away. I would need some help, but not from Ben, he would ask too many questions. Jane would try and talk me out of it. I sent an email to Debbie, asking if she wanted to meet for lunch next week.

The giggling continued from the kitchen until I couldn't bear to listen to it any longer. Wrenching the volume knob up on my retro stereo, I drowned them out with angry rock music. How stupid was I to think I could rely on Ben? We'd had a moment, but it was short-lived, and it was clear I'd been replaced. I could do this without him.

I ignored the tap on the door when it came sometime later, after Amy had gone home, but Ben caught me on my way out of the house.

'Off to the gym?' he called from his room as I passed. The door was never normally open when he was in there.

'Yep.'

'I'll come with you,' Ben offered.

I turned around, sighing, and fixed him with a cold stare.

'I'm not going to Jason's. I'm signing up at a different gym.'

'Oh, okay. Did something happen?' He meant with Jason, but I didn't answer and carried on out of the flat. Ben scampered after me. 'She invited herself in. I didn't ask her. She lives down the road. God, she's been on my case all week!' He rolled his eyes as though I was in on the joke.

'It's okay. Don't worry about it,' I called over my shoulder as I slammed the door behind me. I could imagine the scenario, Ben was too nice to refuse, but I didn't want to get in to it. I had things to do.

25

SUNDAY 28 JANUARY 2018

'He sent me a few texts the following week. You've got my phone, so you can look at them.'

'Anything untoward?' Detective Becker scowls, flicking back pages of her notebook. Her scrawl is unreadable, especially upside down. It's of no use to me.

'Just flirting. He had a nice time and wanted to see me again.'

'And you felt the same way?'

I rub my forehead, eyes on the table.

'Yes,' my voice breaks.

Becker hands me a tissue. 'I'm sorry, Eve, I know this is emotional, but we have to go over everything, so we can fully understand what happened.'

I nod, wishing she'd get to the point. They have my phone, so surely by now whatever is relevant has been taken off it. Do they have any idea what they're doing? Perhaps there's a Convictions for Dummies book at the front desk and I'm being tormented one chapter at a time.

'Okay, so there were a few texts between you over the next

week or so. The next time you saw him after that was last night?'

I nod, blowing my nose.

'Miss Harding has nodded,' Hicks says as he leans in towards the tape recorder. I catch a whiff of his coffee breath and wrinkle my nose. His shirt gapes, exposing doughy pale flesh dotted with dark hairs.

'I saw him at the gym a couple of times actually.' An image of dark red roses flashes before me.

'Okay. We've requested CCTV, so we'll be able to confirm that,' Becker adds.

Go for it.

'So how did last night come about?' Hicks asks.

'He asked me to go for dinner with him. He booked a table at La Casa, but we met for drinks first, at Mangos again.'

'How did Ian seem?'

'Fine, well, then anyway. Normal. He had a lot to drink. More than me.' I engineered it that way. Everything was on track until Ben had turned up unexpectedly. Was he here, in the police station? Providing a statement right now and blowing it wide open? I pray he'll stay quiet.

* * *

Sunday 29 October 2017

Registering at the gym was tedious and it was another outgoing I couldn't afford, but it was necessary. I'd have to cancel the boxing club, it would be a shame, but I couldn't afford both. Pulse gym was almost double what I was already paying, but it was my way of getting closer to Ian. The manager, Ahmed, gave me a tour and the induction, showing me how to use all the equipment. There was no pool, no steam or sauna and no frills. A basic gym, but I had to get used to it. I was going to be working out a lot. I did suggest a punchbag or speedball as we walked around, which seemed to go down well with Ahmed, so I could live in hope.

When I left, I visited the opticians and asked which colour contact lenses would transform my eye colour the most.

'Your eyes are so pretty; most people would kill for that shade of green. I think the blue would turn them a deep turquoise shade. It would complement your hair more than the brown ones.' The female assistant was helpful and showed me all the options.

I bought two packs which could be worn for two weeks before being thrown away. It had turned into an expensive day. Every time I tried to save money, I ended up needing something else.

Reluctant to go home and face Ben, I decided to go for a coffee. Baristas wasn't one of the major players, although the coffee was just as good. Susie, the owner, was a cheery, buxom woman who wore bright red lipstick. I knew from our first conversation that her husband worked away on an oil rig in the North Sea. She'd joke that it was the best place for him. I loved the quaint little shop, but the real pull for me was the small internet café at the back and the lack of cameras inside. I bought a latte and sat searching anonymously for information on crime scene forensics, blood splatter analysis and DNA. My mind raced with possibilities on what I would do if I couldn't get any evidence against Ian. Just how far was I willing to go?

I enjoyed visualising how it might play out. Like watching a movie in my head, but I couldn't imagine doing any of the things I was picturing. For now, I just wanted to watch. I wanted to watch him like he'd watched me that fateful morning. Deciding if I was a good choice. How did he choose? What were his influences: was it the way I walked? My size must have been a factor, easy to overpower. My hair colour even? Maybe he wouldn't like the blonde? Time would tell.

I took comfort from knowing I could stop this at any time. I could go to the police with what information I had. I could tell them I bumped in to him walking along the street and just knew it was him. My faith in the system could be restored, but I knew I might have wasted my chance.

Back home, I crept into the flat; Ben's door was closed. I could hear machine-gun fire, so the Xbox had been dusted off. He sounded engrossed; shouting obscenities at his player. I slipped into my room unnoticed and rang my mum.

'Hi, Mum,' I said, but all I could hear initially was scuffling. 'Mum, you okay?' I asked, louder.

'Yes, sorry, I couldn't get to the phone quick enough.'

'Are you all right?' Sensing something wasn't right, she didn't sound drunk, but she was getting better at fooling me.

'I had a fall yesterday. Patrick took me down to the doctors and they've patched me up.'

'How did you fall?'

'I missed a step coming downstairs yesterday morning. I was at the bottom for three hours before Patrick knocked on the door. He had to break in.'

My heart sank, she must have been pissed or hungover from the night before. She was hardly old and frail.

'Oh god, Mum! Listen, let's FaceTime. I want to see you. I showed you how to do it when I gave you the phone. Remember?' Mum had been pretty good at tech – when she was sober. I'd given her my old iPhone when I'd purchased a new one. Something else I'd bought that I couldn't really afford at the time. It was no wonder my credit card was almost maxed out.

'Okay, you ring me,' she said, hanging up.

I called back and after a few seconds' connecting I saw a view of the white Artex ceiling before Mum's face came into view. I tried to smile, but she looked gaunt, her hair straggly and her eyes bloodshot. Being an alcoholic was taking its toll.

'Can you see me, Mum?' I asked, waving.

She grinned and waved back.

'Your hair!' She clapped a hand over her mouth.

'Do you like it?'

'It's very blonde.' No compliments then. 'Did you get the cheque I sent?'

'Yes, thanks Mum. I've paid the council tax bill.'

'Are you all right for money?'

I nodded, it was easier to lie. I didn't want her to worry about me.

'And what about the other thing? Are you okay?' I gritted my teeth. How could she refer to my rape as 'the other thing? How could she be so fucking insensitive?

'Show me your leg,' I said, changing the subject. The phone shook when she picked it up and she only had the shakes when she needed a drink. Perhaps she was sober? The camera wobbled as she showed me her bandaged shin and the surrounding papery skin.

'It's fine, it'll heal.'

'Make sure you keep it elevated,' I instructed.

Her phone beeped.

'My battery is going,' she said as I heard another beep, then she was gone.

* * *

Monday 30 October 2017

I woke filled with positive thoughts for the day ahead. My new gym schedule was going to start. Everyone who had a gym membership went on a Monday, didn't they? I just had to pick the same time he went. I knew I'd bump into him eventually if I went every day, and it was safer than waiting outside his flat. I guessed it would more likely be after work rather than before. The anticipation made my stomach churn. I was impatient to find out more about him. What he did? Where he worked? It was strange to try and make the pieces fit. Like a double-sided jigsaw puzzle; one side didn't correspond with the other.

Ben was moving around the kitchen, so I was reluctant to emerge from under the duvet. I was still pissed off about coming home to find Amy in my kitchen, which was irrational. There were no rules to say he couldn't bring girls back, but I took an instant dislike to her.

'Morning,' Ben said, shovelling cornflakes into his mouth when I joined him, unable to ignore my rumbling stomach any longer.

'Morning,' I replied curtly. It was half past eight and in half an hour Debbie would be logging on and checking her emails. If I knew Debbie, she'd be on the phone by ten. I didn't want to involve her, but I knew she wouldn't ask any awkward questions.

'You said you wanted to talk? When I got back,' Ben said in between mouthfuls.

'Did I? I can't remember,' I lied.

'What have you been up to then whilst I've been away?'

'Nothing.' It was easier with my back to him as I busied myself making tea and toast. I needed to up my game, I was a rubbish liar.

'Fuck sake, Eve.' I heard the clang of his spoon against the china bowl and spun round. 'What's going on, one minute we're fine, the next you don't want to talk to me,' he snarled.

'That's rich coming from you. Before your course, you hadn't spoken to me for over a week.'

He shrugged and pushed his bowl away. I saw him squeezing his jaw tight. The tension between us was palpable.

'I'm sorry you were attacked. Fuck, I can't even imagine what it must be like to be raped but...'

'But what?' I interrupted. 'But it doesn't excuse me being such a bitch? Or are you just pissed at me because I wouldn't sleep with you?' I spat.

Ben jumped up, his chair scraping across the linoleum. He took slow, steady breaths, gripping the table.

'What the fuck is wrong with you?' He wrenched his coat from the back of the chair and took off, slamming the front door so hard the flat shook.

I launched at the wall, pummelling my fists into the smooth white plaster. Why did I have to say that? Why did I lash out when I was hurt? He would move out, I was certain of it.

My phone rang before any real damage had been done to the wall or my hands. I knew who it would be before I looked at the screen. Taking a deep breath, I answered before it went to voicemail.

'Hi Debbie. How are you?' I said as cheerily as I could.

Three hours later, once I'd popped my repeat prescription for diazepam into the doctors', we sat at a table in the window of Baristas, both nibbling on toasted paninis. I'd planned to spend some more time on the internet, so I was killing two birds with one stone.

'How's the reshuffle been?' I asked, not only as an opener, I was curious. There were never any awkward silences with Debbie, she could fill hours with mindless chatter, which wasn't a bad thing.

'It's been so stressful. They scored us, and we had a round of interviews. In the end, the other poor lady was made redundant, which obviously is good for me, but I'm doing the work of two people now. It's ridiculous! Anyway, how about you? Have you recovered from the attack?' If only it was that simple. Debbie had no idea. The only thing she'd had to recover from was a warning after she leaked sensitive information internally. She was the most tactless human resources representative I'd ever met.

'Getting there. I'm having counselling. How is my replacement, she any good?' I couldn't help but ask; perhaps I needed the ego boost?

'She's all right, not a patch on you though. It's taking her a while to settle in. She's got all sorts of problems; she's going through a divorce and her eldest child has been diagnosed as having autism.' Same old Debbie. No one's secrets were safe.

'That's a shame. It must be tough for her.'

Debbie sipped her latte, a white line of foam painted across her lip. 'How's the job hunting going?'

'I can't do anything while I'm being paid my notice, but I think I might do a bit of temping come the end of November.'

Debbie nodded in agreement. Now would be a good time to slip in the lie.

'Guess what, I'm getting a dog. A pug. My therapist thinks it would be a good idea, give me something to focus on.'

'God, I love pugs, they are so cute with their squishy faces. You won't regret it. A house isn't a home until you have a dog. I wouldn't be without my westie, Molly.'

Forty-five minutes later, after Debbie had told me everything I could ever want to know about being a dog owner, we asked for the bill. I insisted on paying and we gathered our things to walk back to the office. I felt guilty for lying, but I needed Debbie to do me a favour in a few weeks. She was going to help me out with a small part of my plan. So, for now, I was going to be getting a pug.

26

SUNDAY 28 JANUARY 2018

I describe our date last night in detail to Detectives Becker and Hicks. How we had a drink in Mangos before heading to the Italian restaurant. I relay how normal the meal was, how we got through the first bottle of red wine before finishing our main course. I told them I was trying to pace myself, but Ian ploughed through another bottle like it was fruit juice. It loosened him up. He told me he was an only child, that his mother had died when he was young. I almost felt sorry for him. He was good, so convincing. Acting like a normal human being.

It was almost too easy, the conversation flowed between us and there were no awkward silences. I could have forgotten why I was there, until I saw it. Something I said caused his eyes to flash, they rolled dark like thunder. A look I had seen before. Cold and devoid of emotion. It chilled me to the core. A mix of anxiety and revulsion churned my stomach as I sat across the table, watching him saw pieces of his steak. Smiling sweetly and saying all the right things, even managing to flirt when all I wanted to do was run.

'Did Ian know you had been attacked previously?' Hicks asks.

I snort. 'No. It's not really something you mention on a second date. Was I supposed to tell him I was damaged goods?'

He looks sheepish, fidgeting with his papers. *Good, the prick.*

'That's not what I meant, Eve. I was asking if he knew.'

I look away, worried I might launch myself at him.

'What did you have to eat?' Becker asks in redirection. Does she expect me to lie about something so trivial?

'We both had steak.' My voice has an edge to it, but I can't help it. As if asking what we had for dinner brings them any closer to finding out the truth.

I'm sure they will be in contact with the restaurant, interview the waitress. She will report that there was nothing out of the ordinary about our date last night. Any CCTV in the restaurant or the town will confirm the same. They won't know I struggled to finish my meal because I was so nervous about what was to follow. They won't know I almost retched when Ian played footsie with me under the table whilst we waited for the bill. They don't know I was willingly heading into the lion's den, eyes wide open.

* * *

Tuesday 31 October 2017

I eased into a jog, pushing the treadmill to 5km an hour. It was about my pace, maybe a bit slower, but I planned to stay on there for a while. There were six treadmills, and these were always the most popular piece of equipment at any gym. Those and the weights.

There were seven people in the gym, including me. Four men and three women. One of the women was wearing a tiny crop top and shorts. She had more on her face in the way of make-up than clothes on her body. Women like her frequented every gym, they were the girls who never worked up a sweat but wanted cute pictures for their Instagram page.

For the first time ever, I'd made an effort in what I was wearing to work out. My clothes were tight, arms on show, but I was never going to bare my midriff to the world. Before I left, I put on some waterproof mascara and pink nail varnish. I was there to be noticed after all.

An hour in and it was gone six in the evening, but no sign of him yet. I'd been here at the same time yesterday, convinced as it was a Monday he'd show, but he didn't. It had taken all my courage to venture out after dark and by the time I'd arrived I was a bag of nerves. With every step I'd envisaged footsteps behind me. I'd held my rape alarm in one hand and my keys in the other. I was disappointed that after the effort he didn't show, so I had to try again. I needed to see him in the flesh, make sure I hadn't imagined him.

I'd moved from the treadmill to the rowing machine. My shoulders were in great shape from the boxing and it felt good to use them. I was facing the door when he walked in, a towel slung casually over his shoulder. My hands trembled, but I gripped the pulley hard and moved faster, keeping a rhythm as I watched. He filled his bottle at the fountain and got on the treadmill, plugging in his headphones. He glanced my way and I averted my eyes, moving faster and listening to the fan on the rower roar. I felt exposed; would he figure out who I was straight away? The plan suddenly seemed foolish. But my hair was different, blonde and much shorter than it was before. Plus, I had my blue contact lenses in; the turquoise popped against my pale skin. He didn't see much of my face that morning, but the pounding of my chest unnerved me. I had the cover of exercise to account for my panting; trying to take steady breaths to avoid the panic attack which was fast approaching.

Wanting to find an angle where I could watch him unnoticed, I went to fill my bottle, staying by the fountain to have a drink. He was in the zone, staring straight ahead, still running on the treadmill. His face was long with a prominent nose which made him look superior. He had brown cropped hair, no sign of any grey and I struggled to age him. His topaz eyes were as I remembered them, cold, with no light behind. Dead inside. A shiver descended my body, turning my legs to liquid and I held onto the fountain to steady myself. I couldn't believe we were in the same room.

I remained frozen on the spot for a minute before moving to the cross trainer, setting a light programme for ten minutes. My muscles were becoming tired and I worried the adrenaline shooting around my system, coupled with my racing heart, might lead me to pass out. We were opposite each other, across the gym, and I saw him glance my way a couple of times. Surprisingly, I didn't notice him eyeing up the near-naked woman who was now doing yoga poses in front of the wall of mirrors. Every other man in the gym seemed to be; even Ahmed, who waved at Ian as he walked by, couldn't take his eyes off her rear. They were all so predictable; men were creatures of habit, they couldn't help themselves. *Except for you Ian, why? I'd seen you glance at her once or twice, sure. But your tongue wasn't hanging out like the others. Perhaps you weren't turned on by female flesh on show? No, that would be too normal. You were turned on by fear.*

At the end of the programme, I hit the showers and decided to call it a day. Relieved that I'd found Ian. He was going to be a familiar face to me soon. Removing my contacts and placing them in the holder. I would be back again tomorrow but was now looking forward to some dinner and an early night. Fortunately, it was Halloween and droves of parents and their mini monsters were roaming the streets, knocking on doors to 'trick or treat'. It made the area feel safer but all the same I stuck to the main roads and stayed in the glow of the street lights. I bought a Chinese takeaway from our local, two minutes from home, and knocked on Ben's bedroom door as I went past.

'Takeaway,' I announced and a second later he was in the doorway to the kitchen. 'Pork balls or chow mein?' I asked as I opened the foil containers and spooned rice onto plates. I wasn't sure if Ben had eaten, it was past seven, but any left-overs could be used tomorrow.

'Balls please,' he said, getting glasses out of the cupboard.

'I've got wine as well.' I handed Ben the bottle to open. 'Loads of kids out tonight,' I said, knowing we never got anyone knocking on Halloween. No one could be bothered to climb the stairs, and as the door on the street was between two shops, most people didn't even realise it was there.

'What's this in aid of?'

I brought the containers and plates to the table and we sat down to eat.

'A peace offering,' I said hopefully. Today had been a successful day and I was in the mood to celebrate, even if I didn't want to tell Ben why.

'I'm sorry about yesterday,' Ben said.

I stopped, fork halfway to my mouth. 'I'm sorry too. I didn't mean what I said. Are we good?' I wanted us to go back to the way we were, but it still seemed as though there was a crevice between us.

'Of course. Thanks for dinner.'

'What are landladies for, eh?'

Ben rolled his eyes at my sarcasm. 'I didn't describe you as my landlady.'

'How is Amy?' I asked.

Ben coughed, spluttering so much he needed a drink.

'Keen,' he replied with a grin. His eyes streamed, and I had to laugh. I bet she was. Ben was a good catch; tall, dark, quirkily handsome. He was funny and kind. What wasn't to like?

We cleared our plates and by the time we'd finished things were almost back to the way they had been.

I tried to avoid an awkward goodnight by retiring early and not indulging in too much wine. I stopped at two glasses and made sure there was no lingering in doorways. The feelings were still there, for me at least, but to act on them would only confuse Ben and I didn't want to lead him on. He could have a chance with a normal girl, not a crazy one. It didn't stop me lying in the dark and thinking about the kiss we'd shared a couple of weeks ago. It couldn't be helped; the timing wasn't right and now I had too many secrets to hide. Ben wouldn't approve of my plan and it was easier to keep him out of it. Safer too, If anything happened to me, I didn't want to be responsible for dragging him into it.

27

TUESDAY 7 NOVEMBER 2017

'Hello, stranger,' Jason said as I entered the boxing club around 9 a.m., his tone laced with sarcasm.

I bowed my head and raised my palms up in surrender, I knew my absence wouldn't have gone unnoticed. I'd spent most of the week at Pulse, watching Ian, when my body would allow it. I'd started taking supplements and drinking protein shakes and I had to give it to Jason, it was working. My muscles were recovering quicker, I was starting to look toned, almost pumped. I liked this new me. I felt strong, like a warrior. I'd been trying to work out Ian's schedule, so I could work mine around his, conscious not to go every day that he went. I didn't want anyone to notice our training was aligned. He hadn't spoken to me yet and things weren't moving as fast as I'd like, but I couldn't rush it. It needed to seem natural, not forced. Ian showed no signs of recognising me and my anxiety was easing on that front. Wearing the contacts helped; I almost felt like a different person when I put them in. Being in the same room with him still made my skin crawl though.

'Sorry, things have been a bit hectic.' I slung my towel over my shoulder and held my fists out for Jason to tape. There were a couple of people in the gym, including a girl who looked to be in her late teens giving the punchbag a hammering. 'A girl? That's great.' I had been the only one up to now.

'Her probation officer brought her in. We talked about doing a community programme. Getting the waifs and strays off the streets.'

'That would be fantastic.' We moved to the mats and Jason lifted the pads for me to strike. My shoulders felt heavy; after a week of not boxing, I was already losing my agility. Rowing just wasn't the same workout.

'Wanna tell me what's going on? You in trouble?'

I squirmed. What did he know?

'I'm not in need of your programme,' I said, attempting a joke.

We moved in a circle, dancing around each other as I tried to target the pads. And then the idea struck, a little white lie would make this easier.

'There's a guy.'

Jason raised his eyebrows and chuckled. 'There's always a guy!'

Too out of breath to talk and punch at the same time, I sank to the mats and proceeded to tell Jason about a man I'd met in a bar. I knew he was a member of Pulse gym and in a mad moment I'd signed up. I explained that even though it wasn't anywhere near as good as Jason's club, and I missed boxing, I couldn't afford both.

'Hey, I was never going to charge you in the first place, remember? You insisted.'

'I know, I know, but it's not fair to come in for free. You're a business after all, and I can't be in two places at once.'

Jason rubbed his chin, black stubble starting to poke through.

'You're not working, right? Ben said you worked in an office before. How about you come and work here? I could do with some help. I've got no clue about accounts, marketing, promotion, that kind of stuff. There'd be a bit of the maintenance of the gym too, of course, we'd all have to pull our weight, but I want to turn this into something big. Especially if I'm going to get funding for an outreach programme.'

I grinned, watching Jason's eyes light up. He had just made my day. 'That sounds amazing.'

'Okay, let me work out some numbers. It won't be the kind of salary you had, so don't get your hopes up.'

'I won't. I can't do anything until the end of November anyway, as technically I'm still working my notice.' The idea sounded perfect, perhaps I could even do a personal training qualification on the side? I was sure I'd have to subsidise my earnings with some waitressing or something, but getting the chance to work in a job I enjoyed, that would be brilliant.

After finishing at the gym, I picked up my prescription for more diazepam from the chemist en route to my second appointment with Doctor Almara. I'd run out a few days ago but kept forgetting to collect them. I was getting anxious about them wearing off and was pleased when I got two months' worth this time with an appointment reminder before any more would be prescribed.

When I sat down in the orange chair, I reminded myself to play down my buoyant mood. Here, I was a victim of rape, struggling to deal with the trauma. It wasn't a lie, but I didn't want to seem like I was making too much progress. Who knew where my notes might end up in weeks to come?

Doctor Almara sat back in her seat, notepad in lap, her face impassive as I told her about my redundancy and how the circumstances around that had left me feeling low.

'Maybe you should try and focus on the positives of the situation. A new start, a chance to begin again, somewhere different. You can be whoever you want to be. How are the feelings of anxiety? Are they lessening with the medication?'

'A bit. It's slow but I'm making progress. I managed to go outside in the dark, which is something I've been avoiding.'

'And how did that make you feel?'

'Nervous at first and then angry at why I should have to feel scared.'

'These victories are important. Small steps lead to big changes. You should feel proud of yourself. May I ask what led to the change of appearance?' She waved her hand towards my hair, the beginnings of a smile on her lips.

I ran my hand through the platinum strands. 'I wanted a change.' *I wanted to look different, no longer Eve the victim.*

'Has it made you feel better?'

'Yes.' I wasn't going to tell her about my plans for Ian. They would make me feel more than just 'better'.

She asked if I had started writing a journal or drawing yet. I told her I hadn't, but it gave me an idea and I bought a notebook on the way home.

* * *

Monday 13 November 2017

I was making slow progress with Ian at the gym. He still

hadn't spoken to me, but we had moved on to nods of acknowledgement and a smile. Mine was forced, but his was at ease as we passed on my way to the water fountain. I knew I'd get there, he chatted animatedly with some of the other regulars; I just had to bide my time.

I tried to get to the boxing club as much as I could. Jason had made me an offer, even drawing up a contract with flexible working hours, paid holiday and mandatory pension contributions. It was a significant drop in salary, but I expected that. It was a well-known fact that the fitness industry wasn't the best paid. I'd look around for waitressing or some other evening work if I couldn't manage.

I exchanged texts with Debbie and we met up at Baristas for lunch again. She seemed back to her old self now most of the restructuring was complete. I was happy to hear Stuart had managed to keep his job and asked Debbie to pass on my best wishes. We both ordered jacket potatoes and I was salivating when Susie delivered them, steaming hot, to our table. I'd been eating like a horse all week.

'How do you get to stay so tiny?' Debbie complained as I shovelled in layers of butter and cheese. She opted for the less fattening plain jacket with beans

'I'm in the gym almost every day now. I've got a job at the boxing club, starting at the end of November. I'm going to have a complete change of career, maybe do a qualification in personal training,' I said between mouthfuls.

'That's certainly a change! My brother's a personal trainer, sees loads of bored rich housewives. Says they're lazy cows. Do you know, he's been propositioned three times since he started?' Debbie shook her head in disgust.

'Oh, I forgot, check out Doug,' I said, showing Debbie a

photo of a pug puppy I'd borrowed from Google images a couple of hours before.

She shrieked, practically ripping the phone out of my hand to have a closer look. 'He's gorgeous! When are you picking him up?'

'Not until Christmas, he'll be ten weeks then.'

She handed me back the phone and scooped some beans up onto her fork before picking her own phone up and showing me around twenty photos of her westie. To be fair, it was a cute mass of curly fluff.

'I remember what I wanted to ask you, Debbie. Could you do me a massive favour?'

'Of course,' Debbie said, flushing with pride.

'The camera you've got for Molly, I want to get one for Doug when he comes home. Did you say it was from eBay?'

'Yes, the PetCam, oh, they are good.'

'I don't have an eBay account, I'm rubbish at that sort of thing. If I give you the money, would you order me the same one?' I lied, taking out my purse and retrieving some notes.

'Of course, it's twenty-five pounds I think, but I'll order it and you can pay me when it comes.'

'If you're sure? I'd really appreciate it,' I said, smiling at Debbie.

'Absolutely.'

We talked some more about various pet shows and festivals that were good to go to. She'd taken Molly to Paws in the Park in Ardingly earlier this year, suggesting next year we could go together. Our plates had been clear for a while, the bill paid for by Debbie this time, and we were just finishing our drinks. She was complaining about her husband, Darren, failing to help around the house, when she absent-mindedly tapped her phone, the time flashing up on screen.

'Oh god, I better go. I've had over my hour. It's been lovely to see you. I'll text you when the camera arrives, and we'll meet for lunch again. Good luck with the new job.'

'Thanks for lunch. Take care and I'll see you soon.'

Debbie squashed her enormous boobs against the side of my face in an attempt at a hug, as I patted her back awkwardly. Then she left the café and wobbled up the street towards the office on her high heels before disappearing around the corner. My face ached from all the smiling.

Susie made me another coffee and I ordered a Belgian bun, devouring every crumb as I sat at the back, googling crime statistics for Sutton. It occurred to me, over lunch, that I still didn't know if the blonde girl had reported Ian to the police. Just how many attacks, attempted or otherwise, had there been? The statistics weren't helpful, just numbers from last year, nothing for 2017 yet. I tried the local newspaper instead.

My own attack had filled the second page, a piece with a picture of the entrance to Grove Park. Thankfully my name wasn't mentioned, only my age. The report began 'a twenty-five year old woman was raped in Grove Park in broad daylight at approximately 8 30 a.m. on Sunday 24 September 2017. The attacker, unknown to the victim, was described as around 5'7", white, stocky and aged between twenty and thirty years old. He is still currently at large. Detective Sergeant Emmerson of the Metropolitan Police said: "I would like to reassure the public that we are doing everything we can to trace and arrest this man. We believe him to be dangerous and we are appealing to the public to come forward with any information they may have."'

It felt strange reading about an event that I'd experienced, written with so little emotion, just the facts. I carried on scrolling, then ran a search for 'assault' on the newspaper's website. There were plenty of bar brawls and closing time punch-ups but nothing from the end of October. I searched further back, looking at the summer months. A sexual assault on a teenager in an alleyway, in July, after a night out looked like it could be one of his. There was also another attempted attack in June. A lone-women walking home after visiting her friends in the early evening. That one was in daylight, but her attacker had fled the scene after she screamed. Looking at the locations, they were all nearby. I had no idea how long Ian had been stalking the streets of Sutton, but now I was convinced I wasn't the first.

28

WEDNESDAY 22 NOVEMBER 2017

By the middle of the third week, Ian's routine had become clear. He visited the gym most Sundays, Mondays, Wednesdays and Fridays, always a variation on the same exercise plan. Generally starting with the treadmill, he would run for thirty minutes, then row for twenty, followed by some free weights. It appeared, from watching him interact, that he was friendly with other members. It didn't seem like he treated women any differently from men. On the face of it he looked like a gentleman. I'd seen him open the door to allow them through first and witnessed him let Laura ahead of him in the queue for the water. He seemed to know Ahmed well and often chatted to some of the other regulars. I had built up to smiling at everyone with the occasional hello but hadn't spoken to him yet. My social skills were lacking.

Interaction with strangers didn't come easily to me. Trying to interact with the man that had brutalised me was even harder. I used my time to watch his every move, study his face, his mannerisms and expressions. I strained to hear conversations he was part of. On the surface he looked and acted like a regular guy which I found hard to rationalise. Ian was confident but from a distance he seemed smug to me, although no one else appeared to notice.

It was Wednesday when Ian said hello for the first time as we passed each other. Perhaps as a result of my skimpier gym clothes? I had been shopping in the morning, after having my roots done, my scalp now baby pink, and invested in a skin-tight black vest and some bright orange shorts. They were so short, they could have passed for hot pants. Three weeks of reconnaissance and I knew I had to up my game. The new outfit seemed to have worked. Pushing myself to keep moving when he spoke, my body stalled, and I was rooted to the spot. I mumbled hello back and blushed.

To an outsider it would have looked as though I had a crush but having to mask the revulsion was challenging. I could feel my throat closing, not wanting to breathe the same air as him. It hit me then that he was my rapist, without a doubt. It was the closest I'd been to him face to face. There was no mistaking his eyes. They were like no other. Desolate and detached, just a void. Grateful for the contact lenses and hair to mask who I was. I toyed with the idea of abandoning the plan altogether, but he was a predator, stalking women and subjecting them to disgusting acts of sexual violence. He'd degraded me in the worse possible way and I hated him so much my insides burned with it.

How many other women had he attacked whilst I'd been getting closer to him at the gym? The blonde woman hadn't reported hers, or if she had it wasn't in the papers. I squeezed my jaw tight, my entire body reacting to his presence. Being in the same room as Ian was just about tolerable. Up close he made my temperature spike, anger mixed with fear. I made sure I left the gym whilst he was still mid-workout, it was no different to any other day, but I felt spooked.

Detective Emmerson hadn't been in touch, but that wasn't a surprise. I guessed she had no news to give me. I wished I could reach out to the blonde girl in the alleyway, offer her comfort and support. I was doing this for her, for me and all the others whose lives had been ruined.

* * *

Thursday 23 November 2017

The following day when I saw Ian at the gym, I approached him. He was by the water fountain, waiting for the weights to become free, so I went to fill my bottle. I nodded and said hello, briefly locking eyes before concentrating on filling my bottle. I hoped he would open a line of conversation. The tap ran slow. Seconds passed and an awkward silence filled the space. Was he not attracted to women in real life scenarios?

'They need more weights in here.' He sighed but showed no sign of irritation.

I swallowed hard, I could do this. All I had to do was open my mouth and reply. My hands trembled, and I concentrated hard to ensure the twitch in my leg wasn't obvious.

'Yeah.'

Great job, Eve.

I tried again. My tongue feeling too large for my mouth. 'Maybe Ahmed could get rid of some of the mats and put more weights there. I only see them being used by Yoga girl.'

He chuckled whilst I berated myself for inventing a new superhero.

'Good idea. I mean, who stretches to that extent anyway?' He winked at me and my stomach dropped.

'I guess it depends who's watching.' It was out before I could stop it, but he laughed. I could do sarcasm, I used it daily anyway and he seemed to like it.

'I think you might be right. I'm Ian.' He wiped his hand on his towel and held it out for me to shake. I hesitated for a second longer than I should have. I didn't want him to touch me ever again, but if I couldn't bear it, this plan wouldn't work. With gritted teeth hidden behind my smile, I gripped his hand and shook it firmly; not one of those limp handshakes. Those made me want to wash my hands afterwards. Although, I always wanted to wash after any human contact. After his handshake I wanted to bleach the skin off.

'Eve,' I replied. His eyes fixed on mine and I hoped he couldn't see the edges of my lenses. We stood for a couple of seconds trying to read each other. I held my breath, ready to be exposed at any moment. I couldn't tell what he was thinking. Perhaps we were both dead behind the eyes?

'Pleased to meet you,' he said, and nodded towards a vacant weights machine. 'I best grab that while it's free.'

I nodded, and he walked away. Contact was made, and I'd survived.

I left for the showers shortly after; turning the water as hot as I could bear. I scrubbed my skin, especially my palm, but it still felt dirty. I was sure that would be the way of things from now on.

I met Debbie for dinner after leaving the gym. Relieved to take my mind off Ian's handshake. I was feeling braver when out in the dark, now I knew who to watch out for. The nights were really coming in and by four o'clock the sun had set. I was arriving at the gym in darkness and leaving the same way. Always with my rape alarm to hand; I never went anywhere without it. The shops were filled with all things Christmas and the tapas restaurant Debbie and I dined at even had their decorations up. A twinkling tree stood in the window.

'It's a bit early for all that, isn't it?' I grumbled. I hadn't been to the restaurant before. Debbie had frequented it with her husband and said the food was delicious. We ordered three different dishes each and dived in, trying everything. I passed on the squid when Debbie lifted the plate to offer me some, the smell making me baulk.

'I brought the camera.' She passed a carrier bag across the table and I had a quick peek inside. The box was small and felt light, exactly what I wanted.

'Thanks so much for doing that for me.' I handed over the cash, gushing of how I couldn't wait to see Doug the pug wandering around the house when I was out. Inside the bag, she'd included a copy of the order, so I could see how much it was. It was a sweet gesture, but I didn't believe for a second that she would rip me off.

My redundancy had been paid, although most of it had been swallowed up repaying the debt and this month's bills. Ben had insisted on helping and paying a little more in rent, knowing I was taking a pay cut to work for Jason. I was touched by his generosity, but he was adamant I wasn't charging enough anyway and waved away my squirming. It was wonderful to be finally free. I cut up all but one credit card, only to be used in emergencies, which I gave to Ben to keep so I couldn't be tempted to use it.

As Debbie dominated the conversation with gossip from the people I used to work with, I could see she was faking her confidence, as did I. She used her bubbly personality to hide behind. We agreed to meet again in a few weeks. We were an unlikely pair, but I couldn't help but find her endearing.

At home, Ben and I were teetering on the edge of a platonic relationship. Some of our exchanges were fun and relaxed, but as soon as there was any intimacy; or conversation that strayed into awkward territory, a wall shot up between us. We'd been to the cinema the weekend just gone and had an uncomfortable brushing of hands as we shared an enormous tub of popcorn. The fact it was dark didn't help and the action film we'd chosen to see had a frantic sex scene in the middle, unbeknown to either of us. I could sense Ben cringing in his seat as I slid lower into mine, glad the darkness hid my rosy cheeks. I wasn't sure if he'd been out much with Amy. He didn't mention her, and I didn't pry. There'd been no sign of her at the flat. Not when I was there anyway.

He did ask why I hadn't been to the boxing club and what prompted my move to a new gym. I could tell he was convinced something was going on between Jason and me even though I assured him there wasn't. Once I'd finished with Ian, I would be free. Then I could see what developed with Ben. If he was interested of course, but by then I wasn't sure he would be available.

29

SUNDAY 28 JANUARY 2018

'Did he invite you back to his apartment?' Detective Hicks asks.

'Yes, once we finished dinner, he invited me back for a drink.'

'How did you get there?'

'We walked. As I said before, it's so close it's not worth getting a taxi,' I reply. My stomach rumbles but I ignore it.

'Can you talk us through what happened last night from when you arrived at Ian's apartment?'

I open my mouth to speak but Becker interrupts me.

'This was around eleven, right?'

I nod and Becker notes down the time. Her jaw is clenched as though she's stifling a yawn.

'We got there, and Ian put some music on before he went into the kitchen to make drinks. We were talking about what movie to put on.'

'Did you follow him in to the kitchen?'

'Yes. Well, I stood in the doorway. Ian was putting everything on a tray to bring back into the lounge. He wanted us to have gin and tonic. That's why the knife was there, he used it to slice the lemon.'

'He sliced the lemon?' Hicks confirms.

'Yes,' I sigh.

'Okay, please continue,' Becker says.

'I sat on the sofa and he put the tray on the coffee table. He knelt on the carpet, sliced the lemon and poured our drinks. He sat on the opposite sofa and was flicking through the Sky box for what to put on.'

'What happened next?' Hicks's eyes drill into mine, trying to ascertain if I am telling the truth. I have no reason to worry.

'I got up to use the bathroom. I was feeling a little tipsy and I wanted a moment to gather myself. When I got back, Ian had moved onto the sofa I had been sitting on and was holding my drink out towards me.'

'Why do you think that was?' Becker asks.

'I don't know. It tasted funny, but I didn't say anything, I just took a sip and held my glass in my lap. He drank his quickly and wanted me to keep up. Something didn't feel right.'

'How did Ian seem?'

'Weird, hyper maybe. He was agitated.'

'And what did you do?'

'I had another sip of my drink, to be polite more than anything, then I told Ian I wasn't feeling well and was going to call a taxi. He said he would do it and took his mobile into the kitchen, but I don't think he called anyone. When he came back, he was pushing me to finish my drink and snapped at me when I refused.'

'What did he say?'

'He said I was no fun. I stood to leave, but he pulled me

back onto the sofa. I tried to push him off me, but he was too strong.' Tears come thick and fast, no acting required. I will never forget last night as long as I live.

'Do you want to take a break?' Hicks asks, his face full of concern. It isn't something I've seen from him so far and it takes me by surprise.

'No. I don't want to have to keep reliving it over and over.'

They remain quiet while I blow my nose, waiting for me to continue. I have their full attention now.

30

FRIDAY 8 DECEMBER 2017

I was so focused on Ian, I'd forgotten Christmas was fast approaching. Without the obligatory office party to remind me – Debbie had said they were having a low-key do in Kingston and not even partners were invited – it had passed me by. It was Mum that reminded me, she mentioned it on the phone. She'd rung to tell me she would be posting my Christmas present as a neighbour had invited her for dinner, unless I wanted to join them? I couldn't think of anything worse.

I didn't care much for the festive season and what I wanted I wasn't going to find wrapped underneath a tree. At least I wouldn't have to sit across the table from Mum, eating roast dinner out of a box, as she reminisced about 'happier times' like last year. I politely declined her invitation and said I would see what Jane was doing. Jane, it turned out, was celebrating the festivities with Doctor Lush's parents, whom she was meeting for the first time, at their home in Cobham. She'd used the 'L' word when referring to Graham on more than one occasion and I thought she might blow off travelling because she couldn't leave him behind. It looked like it would be Christmas for one here at the flat, not that I was really bothered. It was only one day after all.

With Christmas now on my radar, I made the effort to go into town and buy Mum a gift I could send her. I found a mint green cashmere mix jumper from M&S which would keep her warm. Whilst perusing, I discovered a dark brown leather satchel for Ben to replace his scruffy rucksack, which I hoped he'd like. More fitting for a man wanting to run his own security firm. I chanced upon some fluffy slippers in the shape of westies for Debbie but I couldn't find anything for Jane. When I got home, I had a look on my laptop and ordered a beautiful silver personalised fob watch with her name engraved that could be fastened to her nurse's uniform. I knew she'd love it.

Now that my notice period had ended, I had officially started work at the boxing club, focusing initially on a promotion to bring in business. I spent my days canvassing, promoting the club on social media and even managed to get a slot on the local radio station. The rate of sign-up had almost doubled each week and Jason was thrilled. I began work early in the morning, making sure the gym was manned from seven; lights and heating on, hot water ready, before tidying up from the evening before. I finished around two after Jason came in, so we could have a handover. It was early days, but I was enjoying it.

At five o'clock I headed to Pulse. Fridays were always busy, but I went regardless of whether I wanted to or not. The atmosphere today was jubilant, and everyone was chatty. Ahmed had put up some tinsel, which brightened the chrome and white décor, injecting a bit of colour. Ten minutes into my run on the treadmill, Ian got on beside me, his pace matching mine. There hadn't been much progress since our initial hello, but I wasn't giving up. We exchanged smiles, but then I focused on my run. The last thing I wanted to do was fall off the treadmill and make an idiot of myself. I finished before him and went to get a drink to cool off before embarking on the cross trainer. The air felt electric, like something was going to happen. I was right, Ian followed soon after and I tried my best to relax my shoulders as he approached.

'Hey, are you coming tonight?' he asked.

'Where?'

'The pub, it's our Christmas drink. Did Ahmed not mention it?'

I shook my head and took a sip of water. My stomach gurgled loudly.

'He must have forgotten. Come with us, we're going in about half an hour.'

I must have looked apprehensive as he continued with a chuckle.

'There's a group of us. We normally go to the pub around once a month. You should come.'

'I don't want to impose,' I said.

'You're not. Come. I insist.'

I nodded, and he left to use the rowing machine.

An hour later we were sitting in the Half Moon pub, on the corner of the high street, five minutes from the gym. We gathered at a large round table near the entrance and I sat in view of one of the cameras that I'd clocked when we walked in. Ian pushed Ahmed out of the way to sit next to me, which he got a ribbing for. Ahmed offered to buy the first round and I ordered a Coke.

'Not drinking?' Ian's face sagged slightly.

'No, I can't stay long. I've got a... thing.' I sounded aloof, but not on purpose, I didn't know what to say.

'A date?' he asked.

'No, not a date,' I replied. Ben was cooking dinner, which had become a weekly event on the nights when he wasn't working. Tonight, he was doing an Italian theme and any dish based around carbs was good for me. I couldn't deny I was looking forward to spending time with him.

The conversation turned to supportive running shoes. Laura had bought some Brooks trainers, but she was struggling with painful hips when she ran.

'I'll give you the number of my physio,' Beth piped up. She was a tall, wiry woman, all bone and sinew.

'Do you think he'll be able to help?' Laura asked, knocking back her lager.

'Sure, he'll probably give you some exercises to loosen your hip muscles. They're renowned for being tight when you do an office job.' Ahmed knew his stuff.

I remained quiet. I wasn't overly knowledgeable on exercise and it seemed to be the topic of choice. Although I was able to talk about the benefits of boxercise, and how getting a punchbag installed might bring in some more customers. Sam, aka yoga girl, pouted and suggested an investment into yoga blocks instead. I tried to hide my eye roll, but Ian caught it and smirked, sharing the joke.

The conversation was dull, and after I finished my drink I thanked Ahmed and Ian for the invitation and made my excuses. When I stood, Ian let me out and followed me to the door, holding it open. A sharp intake of breath escaped my lips when he stepped out after me. But there were too many people around for him to try anything.

'Do you fancy doing this again? Maybe just the two of us next time?'

The words stuck in my throat as Ian surveyed me.

'I'd love to.'

His face relaxed, mouth morphing into a grin. 'Brilliant. I'm away over Christmas, so perhaps in the New Year?'

Although it was what I wanted, I couldn't help but feel I'd been given a reprieve. I nodded, my head bobbing a bit too enthusiastically.

He held his phone, to take my number, which I gave him. Then flicking his finger upwards, he closed his open apps, pausing over Facebook. 'Are you on here?'

'I am, but I hardly ever post anything. To be honest I try and avoid social media.' I smiled, it was true, but I was smiling because he'd just given away his last name without me even having to ask. Ian Shaw.

'I know what you mean. I think I'm getting too old for it.' He chuckled and then the silence stretched out between us. 'Well, have a nice Christmas.' He held my arm and leaned forward to kiss me on the cheek. My insides squirmed, legs twitching as though they wanted to carry me away.

Forcing a smile, I wished him the same and turned to head for home, praying he was going to go back inside the pub. My teeth chattered as I walked, although I wasn't sure whether it was from the chill in the air or the one in my veins. Fear pulsed through me. Turning to look back, I saw he was still at the door, only just moving to go back inside. He'd watched me walk all the way down the road. It was creepy. I'd half expected him to try and follow me home and even though I knew he hadn't, I kept looking behind me every few steps just to be sure.

As I turned the corner, I broke into a jog and was home in less than five minutes.

'Blimey, hungry eh?' asked Ben, who was passing the hallway just as I burst through the front door.

'Something like that,' I called, racing into my bedroom to remove my contact lenses. I couldn't let Ben see. I don't think he'd buy that they were for cosmetic purposes. Especially as I was wearing them to the gym.

The smell of garlic bread filled the flat, but I needed wine to calm my nerves before I ate. I sat, grateful Ben had already poured me a glass. It was harder to interact with Ian than I thought. Did he have a split personality? On the surface he appeared normal, a nice guy, but I knew it was a pretence. My brain ached trying to process it, but it had been a successful evening. Ian had asked me out, so I was one step closer and I had a few weeks to prepare myself to be alone with him, which I was certain I would need.

'You okay, you're quiet?' Ben said, placing my pasta in front of me, breaking my thoughts.

'Sure, I'm fine. This looks delicious, thank you.'

'Just carbonara,' he said, tearing off a chunk of garlic bread.

We ate, chatting about our day and Ben's plans for Christmas.

'I thought you were going to your mother's?' Ben dropped his knife and fork on the table. His eyes wide, he looked guilt-ridden.

'No, she's going to her neighbour's house. Do you have plans then?' My face fell. I knew Ben's parents lived in Spain. Perhaps he was going to spend it there or with his sister? Stupidly I'd assumed we'd spend it together and I felt my neck flush.

'Amy asked me to hers. I just assumed you'd be going to your Mum's like last year. If I'd have known...' he trailed off.

I knocked my glass accidentally, wine sloshing over the edge. Ben winced, looking everywhere but at me.

'It's fine, don't worry about it. I'm not bothered honestly,' I lied, forcing a smile. Mopping up the spill with some kitchen roll before putting my hand on his forearm to reassure him.

'I wish you'd said sooner. She only asked me yesterday,' Ben grumbled, pushing his pasta around the bowl.

'You two a thing officially now then?' I didn't want to ask but I couldn't help myself. A pang in my chest told me all I needed to know. I wanted Ben and I didn't want anyone else to have him, but I was too fucked up to do anything about it.

'Sort of.'

I could tell he didn't want to talk about it, so I gratefully changed the subject.

'Shall we put some decorations up after dinner?'

Ben agreed, saying he would dig them out after we'd eaten.

I tried to keep the rest of the evening buoyant, but the mood dwindled and once the decoration box was empty we said our goodnights and went to bed.

* * *

Sunday 28 January 2018

'He was on top of me, grabbing my breasts and pulling at my clothes. I was crying and saying no, begging. We struggled, and I managed to push myself off the sofa and onto the floor. We hit the coffee table on the way down. That's when I felt his hands around my throat.'

My fingers flutter across my neck, I think the dark purple blotches are more obvious now. Skin is still tender.

Hicks stares at my throat and I see disgust reflected in his eyes. I can tell he's old school. A gentleman, someone that abhors violence against women.

'Why do you think it escalated so quickly?' Becker asks.

'I think he panicked that I was going to leave. When I stood up, that's when he got physical. I'm sure he put something in my drink as he was frustrated I didn't want it.' Hicks and Becker exchange a glance, but I can't read them. The doctor, Joyce, took a sample of my blood during my examination. Did they find anything in it?

'Take your time,' Hicks says and I realise I've been staring into space.

'He squeezed my throat, with one hand at first, trying to undo my jeans with the other, but I was fighting so much he couldn't do it, so he used both hands and that's when I struggled to breathe.'

'Do you think he wanted to kill you?' Becker asks.

'Yes, and he would have done too. I was terrified, fighting for my life.'

'What happened next?'

Tears stream down my cheeks. This is exhausting.

'My hand was pulling at his fingers, trying to loosen his grip. Everything was going fuzzy. He grabbed one of my wrists over my head and held it down. I was trying to reach out for anything I could with my free hand.' I wave my arm around demonstrating. 'I knocked the tray on to the floor and I was trying to grab it to hit him with, but I couldn't reach it. My fingers touched something, and I scrambled around trying to get hold of it. I didn't know it was the knife.' I sob into my palms, tears running down my wrists. My back heaving. Hysterical comes easy, I am hysterical.

It was hard not to panic as I felt my vision fade out; I had the knife in my hand, but I needed to hit the spot, the axillary artery under the armpit was the first choice. Not as horrific as the neck, more of an accidental severing than a deliberate one.

'Can I get you some water?' Hicks offers, and I shake my head. I'm hungry, but now is not the right time to ask when lunch is.

'So, you had the knife in your hand?' Becker says, urging me on. Her face is impassive. She's good at this.

'Yes, and I stabbed him with it.' I shudder, but this one is real. There was so much blood.

'Where on his body did you stab him?'

'I don't know, I don't remember. I stabbed upwards, wherever I could. Just to get him off me. I nearly passed out, but when he let go of my neck and I could breathe again, I was able to wriggle out from underneath him.' I had waited a couple of minutes, watching Ian's life ebb away. Just to make sure he couldn't be saved. Then I ran downstairs screaming, barefoot and covered in blood, into the night.

31

MONDAY 25 DECEMBER 2017

Christmas morning was a quiet affair, I woke early and went for a run through the deserted streets, which was blissful. A frost had descended overnight and everything sparkled, nature's way of celebrating. There were hardly any cars on the road and I saw no one except for the Indian shopkeeper who was taking an early delivery of bread and milk. He called out to me as I jogged past.

'Merry Christmas.'

'And to you.' I waved, returning his jubilance.

I wasn't sure if he celebrated or not. I guessed not if he was going to be working in his shop all day.

I ran three miles, thinking of all the children who would already be up, excited to see their presents under the tree. I thought of all the parents fuelled by coffee for the next few hours. Maybe someday I would have a family? Though I wasn't sure I could handle the responsibility.

Ben and I had planned to eat breakfast together and he bought a bottle of Bucks Fizz and some pastries. He was getting picked up at ten by Amy's brother, so he could have a drink and not have to worry about his car. I didn't ask whether he would be spending the night, it wasn't something I wanted to think about. His overnight bag by the door alongside a gift bag of neatly wrapped presents told me all I needed to know. The croissants were already in the oven when I got back from my run, but I had a quick shower before we ate.

'I got you something,' Ben said, tiny red blotches appearing on his cheeks. He pushed a small silver box decorated with a red bow across the table.

'Thank you,' I said, lifting the lid and opening a fold of tissue paper to reveal a silver necklace with a circle pendant. Engraved on the pendant were the words 'still I rise' and, underneath, a semicolon. My eyes watered as I stared at it. It may have been the best gift I'd ever been given.

'It's the semicolon, you know, apparently it's the sign for "survivor",' he explained.

'Yes, I've seen it before. I love it, thank you.' I took it out of the box and put it on, my fingers caressing the pendant. I wiped my eyes and felt foolish for getting emotional. I had to restrain myself from jumping onto his lap. Oblivious to my struggle, Ben relaxed now he knew I liked it, but his face remained red. 'I got you something too.' I went to grab his satchel which I'd wrapped the night before, tying it with green ribbon.

He cleared space on the table and opened it, tearing the paper off like a child.

'It's wicked, thanks Eve. I love it.' It was always nerve-racking giving presents, unsure whether you'd made a good choice or missed the mark. From the look on Ben's face, I had got it right. He awarded me a kiss on the cheek for my efforts and my stomach flipped. God I was tragic. He wasn't mine to lust after.

All too soon it was ten o'clock and Ben hugged me goodbye. I squeezed him tighter than I should have, resisting the urge to pull him in an embrace and make him stay.

'Will you be okay?' he asked.

'Of course, I'm going to start drinking at lunchtime, I've got snacks and movies. I'll be fine. Go and have a great time.' I felt like his mum sending him off, but I wanted to get him out of the door as I was struggling to hold it together. It was silly, but it'd been an emotional morning. Ben was a good friend and, perhaps, if I admitted it to myself, I loved him.

The rest of Christmas Day was spent mooching around the flat, carrying a tin of Celebrations wherever I went, making my way through them one chocolate at a time. When dusk came around, I felt so sick I couldn't bring myself to eat anything more than a couple of crackers with cheese. I rang Mum to wish her a merry Christmas, but she was three sheets to the wind. It sounded like she was in the pub, a rowdy group singing The Pogues' 'Fairytale of New York' in the background, and I couldn't get much sense out of her. I had a text from Ian wishing me a merry Christmas at around eight in the evening. I waited until just before I went to bed to reply, wishing him the same.

Ben still wasn't home by the time I'd watched *Home Alone* and *Scrooged*, so I assumed he was staying out. In the end I went to bed with a bottle of Baileys, trying to calculate how many calories I'd consumed. Sod it. It was Christmas after all.

* * *

Thursday 4 January 2018

During the holidays, the days blurred into one. The rest of the festive season whizzed by; Ben went back to work the day after Boxing Day and normal service resumed. Jason didn't want me back at the gym until the second of January and I was grateful to have a bit of downtime. New Year's Eve was a washout, it poured with rain and I stayed in to watch fireworks out of Ben's window whilst he was at work. He'd suggested it, a better view from his side apparently. I resisted the urge to look around his room. Poor Jane had to work too. She sent me a selfie of her amongst a group of nurses, all wearing party hats, and blowers in their mouths. In the photo, which didn't come through until the following morning, she was pointing to her fob watch pinned to her uniform

There were no resolutions. I couldn't plan anything whilst I still had Ian hanging over my head. But I did allow myself to look back at how far I'd come, mainly in the last few months. Physically and mentally I was stronger. I was no longer Ian's victim. I'd taken control of my life, changed my job, paid my debts and was moving on. I'd even cut right down on smoking. No longer using it as a crutch to get me through the day.

However, I was thinking of seeking help for the caffeine addiction I'd developed from spending so much time at Baristas. If I wasn't at the boxing club or at Pulse I could be found browsing the internet with a latte, telling anyone who appeared interested that I was writing a book. The news delighted Susie, who said she'd suspected for a while that was what I was up to. If only she really knew.

32

WEDNESDAY 10 JANUARY 2018

I'd taken the day off work as my third appointment with Doctor Almara had been booked in for the morning, promising Jason I'd spend a few hours in the afternoon leaflet dropping the roads in the area, advertising the boxing club's no registration fee.

I finally told Doctor Almara the details of my attack, feeling lighter as a result. She didn't shrink away in horror, or eye me with pity. Instead she focused on all the changes I'd made to assist in my recovery. Impressed to see I was no longer restricting my movements to daylight hours and embracing the change in job.

'Are you still having issues with temper flare-ups?'

'Sometimes.' Whenever I thought about Ian, I pictured beating him to a pulp, but I didn't tell her that. She booked me in for another appointment but said, depending on that, she would be happy to sign me off. I'd made progress.

I'd been to Pulse on and off over the Christmas period. I didn't want anyone to think I only went when Ian was there.

It was different going alone, with no purpose other than to exercise. I didn't have to watch what I did or said. I could just be myself. But it wasn't long before he was back, and he seemed keen to see me, interrupting my weights to chat.

'Did you have a nice Christmas?' he asked.

'Yes, quiet but good. You?' I wanted to know where he'd been over Christmas. Did he have any family?

'Lovely, thanks, nice to get away.' I was just about to say, 'anywhere nice?' but he interrupted me. His fingers drummed on his thigh. 'Are you free Friday?' It was only two days away. A shiver trickled down my spine, but I had no reason to delay. Perhaps Friday would give me my first insight into the man behind the monster.

'Sure.' I chewed my lip.

'Shall we go for a drink? I'll meet you here at, say eight?'

I nodded, but before I could speak, Ahmed hijacked our conversation, so I returned to the chest press. I had a couple of days to decide what to wear and, more importantly, what I needed to take. Safety was my main priority, but as we would be out in public, I wasn't overly concerned. Attacking someone who could identify him wasn't his style, too exposed. Speculation, of course, but I believed he hid behind the balaclava.

* * *

Friday 12 January 2018

I stood in front of the mirror on Friday night appraising my appearance. I wore black skinny jeans and a red cold-shoulder top I'd purchased in the week. Everything off the sale rack. The red looked great against the platinum blonde and Ben's expression made the splurge worth every penny.

'Not so bad out of my PJs, eh?' I said, striking a pose.

'You look great. Where are you off to?' His eyes narrowed.

'Just out.' I added, 'I have a date.' There was no harm in the telling the truth, Ben was still seeing Amy and our relationship was firmly back on the platonic side.

'Be careful,' Ben said, which irked me. Why couldn't he have said 'have fun' or 'don't do anything I wouldn't do', but I knew he was looking out for me.

The closer I got to the gym, the more my flesh crawled. I was much more comfortable being outside. But no matter how many times I walked the streets in the dark, I still felt vulnerable and exposed. As I approached the red-brick building, I could see Ian stood underneath the neon Pulse sign. He looked smart in a shirt and jeans, his hair full of wax and styled like I'd not seen it before. I didn't get it. He was good-looking; surely, he didn't struggle to get a date? Why did he need to attack women to get his kicks? Didn't they say something similar about Ted Bundy too?

'You look gorgeous,' he said, giving me a kiss on the cheek. He exuded confidence, which intimidated me straight away.

'As do you.' *I could do this. Relax, just be yourself, your best self. Go with the flow.*

Ian led me to Mangos, a wine bar, and selected a table at the back with high stools, away from the speakers. Everything was silver and black, it reminded me of a dominatrix's boudoir rather than a bar. Ian went to get our drinks and returned with two mojitos, without asking me what I wanted. Did men truly believe women liked having their choice made for them? Egotistical bastards. I certainly didn't, but I smiled sweetly on his return and sipped at the cocktail. I couldn't deny it was nice, but it wasn't what I would have chosen. Ian settled into his seat, looking pleased with himself. My hero.

'Where did you go over Christmas; were you visiting family?' I asked, desperate to know.

'My dad lives in Oxford, he's in a care home. It's just me and him now so I always go and spend a few days there at Christmas. In a hotel that is, not in the care home.' The monster had a heart?

'That's very sweet. How old is he?'

'Sixty-five but he's got dementia, diagnosed a few years ago. Early onset. He began wandering around all over the place. Getting out at night. It's the best place for him, round the clock care.' Ian said flatly. His tone jarred me. Not quite as sincere as I thought.

What's his name?' I asked.

Ian's smile faded. 'David. So, what do you do? I don't think I've ever asked,' he said, changing the subject.

'Well, I was in marketing, although I'm in between jobs at the moment. I got made redundant before Christmas so just taking a bit of time to figure out what I want to do next. What about you?'

'I'm an Account Exec for Dunnes Advertising.' That explained the fancy apartment block. Did he drive a Porsche too?

'How old are you?' I blurted out without thinking and he nearly choked on his drink laughing. It struck me he could be a bit older than I first thought.

'Thirty-two. You?'

'Twenty-five,' I replied. Why was he not married? Because he was a fucking rapist, that's why.

'We haven't done favourite colours yet.'

'Purple.' I didn't hesitate.

'This is like speed dating with quick-fire questions.' I could see he was being sarcastic.

For the next hour, I let him dominate the conversation and went with the flow. He wanted to find out about me, where I lived; what I did for fun, where my parents were? I didn't give any specifics, instead skirted around the truth so I couldn't be caught out later. There wasn't much in the way of flirting, although I was no expert. Jane always said you should leave them wanting more, so at around half ten and three mojitos later, I made an excuse to leave, telling Ian that I needed to get up early in the morning. He offered to wait with me for the taxi and didn't seem perturbed that I didn't want to go on anywhere else.

Throughout the evening he'd been a perfect gentleman, helping me on and off with my coat and insisting he went to the bar for drinks. I wasn't allowed to get my purse out once. Everything I'd learnt, apart from the obvious desire to be in control, I found difficult to reconcile with the predator I knew him to be. I stared at his eyes, fascinated by their lack of depth. He appeared empty, devoid of emotion, but he put on a pretty good act. I could see how he had everyone fooled. The charming successful bachelor. I bet he did charity work too.

When we got outside, it was freezing. A bitter wind whipped around us, and my teeth chattered uncontrollably. Ian offered me his coat, but I declined. The taxi stand had a small queue, but no cars came by in the few minutes we waited. It was only a short walk back to my flat, but there was a difference between walking home alone at seven o'clock at night, and at ten o'clock. Especially knowing Ian could follow me.

He frowned at my shivering and pulled out his phone. 'I'm ten minutes away, come back to mine and I'll book an Uber. You can wait in the warm.'

My heart leapt into my throat and my mind raced for reasons not to.

'Umm,' I said, to make it look as if I was considering it, buying some time. What the fuck was I supposed to do? If I declined, it looked weird. Why wouldn't I go back there? Because I wasn't going to offer myself to him on a plate, that's why. Then I remembered I'd packed the PetCam in my bag, just in case I had the opportunity to plant it. 'Okay.'

'Great,' he said with a smile, steering me by the elbow. Perhaps he thought the alcohol had gone to my head. Or maybe he wanted to get me back home for a repeat performance? The thought made my blood run cold.

* * *

Sunday 28 January 2018

I screamed outside in the bitingly cold air for a full minute until someone came out to see what had happened. A middle aged man emerged from one of the houses over the road; no one from Ian's apartment building came out at first.

'Mr Woodcock,' Detective Becker says, checking her notes.

I had no idea what his name was, but he had kind grey eyes and a sizeable belly you could rest your pint on, or so my dad would have said.

'He was the first one to find you?'

I nod, wiping my good eye. Now they are both swollen and sore. I must be dehydrated with the amount of tears I have shed, I should have grabbed the offer of water when I had the chance.

'Yes, he called the ambulance and gave me a coat. He tried to get into the building, I told him Ian was hurt, but no one answered their buzzers.' I sniff.

'How long did the ambulance take to get there?'

'I don't know, it was quick. The police arrived at the same time, by then neighbours had come out and they got in to Ian's apartment. They sat me in a car, until I was brought here.'

'Okay, Eve, you've done brilliantly. Is there anything else you can remember? Anything you want to add?'

I shake my head. What happens next? Am I going to be charged?

A light tap on the door interrupts Hicks. A young uniformed officer pokes his head round.

'Detective Becker, can I borrow you for a minute?'

Becker stands to leave and Hicks pauses the recording.

'Do you want a drink or anything?' he asks.

'Please, and can I have something to eat too?'

He checks his watch and sees it's midday.

'Sure, I'll be right back.'

He disappears out of the room and I see the young officer outside through the window in the door. My stomach cramps, but I'm not sure if it's nerves or hunger. I didn't finish the bacon roll from this morning.

When Becker returns, she looks resigned and her downcast expression troubles me.

Hicks comes back a minute later with a pre-packed

cheese sandwich, which he places in front of me. I open it and take a bite. It's good.

'Eve, once you've eaten we're going to go back out to the desk where you will be formally charged with murder.'

Suddenly I'm not hungry any more.

33

FRIDAY 12 JANUARY 2018

We got to Ian's apartment in less than ten minutes, the crisp air making us walk faster. I thought about the film *The Green Mile*, that long corridor on the way to the electric chair. That's how I felt, like I was walking towards my demise or maybe into an ambush. I tried my best to act naturally and, on the way, we talked about our shared interest in keeping fit. He told me he enjoyed rugby, playing every Saturday for a local team. It was why, he said, he was often covered in bruises. A perfect cover. Vanity made him wear a cap to avoid cauliflower ears. I vaguely remembered seeing men wearing them on television, but rugby was a sport I didn't understand bar the ball having to cross the line to score. He suggested I come and watch. I'd rather watch paint dry, but I giggled and agreed all the same. I was being good, little compliant Eve and he liked it.

'Are you seeing anyone at the moment?' he asked.

'No, not for quite a while,' I admitted. 'You?'

'No one special,' he said with a nonchalance that made me want to punch him in the face. I was sure he'd 'seen' more of me and his other victims than we'd ever have let him by choice.

Fear clouded my judgement the closer we got to his flat. The conversation had stalled, and we were walking in silence. Was I going to my own execution? Despite my apprehension, I was curious to see inside. I had expectations of chrome and gadgets galore. I wasn't disappointed, it was minimalist, light and airy with plenty of space. An open plan lounge/diner with a hard wood floor and white walls. The lounge area had an enormous television mounted onto the wall in front of two brown leather sofas surrounding a coffee table on a plush cream rug. The walls were bare except for a large framed black and white *Scarface* poster in the dining area. I looked around in awe at a living space so different in style to my own eclectic tastes.

'Wow. It's lovely.'

'Thanks, it's still quite new. I bought it when it was being built, so it's only a year old.'

'You're so tidy,' I said, unable to see anything that looked out of place.

'I have a cleaner who comes in twice a week. She was here this morning.' There was no hint of embarrassment at the admission.

'Lucky you.'

'I've got beer in the fridge, or would you prefer a coffee?'

I hesitated, not wanting to prolong being here with him any longer than I had to.

'Coffee, please.'

He took my coat, hanging it up by the door. I looked at it longingly, my escape route. I tried to control my breathing as my anxiety spiked at being alone with him.

'Okay, I'll order a taxi to come in twenty minutes.' He

walked out of the lounge and into the kitchen, and I heard the tap being run. A second later the kettle began to boil.

I didn't have time to worry. Scanning the room until I found what I was looking for. The sleek black modem was slotted into a glossy bookcase, its lights blinking. I swiftly took a picture of the security key sticker with my phone. Pausing to listen, I heard clinking of mugs and the kettle whistling.

'Could I have sugar in mine, please,' I called over the noise, my voice higher than intended. I needed to buy another minute.

Rummaging in my bag, I pulled out the PetCam which I'd broken out of its plastic casing at home to make it smaller. I wanted to be able to watch Ian's comings and goings, to see what he got up to.

On the third tier of the bookcase there was a small space on top of *Great Expectations*, it was there I wedged the camera. A layer of dust confirmed my suspicions. The book, along with other classics like *1984* and *The Great Gatsby*, were for show and rarely moved.

Perspiration prickled my neck, I was running out of time. I pulled the slim cord down the side of the bookcase and plugged it into the power, tucking the cord out of sight. Any second now he would be back in the room. I could feel my underarms starting to sweat, my skin clinging to the red polyester fabric of my top. Luckily, a large-leaved pot plant shielded the plug from view. A bead of sweat drizzled down my side as my pulse continued to race. I had done it.

I dashed away from the bookcase and pretended to survey the view out of the window. Ian came back into the room and handed me a cup of coffee, which I accepted gratefully, wishing I had asked for a beer now I'd warmed up to the point of perspiration.

'Nice view,' I said, more to make conversation than because it was. There wasn't much to see other than the arched railway bridge illuminated by street lights.

He smiled and sat on the sofa, using a remote control to close his blinds.

'Can I use your bathroom please?' I was being overly polite, but I couldn't help it. I was nervous, scared to say anything which could be misconstrued. I didn't want to upset him in any way. It hit me just how vulnerable I was.

'Sure, it's by the front door.'

I took my bag and locked myself in the small toilet. It smelt of bleach and a manly woody fragrance. I sat on the toilet seat and unlocked my phone, connecting it to the Wi-Fi using the security key I'd photographed. Once connected, I linked the PetCam to Ian's Wi-Fi and used the app I'd downloaded at home to view straight into the lounge area. Ian was waiting for me on the sofa, I could just about see him fiddling with his phone, but the picture was good and clear.

I flushed and washed my hands, putting on lipstick before I left so there was a reason for me to have taken my bag into the toilet.

Ian smiled when I returned, perhaps assuming the lipstick was for him. I resisted the urge to glance at the bookcase, paranoid the LED light I'd covered with electrical tape at home would still be seen. I knew it wouldn't, but I panicked anyway.

I sat on the opposite sofa, my coffee cup still steaming. I wanted to keep as much distance between us as possible.

'You know,' Ian said, 'I'm sure I've seen you somewhere before.'

I spluttered as I sipped my drink, the hot liquid escaping down my throat. Was he playing with me? His eyes were like slits, but he wore a smirk.

'I don't think so, I'm sure I would remember,' I said, searching for a change of subject. 'I'm sorry for rushing off early tonight. I'd love to do this again?' I added.

Ian's eyes flashed to the floor. The corner of a metal cash box poked out from under the lower level of the coffee table. I quickly averted my gaze. What was in there? Had he seen me looking?

'I'd like that. Dinner next time?'

'Sure.'

'Where would you like to go?' He leant forward, placing his mug on the coffee table. I followed suit with mine, although I had failed to use a coaster. He rectified that in seconds and I just caught myself before I rolled my eyes.

'I'll let you choose, I'm sure you know where the food is good. I don't get out much,' I said, playing to his ego.

He rubbed his chin, but a buzzing from his phone interrupted him as he was about to speak. He snatched it up, turning away from me. The box had been pushed fully under the table, out of sight. There was something in there he didn't want me to see.

'No problem,' he said, 'taxi's here.' My shoulders relaxed. Finally. Why hadn't he tried anything? He'd had the perfect opportunity.

We stood and for the second time Ian helped me on with my coat; brushing my neck as he adjusted the collar of my jacket which had turned inward. My neck tingled, skin on fire, but not from pleasure. His hand pressed into the small of my back, guiding me out of the door and navigating the steps until we were out of the building. He opened the taxi door for me and I stiffened as he drew me in for a kiss, his tongue penetrating. I knew I was awkward, I couldn't help it, even with the alcohol. It was over in a second and Ian wished me goodnight, closing the car door between us. Before I knew it, I was being driven away; the taxi driver looking on in amusement as I wiped my mouth with my sleeve.

34

HIM

Something about her made me curious. She intrigued me from the moment I saw her. The way she carried herself; her slight frame and elfin features. Eve. Such a pretty name for a pretty girl. Now we've gotten to know each other; we've become friends and perhaps maybe something more. I want to find out her secrets and the things that keep her awake at night.

She's dyed her mousy hair and even her eyes are a different colour; but she smells just as enticing. Fear emanates from her, like a bitch in season and the scent sings to me. She's nervous, wary, but I can tell she's not worldly. Not like those other girls, faces painted; the fake whores pouting for likes on Instagram. Could it be her lack of experience that makes her tremble? Or, has she hunted me down? Is it a coincidence or has she worked out I'm the one who took her behind the café? I can't tell. Not yet. This is going to make for an interesting game. But either way, now I get to taste her again.

35

SATURDAY 13 JANUARY 2018

I couldn't sleep, wired from the evening's events. Too hyped up from the adrenaline pumping around my body. I'd done it. Palpitations developed every time I relived hiding the camera with seconds to spare. He didn't catch me though and now I had a window into his life. It felt good having one over on him, having the upper hand. Ben was at work and I took one of his beers from the fridge, sure he wouldn't mind. I needed to relax but was jittery and unable to settle. I considered taking two diazepam, but I wanted to remain alert. The PetCam app had been streaming continuously on my phone since I came through the front door. I'd chewed my nails down to the quick, but all I was watching was Ian's empty sofa. He was nowhere to be seen. Had he gone to bed? Unless he'd gone out on the prowl? The idea made me nauseous.

I had no way of knowing what he was doing unless I contacted him. It was gone eleven now, but I had his number. I tapped at my screen, composing a text.

`Had a lovely time tonight. Looking forward`

to doing it again. Off to bed now. Eve x

I waited for my phone to buzz back, but it remained silent.

I finished the beer, took off my make-up and cleaned my teeth. Checking my phone every few minutes. It wasn't until I got into bed that my phone finally vibrated.

I'm in bed too. Big game of rugby tomorrow. Looking forward to dinner soon. See you at the gym. X

Whether or not he was in bed, I couldn't know. I couldn't be responsible for what he did, it was down to the police and they'd failed to catch him. Which is why I was going to deliver some justice of my own.

By lunchtime the next day Ben questioned why I was so glued to my phone and I had to lie on the spot. The best thing I could come up with was a dating app, which I instantly regretted as his face darkened. I'd never been good under pressure, especially at lying.

In truth, I couldn't stop watching the window into Ian's life, although there had barely been any activity; only a couple of flashes of him walking past early this morning, wearing his rugby kit. I knew he'd be out most of the day. Being a voyeur was addictive. In the end I forced myself to put the phone down.

'What are you doing this weekend?' I asked Ben.

'Not a lot. Amy is on a hen weekend in Brighton, so I'll be

just chilling. How was your date?'

'All right.' I didn't want to elaborate; Ben would see straight through me. Thankfully he didn't push for more information.

'Fancy a movie and a takeaway tonight? Or I could cook, we haven't had a themed night in a few weeks.' No, we hadn't, not since Amy came along anyway.

'Takeaway would be good,' I replied.

Whilst Ben was out collecting the curry, I opened the app to see if Ian had returned and almost jumped when I saw him sat on the sofa, a laptop across his knees. The PetCam had a microphone you could talk through as well as playing audio. When the app was opened, both features were set to mute. I unmuted the audio, so I could listen. Sounds of sex filled the room, slapping of skin on skin and a woman squealing. I baulked, wrinkling my nose. He was watching porn on his laptop. Not that different from other men after all. Cheeks flushed red with guilt for prying, watching his arm jolt up and down as he pleasured himself, I couldn't tear my eyes away. After a minute, when I was just about to close the app down, the squeals turned to screams. A different sound came through the speakers. Crunching of bone and swear words spat venomously. On the laptop screen, it looked as though the man was now beating the woman. Something which had started out as sex had turned into a vicious attack. She was crying for help as punches rained down on her. My eyes brimmed with tears, the phone quivering in my hand, but I couldn't wrench myself away from the horror. Ian's arm was moving faster, his excitement palpable. It sickened me, how could someone enjoy watching such violence? Ian groaned, and I guessed he'd ejaculated. My throat constricted, and I thought I was going to be sick.

I didn't hear Ben enter the flat. When a voice came from behind me, I jumped out of my seat.

'Are you watching porn?' he asked, the corner of his mouth turned up into a half-smile.

I closed the app and threw the phone onto the carpet. 'No. Just one of those stupid horror things that make you jump,' I lied, wiping my eyes.

Ben went into the kitchen, the smell of curry turning my stomach as it wafted past. I rushed to the bathroom sink.

'I bought elderflower gin, it was on offer. Didn't you say you wanted to try it?' Ben called, oblivious.

'Brilliant, pour me a glass would you,' I called back, sucking in air as the nausea subsided. I stared at my ashen face in the mirror. What was I doing? I was going to be found naked and dumped in an alleyway if I kept going down this rabbit hole. It was clear violence turned him on and that petrified me. Had he fantasised doing that to me?

'It's on the table,' Ben called back.

I splashed water on my face and returned to the kitchen. I was safe here with Ben. For now, anyway.

'Best Indian takeaway, bloody annoying they don't deliver though,' Ben said, thankfully unaware of the torment I was trying to hide.

I pushed the dhansak around my plate, willing my hunger to return.

'Are you okay?' Ben asked.

I nodded, forcing myself to make conversation. 'So, Amy's on a hen do then. Are you going to the wedding?' Glad to change the subject, I forced a forkful of curry into my mouth, chewing rhythmically.

'Yep, it's two weeks away and I've got to get a suit. She's already stressing about what to wear.'

'It's what us women do.' Well, most women, normal women. Not so much me.

'I'm just hoping she doesn't catch the bouquet.'

I choked on my food then, spluttering as it lodged in my throat.

'Otherwise you'll be right up shit creek!' I croaked.

My mood lifted a little and we joked good naturedly about the sort of wife Amy would make. We'd lounged on the floor, eating left over poppadums and watching *Anchorman*. I didn't want the evening to end. For a while I forgot about Ian.

Saying goodnight to Ben was always difficult, especially after the kiss that seemed like it had happened years ago. Would it ever be repeated?

My bedroom was cold after the warmth and laughter of the front room. Under the duvet, I was terrified to open the app but compelled to at the same time. Hesitating, I opened the portal to Ian's living space, relieved to see he wasn't in view. I didn't think I could go to the gym tomorrow. I couldn't look him in the eyes so soon without revulsion etched across my face. How could I hold a conversation with him? How do I attract this predator without becoming his prey once more?

Sunday 28 January 2018 – DC Becker

Hicks's forehead crumples as he scans the preliminary lab results which have just been sent through. The ingrained lines doubling, the harder he frowns at the page.

'Why would she lie?' I ask.

He shrugs, he's not interested in debating, but I can tell something is troubling him.

'She's admitted killing him. There's no reason for her to lie,' I continue.

'I think she's lying about how it went down. Something's not right. I've got a feeling.' He's still frowning, patting his stomach to indicate the bad feeling is coming from his gut. 'Did she deliberately mislead us with her name?' he continues.

'That was our mistake, not hers,' I say dismissively and gesture towards the paper he's holding with the lab results.

'Nothing surprising, his blood type on her, there's tissue under her fingernails, but still waiting on DNA confirmation, but I think we're safe to assume it's him. Both fingerprints have been found on the knife, in different places, conducive to how she handled it. No trace of her so far in the kitchen, only prints in the bathroom and living room.'

The girl looks too fragile for this and I'm concerned for her state of mind. I can tell Hicks thinks she's too contained, but I believe she's in shock. Knowing she was raped only a few months ago, she must have some residual post-traumatic stress. It's no wonder she reacted like she did. I would have done the same. Working these kinds of cases never gets easier. Looking at her is like looking in the mirror at myself twenty years ago.

'Have you seen the papers?' Guy, the newest member of our team, comes rushing in to the kitchenette, flapping the *Daily Mirror*. I scan the text before handing it to Hicks.

'Shit,' I sigh, this could change things. 'Has the boss seen it yet?'

Guy shakes his head. He's on loan from another station, pending a transfer after buying a house in the next county. I like him, but Hicks isn't too keen, although he takes a while to warm up to anybody. I can see why he rubs Hicks up the wrong way, Guy is like a puppy, constantly bouncing and requiring attention.

'Who do you think leaked it?' I ask.

Guy's eyes glint at the possibility of an internal leak.

'No idea.' The headline is 'Victim Arrested in Rapist's Killing'. A photo of a brunette Eve holding a cocktail is framed by three paragraphs of outrage on the miscarriage of justice.

'The press will have a field day with this, it's like the pensioner and the burglar all over again,' I say. My left eye begins to twitch, it always does when I'm tired. At six o'clock this morning, I was singing 'Twinkle Twinkle, Little Star'. I can count the number of hours sleep I've had in the past twenty-four on one hand.

'#ReleaseEve is trending on Twitter,' Guy adds.

I shake my head; social media is always the thorn in our side.

He hands me a folder. 'Psychiatrist's report. She's only been a few times. The doctor wouldn't supply recordings without a warrant but has written an outline of her mental state.' This is something I'm looking forward to reading.

'Thanks,' I reply, turning my focus back to Hicks. 'Was anything found at either home address?'

His eyes dart back to the sheet.

'Rohypnol was discovered at Mr Shaw's address, and there were traces of it in Eve's saliva sample. Preliminary scan of his laptop shows he streams some pretty violent porn on a regular basis. A journal was found at hers, Lisa is going through it now but said nothing untoward.' Hicks pauses, and Guy jumps in.

'Financial and phone records aren't out of the ordinary

either. They communicated by text a few times, typical of a couple going out.'

Hicks scowls at the interruption. He's grumpy today.

'Thanks, Guy. So, evidentially, it looks as though she's telling the truth. Can you see what you can find out about Ian Shaw. Any previous? Ask them to run his DNA through the system, if that hasn't already been requested. And can you check the report for the CPS please, make sure it's got all the findings in it so far?' I ask.

Guy nods, scribbling the instructions on a notepad he cradles like a clipboard.

'Already searched through the database for Ian, makes for interesting reading. I've sent the file over to you both,' he says, before hurrying out of the office.

'God, he's so bloody keen,' Hicks grumbles.

I ignore him.

'We need to probe Eve more, perhaps ask some difficult questions. Are you up for that?'

Hicks grunts in agreement and takes a loud slurp of his tea. He is much better at squeezing information out of someone than I am, that I'll willingly concede. He tucks in one side of his shirt which has worked its way out over his waistband. I'm sure he was wearing the same one yesterday. My nose wrinkles, I can't help it. Personal hygiene should be a minimum for this job. Hicks is a good detective though and his gut has been a contributing factor in some other cases we've solved together. On the surface this looks like a clear-cut case.

We head back to the interview room, but we're stopped in the corridor by Guy.

'Glad I caught you. More results just in: blood splatter and initial crime scene DNA.'

36

SUNDAY 14 JANUARY 2018

Ian sent a text on Sunday afternoon, to see if I was okay. I didn't go to the gym, I couldn't face it, instead I managed a four mile run, a personal best for me as it was the furthest I'd ever done. It helped clear my head. Listening to the sound of my feet pounding the concrete, I let my mind drift. I did all my best planning whilst running, going through scenarios in my head, exhausting endless possibilities. On the way back, I stopped in to see Susie at Baristas, excusing my sweaty mess. I was the only customer, so I needn't have fretted.

'Don't worry about it, love. Fancy a pastry? I'll only have to eat them myself, won't be fresh tomorrow. Free to you.'

I hesitated but then accepted, I hadn't had any breakfast. I put a couple of quid in the tip jar and paid for my latte. I devoured the cinnamon roll, flaky pastry covering me like a blanket.

'All right, big tits! Americano please,' boomed a voice behind me, an accent which sounded like they were from the East End. They were a long way from home.

My head snapped round, even though I knew it was not

directed at me. My décolletage could never be described as big.

'Coming up,' Susie replied in her usual chirpy manner. Turning her back to us, she seemed unfazed as the machine churned the coffee.

I threw a filthy look in the direction of the man who had spoken. He was dressed casually, a long-sleeved polo shirt over a bulging belly, jeans and trainers. Unshaven and carrying car keys, a large gold watch adorned his wrist. He gave me a toothy grin, oblivious to the offence he had caused.

'I only come in here because of her tits, you know. She's got a lovely pair.' As if I wasn't in on the joke.

'Tosser,' I muttered, turning back to my pastry.

'What's your problem? You a dyke?' He spat on the floor of the coffee shop and I stood up, mouth gaping.

'You're a pig,' I said, temper flaring. I felt the vein bulge in my neck.

Susie rushed to pass the man his coffee in a takeaway cup.

'Go fuck yourself, pipsqueak.' He launched forward, arm pulled back, like he was going to punch me and fell about laughing as I recoiled. My face steamed but he sauntered out of the shop, whistling to himself.

'What a wanker,' I growled, taking a napkin from the counter and bending to wipe the spittle.

'I know, he's in most days, Bob the cabbie, always the same.'

'You shouldn't let them talk to you like that,' I said, but then looking at Susie's large chest, emphasised by the low-cut purple top she was wearing, I saw I was fighting a losing battle.

'Ah well, doesn't matter. Are you doing research today?' She gestured towards the back of the café. The four computers spaced out on a high bench, each with stools tucked neatly underneath. I always used the one on the far left, furthest away from the counter.

I nodded, damn right I was.

'I'll put the lights on back there. How's the book coming along?'

'Slow.'

'Then I'll bring you a hot chocolate,' Susie replied, squeezing my shoulder. She reminded me of a perfect mum, always wanting to take care of everyone. So different from mine. It was such a shame she didn't have any kids yet, but her time would come. Perhaps when her husband was home from the rigs.

I headed to the back of the café, my blood still boiling from the customer who had just left. What right did he have to talk to either of us that way? Why did men think they could say whatever they wanted with no consequences? Treat women any way they felt like? I had to stop myself from following him, although I fantasised about it for a while. Leaving a present on his doorstep, faeces in a bag set alight, or I'd heard brake fluid poured on a car melted the paint right off. Revenge stoked the fire within me and I liked it. Maybe a bit too much. Something had to be done. I had to make a stand. They had to pay, but Ian was first.

I turned my attention to the search engine on screen and began to type. If I was going to do it, it had to be right. Every possible outcome had to be anticipated, every loose strand tied up. There could be no room for error otherwise the consequences didn't bear thinking about.

I stayed for another hour, making mental notes. No pen and paper for me. I wasn't stupid. When Ian texted me later asking how I was and telling me his team had won at rugby the day before, I left it a while before replying. I was deliberating on what to say. I sensed he liked the chase and I was happy to oblige. After a few hours, just before bedtime, I responded.

`Well done. Sorry, been out all day. See you tomorrow. X`

Hopefully it would be enough to pique his interest. When I saw him, I would make something up, a day out shopping with a friend or visiting relatives, but for now he could wonder. I called Jane briefly, she'd been on shift this weekend and had a tough week by all accounts, covering for a colleague on the oncology unit. Doctor Lush was throwing her a leaving party on Sunday 28 January and had hired the upstairs of a local pub. I could hear her wavering about going, although she wouldn't admit it. She'd fallen for him hard. I promised I'd be there if I didn't manage to catch up with her next weekend. There was no way I was going to miss saying goodbye to my best friend and wishing her well on her travels.

* * *

Monday 15 January 2018

The tables were turned when I arrived at the gym at five o'clock on Monday to work out. I'd spent all day buried in Jason's accounts, trying to make sense of the mountain of receipts he'd shoved in a drawer and enter them into a spreadsheet. I was starting to regret the decision to work at the boxing club. I hardly had any time to train and my job description seemed to involve everything from cleaning the showers and washing the towels to strategising a marketing campaign. I didn't mind variety, but it was a joke.

I started off on the treadmill, knowing Ian would normally arrive around half an hour after me; he'd told me he worked until five and came straight there. An hour later, I was already on weights, the last part of my workout, and he still hadn't showed. I toyed with asking Ahmed but didn't want to appear clingy. Ian hadn't responded to my text the night before. He said nothing about not being be around. Maybe he'd got caught up in something at work?

I dragged it out for as long as I could before going home to a microwave meal. I stared at my phone after dinner, willing it to beep. It was strange being desperate for contact from someone you despised. There would be no butterflies when he finally got in touch, just relief. Ben would have found it amusing for sure, watching me getting uptight, but he was working tonight, and I hadn't seen him all day.

I switched the television on, looking for some distraction when a text came through from Ian.

`I'm outside.`

What the fuck? Outside where? Seconds later there was a loud knocking at the door. I jumped, my body quivered, alerted to the fact something was wrong. I checked my phone again, unable to put the two together. Ian was here? He couldn't be. He didn't know where I lived, did he?

Normally when I was alone I wouldn't answer the door, but the television was blaring, and I knew it could be heard from the hallway outside. I wore the pyjamas mother had sent me for Christmas, pink fleece with tiny penguins on. Not the best outfit to speak to a stranger in. It had to be a stranger surely, Ian must have meant the text for someone else and it was just a coincidence someone was at the door. I crept closer , tiptoeing along the carpet, and almost screamed when I got close and the knocking resumed, impatient this time.

'Eve, it's me.' Ian's voice travelled through the solid wood door and I clapped a hand over my mouth, backing up. Frozen for a few seconds as my mind raced at the same speed as my heart. How had he found me? Fuck, I had to get out of here. No time.

Rushing to the bathroom, I twisted the caps off the contact lens case, struggling to put them in with shaking hands as the seconds ticked by. I couldn't answer the door without them, it would be suicide. More knocking came, urgent. He wasn't going to go away.

Rushing back to the front door and steeling myself, I swung it open; a huge bouquet of dark red roses was pushed towards me. Ian didn't strike me as the romantic type. My heart racing, I gasped as I took them from the outstretched hand. I lowered the blooms to inhale their fragrance. It seemed like the right thing to do. My hands still shaking. Even framed by the beautiful petals, his eyes were evil. Cold, heartless and cruel.

'What took you so long?' he said, grinning.

* * *

Sunday 28 January 2018

'The question is, did you mean to kill him?' Hicks asks, staring intently at me.

I hold his gaze, refusing to blink. The interview has

stepped up a gear since the break. Detective Hicks looks like he has a point to prove. I have to hold my own. Terry, the duty solicitor, advised me against answering any more questions and reverting to my right to give no comment. Defiant, I told him I was going to tell the truth. He looked bewildered. Anyone would think I have a problem with authority.

'No, I did not.' I will not allow myself to be rattled, I've come this far.

'But you do have anger issues?' he continues.

'Do I?' Where is this going?

'Apparently so, according to the report from your psychiatrist.' He removes some papers from a folder he brought into the room a few minutes ago. Damn it Doctor Almara. Whatever happened to patient–doctor fucking confidentiality? '*As well as considerable emotional trauma, Miss Harding appears to have repressed anger issues due to the unresolved sexual assault which happened in September 2017. No offender being found has contributed to these feelings of rage which she has confessed to*,' he reads.

'That's not fair,' I stutter. I hold my hand out for the sheet, so I can read the words myself.

Hicks hesitates before obliging. Becker watches our exchange, a flush creeping up her neck. She's squirming in her seat. I know I have her on side. He doesn't trust me though.

'Yes, I was angry, wouldn't you be? Angry at the system. Angry at the man who did it to me,' I try to explain, but he cuts me off.

'Rage. She clearly writes you have admitted to feelings of rage.'

I remain silent. I won't justify myself any further, but Hicks looks pleased with himself. He thinks he's got me. *Give me five minutes alone and I'll show you my rage.* I dig my nails into my palms under the table, stopping short of drawing blood.

'Could you explain to us again how you stabbed Ian?' Becker asks.

'I told you, I was on my back. He was on top of me with one hand around my throat, the other holding my wrist. I searched around with my free hand, trying to find something to use against him. I knocked the tray off the table and then I felt the knife.' I demonstrate with Hicks's pen, imagining driving it into his wrinkly flesh for a second. 'And brought my hand up to get him wherever I could,' I continue.

'You stabbed him in the axillary artery which runs underneath the armpit. Was that intentional?'

Yes, of course it was, you moron. How else was I going to get him to bleed to death in minutes without it looking like I meant to? It was the reason I didn't choose the neck or the thigh. Too obvious.

'No, I just wanted to get him off me. To escape. He was trying to strangle me.' I point to the necklace of bruises that circle my skin. Glaring at the detectives in turn.

'Did you have sex with Ian?'

'No?'

'The lab found semen on your vaginal swab.'

I fold my arms. Shit, this doesn't look good.

'We're running the DNA, but it takes time. Why don't you just tell us whose it is?' Becker asks, her eyes like slits. Now I look like the town tramp, but there's no point in getting caught out in a lie.

'I slept with Ben, my flatmate. We got drunk, one thing led to another. It was a one night stand that we both regretted in the morning.' I sigh and look up to the ceiling. When will this be over?

'Let's have a break,' Hicks says, rubbing his grey whiskers. A shave is long overdue.

'Can we get Eve some more water please?' Becker asks the officer by the door. Thank goodness, I need to rehydrate.

37

MONDAY 15 JANUARY 2018

'I-Ian?' I stuttered, stepping back, a mixture of terror and embarrassment washed over me.

'I know, I'm sorry to arrive unannounced. Nice pyjamas!' he said, taking note of my reaction. He chuckled, ignoring my mouth hanging open, and stepped past me into the hallway. Vampires had to be invited in, didn't they?

I clutched at the neck of my top to check I'd buttoned all the way to the collar. I felt exposed.

'I won't stay long. Quick cup of tea?'

I nodded, still unable to speak. What the hell was he doing here? He must have followed me home from the gym. The claret petals fluttered in my trembling hand and I began to feel faint. I remained rooted to the spot by the front door, worried I'd fall if I moved.

Ian laughed, mistaking my distress for surprise, and took the flowers from me. Striding down the hallway, looking right and then left until he found the kitchen. Seconds passed, and I was yet to follow him. I lingered, gazing out into the stairwell down to the street, feeling the chill from the air outside wafting in. I considered running into the street and the muscles in my thighs twitched in anticipation, but the bubbling kettle brought me back to my senses, propelling me to move. I closed the front door and hurried to my bedroom, unhooking my dressing gown from behind the door and tying it tightly.

'Sorry, you caught me off guard. Obviously,' I said, forcing a smile and gesturing to my dressing gown.

He waved away my embarrassment and continued to hunt around the kitchen cupboards for mugs.

Autopilot kicked in and I took the flowers over to the sink to unwrap the cellophane. 'Thank you for the roses, they're beautiful.'

'You're welcome. I couldn't resist, so dark, like blood.'

I shivered at his choice of words. An avalanche of dread crashing down upon me. I was trapped, alone with him. Ben wouldn't be home until the morning. Did Ian already know that? Had he been watching the flat?

'I'm sorry I wasn't at the gym today. I had to work late, but I wanted to see you.'

'How did you know where I live?' I asked, keeping my tone light. It was easier to maintain composure with my back to him; fear would be obvious in my eyes. I heard water being poured and then the fridge opening. I took the scissors out of the drawer and snipped the stems. Taking my time. If he was going to attack me, he would have done it by now. His DNA would be all over the kitchen and the flowers. Despite that, I held the scissors tightly in my hand.

Play it cool; he's paid you a surprise visit, nothing more. Remember, you don't know he's a rapist.

'If I told you that, I'd be giving away my secrets, now wouldn't I?' He laughed, and I smiled, to show I was in on the joke, but his tone made me uneasy. It must have been Ahmed, either that or he'd followed me home? I left the scissors on the side for easy access and placed the roses in the only vase I owned. It quivered as I put it on the table. They were stunning, belonging to a gothic fairy tale. Ian saw me staring at them and smiled, more to himself than at me.

'I knew you'd love roses.'

He was across the kitchen in one swift movement, face inches from mine. Backed into the corner, nowhere to escape to. My chest tightened, fingers gripping the worktop to keep myself steady. He pushed a blonde strand of hair behind my ear, his lifeless eyes searched mine as though he was looking for answers. I knew he enjoyed having the upper hand. He liked to be in control, in every way and I was no match for him here.

'I can't stop thinking about that kiss.' He leaned in, his lips brushing mine. I squeezed my eyes shut and prayed for Ben to walk in unexpectedly. Ian held the back of my head in place, fingers in my hair. I was going nowhere until he was done with me. I held my breath when his other hand wrapped around the cord of my dressing gown, tugging it gently. He was going to undress me, here in the kitchen. My brain was steaming ahead, thinking of ways to escape, excuses to stop. All the time trying to pretend I was enjoying his tongue dancing in my mouth. I tried my best to get involved, not to be stiff. But not so much for him to take things further. Finally, after an age, he pulled away, licking his lips as though he had just stopped short of devouring me entirely.

'That made it worthwhile,' he said, releasing his grip on my dressing gown and stepping away to pick up his tea.

My lips tingled from the pressure, chest flushed red. *You're disgusting*, the voice in my head spat.

'You're very quiet?' Ian said.

'I'm sorry, you've just thrown me.' I said, my hand touching my lips.

Christ, Eve, get your shit together otherwise he's going to figure out something is wrong.

I slurped the too hot liquid, my mouth stinging. The burning was a welcome cleanse, dissolving the taste of Ian. I sat at the table and he followed, sitting opposite me. It was strange seeing another man in Ben's chair.

'How was your day?' I asked, making conversation.

'Nightmarish, we almost had an account pull out of a contract, which is why there was a crisis meeting. I should have gone to the gym to be honest, relieve the stress, but I wanted to see you.' His eyes flickered to my closed bedroom door, which could be seen from the kitchen.

'You could always go for a run?' Images of him sprinting away whilst I hid behind the parked car flashed into my mind.

'Bit late now, I might before work in the morning.' He finished his tea, mine was still a touch too hot to drink, but I persevered regardless. He stood and put his empty mug in the sink, turning back to me. I didn't move, eyes fixed on him. Was he going to drag me to my bedroom? Force himself on me? 'I'll let you get to bed.'

I pushed myself up and walked Ian to the door, relief washing over me. I thanked him again for the flowers. In a few more seconds, I would be able to relax. He would be out of my home and I would be safe with the deadbolt across the door. Although now he knew where I lived, I didn't think I'd ever feel safe again.

'See you Wednesday?' I nodded, waiting for the kiss I knew I would have to endure. When it came, he cupped my face in his hands and there was less urgency, but I was grateful when it ended.

When he left, I locked the door and checked every window, making sure the flat was secure. I needed a drink stronger than tea. I threw away what was left of mine and poured a large elderflower gin. Sitting at the table, I retrieved my packet of cigarettes from the fruit bowl. I hadn't smoked in days, but I lit one, sucking in the smoke, using the taste of tobacco and gin to rid the memory from my mouth. How far was I going to let this relationship go? How far was I willing to go with the plan?

38

TUESDAY 16 JANUARY 2018

I slept past my alarm the following morning and had to drag myself to work, it had been a fitful night. I kept watching the app but didn't see Ian return home. The barren image of his living space had been burnt into my retinas. Where was he? What dark road was he wandering along? Who was he following?

I was grateful he didn't push me further last night. He could have and what would I have done, here alone? So confident to the point of being cocky, it was intimidating. I found myself shrinking whenever I was around him. Although who I was around Ian wasn't the real me. It was the submissive Eve, who was happy to relinquish control. The sort of girl Ian liked. One he could easily manipulate.

I popped home at lunchtime. Ben and I rustled up beans on toast after he had discovered the fridge was empty and our stomachs rumbled in joint protest. I promised to go shopping in the afternoon and Ben tried to give me some cash, but I refused.

'I'm doing all right for money at the minute. If I need it, I'll shout. I promise.'

He shoved the notes back in his wallet.

'Amy's been hassling me about coming for dinner,' Ben admitted.

I raised my eyebrows, glad my mouth was full, and I wasn't about to speak before I had a chance to initiate my filter.

'Oh? Let me know when and I'll make myself scarce.'

Ben rolled his eyes. 'No, you idiot, she wants to come for dinner, with all of us. Together.'

Oh God, could I sit through that?

Ben sniggered, reading my thoughts. 'It won't be that bad.'

I hadn't been able to hide my expression fast enough. Being a gooseberry, in my own kitchen and having to be polite whilst she hung off his every word sounded like torture.

'Okay, you're cooking though. You can cook for your harem.' I smirked, and Ben's ears tinged pink. I was sure he was going to hate it as much as I was.

We left soon after; he had some errands to run before work and I had to get back to the club.

That evening, after a dinner of pasta carbonara, I settled in front of the television to write some more in my journal. Checking the dates against the calendar on my phone. I needed to get into the habit of doing it daily, but nothing about my life was routine any more, even the visits to the gym.

I opened the PetCam app, expecting to see another view of Ian's empty sofa, so was surprised to see Ian sitting with the laptop on his knees. Muting the television, I turned the volume on the phone right up and switched on the speaker. He was talking to someone. Who was there, was it a woman? My skin prickled, but then I saw his neck crooked to the side, holding the slim phone against his ear with his shoulder. The speaker wasn't great quality and I could barely make out the words, but I heard Ian say 'account' and 'premium'. He must still be working.

Mesmerised, I continued watching. He finished his phone call and started tapping the keyboard. Perhaps he was sending emails. It was frustrating not being able to see the screen this time. He was sitting on the opposite sofa and the screen wasn't in view. After a few minutes, he stretched and put his hands behind his head. He swore, then snapped shut the lid of his laptop and threw it on the sofa. He strode out of view, returning a minute later, unbuttoning his shirt as he stared at something, eyes glazed. What was he doing? A nervous twitch erupted in my eye as I glared at the screen. He left the room and I sat, willing him to come back into shot.

Minutes passed, and I smoked two cigarettes back to back before he returned, now dressed in dark clothing. I sat up straight. Was he going running? Or... Fuck. He was going out on the prowl.

Jumping up, I ran into my room and pulled on running leggings and a black hoody. I had to stop him. I had to do something. I couldn't let him go out and attack another woman. Adrenaline pulsed in my muscles as if they knew I was about to run the mile journey in as few minutes as possible. I didn't know what I'd do when I saw him. Would it blow everything?

Grabbing my phone and keys, I was a few steps from the door when a knock came from the other side. I ignored it; I had to get going. I hopped from foot to foot, considering using the fire escape stairs, but the knocking persisted.

'Miss Harding?' a voice called.

I instantly recognised the cool tone with a hint of middle class. She had terrible timing.

I opened the door.

'Detective Emmerson. Sorry I was just getting changed.'

'Hello, Eve, are you on your way out?'

'Yes, I'm just off to the gym,' I replied.

'Can we have a chat, it'll only take a few minutes.'

I sighed and stepped back from the door, defeated. Emmerson stepped across the threshold. Her blonde hair bobbing as she moved. For a second, she looked like she was walking bowlegged and then her long beige mac parted, and her bump was obvious.

'Congratulations,' I said, gesturing towards her belly, the navy fabric of her wrap dress stretched tightly across it.

'Thanks, I seem to have bloomed in the past few weeks. I feel like a whale.' She rubbed her stomach. Why do women always do that, constantly rubbing their stomachs when pregnant? She followed me into the kitchen and I wanted to smoke but refrained. I didn't offer her a drink. We weren't friends and I wanted her gone as soon as possible. 'I wanted to stop by on my way home. There was an attempted attack on a Saturday back in October, but the victim has only just come forward to report it. It happened closer to town, the girl was walking home the morning after staying over at her friends. Around the same time of day you were attacked.' The image of the petite blonde crouched by the fence flashed into my mind.

'Is she okay?'

'She said an alarm spooked her attacker and he ran off. She didn't get a good look at him, but he was wearing a balaclava and carrying a knife.'

Thank God, she didn't get hurt. What would have happened if I hadn't been there? I knew the answer to that already.

Emmerson eyed me as though trying to read my thoughts.

'It's going to be in the local press this week, I believe, with an e-fit. I wanted to speak to you before you saw it.'

Why wasn't I offered an e-fit? Was I not a credible witness?

'The victim saw he had dark hair. So even with the balaclava covering his face, we now have skin, eye and hair colour, as well as height and build. We're officially connecting this attack with yours, and potentially others, too.'

'It sounds like he's not going to stop.' I couldn't keep the tremble from my voice.

'I think you're right, Eve. Not until we stop him.' The 'we' made me start. She couldn't know what I was planning, surely?

* * *

Sunday 28 January 2018

I am left alone for a few minutes, apart from my guard, while my solicitor speaks to the detectives. I nurse my tea and allow a second to wallow. What if I never get out of here? What if I've made a terrible mistake?

Hold your nerve, Eve, just for a bit longer.

It's so frustrating not knowing what is going on outside this room. I have an idea of what lab results they've received, other than what they've declared. I'd tried to think of everything, but now I've been charged, there is no turning back.

There was always a possibility I would be. A likelihood even. My solicitor wants me to 'no comment', but there is enough evidence to put me away, it's intent they'll struggle to prove. Thoughts whirl around my brain and I itch for nicotine.

'Could you please take me out to the yard for a cigarette?' I ask the officer.

'I'm afraid there's no smoking anywhere inside the station.'

My shoulders sag.

'But I can take you out for some fresh air?' he continues and I award him a grateful smile.

The detectives and my solicitor are nowhere to be seen. The custody officer is a jolly guy with rosy red cheeks who smiles at me as I pass. My experience of the police so far has been a pleasant surprise. I wasn't sure it would always be though.

Cold air rushes through the door as it is unlocked, and I move out into the tiny yard. I can't believe how much I've taken for granted just being able to go outside. Freedom is underrated, that's for sure. With a view of the sky, I am calmer, the future doesn't look so bleak when I go back into the interview room.

'In your bag we found a rape alarm. Why did you not use this when Ian attacked you?' Hicks asks when the interview continues.

'My bag was on the side by the front door, I'd left it there when we came in. I couldn't get to it.'

'What do you think made Ian snap? Do you recall?' Becker presses.

Why are they revisiting this again? The same thing over and over; are they trying to catch me out?

'He was fine until I didn't want the drink and asked to go home.'

'Do you think his plan all along was to rape you?'

'I don't know.' *Isn't it your job to connect the dots, detectives?*

'Did you plan to have sex with him?' Hicks asks, his eyes narrowing.

'I don't see how that is relevant,' my solicitor interjects, but I talk over him.

'No, I hadn't planned to. It was only our second date.' I purse my lips.

'Why did you agree to go back to his?' Becker asks.

I glare at her, my outrage obvious, but she doesn't flinch, our eyes lock. Hers are watering and I see something in them. Pity? Empathy?

'Because he invited me to, for a drink. I'd been before, and he was a gentleman then. I thought I'd have a drink or two and he'd call me a cab, like last time.'

'Did you know Ian had a history of violence?'

Yes, I did, but not a documented one.

39

TUESDAY 16 JANUARY 2018

I jogged towards Ian's place and around the outside of the park, not daring to go in. Gripping my rape alarm the entire time and staying only on main roads. I wanted to find him, but I had to stay safe, now I knew what monsters lay in wait for the unsuspecting. Hands slippery with perspiration, I threaded my keys through my fingers to use as a weapon if I needed to. I hadn't been jogging in the dark and the rush of air past my ears as I moved made it hard to hear. I looked all around, but I couldn't find him or any evidence of an assault. There were no sirens or flashing lights, the streets were quiet. If only Emmerson hadn't kept me talking.

Frustrated, I returned home, checking the PetCam straight away but Ian was nowhere to be seen. Defeated, I went for a hot shower and found some whisky stashed under the sink. I don't remember how it got there, maybe it was from the housewarming party I'd held when I moved in and started working at Drive. My lame attempt at making friends in the area. The flat had been filled with airheads from the office, ones Debbie had rounded up for me. I didn't have anything in common with them, their fake eyelashes and ridiculous drawn-on eyebrows. It was like I'd landed on an alien planet. The party wasn't a raging success, although Debbie stuck to me like glue from then on, whether I liked it or not.

The whisky burnt my throat on the way down and warmed me through. It tasted vile though and one was enough. Unfortunately, it didn't help me sleep. I stared first at the ceiling, then at Ian's empty sofa until I switched my phone off.

* * *

Wednesday 17 January 2018

Ben came home from work the next morning in a panic, just as I was on the way out of the door to go to the club, confirming tonight he was doing the dinner for Amy and could I be around? I agreed, resigned to my fate.

'I'll pick everything up. What are you drinking?'

I wanted to say, 'the strongest alcohol you can find', anything to numb the pain of the evening, but Ben was stressed enough already, and I didn't want to add to it.

'Anything, whatever Amy likes.' Hideous, it was just going to be hideous. I hadn't forgiven her for pinching him right out from under my nose. Even though at the time I didn't know I wanted him. She knew though. I could tell the way I caught her looking at me. I knew she saw me as a threat.

On the way into work, I stopped at the shop, buying all three local papers and scouring them over lunch for the piece on the attack.

Typically, the piece I was looking for was found in the last paper. Page five featured a half-page spread with a large e-fit, dominated by the balaclava. She hadn't got the lips right, his were thinner and his mouth smaller. The eyes were similar, but Ian's were remarkable by their lack of depth. Their topaz blue colour, although attractive, was flat and lifeless. It didn't look like Ian. I imagined him cutting out the article and adding it to a scrapbook, sneering at the police incompetence. Was he the sort to take mementos? Ian hadn't taken anything of mine. Not yet anyway.

I hoped I would see him at the gym later, I needed to start moving things along. Although I'd promised to be home for seven so my workout would be shorter today. Perhaps I should invite him? We could double-date: 'Hi Ben, Amy – this is Ian, my rapist boyfriend I've just started seeing.' It would be amusing if it wasn't true.

When I arrived at the gym, Ian was already there, deep in conversation with Ahmed by the weights. I smiled and waved, and he grinned back, giving me a wink. I saw a playful nudge from Ahmed and could almost hear him being pumped for information. I ignored them and got on the treadmill to run, choosing the one nearest to them so I could keep them in sight. I never ran with headphones, but the noise from the treadmill drowned out everything. The rhythmic beat was soothing. Dinner with Amy and Ben was fast approaching, and I was sulking about the whole thing. I hated doing things I didn't want to do, but I owed it to Ben to try. Ian walking past, winking, broke my concentration. I almost tripped over my own feet. He got on beside me and seconds later we were jogging in time.

'You're early today,' he shouted over the hum of the machines.

'I have dinner plans.' I was jogging too fast to talk but

pride stopped me from slowing. If he could do it then so could I.

'Oh?' he said, raising an eyebrow, a playful smirk on his lips.

'My flatmate and his new girlfriend.' Although she wasn't new any more.

'Want rescuing?'

'I wouldn't put you through it. Actually, you never did tell me where you got my address?' It was a safe environment to ask again. He didn't intimidate me here.

'I couldn't possibly reveal my source.'

Ahmed, he must have got it from him. Ahmed had the addresses of every member of the gym. Surely it was illegal, data protection existed for a reason, but I didn't want to consider the alternative. That he had followed me home. I considered going to the police. Detective Emmerson seemed to have a renewed vigour for the case, but I didn't hold out much hope. Ian seemed to be able to move around as he pleased without fear of detection. Perhaps if I was in his shoes, I would be as arrogant. No, it had to be me. The police weren't going to find him anytime soon. I had to deliver him to them.

As I was getting dressed later, still damp from my shower, a text came through on my phone from Ian.

`Wait outside for me`

No please or thank you, just a command. Did he have any idea how he comes across? I couldn't refuse, just had to go with the flow. Inching ever closer to my reward.

Outside, the bitter night air stung my face, gusts of wind

blowing my hair every time I changed direction. I didn't see Ian until he was right in front of me.

'I thought you were dancing.' He grabbed me around the waist and pressed his body against mine, swaying to music neither of us could hear. His chest felt solid, ice cold against mine. My jaw clenched at the proximity, every fibre of my being wanted him off me.

'Trying to get my hair out of my face,' I said, tucking a handful of it behind my ear unsuccessfully.

Ian moved me backwards to an alcove at the side of the building, out of the wind. 'Better?'

I nodded but was uncomfortable at being shielded from the road. The alcove was dark and tucked away, hidden in the shadows. Anything could happen, and no one would see. Just like behind the café. I blinked away the memory, legs trembling.

'When are you free for dinner?' he asked, still with one hand around my waist.

I bit my lip.

'The weekend?' My voice high pitched, giving away my nerves.

'Okay, I'll book a table. Saturday?'

'Sure.'

'You're a mystery, Eve. I can't wait to find out your secrets.'

I shivered and stiffened in his arms as he leaned towards me. I tried to relax as he spent the next few minutes pawing me in the dark. Pressed against him in a passionate embrace while I was trying to find my 'happy place'. The feel of his hands over my body made me shudder and I counted in my head until it was over. Praying he wasn't going to take it too far. I didn't want to anger him by pushing him away A fumble in the dark, groping and stolen kisses that filled me with revulsion. I felt soiled and the urge to go back inside the gym to shower him off me was strong.

'Get a room,' came a deep voice from behind Ian. He pulled away and we both looked at the man walking past; clutching a can of beer and chuckling to himself. My knees buckled, grateful for the interruption.

'What fucking business it is of yours?' Ian spat, which made the man laugh even more.

'Ooooooohhhhhh,' he replied in a high pitched mocking wail.

'Fuck off,' Ian said dismissively as the man staggered where he stood.

'And if I don't?'

Ian moved as quick as a flash, my grip on his sleeve lost. Seconds later, the man was on the ground, with Ian leaning over him. Pulling his arm back, Ian slammed his fist into the man's face, twice. I gasped, watching blood fly from his mouth. Teeth awash with red drool. My veins filled with ice as the scene played out before me. I stood frozen, powerless to intervene, as the man's head bounced off the concrete, eyes rolling back into his skull.

Ian stood up, smoothed his hair and stepped over the man as though he had always been there. My body shook, unwilling to respond to my brain screaming at me to run.

'Come on, let's get you home,' he said, putting his arm firmly around me and leading me away.

We walked for five minutes, neither of us speaking. Was that on Ahmed's CCTV? I knew there were cameras at the front, but what about the sides? We headed towards my flat before I mustered the courage to disentangle myself from him.

'You don't need to walk me, I'll be fine from here,' I said, my voice drifting away into the wind.

Ian looked at me, trying to read my staged smile.

'I'm sorry I lost my temper,' he said, not sounding in the least bit sorry.

'He was an arsehole,' I offered, to appease him.

Ian's face relaxed and a smile played on his lips. I had said the right thing.

'He was,' he replied simply. He kissed me goodbye and turned back in the direction of his apartment.

I shuddered, chilled to my core but it had nothing to do with the winter temperature. Should I go back and see if the man was all right? How badly had Ian hurt him? I began to jog towards home, pausing as I passed a phone box. Stepping inside, I dialled for an ambulance, reporting a bleeding man outside Pulse gym and hung up, not giving my name. It was all I could do. I didn't have time to process it. I was due back home to enter another charade.

40

WEDNESDAY 17 JANUARY 2018

When I arrived home, I could hear them in the kitchen laughing. Ben had pulled the table out from against the wall and positioned all the matching chairs around it, so it seated four instead of two. Tonight, the table was covered in a cream cloth, with candles at the centre, and laid for three, each place setting had a folded napkin and wine glass. Ben had made an effort. A pang in my chest reminded me he had done it for her, not me.

'Just in time,' Ben said, pouring me a glass of wine. The bottle was two thirds gone already. I must have missed the pre-dinner drinks or was the alcohol for Dutch courage? What was I walking into?

'Be right in.' I dumped my gym bag in my room and quickly removed my contacts in the bathroom. One of these days I'd forget, although it didn't matter so much if Ben saw them. I sat on the toilet, gathering myself, trying to slow the race of my pulse. Unable to comprehend what I'd just witnessed. I couldn't focus on it now, not with them waiting. I flushed and washed my hands and arranged my mouth into a smile.

Entering the kitchen, I took the glass Ben held out to me, draining it in one go. He raised his eyebrows at me, but I ignored him. I needed the alcohol to take the edge off.

'Hi Amy, how are you?' I asked.

'Fine, thanks. Have you just been to the gym?' Her nose wrinkled ever so slightly, and I smoothed down my static hair.

'Yep, working up an appetite. Smells delicious, what are we having?' I feigned a smile at Amy, who stretched her thin lips upwards a degree in return, her glare remained stoic. Had this been her idea or his? Was there an agenda to this dinner I wasn't aware of? I wasn't bowled over by her warmth, that was for sure.

'Stew, it's been in the slow cooker all day.' Ben grinned, looking pleased with himself.

'We have a slow cooker?' I asked.

'We do now,' Ben said, spooning stew into bowls. I caught a glimpse of Amy stiffen at the use of the term 'we'. The smell reminded me of winters with Mum, quelling hunger pains after a day playing out in the streets.

Amy bustled around my kitchen as I looked on, slicing the French stick and placing it in the bread basket. I sat, redundant. They moved around each other with ease. It made my throat tighten, I refilled my glass and swallowed a large gulp of wine.

'So, what have you been up to, Amy?' I asked, trying to generate a conversation.

'Work has been hectic, hardly any down time. All work and no play,' she said, reaching for Ben's hand. 'I don't see

Ben as much as I'd like.' She frowned at him and stuck out her bottom lip like a child. I held in a snigger.

'It's the shift work,' Ben interjected, but I knew that already. I barely saw him either. It was one thing Amy and I had in common. Maybe the only thing.

Ben delivered the bowls to the table and my appetite arrived on cue as soon as it was placed in front of me. I scooped up the stew with crusty bread slathered in butter, it tasted delicious.

'Do you work in security too?' I asked.

'Yes, I'm the head administrator for the South East, I have to do all of Ben's paperwork for the warehouses. Make sure licences are up to date, insurances, rental agreements, that kind of thing.'

'Sounds busy.'

Amy nodded, her mouth full.

'How's Jason?' Ben asked, dipping his bread in his bowl too.

'Fine, working me hard. Says he wants to get together for beers and he'll text you,' I said, listening to the conversation that followed as Ben told Amy who Jason was. I concentrated on eating, zoning out momentarily and chewing blissfully. I thrust the incident with Ian to the back of my mind. I could dissect it later. Amy's voice blurred into the background. It wasn't until Ben refilled my almost empty glass my focus returned, and I tried to get back in on the thread of the conversation.

'So, we don't know how much we can afford, but looking around at the estate agents online, we might be,' Amy chimed.

'I'm sorry, what?' I butted in. Silence fell over the table and they both stopped to look at me.

'Not straight away, there's no rush,' Ben said, before his eyes returned to his bowl.

'But we'll see more of each other if we live together.' Amy smiled but had her jaw clenched tightly. She placed her hand on Ben's arm as if in ownership and narrowed her eyes at me.

'You're moving in together? Isn't it a bit soon?' I said, incredulous. I meant to provoke, and she bit, as I knew she would.

'Why shouldn't we?'

I shrugged, I wasn't going to get drawn in to that conversation. My stomach sank as I thought about how I would pay the mortgage by myself. I'd have to get a lodger. I didn't want Ben to move out; I didn't want to be here without him and there was no way I could live alone.

A hush fell as we resumed eating until Amy piped up.

'Are you seeing anyone, Eve?' Her tone was sickly sweet, and it was my turn to bite.

'Yes. Well, kind of.'

'Who?' Ben asked, and Amy glared at him.

A violent psychopath if tonight was anything to go by.

'A guy I met at the gym, we've only been out twice. He's taking me for dinner on Saturday.'

Ben lowered his eyes back to his bowl. Amy had won, she'd goaded me, and I'd taken the bait. Now he was hers and she knew it. Before long he would move out and I would be alone. My appetite left as soon as it had arrived, and I excused myself to use the bathroom.

I stared at my reflection in the mirror. What was I supposed to do? I couldn't tell him what was going on. I couldn't drag Ben into this thing with Ian. He was a decent guy, the best kind. He deserved to be happy. The timing for us was all wrong. But surely Amy wouldn't last. Six weeks into dating and she was already trying to mastermind their future. Did Ben not remember what happened to the pet rabbit in *Fatal Attraction*?

When I returned to the table, they were holding hands and my dinner almost made a second appearance. We exchanged pleasant conversation for the rest of the night, but it was stiff and polite, missing the banter than Ben and I shared when we were alone. I continued to drink, the second bottle of wine consumed quickly between the three of us. Everyone using it as a crutch to get through an excruciatingly painful evening. Amy grew louder and more obnoxious with each glass and at times I had to bite my tongue, worried I would say something to upset the happy couple.

At around ten, I could stand it no more. I excused myself, feigning a headache from 'too much wine', thanking them for a lovely evening and returning to the sanctuary of my room. I lay in the dark for a while, my thoughts turning back to Ian. What on earth had possessed him to hit that guy? He was only having a laugh. Why did he not shrug it off, tell him to get stuffed and walk away? The abrupt attack came out of nowhere. Was the guy okay? His face was covered in blood. There was no need for that level of violence and it reminded me what he was capable of. And what I was getting myself into.

Later, even with my headphones on, I could hear Amy's exaggerated moans of pleasure as they had sex next door. Bitch. It was for my benefit and it felt like I was having my heart removed with a spoon. I think Ben had deliberately delayed her spending the night for that very reason. He didn't want to rub it in my face that he was with someone else. I tossed and turned, but there was no chance of sleep. My phone buzzed; it was a text from Ian.

How was dinner?

I opened the app and saw him sat on the sofa in front of the television, drinking a bottle of beer. I wasn't sure whether to respond, but watching him continuously check his phone made me cave in.

Painful!
Want me to come over?
I'm already in bed.
I'll be right there 😊

I dropped the phone in panic and it bounced on the carpet, knocking over a glass of water I kept by my bed. I rushed to get my towel from the bathroom to soak up the excess liquid seeping into the carpet. My heart raced, had I just invited him here? Into my bed? God no. The screen of my phone had locked, but I could see another message from Ian had come through. I keyed in my code, stumbling over the digits.

I'm just kidding

I let out a sigh and waited for the shakes to subside. My stomach churned like I'd been on a roller coaster. I knew I had to text back, I didn't want to leave it too long but was unsure what to write. My phone beeped again.

Have I scared you off?

Yes, was the true answer. As I was typing a reply another message came through.

```
I'm sorry about that bloke. He pissed me off
and I lost it.
It's okay,
```

I replied quickly, although it wasn't.

```
Too much going on at work. Feeling the pres-
sure. Need to let off some steam.
I understand.
I'm looking forward to dinner.
```

He signed off with a kiss and I held down the icon of the PetCam app, deleting it from my phone. I didn't want to watch him any more. I wasn't sure I wanted anything to do with him.

* * *

Sunday 28 January 2018

I shudder as though someone has walked over my grave. The hairs on my arm stand to attention. He has a criminal record? He was known to them?

'No, I didn't know,' I whisper.

'Ian holds a conviction of ABH on his ex-girlfriend from 2009.' Becker taps a brown file on the table. She slides a photo out and places it in front of me. A once pretty girl looks out at me with one eye, the other is bruised and swollen shut, just like mine. We could be twins. Her nose looks too big for her face and sits at a funny angle; blood crusted in her nostrils. Jesus, he was a vicious bastard, even at twenty-two.

'You didn't know?' Hicks asks, and I sense his scepticism.

His eyebrows so high they are clambering off his wrinkly forehead. 'Do you think perhaps he deserved what happened to him?' Hicks continues, his tone more urgent to the point of being aggressive. He is going for it. 'Is that why you killed him, Eve?'

My mouth gapes and for a moment I'm speechless. Becker touches Hicks's arm to reel him in but is shrugged off.

'I object to these questions and my client will not answer them,' Terry interjects. Finally, he's woken up, but Hicks dismisses him, raising his palm like he's directing traffic.

'Did you think you were doing the world a favour? For all those women who'd been attacked, like you were last night and four months ago?' He looks so smug that I almost lose it. We glare at each other, his lip is curled back in part snarl, part smirk.

'If you felt like that, Eve, it would be understandable. He hurt you and we're just trying to get to the truth.' Becker speaks softly, breaking the loaded silence.

'I am telling the truth.'

'I think now is a good time to break for lunch.' Becker stands and waits for Hicks to join her, which he does deliberately slowly, throwing me a pointed look before shuffling out of the room.

41

SATURDAY 20 JANUARY 2018

When Saturday came, I was a bag of nerves. I considered calling off the whole thing. I didn't know if I could go through with it. Sitting down for dinner with my attacker would be hard enough, but what I had to do later, maybe it was asking too much?

The knot in my stomach prevented me from having any breakfast or lunch and even a quick two mile run did nothing to stave off my nerves. By the afternoon I was burnt out and had a long soak in the bath, closing my eyes to stave off the headache threatening to descend. Ben wasn't home. I assumed he was at Amy's, but I was glad he wasn't around. I didn't have to pretend I was fine when it was obvious I wasn't. Baking in the steam, I jumped when a loud thud came from somewhere outside the bathroom door. Water sloshed over the side of the bath, forming a puddle on the linoleum.

'Ben?' I called out. Maybe he had returned home. Sharing a house with a man meant I always locked the bathroom door whether he was in or out. There was nothing worse than being caught in the buff.

The thudding came again, harder this time. It must be the front door. Fuck's sake. I hauled myself out of the bath and wrapped my dressing gown around me. The fibres soaking up my wet skin. A high-pitched cry came through the door.

'Eve, it's Mum! Hurry up, I need a piss!'

I groaned. What was she doing here? That was all I needed. I unlocked the front door and she hurried past me, already unbuttoning her trousers.

'You took your time!'

Sighing, I shut the front door, coming around the hallway to see a pair of wrinkly knees on display. She hadn't even bothered to close the bathroom door. Thank goodness Ben wasn't here, it would be a lovely introduction to my mother.

I went into the kitchen and boiled the kettle. A minute later the toilet was flushed, taps run, and she came in.

'Five hours! Five bloody hours it took to get here. The A11 was screwed again. Stationary traffic for miles. Bloody overturned car! I needed a wee half an hour from home! Anyway, how are you, love?' She pulled me against her, the smell of gin permeated her breath. It was her signature scent these days. It was so bad that she could only function with alcohol in her system. She wouldn't have been able to make that drive without a few glasses.

'I'm good, Mum, how are you?'

Holding me at arm's length, she looked me up and down. 'Jesus, girl, you need to eat something. You're a bag of bones and that hair – well, it looks better in the flesh than on the phone.'

I hadn't seen Mum for around six months, not since I visited for a week last July. I'd envisioned a week on the Norfolk broads, enjoying the weather, but I spent most of it clearing out the house, getting rid of empty glass bottles and rotting food. Not to mention giving the place a good scrub. She wouldn't let me get her any help and I couldn't bear to see her living in squalor, so I hadn't been back since. I contacted the doctors and Alcoholics Anonymous, but I was told she had to take the first step, I couldn't do it for her.

She sat down at the table, rummaging in her handbag for cigarettes. The miniatures she always carried clinking as she searched, eventually finding them. Handing her the tea, I sat down opposite, taking two cigarettes out of her pack and lighting one after the other.

'Smoking again?'

'I keep quitting, then starting again.'

'How are you really?' She sucked on her cigarette, fingers stained a permanent brown.

'I'm okay,' was all I could manage as I tried to stop the floodgates from opening.

'Are you sure? After what happened?'

A single tear dropped from my eye, the culmination of stress and worry, the debt, giving up my job and, of course, Ian. I tried to hold it all together as my mum reached over and rubbed my arm, staring intently at me. I felt under the microscope.

'I'm working through it.' I smiled and wiped my eye.

My mother looked quite well, considering. There were tell-tale signs. She still had the shakes, she couldn't conceal those, and her eyes were tinged yellow, but there had been a drastic improvement since I last saw her. Was that Patrick's influence?

'You look well, Mum. Almost fighting fit,' I said, changing the subject. No matter how I felt about her drinking, or some of the things she'd said and done when drunk, she was still my mum.

'I don't know about that. Listen, I've got my bag in the car. I thought perhaps we'd go out for dinner, or order in? I brought gin.' I'd bet my last pound the bottle was already open, swishing around in the footwell of her Corsa. Given Mum's penchant for alcohol, it was a wonder I drank at all. But it hadn't always been like that. It'd only started when Dad died; it was her method of coping with losing the man she'd been married to for thirty-odd years. I could understand.

If she was intending on staying, I'd have to cancel Ian. I couldn't leave her here by herself. Especially with what I was planning. My shoulders automatically relaxed, rolling back into their usual position. The rock in my stomach slowly dissolving. I'd had a reprieve. For tonight at least.

'Let me get dressed.' If I was lucky it would only be for a night and even I could put up with her drunken antics for one night. There had to be a reason for her to drive all this way? What did she want to tell me? She had said before she had some news, but we never got around to it.

In my room, I pulled on my grey loose fitting boyfriend jeans but hesitated on what to pair with them. When I was younger, Mum always berated me for my tomboy style, wanting me to dress more like a girl. Cursing my lack of backbone, I picked a soft pink jumper that was hanging up in my wardrobe. Thrust to one side, the tags still on, it might give me an easier ride.

When I returned to the kitchen, my mother nodded approvingly and held out her car keys. Obediently I went downstairs to retrieve the holdall from her car. It was a mess inside; bottles and empty crisp packets littered the floor. The stench of neat alcohol reminded me of science class in high school. If she'd been pulled over, she would have been buggered. A sniff of the interior was enough to get you tipsy.

'Mum, I'll put your bag in the front room and pull out the sofa bed,' I called when I returned, grabbing sheets from the airing cupboard and making up the bed. Wondering if I'd be helping her into it later.

'That's fine, I can sleep anywhere.'

I remembered I needed to text Ian. It was already six. It was shitty to let him down at such short notice and I hoped he wouldn't be too angry.

'Where's your lodger?' Mum called.

'I think he's out with his girlfriend,' I replied, distracted. Focused on my phone, I began to type.

Sorry, will have to postpone. Just had Mum turn up! Five-hour journey down, no warning! Really sorry to cancel so late. x

That would have to do. When I returned to the kitchen Mum was in full flow, moaning about her neighbour's cat which kept shitting in her front garden.

'Let's have something stronger, shall we? It's a celebration after all. We haven't seen each other in a long time.' Mum disappeared from the kitchen, returning with the bottle of gin from her holdall. This was how it started. In a few hours I'd be putting her to bed whilst she barraged me with abuse. That was the extent of our quality mother and daughter time together.

Sighing, I gathered glasses, a bottle of tonic for me – she didn't bother with it – and ice for a toast at the table.

'To us,' she said, clinking my glass. If only I could fast-forward to tomorrow. I prayed Ben wouldn't come home tonight. Watching my mother get wasted would put him off me for life. 'Down the hatch,' she said, knocking it back in one.

I sipped mine, one of us had to keep a hold on reality.

She asked after Jane and I gave her the low-down on her travelling plans, her party being next week.

'She bagged herself a doctor then, lucky girl. What about you? I haven't heard you talk of a boyfriend for ages.'

'There is someone, but it's early days.' Unsure if I was talking about Ben or Ian, or perhaps both.

'I have news.' She leaned in as though she was going to tell me a big secret, her nose growing pink. 'Patrick's asked me to marry him.'

My glass stopped inches from my open mouth.

Ignoring my look of utter disbelief, she carried on. 'We're going to move in together, into his cottage. I stayed there for a few days over Christmas and we got on so well.' So much for Christmas with the neighbour then?

'What? You're going to sell the house then? But said you didn't want to sell it because you'd lived there with Dad?'

'Well, your dad isn't fucking here any more is he,' she hissed, pouring another drink, the gin slopping over the edge. Her words were like a slap in the face, stinging as much as her palm. She finished her second shot of gin and poured another without hesitation. The bottle was almost half empty, obviously opened before her arrival. 'I need someone to look after me. Patrick's nice, and we have a laugh.' I recoiled but she didn't notice, barely pausing for breath. 'I'm fifty-four this year and it's time I put myself first.'

Swallowing the rest of my gin in one, I refilled my glass. It was going to be a long night.

* * *

Sunday 28 January 2018 – DC Becker

'What the hell was that about?' I hiss as soon as the interview room door closes behind us.

Hicks ignores me, carrying on down the corridor towards the kitchenette. I grab him by the arm, harder than I intend to, and his head whirls around. We stand in the doorway glaring at each other. He's going to blow this whole case if he isn't careful.

'I said, what was all that about?' I try again, my voice hushed as though we are sharing a secret.

'I'm trying to get her to admit it.'

I roll my eyes. 'She has admitted it!' I hiss through gritted teeth, the vein in my neck pulsating.

'It's premeditated. I know it.'

'What are you talking about?' I sigh. I'm too tired for this. I just need to get Lily sleeping through and then it'll be better. Whose idea was it to have a baby at forty?

'She knows it and I know it. It's premeditated. I'm trying to break her.' A fool's errand is what it is, but as usual, Hicks is like a dog with a bone.

'Just don't fuck up the case. We need that interview recording, don't make it inadmissible in court,' I snap, rubbing the back of my neck. Sometimes he's hard work.

He backs out of the kitchen, away from me, as though struck by an idea.

'Where are you going now?'

'Digging,' he calls back over his shoulder.

I hurry after him, unable to let it go. He shoots me a look of contempt, fleeting, but I catch it. I don't give a shit. After all these years the feeling is mutual.

'You know I'm good at this. Give me one more go at her,' he says, softer now, his eyes imploring.

'Fine. I can delay collection for a couple of hours or so, then she's out of here.'

He nods, quickening his pace and leaving me behind. I can't hold it against him, he wants to retire this year, just before his sixtieth birthday, and every case must be wrapped up neatly with a bow. He's told me before he doesn't want any unfinished business before he goes; he's planning to buy a barge and spend his retirement sailing the canals with Sandra, his wife of forty years. I can't see this being one of those cases that will come back to haunt him.

My desk is piled high with paperwork. A map of the local area sits on top, with an orange circle highlighting an area of approximately half a mile.

'Phone triangulation for Eve; for yesterday.' Guy manifests behind me like a ghost, making me jump. He's so keen, eager to climb the ranks. I bite down on my molars and stifle a smile. A thought tries to push its way through the fog as I eyeball the map.

'Guy, can you get whoever did this on the phone please and transfer them through?'

'Sure, will do, he gives a quick nod and is gone.

While I wait for the call, I rummage in my drawer for some pins. A red pin is pushed through the location of Ian's apartment, another through Eve's. Ian's sits inside the circle to the left; Eve's is outside. I stare at the orange, absorbing the road names within, my eyes shifting in and out of focus. I'm so tired. The desk phone rings, jolting me back to the moment.

'James, I'm putting you through to Detective Becker,' Guy

says, then I hear a click and the obvious background sound of a call centre comes through.

'Hi James, thanks for producing the phone triangulation for us. I was wondering, could you have a look at the last four months on that account?'

I hear him sigh down the phone.

'That might take some time. You want printouts for every day? What is it you're looking for?'

It's my turn to sigh and I massage my temples, keeping the headache at bay.

'I'm not sure yet. No, I don't need a printout. I'm just looking for anything out of the ordinary, any patterns or usage spikes,' I reply. Something about the way Hicks is so convinced of Eve's intentions unnerves me. Could I be wrong about her?

42

SATURDAY 20 JANUARY 2018

My mother regaled me with tales of Patrick, how they'd met and, more revoltingly, how he didn't need Viagra, even at sixty. All I could think about was Dad. There was no denying I was a daddy's girl and his untimely death destroyed our little family. I lost both parents overnight. Four gins down and I was struggling to hold my tongue. The urge to shake my mother by the shoulders was compulsive and I balled my hands into fists under the table.

'I came here to let you know, because when I sell the house I'm going to send you half. It would have been your dad's half and it'll make a huge dent in the mortgage of this place.'

'I don't care about the money.'

'Don't be so ungrateful,' she snapped, slapping her hand on the table. She wasn't slurring yet, but it wouldn't be long. I needed to turn this conversation around. I needed to get her some food to soak up the alcohol. 'You'll like him. I promise. I'm drinking less, he's trying to help me stop altogether.'

'Really?' I said, hopeful that Patrick had made headway where I couldn't.

'Yes. I know I have a problem.' *No shit!* 'Also, I want you to be my bridesmaid.'

'What?' I said, incredulous. I rose to my feet, ready to let her have it. The image of me as a child, in a pale blue dress holding a posy, from when her and my dad renewed their vows clear in my mind. Before I had the chance to unleash the anger I had been withholding, there was a knock at the door. I didn't move, glaring at my mother who was oblivious.

'Are you going to get that?' she asked, filling her glass yet again.

I stormed out of the kitchen and into the hallway. A thought made me stop dead in my tracks. What if it was Ian? What if he'd turned up again uninvited? I dashed back to the kitchen and kneeled, so I was the same height as Mum.

'Mum, listen. This is really important. I think the man I like, you know the one I was telling you about is outside the front door. I'll explain later, but when I met him I was wearing coloured contacts. He thinks my eyes are blue. You mustn't say anything about my eyes.'

Mum was looking at me, confused. 'You kids these days.'

'Mum, it's important, okay. I'll be your bridesmaid. Just don't tell him I'm wearing contacts, understand?'

'Okay, okay.'

Another knock came from the door as I quickly put in the contacts, hiding the case in the bathroom cabinet.

I ran to the door and threw it open. My gut had been right. Ian stood in the communal hallway holding a bulging takeaway bag in one hand and a bottle of wine in the other.

'I must get you a doorbell, you know,' he said, stepping

over the threshold and kissing me on the cheek. I was too flustered to be afraid.

'Didn't you get my text?'

'I did,' he said with a glint in his eye and before I could stop him he'd made his way to the kitchen. 'Hello,' he said in an enthusiastic voice that made me cringe. He sounded like he was talking to a child. Mum would hate him, I was sure. She'd see straight through him. It would be exhausting trying to defend him to her later, I could tell.

'Mum, this is Ian,' I said, leaning on the door frame for support. Could tonight get any worse? Now my mother and rapist were going to sit across from each other to eat a meal at the strangest dinner party I'd ever been to.

'Lovely to meet you, Ian. Are you my daughter's lodger?' she asked, and I snorted.

Ian frowned at me.

'No. Boyfriend, I guess you could say.' My skin prickled.

'Oh. That's interesting. I was just telling Eve that I'm getting married, she'll have to bring you to the wedding.'

Ian began unloading the foil cartons from the bag and I got the plates out. My anger steadily rising as I digested the boyfriend admission.

'I take it you haven't already eaten?' Ian whispered. I shook my head.

A few minutes later we were gathered around the table and tucking into the Chinese takeaway Ian had delivered. The gin bottle was almost empty, but Mother had no problem moving straight onto the wine. I listened to Ian charm her with ease. He seemed to know exactly what to say. She lapped up every word of what he did for a living and how we met.

'Well, Ian, you sound quite taken with my daughter. I

think she would be a catch for anyone. Perhaps with a bit more meat on her bones.' If Ian was surprised by my mother's barbed comment, he didn't show it. I didn't retaliate, there was no need. Ian came to my rescue like a knight in shining armour.

'I think she's beautiful.' He smiled at me and stroked my arm for show, all for her benefit. I wasn't sure whether to be sick or grateful.

My mother did her best to embarrass me throughout the course of the evening. First, she told Ian how, when I was six, I'd wet myself in a corn field as I was adamant that I could pee standing up just like my father. When that didn't get a reaction, she followed it up with how I'd got into trouble at high school for making a pass at my teacher. All variations of the truth, but there was no point in correcting her whilst she was in full flow. I was too nervous she was going to tell Ian about the contact lenses just to be vindictive. I sat at the table refilling my glass, becoming more intoxicated as I listened to her subtle jibes; while Ian defended me with compliments. It was like watching a game of tennis. The conversation was so strange, the polite match of one-upmanship, which I was happy to see Ian winning hands down.

In the end my mother gave up and said she was going to bed. The evening had been much tamer than I expected, no hurling of abuse or furniture. Ian seemed to have defused the situation every time I thought she might kick off. The gin bottle now empty, she stumbled off, taking her clinking handbag with her into the lounge before shutting the door.

Ian stared at me and shook his head. 'She's something else.'

'Tell me about it.' I replied, although he had a cheek.

I was exhausted, the battle had been won tonight, but it

was bound to continue tomorrow morning. I wanted Ian to leave so I could go to bed, but instead he poured us both a glass of wine. Mixing wine with gin was making my head fuzzy, I hadn't drunk this much alcohol in ages. I drank it anyway, partly to be polite, partly because I was grateful he'd seen her off.

'I'm sorry about my mother.' I wasn't sorry but I had to keep him onside, play my part of submissive Eve.

'Don't worry about it. I know how to handle people like that.' He looked pleased with himself, but I wasn't in the mood to inflate his ego.

'Thanks for the Chinese.' I stood and lingered by the door, gazing at my bed, across the hall.

'You're welcome.' Ian joined me in the doorway and kissed me hard. My head throbbed, and the room tipped, like I was on a boat at sea.

'I'm really tired, Ian,' I said, trying to wriggle out of his grasp, but he manoeuvred me into my bedroom. I didn't feel sober enough to put up much of a fight.

'Let me put you to bed,' he said, easing me down on top of the covers. We kissed again, his hands roaming under my jumper and caressing my breasts. His touch was oddly gentle, not how I expected him to be, the alcohol dulled my ability to reason. It wasn't until his hand reached inside my jeans that I came back to earth with a thud. What the fuck was I doing? The lines were blurred, and I had to get my head straight.

'Ian, stop.' I mumbled as he kissed my neck, pushing his fingers into me. I forced his hand away. He sat up panting, eyes wide and teeth bared. The mask slipped for a second and for the first time I was truly afraid of him. Quickly, he composed himself. Running his hand through his hair, he smiled tightly.

'I'm sorry. Too soon?'

'Yes, sorry.' My stomach gurgled from the alcohol sloshing around.

Ian straightened his clothes, then bent down and kissed my forehead.

'I'll let you get to bed. I'll ring you tomorrow.' Then he turned and walked out of the room, closing the bedroom door behind him.

I sat in the darkness listening. Seconds later I heard the front door close. What had I done?

* * *

Sunday 28 January 2018

Terry sits across the table from me, munching on his free sandwich courtesy of the custody officer. We are alone in the interview room. This is our lunch break and there are no tapes recording us now. I nibble at my cheese sandwich from earlier, managing half of it by the time he has scoffed the lot. He licks his long fingers and a wave of nausea hits me.

'Right, let's get back to it shall we.'

I nod, although I'm unsure of what he wants to get back to. At this moment, my fate is sealed. My bravado from last night is slipping in the cold light of day.

'What's going to happen to me now?' It comes out like a whimper.

Terry runs his hand back and forth over his bald head, sighing. It's not good news.

'Due to the seriousness of the offence, plus you've admitted to inflicting the wound which resulted in Mr Shaw's death, you have been charged. So, later today you'll be remanded into custody. You will have an appearance at a Crown Court, which could be as early as tomorrow, where they will read the charges against you. They may ask for an initial plea.'

I close my eyes as my stomach plummets.

'I have to warn you that the likelihood of bail being permitted is low. To that end, I think it would be wise to build a case of self-defence and I strongly suggest you plead not guilty to the murder charge. I don't think they have enough evidence to prove intent. It's likely it'll be downgraded to involuntary manslaughter.'

'How long could I get if found guilty?' I ask, although I'm not sure I want to hear the answer.

'For murder? Could be anything up to life imprisonment, but I believe in this case, unless they can prove intent, you'll be looking at a maximum of five years. Out in half for good behaviour.'

I lean forward and rest my head in my hands. I have no more tears left to cry. Anger boils inside me, firing up from the pit of my stomach. It's not fair. He was a monster. He would have raped me again, then killed me. I know it. I kick out at the table leg and Terry jumps back in his seat.

'I'm sorry,' I say.

He gives me a pitying smile, one that says, chin up, it's not all bad. He has no idea just how fucked I am.

'You could plead guilty in the hope of getting a lesser sentence. However, I think with the evidence I've seen so far, we have a good case for self-defence.' He takes his glasses off, holds them by the wire rim and proceeds to polish them with a hanky retrieved from his pocket. 'You were attacked last year?' he asks.

I nod.

'Good. Well no, not good. I'm sorry, I didn't mean it like that,' he stumbles on, 'what I mean is, that it adds weight to your self-defence case.' His cheeks redden. Jesus, where did they find him?

'I need to think.'

'Yes of course. I'll get in touch with any potential witnesses as soon as possible. Do you have any questions at the moment?'

My mind whirls with thoughts of years incarcerated and life in a female prison. I shake my head, this isn't what I'd bargained for, but it's too late to turn back now. Whatever happens, I don't regret it. The world will be safer without that scum in it.

43

SUNDAY 21 JANUARY 2018

As tired as I was, sleep didn't come for hours. The alcohol combined with Szechuan chicken and rice sat in my stomach like a brick. I stared out of the window, unease creeping over me like spiders on my skin, as I listened to my mum snore like a train from the lounge. Ben would get a shock when he came back if she was still at it. I'd survived the evening with my mum, thanks partly to Ian. Disturbingly, him being there made it easier.

I couldn't believe she was getting married again. Would she change her name? No longer be a Harding? My father's name dropped after all the years they were married? She was like a different person since he died. Morphed into someone new, someone who only cared about herself. Could Patrick save her? Could I trust her when she said he was trying to help her stop drinking? I never knew what to believe. I stayed with her for a couple of weeks after Dad died, both of us holed up in shock. I missed the signs then, assuming it was grief and would eventually pass. When she was drunk, which became most of the time, she'd be violent. Smashing up the house, hurling abuse at everybody, you couldn't reason with her. She'd forgotten I was grieving too. In the end it became too much, and I came back to Sutton. I spent the next month waiting for my phone to ring. For her local doctor to call and tell me they'd found her dead; that she'd drunk herself to oblivion. She was still going though and now she'd found herself a husband. I was sure his son owning the off-licence wasn't a coincidence, probably how they met but I hoped she'd turn things around. There was no way I'd be going to the wedding. I couldn't watch her marry Dad's replacement. I wanted her to be happy, but it would hurt too much. I had my own shit going on with Ian to deal with.

Him turning up again out of the blue was worrying. It was starting to become a habit. Perhaps he was checking I was telling the truth. It was amusing to watch him run rings around my mother. Thankfully she kept quiet about the lenses. It struck me when she was airing all my flaws that I was sat at the table with two people that had caused me more pain than anyone else. My life was so fucked up.

When I woke, I heard banging in the kitchen and it was a few seconds before I remembered my mother had stayed over. Dragging myself out of bed, I ventured into the kitchen, surprised to see her frying eggs on the stove. She wore an oversized T-shirt that just covered her backside, sinewy legs on show and a cigarette hanging from her lips. Patrick must think her a delight.

'Morning sleepyhead,' she said, nodding to the coffee waiting for me on the table. Hers already half empty and the ashtray full. I opened the window to disperse the lingering smoke. It was going to take ages to fumigate the flat when she went.

'Morning.' I glanced at Ben's door. It was still shut and for once I prayed he had stayed at Amy's.

'Your lodger didn't come home then?'

'No, he works nights, Mum.'

She whistled at that. 'Something wrong with people that work nights, mark my words. You be careful, pet.'

I rolled my eyes in response. Ben was harmless. If only she knew the things Ian had done as she sat across from him last night. Mother didn't wait for a response before carrying on the conversation single-handedly.

'That Ian was lovely, quite a catch you've got there. Looks like he's got plenty of money.'

I sighed.

'He didn't stay over then?' Did she think she would be greeting him in the kitchen wearing nothing but a T-shirt? The thought made my throat constrict. Was she that desperate?

'No, he plays rugby at the weekends.'

She nodded. 'I'm going to head off after breakfast,' she said, deliberately avoiding my eye. I wasn't surprised she was eager to get home. She would need to start drinking, topping up the alcohol level from last night. She'd have a bit this morning, to take the edge off. She'd need some to stop the jitters, but not too much if she was to drive straight.

'Okay,' I replied.

She popped bread into the toaster and turned to face me.

'I'll post down an invite for the wedding. You'll come, won't you?' Her voice shook, I'd never seen her so vulnerable.

I looked away.

'Sure.' I lied.

There was a minute of awkward silence before the toaster clicked and she spooned the egg onto the bread.

'Here you go,' she said, placing the food in front of me. I couldn't remember the last time she'd made me breakfast. She must desperately want me to come to this wedding.

I didn't fancy the eggs but was keen to get her out of the flat. The quickest way to do that was to be civil and eat the damn breakfast. It wasn't long before we'd both given up, our plates still half full, and lit cigarettes.

'I'll get you a towel for the shower, Mum,' I said when I'd finished my cigarette.

Scraping the plates into the bin, listening to my mother singing in the shower. I wanted to believe she was making changes. Although last night didn't turn into the violent stand-off I'd expected, she would never be the mother I remembered from my childhood. That one was dead. This one would be too if she carried on drinking.

Half an hour later, I waved her off and sat at the table, enjoying the air blowing through the house. I'd opened all the windows and was contemplating having a drink when Ben arrived home.

'Hiya,' he said, entering the kitchen with a spring in his step. He must have got laid last night.

'What happened to your face?' Ben had three scratches from the end of his eyebrow right down to the corner of his mouth. They looked red and angry.

'Oh, Amy's dog got the better of me this morning,' he replied, avoiding my gaze.

'I'm glad you stayed at Amy's.

'Really? Why?' He frowned. Was he expecting a fight?

'My mother turned up last night. She's just gone, thankfully, but fucking hell she's a nightmare.'

'Are you all right?'

I nodded. Now wasn't the time to go into the history of our broken relationship.

'Have you been out?' he asked. Then realising I was still in my pyjamas continued, 'There's been some sort of fight or something last night. Girl got beaten up down the road.'

A shiver ran down my spine, something about Ben's news rang alarm bells.

'What happened?' I asked.

'No idea, but it was a bloke apparently. Bastard. Who would beat up a girl?' His voice tailed off and he gave his head a little shake. I didn't respond, I was too busy trying to process the news. It couldn't be Ian, could it?

'How do you know? Are the police there?' I asked.

'No, it's been cordoned off. I heard a woman mention it as I walked past. She's in the hospital apparently. It was her niece, I think she said, Sophie Whitaker. Does the name ring any bells?'

It was my turn to shake my head. I didn't know her. But I was going to.

44

SUNDAY 21 JANUARY 2018

The automatic entrance of the hospital reception creaked open painfully slowly. A queue of people at the front tried to push their way through the doors as they were still parting. I could see the receptionist scowling at our impatience. Hospitals weren't somewhere people wanted to be. Everyone looked miserable, wishing they were somewhere else. The sickly smell made me gag. It's the antiseptic, smells the same in every hospital. Combined with the sterile white walls that close in, regardless of the cheerful art displayed. The whole place made me twitch. Too similar to the psychiatric units I'd seen in films. Perhaps I wouldn't be allowed to leave once they'd realised how mad I was.

I approached the desk, smiling at the receptionist who didn't return the favour.

'Could you tell me what ward Sophie Whitaker is on please?'

She tapped her keyboard and waited, lips pressed tightly together.

'Chiltern ward.' Her tone was clipped.

'Thank you.'

She didn't break a smile. What was it with doctors and hospital receptionists? Everyone I'd ever encountered had a facial expression that resembled a bulldog chewing a wasp. Like they'd completely forgotten how to turn up the corners of their mouths, and this from people working in the care profession!

I checked the board by the lift and saw Chiltern ward was on the second floor. The hospital was busy as visiting hours were in full swing and I nearly bumped into a man on crutches coming around the corner. I wasn't sure what to say to Sophie, or how to ask, but I had to find out if there'd been a sexual assault. I needed to know if it was him.

I pressed the buzzer, was let into the ward and went to the nurses' station. This time a portly nurse, wearing a blue uniform stretched tightly over her curves, greeted me with a smile.

'How can I help you, my love?' She had a rich Nigerian accent and I couldn't help but smile, her warmth was infectious.

'I'm looking for Sophie Whitaker please.'

'She's in the last bed by the window. Her mother is with her now.'

'Is there somewhere I can wait? I mean, I don't want to intrude.'

She pointed to a row of blue plastic chairs bolted to the wall and I took a seat.

'Thank you.'

Around fifteen minutes later a smartly dressed lady in her late forties approached the desk. I raised my magazine an inch, so it shielded my face, pretending to be engrossed.

'I'm just popping to M&S, she wants some more flapjacks,' she said, clutching her purse to her chest. Her red lipstick had bled into the creases around her mouth and her attempt at putting a face on didn't mask the dark circles beneath her eyes. It was a face so unlike my mothers, not tainted by alcohol but haunted by the pain her daughter had experienced.

'They are addictive,' the nurse replied, flashing an enormous smile. As she walked past, the nurse winked at me and nodded towards the back of the ward. The lady must have been Sophie's mother. I was alarmed at how young Sophie might be and my legs were heavy as I made my way down the ward. I approached the curtain which was half drawn and peered around. A puffy face, a mixture of pink and purple tones, looked up at me. It was awful, her features were so swollen, I couldn't tell what she was supposed to look like or how old she was, but I'd guess she was still in her teens. Caught between not bearing to look and unable to tear my eyes away, I was dumbstruck that someone could do that to another human being, a mere girl.

'Hi,' I mumbled, scooting down to sit beside her. The chair still warm beneath me.

'Hi?'

'I'm sorry to turn up without warning, but I wanted to come and see you.'

'Okay,' Sophie said slowly. She stared at me, trying to work out who I was and why I was there. I shook my head to clear my jumbled thoughts. Meeting Sophie was more difficult than I'd anticipated.

'My name is Eve. I was attacked back in September,' I admitted.

Her eyes flashed interest then – from the one I could see anyway.

'Can you tell me what happened?' I asked.

Sophie shook her head, her bottom lip trembled and then a tear dropped onto the starchy white sheet. 'I don't know exactly.'

'Did he... Did he touch you?' I stammered. I had to know, but Sophie shook her head.

'He just hit me. He kept on hitting me.' Her voice clogged from holding back tears. She looked broken, like she'd been beaten with a baseball bat. I couldn't believe someone's fists could do so much damage.

'Excuse me?' came a peeved voice behind me. Her mother was back, laden with snacks.

I stood immediately, smoothing my hair as she looked me up and down. Heat continued to rise in my cheeks at being caught somewhere I shouldn't be.

'I'm sorry,' I said, turning to leave, but Sophie's voice stopped me.

'Did he do the same to you?' She sounded so fragile.

'No,' I replied, not wanting to share my story. I think she understood as our eyes met and we regarded each other as victims, bound together. It couldn't have been Ian. There was no sexual assault.

Her mother stared wide-eyed at me.

'I hope they catch him,' I said and reached down to touch Sophie's hand. My heart broke for her and all the other victims that had to suffer the bruises and the pain that men inflicted. Even when she was healed she wouldn't be fixed on the inside. I knew that for a fact.

Her mother followed me out of the ward and down the corridor to the exit.

'Did that same man attack you?' she demanded. Hands

wedged onto her hips, blocking the door. She wanted answers, a lioness protecting her cub.

'No, not the same man. I was attacked yes, but it was different,' I tailed off.

She stared at me, lips pursed.

'Did she see him?' I asked, eyes wide, but she shook her head.

'No, he came at her from behind. Drunk they think, knocked her to the ground and laid into her like a fucking animal.' She rummaged around in her handbag for a tissue and began dabbing her rapidly filling eyes.

I shook my head, unsure how to respond.

'I don't know what could have possessed him to attack a girl. A complete stranger,' she continued.

I wanted to leave but she was still blocking the door. There was nothing I could say that would make it okay. All I could hear was beeping from a monitor a patient was hooked up to, timed exactly to the sound of my own heart thudding.

'She's got a broken eye socket and a fractured skull.'

I winced. Mrs Whitaker looked to be in a world of her own, staring into the distance.

'You are perfect,' she whispered to no one.

Ice shot down my back and I stood to attention.

'I'm sorry, what did you say?' I asked, bringing her back to the moment. Her eyes focused on me and she sighed. She looked like she hadn't slept a wink.

'That's what he said to her before she lost consciousness. "You are perfect".'

'I have to go. I'm sorry,' I said as the room blurred. I squeezed past her and pressed the door release button. Hurrying to the exit, outside into the fresh air. When I reached the doors to the smokers congregated under the canopy, I slumped against the wall. Doubled over like I'd been winded. *You are perfect.* It wasn't a coincidence. Ian had said the same words to me.

* * *

Sunday 28 January 2018

I've been doing laps of my cell for around half an hour now, after I managed a short nap. Time seems to move at a glacial pace as soon as the door is locked. It feels like I've been here for days. There's no way of knowing what the time is. Only the light from the window dictates night or day. It must be late afternoon now. I'm not sure what is going to happen. Will they want to interview me again? I've been charged now and I'm not sure what more they can ask? There's a lead weight in my stomach, pushing me down. I'm waiting for the door to swing open and to be carted off to HMP somewhere. I don't know where the nearest female prison is. I have no idea where any prisons are.

All the hanging around is making me twitchy. Like I'm due to sit an exam I haven't prepared for. I'm used to the smell of urine radiating from the floor now. No matter how many times the cell is cleaned, I'm sure it remains, ingrained in the cracks. Yet I don't want to leave here. I'm afraid of where I'll be sent.

The grey plimsolls they've given me are too big and rub at my heels, but I persevere with my walk. Around and around in circles with no purpose, a bit like my life. What a disappointment I must be to my mother. I wonder if anyone has told her? Jane maybe? Ben? Will she be sober enough to comprehend?

Perhaps I didn't think it through, got too cocky. I knew it wasn't without some risk. A few days ago I thought I had nothing to lose. Now I realise exactly what losing everything will mean. I'd hoped to be home by now, celebrating my release with copious amounts of alcohol. Looking to the future and putting everything behind me. I thought I was smarter and maybe that was my downfall.

Looking around the walls, I better get used to this space. What is it, 8' by 12'? The urge to run ripples through me, to feel a breeze fluttering my hair as I head towards the horizon. I may not run again for a long time. At least not anywhere green, beyond the confinement of prison walls.

45

SUNDAY 21 JANUARY 2018

I stopped off on the way back from the hospital to see Susie at Baristas. I caught her just before closing. She locked up and we sat at the back with a latte and a toasted teacake.

'I haven't seen you in a couple of weeks, Eve, you been busy?' Susie asked between mouthfuls.

'Yes, I'm sorry. I've been working at the boxing club.'

'Oh, don't be silly, pet, I didn't mean anything by it. I'm glad you've popped in. It's nice to see you.' Susie was always smiling, it was so refreshing. Life was always better after a chat with her. I wanted to tell her how my stomach was in knots. How the guy I was seeing was a violent sexual predator and what I was planning to do about it. If only I could. 'Still writing your crime novel?' she asked, bringing my attention back to the table and the teacake I'd barely touched. I bit into it, the warm butter escaping down my chin.

'Yes, but it's slow going.'

'It'll come along. Just keep writing, it'll happen eventually.'

I raised my eyebrows and she chuckled.

'I had a thought about rebranding. What do you think of the name "Roasted"?'

It was my turn to laugh then. I wasn't sure whether she understood the term and how it was used now.

'Told you I was down with the kids,' she said with a wink.

'Very catchy, I like it,' I admitted. My phone buzzed in my handbag. A text had just come through from Ian. Susie noticed me shifting uncomfortably in my seat.

'Bad news?'

I must be so easy to read.

'No, but I'm going to have to get off. Thanks for the chat, Susie.' I put a few coins in her tip jar on my way out as she hadn't charged me for the coffee or the teacake.

'Don't be a stranger,' she called as I unlocked the door, the bells chiming above my head.

Out on the street, I opened the message.

Hi beautiful. How are you?

I stared at the message, unable to believe this was the same beast that beat up an innocent girl last night. He was unhinged, without any moral code, and it was my fault for pushing him away. I typed back.

Fine thanks, Mother just left thank god. How are you?

Great. How about this Saturday for dinner?

My stomach flipped. Every time we set a date I felt like I was arranging my funeral, but he had to be stopped, it couldn't wait any longer.

`Sure.`
`I won't see you at the gym. I've had to go to Oxford today.`
`Is your dad okay?`
`No, he's had a fall. They've taken him to hospital. I'll be gone for a couple of days at least.`
`I'm sorry to hear that. Hope he feels better.`

I wasn't sure if I was relieved or disappointed that I wasn't going to see Ian for a few days. My head was all over the place. I had to stay focused. I knew it was him, all I needed to do was stick to the plan. I had wanted to look at his knuckles. Surely if he'd delivered a beating of that magnitude he was bound to have some marks? Maybe that was why he'd left town in a rush? Perhaps his dad hadn't had a fall at all? Maybe if I could find where his dad was I'd be able to check if Ian was there? It was too risky to do any searches on my phone or laptop at home and as Susie's shop was now shut it would have to wait until tomorrow. Frustrated, I headed home.

The presence of Ben, sat at the table shovelling pasta into his mouth, irritated me as soon as I arrived. For once I wanted the place to myself.

'Haven't you moved out yet?' I joked and watched as Ben frowned at me.

'What's up with you?' He pushed his bowl away and sat back, folding his arms.

'Nothing, just thought she would have had you all packed up by now.'

'Oh, fuck off,' he said, rolling his eyes, a grin slowly spreading across his face.

'Don't rush in to anything, Ben,' I said before I could stop it slipping out. His face softened and for a second, I panicked. I was going to cry. I turned away and poured myself a glass of water.

'I won't,' he said from right behind me. So close I could feel his breath on my neck. I turned round to be pulled into a bear hug. My instant reaction was to fight the affection, the closeness, but instead I melted into him. It was good to be held after what had been a shit couple of days.

Determined not to cry, I pulled away, attempting a joke. 'Don't want to have to get her thumbprint tattooed on your forehead now.'

* * *

Monday 22 January 2018

The next day I couldn't be arsed to go to Pulse. Ian wasn't going to be there, and I'd used up all my energy at the weekend. Plus, I had work to do at the gym. There was a mountain of towels that needed washing. I had to make sure I was around for the plumber who was finally going to look at the hot water tank and I had to collate the sign-on report for Jason, so he could see how we were doing on the membership front. Our handovers were getting shorter and shorter, with Jason generally turning up about ten minutes before I was due to leave. I thought he was leaning on me a little too much but without another job to go to there wasn't much I could do.

When he finally arrived, I was folding up the towels, all

fluffy from the industrial sized tumble dryer. He came in to help and I gave him a rundown of the day so far, including what the plumber had charged. The figure made him wince.

'How's Ben? I haven't seen him in a while,' he asked, when I'd finished my update.

'Fine, he's all loved up with Amy.'

'Who's Amy?' Jason stopped folding to stare at me. Ben obviously hadn't told him about her.

'A girl from work he met on a training course.'

'I thought you two had a thing?'

I shook my head, not unless you could call one kiss 'a thing'.

'Oh, I must have got it wrong then. I thought you were his girlfriend.'

'Really? No. We didn't have a thing,' I mumbled. Jason's words made my stomach flutter. It was too late now anyway.

Jason and I finished the pile and put them in the cubby-holes by the door.

'Right, I'll let you get on. See you tomorrow,' I said, hurrying out of the club and towards the library, so I could search the internet without Susie peeking over my shoulder.

When I arrived, I was frustrated to find all the machines upstairs full. Bloody jobseekers and students doing their coursework. I wandered back downstairs to look at the thrillers until someone came down. I nipped back up to find a computer now free. An hour later, I had a printed list of all the care homes in Oxford. There were over twenty of them. I would be spending the rest of the day on the phone, but that I could do in the privacy of my room.

* * *

Sunday 28 January 2018

I'm back in the interview room again. Collected from my cell without warning. I've been waiting for five minutes, but no sign of Hicks or Becker yet. What are they going to ask me now?

I've just caught my solicitor playing Candy Crush on his mobile phone out of the corner of my eye. I'm going to prison for sure. At least I'm not hungry. They delivered a microwave bolognaise pasta dinner, still in its beige tray fifteen minutes ago. It was lukewarm and I'm sure it contained as much meat as a tofu salad. I'm not one to complain though. I've been a waitress; I've seen what happens when food is sent back to the kitchen. I had counted one hundred laps of my cell when Jamie brought it in. I had no idea it was even dinner time.

He seems nice, a friendly face, a bit of blond bumfluff on his chin. He's younger than me I think, early twenties. But he doesn't speak, just smiles. He must be part of the custodial officers, perhaps a junior? Tasked with moving people around, delivering food and the like. Making sure none of us are tempted to escape.

The door opens, and Becker comes into the room, followed by Hicks, who won't meet my gaze. Will he interview me? He should be reprimanded for his interrogation methods. I can't understand what he's so angry about. I've done the world a favour. It's a safer place now. He's the one that's supposed to catch the criminals. He looks like he couldn't even catch a cold.

'Eve, we wanted to give you one last opportunity to tell us anything you may have overlooked from last night,' Becker says, once she has set the recorder. She doesn't look quite so immaculate now. Her hair is starting to frizz out of the bun, the hairspray no longer holding, and there's a coffee stain on the cuff of her blue shirt. I bet they can't wait to get me out of here.

'I've told you everything.'

'We've had some more information come in and that's not quite true is it.' Hicks speaks this time. It isn't a question.

I remain silent. My solicitor gives me a sideways glance. Perhaps this is the time to start exercising my right not to speak?

'This will be your last chance to get on record what happened. Because changing your story later will not be viewed favourably in court,' Becker continues, emphasising the 'not'.

I will myself to keep still, any fidgeting will give me away. What do they know? Is she bluffing? I can't be sure. Now is the time to hold my nerve. I briefly glance at the door. I can't help it. It's a knee-jerk reaction to seek an escape route; and I see him, fleetingly, passing the door.

I feel a numbness cascade through my fingers. Why is Ben here?

46

MONDAY 22 JANUARY 2018

Finding Ian's dad had been a mission. I called seventeen care homes before I had any success. In the beginning, I was told they weren't allowed to give out any information, but then I began claiming I was David Shaw's niece. By the eighteenth call, to Nuthatch House, I was more than a little bored but had my patter perfected.

'Hi. I wonder if you can help me. I'm looking for my uncle, David Shaw. Is he a resident here?'

A gruff man with an Eastern European accent answered and he didn't sound particularly friendly. 'Yeah. Why, do you want to come and see him? Visits are by appointment only.'

I was so surprised I'd finally found him that I hesitated in my reply.

'Yes, yes I do want to come and see him. Is he okay, I heard he'd had an accident?'

The man snorted. 'Listen, love, he's ten feet away from me, watching television in the communal room. He's fine.'

'Thank you,' I replied, feeling oddly relieved for the man I'd never met. The father of a monster. Now I knew Ian was lying. Where was he? Laying low at home waiting for his knuckles to heal or did he really go to Oxford?

'Hang on. Who did you say you were? You must know Ian? Does he know you're coming to visit?'

Fuck. Whoever he was, he knew Ian. If he found out someone was falsely identifying herself as David's niece, he might know it was me. I ended the call. My fingers trembling as they slid across the screen. Shit. What an idiot. He wouldn't call Ian, would he? I was glad I'd withheld my number. I prayed it would be forgotten when he next contacted them or that someone else would answer the phone if he called to check in on his father. It didn't sound like the most welcoming place.

My eyes darted around the room, turning the call over in my mind. Why could you only visit by appointment? That was odd. I had no experience of care homes, but I'd assumed they would have visiting hours, the same as a hospital? Booking an appointment to see your loved one sounded strange, suspicious even. Why couldn't you just drop in unannounced? I had to use the internet again but didn't dare use my home Wi-Fi or laptop for any of these searches. Especially now I knew what I was looking for.

I slipped on my trainers and headed back to the library. At the café I treated myself to a coffee and a flapjack as there had been no time for lunch at home. Most of the computers were free when I arrived this time. The whole library was quieter. Armed with my refreshments, I slid into the chair in the corner unnoticed. When the search engine opened, I typed in Nuthatch House. The computer whirred for a few seconds, the small circle spinning endlessly in the centre of the screen. Then a message, 'Firefox is not responding'. God these were ancient, the yellowing plastic and boxy monitors were relics. The library could do with an injection of funding to update its equipment. Finally, a long list of results loaded. At the top were two from national newspapers. I clicked on the first link, drumming my fingers on the desk. It was slow to load, and I bit into my flapjack. The sweet oats clogging my dry mouth until I washed them down with coffee. Wincing as the molten liquid burnt my tongue.

'Nuthatch House of Horrors' in bold black letters filled the screen, followed by the tagline 'Care Home from Hell'. I read quickly, devouring the words and scrolling down as fast as the prehistoric machine would allow. At least Susie had computers from this decade. I consumed the information in parts as the page loaded. There had been an investigation into the methods used by the staff. Their lack of training questioned after a patient died of dehydration. Further down the page there were reports of patients being left in their beds, soiled, for days. In later findings it was concluded that residents were only being given one meal a day. When journalists infiltrated the care home to record these incidences undercover, they found an elderly Alzheimer sufferer chained to her bed as she was prone to wandering.

It was horrific reading and I couldn't believe the level of cruelty inflicted on these vulnerable people. How could Ian allow his father to be homed there? Surely, he must have read these reports? Investigated, before charging them with his father's care? I would have. Ian was heinous, that was certain, but what did his father do to him?

I clicked on the second link and it was much the same as the first. Infected bed sores, and physical punishments handed out when patients did not do as they were told. I sat back and stared, open mouthed, at the screen, unable to believe what I was reading. The news reports were from only two years ago. How long had David been there? Was Ian from Oxford originally? Why was he housed so far away?

Another idea hit me, and I searched for Oxford and sexual assault. The fourth link began 'Thames Valley Police are appealing for witnesses following a violent sexual assault on a university student on the way home from a Christmas party on Tuesday 22 December.' The details were sketchy; the psychology student had been jumped from behind. Could it have been Ian? A different hunting ground but he was in Oxford over Christmas, or so he said. I shuddered, wanting to shake the feeling of discomfort that had attached itself to me. I went back to Google and typed in Nuthatch.

The care home itself had a nice bright website with a well turned out elderly gentleman in a wheelchair with a gorgeous young nurse beside him on the homepage. It was too perfect, a stock photo for sure. Apparently, Nuthatch had been refurbished and all staff trained to Level 3 NVQ in Health & Social Care. Somehow, I didn't believe that. The man I'd spoken to sounded more like a nightclub bouncer. I'd be surprised if they ever recovered from the damage to their reputation.

Leaning back in my chair, I tried my coffee again, which had cooled. I frowned at the screen; it might be worth a try. I opened a new tab and this time typed David Shaw in the search engine. Again, the machine whirred, and I used the waiting time to finish my snack. Lots of results came up for Facebook and I scrolled past them. Nothing jumped out at me. There was an accountant in the Isle of Wight and a solicitor in London that both had web pages linked to their names, but I couldn't find what I was looking for. David Shaw was a common name, there would be hundreds, maybe thousands.

I typed Oxford next to the name and hit enter again. On page three of the results another news report caught my eye. This one published in 1992 by the *Oxford Times*. I clicked the link and rubbed my eyes as it loaded. They were sore from straining at the dimly lit screen.

Another headline filled the space, this one made me queasy: 'Boy found locked in cupboard'.

A man by the name of David Shaw had been arrested in Donnington after neighbours heard the cries of his son through the walls. The boy was six, according to the report, and was found malnourished whilst his father was at work. The mother had died of cancer and no other siblings were mentioned in the article. I shook my head. It was disgusting.

Clicking back and scrolling further down, I saw a later report from the same year stating David had been sentenced to five years imprisonment. It wasn't enough. Sentencing never seemed to fit the crime. Always either too lenient or too severe. The boy wasn't named for obvious reasons. Could he have been Ian? Could Ian have been locked up and starved?

I rubbed at my temples and lowered my head to stretch the crick in my neck. It must be a coincidence. There were lots of David Shaw's, Oxford was a big place. I got up, pushed my chair back and stretched my legs, in search of a bin. I found one by the stairs and took a slow walk back to the computer section. The top floor of the library was empty apart from one librarian stacking shelves. Deciding to call it a day, I began to close the tabs on the computer one by one. As I lingered on the care home website and the fake smile of the blonde model; it dawned on me. I couldn't believe I hadn't seen it before. It was no mistake that David was at Nuthatch. Ian had put him there on purpose. As punishment.

47

HIM

I lost control, I admit it. By the third blow, the girl had lost consciousness, but I couldn't stop. Rage propelled me on until I could no longer feel my hands. She wasn't so pretty by the time I finished. All the time picturing Eve's sweet face, her full lips, split and bloody. Still the frustration lingers, even after I used that girl as a punchbag. I'm not sure how long I'll be able to control myself. No matter, she'll be worth waiting for.

Once I've spent my weekend with Eve, I'll take a few days off. I know my father will love to hear a detailed account of how I spent my weekend. He'll twitch and moan and maybe even cry, but I know deep down he'll enjoy it, almost as much as I will reliving it. I'll tell him how perfect Eve was, just as he told my mother all those years ago.

I just have to figure out what to do with her. I cannot let her go. This time I'm going to take more than her body. She will be perfect.

48

MONDAY 22 JANUARY 2018

Left reeling by Ian's possible motive to entrust his dad to Nuthatch, I walked home, mind racing. Images of him tipping staff with banknotes each time he visited flooded my thoughts. Ensuring his father was neglected or abused at every opportunity. A cruel smile and sly wink alongside a commissioning handshake to the Care Home Manager.

There was no concrete proof; I was assuming he knew about Nuthatch. Guessing that the boy in the cupboard was him. I could be putting two and two together and making five. My 'evidence' was circumstantial at best, but deep down I knew it was him. Everything added up. His controlling nature, the violent porn and aggression. I'd always known. As soon as I saw his unfeeling blue eyes in the gym and the physical effect he had on me. I was frightened of him. My entire body tensed when he was near, reacting for me. It knew before I did.

In a few days Ian and I would have dinner. He would invite me back to his flat. For what purpose, I wasn't sure? What were his motives? To rape me again? To beat me? To make love? I had so many questions and I knew the answers to none. But I would be going back to his flat. I needed to prepare.

Plucking my phone from my bag, I dialled as I walked home.

'Jason?'

'Hello?'

'It's Eve.'

'Hiya, you all right?'

'Yeah fine. I meant to ask you earlier. You don't know anyone that runs self-defence classes for women, do you?'

'No, not offhand, but I can always show you a few moves if you like.'

I smiled, I was hoping he'd say that. 'Brilliant, thanks. Just half an hour or something.'

'Sure, I'll come in earlier tomorrow, before you finish. We can do it then.'

'Perfect. Thanks Jason. See you tomorrow.'

My Tuesday was filling up fast. Work in the morning and Doctor Almara in the afternoon. I had to try and squeeze a workout in too. Just four days until Saturday, the thought made my insides squirm.

At home we were starting to run out of food again, but shopping would have to wait until later in the week. I ran a bath and lowered myself into the hot water, Was Ian with his father now? Or had that been a lie? Maybe I shouldn't have deleted the PetCam app and the window it gave me into Ian's life, but I had a plan and I had to stick to it. Deviation would be foolish, and I had to be smart.

I spent the evening waiting for the sound of Ben's key in the door, but it never came. I had no idea if he was on shift this week or whether he was with Amy, but I missed his company. Jane called me in her break, she was on lates this week and her shifts didn't finish until ten. I could tell she was running on empty.

'Only a few more days to go now, chicken,' I said.

'Yeah, I can't wait. I meant to say, everyone's been asking about my fob watch, they can't believe I have such amazing friends.'

'Just you remember that when you're travelling halfway around the world. Don't forget what I look like, will you.'

'How could I! We'll FaceTime, and I'll write, it won't feel like I'm so far away, I promise.' Her break was ending so we said goodbye. I knew I'd be lost without her when she left. Where would I be when she returned? Knowing what was coming I couldn't help but wonder whether I'd be alive or dead.

49

TUESDAY 23 JANUARY 2018

Sleep came easily for once and the next morning I rose later than planned, rushing around to get ready for work. Starting so early was beginning to wear me down. I busied myself with cleaning chores and did some sparring with Louise, the young girl on probation. She was lovely, if a bit rough around the edges, and she had a cracking right hook.

Jason came in mid-morning and moved some mats onto a large space on the floor, as enthusiastic as ever. I could tell teaching was what he loved the most.

'I've been looking at some bits on the internet to refresh my memory. We covered a module of it in one of the personal training certificates a year or so ago. I'm looking forward to you throwing me around.' He loomed above me and I laughed, looking him from head to foot.

'I don't think that's going to be happening any time soon.' Although if I could hold my own against Jason, I might stand a chance with Ian. I had to learn as much as I could.

'We'll see. Let's do some stretches, a bit of warming up to loosen the muscles.'

I followed the exercises Jason demonstrated. Rolling my shoulders and stretching my arms and hamstrings. Then we faced each other a few feet apart, like we were about to wrestle, and I tried not to giggle. Jason towered over me and although it was silly, I felt slightly intimidated. Ian was smaller in stature, but I'd seen first-hand what he was capable of with Sophie.

'Okay, first one – a good kick in the balls. It'll disable any guy if you kick hard enough.' Jason bent down and picked a protector cup from the floor, like those worn by cricketers, and slipped it inside his jogging bottoms. The bulge obvious. I flushed red, hesitating, not wanting to look at that area.

'You're not seriously expecting me to kick you... there, are you?' I pointed feebly.

'Well, not full pelt. I do want to have kids one day, but yes, go on, give it a go.'

Unsure if I could, I paused. Jason braced himself, so I took my cue and swung my leg back, managing to kick Jason in the thigh. He shook it off, but my face turned scarlet. This was excruciating.

'Might want to adjust your aim.' He smiled, and I tried again. This time my foot connected with the cup. 'Perfect,' he said. 'Okay, I'm going to come behind you.' He moved around to my back, his breath ruffling strands of my hair. My pulse raced, and goosebumps appeared on my skin. I was right there, behind the café, bent over that bin.

You're safe. Jason won't hurt you, I told myself. My body wouldn't listen to reason though and I could feel myself begin to sweat.

'I'm going to put my arms around your chest and I want you to stamp down on my foot and bring your arms up in a praying motion and try to slip them under my arms.'

I nodded in agreement and his arms wrapped around me. I closed my eyes, the room blurring for a second. I was pressed against the wall and it wasn't Jason behind me, it was Ian. His face hidden by the balaclava. Anger brought me back to the moment and I stamped down on Jason's toes as instructed, managing to slip my arms up and break his hold. I jumped up and down, the adrenaline pumping. Thrilled to be learning the moves that could potentially save my life. Perhaps things would have been different if I'd known them then?

'Brilliant,' he said.

Jason went on to show me where to hit to cause the most damage and other ways to incapacitate your attacker, as well as how to free yourself if being held by the arms or shoulders. With my memory of that morning safely locked away, we reversed roles and I tried my best to restrain him. It was impossible, I could barely get my arms around him. I did manage to throw him over my shoulder using my weight as leverage, although I think he helped. Stupidly, I hadn't thought about how much physical contact or exertion would be required and by the end of it I was a hot, sweaty mess. My face pink and shiny, with hair that had become a mass of frizz. Jason merely glistened, he hadn't even perspired properly.

'Thanks so much, Jason, I appreciate it,' I said, guzzling from the water bottle he handed me.

'No worries. It was fun. Fancy something from the snack wagon around the corner?'

Five minutes later, we were hidden away in his office cuddling polystyrene cups of hot tea. The cooling sweat making me shiver, damp on my skin.

'That's handy to have nearby.' I gestured to my bacon roll

as I bit into it hungrily, the tangy brown sauce escaping onto my lap. 'Bugger,' I swore, and Jason handed me a napkin.

'Does quite well from the business on the industrial estate, I think.' Jason tucked into his roll, making less mess. 'So, why the self-defence?' he asked.

My mouth was full, so I had time to construct my answer. 'I was mugged last year and kept meaning to learn some moves.'

'Jesus. There's some fuckers around aren't there.' He shook his head in disgust.

I nodded, glad my mouth was full. I couldn't tell him I was dating one.

'Ben all right?' he asked.

'Think so, haven't seen much of him.'

'No, me either. Must be all loved up.'

A pang in my chest deflated the elation of the morning.

'Guess so,' I replied.

'Are you seeing anyone?' he asked, a smile playing on his lips.

'Yes, well, sort of. It's early days.' *We'll have broken up come the weekend.*

Jason shrugged slightly, more to himself than to me. I wasn't intending to be another notch on his bedpost, although perhaps I was being unfair. He'd been nothing but generous to me, even if he had turned out to be a slave driver.

I showered and left to go to my appointment with Doctor Almara. More prepared after the self-defence demonstration but still terrified of being alone with Ian. Not knowing his plan, if he even had one, unnerved me. It was like playing cat and mouse, but I wasn't sure which one of us was the mouse? This could all be a game to him. After all, physically, I was hardly a threat.

I managed to make it to the psychiatrist's office in time for my appointment and she welcomed me warmly.

'Eve, good to see you. How are you?' Today she wore a striking burnt orange trouser suit, blending into the Moroccan tones of her office. Her smile was wide and genuine, my ears burned as she took me in.

'I'm good, thank you,' I replied, trying to focus on why I was here.

'What would you like to talk about today?' she asked.

'I wanted to ask a question, actually.'

'Okay, go ahead.'

'About behaviour, and where it comes from.'

'In what context?'

'How would you determine if someone was a danger to society?'

The question didn't invoke a reaction, she merely curved the corner of her mouth a little. She leant forward in her seat. 'How do you mean? Dangerous in what way?'

'To others, violent. Say a psychopath, for example.'

'Well, there would be a number of contributing factors and personality traits that could identify a potential psychopath, but there aren't as many out there as Hollywood would have you believe.'

'What kind of personality traits?'

'A lack of remorse or guilt, for example, also the ability to deceive others. They would be charming and excellent at manipulation. A psychopath would be impulsive, unable to accept responsibility for their actions and likely promiscuous, with little empathy for others.'

I took it all in. Doctor Almara was doing her best to not to ask any probing questions.

'Say you were in a relationship with a psychopath. What would that say about you?' I asked.

'Many people find themselves easily charmed by someone with psychopathic personality traits. They are, in general, charismatic people who enjoy manipulating others, so it can be quite easy to fall under their spell.'

I nodded and stared out of the window for a minute. It had started to rain outside, and the tapping distracted me.

'Eve, have you met someone?'

I nodded, there was no reason to lie.

'Do you believe he has some of the traits I mentioned?'

'I'm not sure.' I looked at the floor, not wanting to be probed by those eyes.

She spoke softly. 'Be careful, Eve. You're fragile at the moment and I'm concerned you may get taken advantage of. Let things develop gradually. As we discussed before, you need to make sure you're comfortable before any relationship becomes physical. Otherwise there is a possibility it could hinder your progress.' Her genuine concern warmed me like a blanket. I was touched.

We spent the rest of the session discussing my recovery so far. She commented that I seemed focused and asked if this was the result of meeting someone new. She was right. I was focused. Resolute on getting my life back. On righting the wrongs that had been done to me, the girl in the alley and Sophie. And any others. It was easy to suggest Ian's behaviour was because of his treatment as a child, but there were thousands of people who suffered similar parental abuse. They managed to move on and function normally within a community. I could not allow it to unsettle me. I was not going to feel sorry for him. It was not an excuse.

My phone vibrating in my pocket jolted me out of my

thoughts on my way home, hurrying through the streets as the rain became heavier. When I saw it was Ian, I almost didn't answer it.

'Hello.'

'Hi, how are you?

'Good thanks, how are you?'

'Oh, you know, spending quality time with my dad.'

I shivered. What exactly did that entail? 'How is he?'

'Fine, a bit bruised. I've been telling him all about you. He loves hearing about what I get up to.'

There was a pause as I tried to come up with a response.

'Is he able to talk?' I wasn't sure why I'd asked. Visions of Ian whispering awful things into David's ear, tormenting him whilst he was powerless to do anything about it.

'Not very well, he doesn't make much sense. He gets easily confused. Anyway, I just wanted to let you know I'll be home tomorrow. He's out of hospital and back in the care home,' he continued. I knew full well he'd never left.

'Okay. Might see you at the gym,' was all I could muster.

'Can't wait to get my hands on you Saturday.' He chuckled and then the line went dead.

* * *

Sunday 28 January 2018

'Who has access to the internet at home?' Hicks asks.

'Me and Ben, my flatmate.' The additional information seems an overkill considering Ben is here at the station, presumably being interviewed. I'm sure they already know we live together. I need to keep a cool head.

'Your internet usage seems quite low. On the history of websites visited, there's some shopping, a bit of porn, but that's it.'

I roll my eyes. If Hicks is hoping for a reaction he's not going to get one. I remain silent, waiting for him to get to the point.

'No streaming or downloading. Hardly any social media. I thought all young people were into that?' Hicks looks smug, but I'm not going to play into his hands. How old is he? Fifty? Sixty? He looks worn around the edges and the creases in his forehead run deep.

'Not all young people. I'm not interested in seeing photos of what my friends have had for dinner.' That amuses him.

'Would you say you go online a lot? On your mobile or laptop?' Hicks asks.

I shrug. 'Not really.'

'Do you use the internet anywhere else, Eve?'

My jaw clenches ever so slightly before I catch myself. *Relax, don't let him see.*

Hicks stares intently, absorbing every movement I make. It's his job to read people and I am, by my own admission, a terrible liar.

'Sometimes. At work I did.' I keep my voice even.

'There's also an internet café in town, isn't there? Baristas I believe it's called.'

Susie's coffee shop. I swallow, my mouth suddenly dry. My brain is firing, sending signals around my body I'm trying to conceal. I can't give anything away. Especially now. My search history on that machine would be everything they needed.

'Have you been in there before?' he presses.

'Yes, for coffee.'

'Have you used the computers in there?'

I know Susie doesn't have cameras installed, but what if he's sent someone to see her? Someone armed with a photo of me. She wouldn't think to lie.

'I don't think so,' I say, frowning as though I'm trying to remember. I'm worried he can hear my heart hammering.

'I see,' Hicks responds, shuffling the papers he's holding. Becker looks redundant, she is yet to speak. Hicks is leading the interview and it unnerves me.

I bob my legs up and down under the desk. Fuck sake, just get to the point.

'Your phone records have been low too, a few calls to the doctors, work, friends. No more than three or four a day.'

I raise my eyebrows. I know where this is going. Shit. Why didn't I use another phone?

'Until a few days ago, when you had quite an erratic day I'd say. On Monday, you made over twenty phone calls,' Hicks says.

My expression remains stoic, but inside panic swells like a balloon. Sweat prickles underarm as my temperature spikes. I need to head this off.

'I was trying to find Ian.'

'Is that why you called every care home in Oxford? To find Ian?'

Think you've caught me out, detective? Think again.

'Yes. He told me he wouldn't be around as his father had a fall. He was going to Oxford to see him. I wasn't sure he was telling me the truth.'

Hicks frowns at this.

'So, you phoned every care home in Oxford?' He doesn't believe me. It doesn't matter.

'Yes.' I try to resist the urge to stand up and give the smug detective the finger. I can't be convicted for being a clingy girl keeping tabs on her man.

'And you found him? You found Ian?'

'Yes, at Nuthatch Care Home. The member of staff told me he was there visiting his father, David.' My poker face is good. It is hard not to smile. These tiny victories feel amazing given the circumstances. Could this be the light at the end of the tunnel or is Ben about to contradict everything I've said?

'How did Ian react to you checking up on him?' Becker asks, breaking her silence.

I glare at her, she's fed me to the wolf that is Hicks.

'I don't know. He never mentioned it and neither did I. I'm not sure he knew.' I lean back in my chair, drinking in Hicks's grimace. *You'll need to try harder than that, detective.* But deep down, there's a niggling feeling in my gut I can't ignore. It was a mistake using my phone for those calls. How many other mistakes have I made? My shoulders tense. They couldn't seize Susie's computers, could they?

50

TUESDAY 23 JANUARY 2018

I stood still on the pavement, unaware of the people passing me by. Jostling for room and hurrying to get out of the rain. Staring at my phone although Ian was no longer on the line, fat drops splashing down from above. I had visions of Ian's hands around my neck. Is that what he meant? I shuddered involuntarily and managed a few slow steps forward. Annoying those trying to navigate around me.

I was going to die on Saturday. It wasn't cat and mouse. It was lamb to the slaughter.

Get a hold of yourself, Eve. I knew I'd have a wobble in the days before, but I didn't anticipate wanting to turn and run. Could I go through with it? The plan I'd researched and thought about. Spent hours trying to consider every minor detail. The one that in my head was so clear, but the thought of making it a reality terrified me.

My stomach churned with nervous energy and my bladder announced the need to be emptied. I had to get home. The trouble was, I couldn't talk to anyone about what was going on. Not Susie, not Ben, and Jane was leaving the country in less than a week. I wanted it to be over, to be rid of the months consumed by nothing but thoughts of Ian. I longed to be free of him and there was only one way I could do that, but first I was willing to give the police one last try.

When I got home, I shut myself away in my room and dug out the business card given to me months ago, wedged into my bookcase.

'Emmerson,' stated a weary voice after a few rings.

'Hi Detective Emmerson. It's Eve, Eve Harding.'

'Hi Eve, how can I help you?'

'I just wondered if you had any updates at all.'

I heard her sigh faintly.

'No, I'm afraid not. I've got nothing to report. It's still an ongoing investigation and we are looking at other assaults of the same nature in the vicinity.'

'The attack on Sophie Whitaker. Do you think it's connected?'

'Did you go and visit Miss Whitaker in hospital?' Emmerson cut me off.

I remained silent. My attendance had obviously been reported by Mrs Whitaker.

'Please don't get involved, Eve, leave it to the police.'

'But do you think it's connected?'

'There was no sexual assault, so, no, I don't think it's connected.'

Shows what she knew. Emmerson wasn't aware that a frustrated Ian left my house minutes before Sophie was beaten to within an inch of her life. She didn't know that her assailant spoke the same words to her that he had to me. Was I going to tell her? Make her believe that I knew who the predator was? It was the last chance before I took matters into my own hands.

The silence between us stretched out and I heard Emmerson sigh. Perhaps annoyed I wasn't on the same wavelength? Or that I wouldn't roll over and agree? It was on the tip of my tongue. *Just say it. The person you are looking for is Ian Shaw.* But before I could get the words out the silence was broken.

'Eve, I'm going on maternity leave today. I'll be passing your case over to the team and one of them will be in touch to introduce themselves. Please don't worry. We will find him.'

But I did worry. I worried because even with everything I'd learnt there was no hard evidence to prove he was the man behind my attack. No evidence from the attack on Sophie and the nameless girl in the alley. I had nothing to offer the police but a name and now Emmerson was leaving to have her baby; I knew no one would contact me. The case had already gone cold and I was sure she hadn't planned to touch base today. I just caught her off guard. My decision was made; I couldn't walk away.

* * *

Wednesday 24 January 2018

After work, I spent the rest of Wednesday going through the flat, room by room, knowing someone would be here in the coming days. I hadn't kept anything incriminating and got rid of most of what I found. Old receipts, bills and paperwork had been distributed in various rubbish bins around town. The PetCam box, instructions and eBay receipt destroyed too. None of it could be used against me, but I had to be sure. I didn't want to make it easy for the police to build a profile of my life. The place was well overdue for a spring clean anyway.

Ben caught me on my hands and knees digging through the sofa to see what had been stuffed down the sides. The handheld hoover at my feet, ready for action.

'What are you doing?'

'Spring cleaning,' I answered and, amused, he left me to it.

Every room was cleaned and picked apart, except for his. It was amazing how much stuff I'd accumulated since moving in. Much of it down to spending habits that I'd done my best to curb lately.

As well as the rubbish, I had three bags of books, clothes and DVDs for the charity shop too, which I dropped off on my way to Pulse. Ian didn't show and for that I was grateful. After a two mile run, I spent the rest of my time on the free weights, lifting as much as I could. Tearing muscle tissue and berating myself for not lifting heavier weights sooner. I wanted to be as strong as I could be for Saturday. I should have done more boxing too; being nimble on my feet would have been an advantage. It didn't matter. What would be would be.

* * *

Sunday 28 January 2018 – DC Becker

'That went well,' I struggle to keep the sarcasm out of my voice. Functioning on barely three hours sleep feels like torture. I should be used to it by now, but it never gets any easier.

Hicks grunts and collapses in his chair, swivelling it

around to face me, legs splayed. He picks up his stress ball from the mess that is his desk, pumping it rhythmically as he chews his lip.

I turn away, my desk is no tidier. Unlocking my screen, I see Guy has sent me an instant message. James, the guy from the mobile phone company, wants me to call him. I pick up my mobile and key in the number. Hicks is still deep in thought and pays no attention as I edge out of my seat and down the corridor to find an empty office.

'James, it's Detective Becker. You called me?' I feel my stomach flutter before he even speaks.

'Hi, yes. That account. You mentioned patterns, right? Well, I've got something a bit weird for you.'

'Go on,' I said, my interest piqued.

'Back in late October, for about a ten day period on and off, the phone is in one spot for hours at a time. It's kind of strange from what I've seen before, that kind of limited movement. Could be work or home address or a friend's maybe?'

'Okay, great. Thank you. Could you send me the location and the dates please?' I give James my email address. The fluttering in my stomach continues and I sense I'm on to something, but I can't work out what. Hicks is right, something doesn't quite fit.

I head back to my desk to find him leaning forward, squinting at his screen. I spend the next few minutes refreshing my inbox until it comes through. The triangulation is very similar to the printout I have from yesterday, but interestingly neither Ian's or Eve's houses are in the orange circle. This time Ian's is just on the edge. I stare at the map, running through each road name in my head, trying to make a connection. There's nothing else there, only housing, with a gym and petrol station on the periphery of the circle. I spot

Western Road, which runs alongside an area of green on the map. It rings bells.

I tap the road name into the database and in seconds a solitary result appears on the screen. Eve Harding indecent assault, Grove Park, Western Road entrance, 24 September 2017. Why would she go back there? For some kind of therapy? It doesn't make sense.

I type in the last date of the pattern from James's email before the movements went back to normal. Perhaps that will enlighten me? There is a DUI and a domestic recorded on that date but also an attempted assault. Alice King: attempted sexual assault on Blackwater Lane. I scan the notes; the attack was interrupted by persons unknown, resulting in the perpetrator fleeing the scene. My eyes flick back to the pool of orange, searching for Blackwater Lane. It's there, right in the middle of the orange circle. The other side of Grove Park.

Hicks was right. She'd found him – not only that, she'd caught him in the act.

51

THURSDAY 25 JANUARY 2018

When I was halfway through my workout on Thursday, I jumped as a hand slid around my waist, quickly followed by lips pressed against my cheek. Ian was back. I set my mouth into a smile before turning around to greet him.

'Hello, gorgeous. Did you miss me?' His eyes remained flat, not matching the words he spoke.

'Of course I did.' Throwing my arms around him for a second before recoiling. 'Sorry, I'm sweaty.' I admitted, using it as an excuse.

'It's all right, I like it.' He winked, and I shuddered involuntarily.

'You just got here?' I asked, and he nodded.

'I'm desperate for a workout, feel all pent up.' He laughed, rotating his shoulders as though he was loosening up for a fight.

'I'm almost done. Will you be here tomorrow?'

'Yeah, think so, as long as there aren't any catastrophes at work.'

I leant forward to kiss him briefly on the lips. I didn't want him to think I was being weird.

'See you tomorrow then.' I sashayed away, hoping he was watching. I had to make myself irresistible. I needed him to ask me to come back to his on Saturday night after dinner. I couldn't assume it was a foregone conclusion. From previous experience of being alone with Ian, I didn't think it would be too much of a problem.

In the evening, I spent over an hour on the phone to Jane. We talked about her packing, which amazingly she hadn't started yet. I wasn't surprised, she always left everything until the last minute. The countdown to her leaving was edging ever closer and my heart ached. She could tell I wasn't myself and kept trying to probe, but I told her I was just sad she was going, that was all. She didn't believe me, she could tell something else was going on. It was impossible lying to someone who knew you so well, but I couldn't tell her about Ian now.

* * *

Friday 26 January 2018

I woke late again on Friday morning with no motivation to get out of bed. My muscles ached from the gym and I struggled to raise my arms above my head to wash my hair. I couldn't face Ian knowing what was coming tomorrow. I'd make an excuse about why I couldn't go to the gym. I was going shopping for a new outfit. He'd like that, me getting all glammed up for our date. His ego would be nicely inflated even before I arrived.

Ben joined me for a quick breakfast when he got home from his night shift. I hadn't seen much of him all week. We'd turned into ships passing in the night, gone were our themed dinners and movie nights.

'How are things?' he asked, spooning cereal into his mouth as I slurped my protein shake.

'Good. Going to look into doing that personal training qualification next week,' I lied to make conversation. To fill the crevice between us. It was as if we didn't know what to talk about any more. The banter had dried up. I didn't want to hear about Amy and, thankfully, he spared me that. At the same time Ian was a topic I wanted to avoid too.

'That's good.'

'Any closer to finding a flat?'

'That's on hold for a bit.'

'Oh?' I shuffled forward in my seat, chastising myself for being so obvious.

'Yeah. Amy just likes to get ahead of herself.' *I couldn't agree more.*

When Ben left to go to bed, my shoulders felt lighter, not because he'd left the room but because he'd seen sense. It was too early for them to move in together. I knew it was none of my business and I had my own motives to want to slow things down, but it had got serious way too quickly.

I stared at Ben's closed door. There was so much I wanted to say but couldn't. It may be the last time I saw him for a while, maybe even forever. It was melodramatic but so was my mood. I couldn't think about it any longer, I had to get to work.

When Jason came to relieve me after my shift, I managed a quick workout, skipping and floor exercises. My arms were too sore to box. I did what I could and when I had no more left to give I returned home. I wanted to make a few phone calls.

I rang Debbie for a catch-up. Ten minutes in, I realised it had been a terrible idea. She droned on about her workload, although she was in no rush to get off the phone to me and back to it. I almost slipped up when she asked me about the puppy. I needed to keep better track of the lies I told. I explained, sadly, that he had passed away. I felt awful lying about something so horrid. I tried Jane again, but it went straight to voicemail and I assumed she was working.

Lastly, I rang Mum who seemed pleased to hear from me. She told me she'd posted the wedding invitation yesterday, so I should get it in a day or two. It was going to be a simple registry-office affair and Patrick couldn't wait to meet me. If only the feeling was mutual. The house had been put on the market.

'It's selling for £400,000. I couldn't believe it.' That's a lot of gin. Although she sounded relatively sober and more positive than I'd heard in ages. I wished my mother well, promising under duress I would be there for the wedding in a month's time.

When I'd had enough of being social, I gave in and poured myself a drink. The sound of ice chinking against glass whilst on the phone to my mother planted the seed in my head. I wanted to numb the dread that had been slowly creeping up on me all day. When I finished the elderflower gin Ben had originally bought, I popped downstairs to get another bottle. Whilst in the shop, I bought cigarettes and crisps which I intended to use to soak up the alcohol as I couldn't be bothered to cook anything.

I thought Ben was working, but when he came out of his room I could tell he was dressed to go out. Probably taking Amy out for dinner. Lucky girl.

'Where you off to?' I asked.

'I'm going for a drink with Jason. Want to come?' He eyed the empty bottle still on the table, moving his gaze onto the newly opened one.

I shook my head. In other circumstances I would have jumped at the chance, but I wanted to drink alone tonight. Also, it would be nice for Jason to have Ben to himself for a bit. 'Tell Jason I said hi. Have fun.'

'Are you having a party for one?' he asked, his lip curled.

'Yep. I'll catch you later for post-party drinks,' I said, raising my glass in a toast.

Ben laughed, his eyebrows raised, humouring me. 'Catch you later. Go easy okay.' He jabbed a finger towards the bottle and I nodded.

A while later I fell asleep at the table, my head resting on my arms. When I woke, the flat was dark and my head pounded. Switching on the light and filling a pint glass with much-needed water I saw it was past eleven. Maybe Ben would be back soon, and we could have a drink after all. I downed the water in one go and poured myself a small shot of gin to take to bed. I hadn't checked my phone all night and saw I had two missed calls and a text from Ian.

`You okay? No gym today?`

He was such a control freak. He had to know everything, where I was, who I was with. I hated him. Tears welled up in my eyes. Tears of anger and frustration but also fear. I could pack a bag and run. I could make an excuse and break things off before anything happened. I could even pretend he wasn't the one and carry on dating him. I snorted at that thought, but the point was, I had a choice. I'd tried to give his name to Emmerson, but I didn't try hard enough. I couldn't blame her.

Her mind was elsewhere. Concentrating on bringing new life into the world, where I was planning to end one. I had to stay strong. Hold onto my anger. He was a monster and he was going to pay. He would be held accountable for what he did to Sophie and the others. I would be the one to do it.

I lay down, running over how I thought things would go tomorrow, again and again. What if this happens? What if he does that? Every possibility thought out. One thing was for sure, if anyone walked out of that flat tomorrow, it wouldn't be him.

52

FRIDAY 26 JANUARY 2018

Ben didn't stand a chance when I knocked on his door in the middle of the night. My mind set on fulfilling a need for comfort, so strong I'd given up with reason. He'd arrived home drunk, crashing through the front door and stumbling into his room. Rousing me from the sofa where I'd dozed off, still clutching the bottle of gin, television playing in the background. I'd waited a few minutes before going to his room. He stood, half dressed, in the doorway, bathed in red light from his lamp. Interrupted as he got ready for bed.

Puffy eyes and cheeks hot, I chewed at my thumbnail, anticipating the forthcoming rejection.

'Are you okay?' he asked, swaying slightly.

I wrapped my arms around his waist and pressed myself against his cold body, nuzzling my head into his chest. His breathing shallowed and I felt a stirring in his groin.

Ben pulled away, as I thought he would. Before he could object, I rose onto my tiptoes and pushed my lips against his. Softly at first but then with urgency. After a few seconds he wrestled me away, holding me at arm's length.

'Eve?' I knew he was thinking 'what about Amy?' but I didn't give a shit about her. I needed him, there in that moment. He had to know how I felt in case this was our last chance. I was tired of hiding it anyway. I forced my lips back upon his, daring him to stop me, but he didn't.

Later, I woke as the sun prised its way through the curtains. Ben snoring beside me and my head pounding, hangover in full swing. I desperately needed the toilet and a drink. Had I been chewing sandpaper last night? Creeping out of bed, I slipped on my pyjamas. Pausing to take in the fleece material. To think I'd worn those as an outfit for seduction. I tiptoed out of Ben's room, easing his door closed so as not to disturb him. I had no idea what this meant for us. No words had been spoken. For all I knew Ben would wake, distraught at the terrible mistake he'd made. I didn't want to wait to see that look in his eyes. To see him choose her over me.

53

SUNDAY 28 JANUARY 2018

I'm taken back to my cell, my interview with the detectives concluded. This must be it now, the questioning finally over. I'm itching for a cigarette and knowing I can't have one is making me irritable. No one has so much as glanced through my viewing hatch in ages. I think it must be a handover of staff, the changing of shifts. The van will be on its way to pick me up.

I sit, jiggling my legs and chewing what is left of my thumbnail. How did it go so wrong? I want to be at home, reunited with Ben. At least he has Amy and I know he will look after the flat for me. I trust him to take care of things while I'm gone. Will I get bail? Will I be allowed home before the trial? Surely not on a murder charge; I don't hold out much hope. Although it's possible, I have no previous record. I can't think about it now; my mind is consumed with thoughts of spending the night in prison.

I am in danger of bringing up the bolognaise. My stomach is tightly wound like a spring and I'm assaulted by repeated hot flushes. Ridiculous, given the icy temperature of the cell. My solicitor is right. I have to plead not guilty and stick with self-defence. I may still be able to walk away from this nightmare. Could I afford a proper solicitor, one that is likely to be able to get me off? Or do I stick with my Candy Crush-playing freebie? Can you put a price on freedom? My brain is overloaded. I could do with some more sleep as I got so little last night, but I am too wired to nap. Dreading the knock on the door, coming any minute. My gaoler leading me away. I heave, unable to hold onto my dinner any longer and just make it to the metal toilet before spraying the bowl with half digested pasta. The acrid smell wafts from the pan. I'm in hell.

54

SATURDAY 27 JANUARY 2018

Feeling awkward, I didn't want to be in the flat when Ben woke, plus there was something I needed to do. I threw on some running gear, grabbed my debit card and phone and headed out into the morning sun. The air was crisp, but there was no frost on the ground. I was so desperate to feel something, anything. It led me to Ben's door last night and into his bed. I didn't give him a chance to say no or push me away. I wanted to erase every touch of Ian's and replace it with Ben's. I wanted my body to know Ben's hands on its skin, to remove the imprint Ian had left last year.

A guilty weight thudded in my stomach as I ran. I'd been weak, selfish even. The boy I loved belonged to someone else, Jane was going to be gone for a long time and Mum was starting a new life with another man. I allowed myself a moment to wallow and think about what could have been. How my life could have been different if I'd never been in the park that morning? If I'd realised how I felt about Ben before it was too late? If I'd tried harder to help my mother.

With a heavy heart, I threw my iPhone into the bin

furthest from the flat before looping back on myself. I'd restored factory settings before I left the house, but I couldn't be sure the PetCam app had truly been deleted. I knew some data could remain, but I thought it would be on the hardware not on the SIM. It was the only way to be sure. On my way back, I stopped off at Carphone Warehouse on the high street and purchased the cheapest android smartphone they sold. I put my old SIM back in and hoped I'd get the hang of how to use it quickly. I walked back from the shop, playing with the new device. Checking my texts, photos and browsing history for anything untoward. I was hoping there wouldn't be a desire to look too hard.

When I returned home, Ben was still snoring, and I lay on my bed, hopeful for a few more hours sleep. All my emotions put away in the box marked 'for later' in my head. I had nothing to lose. I was going to even the scales of justice, or I would die trying.

* * *

Around midday there was a knock at the front door. Ben still hadn't emerged, so I answered it. I hadn't showered since my run and looked a mess. Amy stood in the doorway beaming, clutching a dry-cleaning bag, her face falling instantly when she saw it was me.

'Is Ben in? His phone is switched off,' she said curtly.

'I believe so,' I replied, moving to let her pass.

She knocked quietly on his bedroom door before letting herself in and closing it behind her. I hung around in the kitchen and made myself a sandwich, praying he wasn't inside telling her what we'd been up to last night. After around ten minutes of pacing, they both came out. Ben looked dishevelled, Amy complaining how much he stunk of booze as she entered the kitchen and flicked on the kettle.

'You need a coffee. We've got that wedding in a few hours and you need to get ready,' she said brightly, tipping granules into a mug.

Ben and I exchanged a look as her back was turned. His eyes wide and panicked, like a deer caught in headlights just before it hits the windscreen. I sighed inwardly, relieved he hadn't said anything but also disappointed too. His eyes searched mine. I had to give him an out. Let him off the hook. I smiled and gave the tiniest shake of my head, trying to convey the message that it was okay, I understood. Then I retreated to my room. I had no time to waste feeling nostalgic. I had to focus on the evening ahead. I knew what had to be done and I had to follow through.

I spent ages trying to get my winged eyeliner just right, my eyes watering from the contacts. I wasn't sure why, but it felt like armour. Wearing my war paint, I was going into battle. Getting the line straight was tricky because my hands were shaking. Even a shot of gin didn't help to steady them. Dressed in dark skinny jeans, biker boots and a cream silk camisole with spaghetti straps, I looked tiny. Perhaps even fragile. I'd lost definition in my shoulders since I'd stopped boxing and my bones protruded. Too much skin? Maybe, considering how thin I was. However, the shade was perfect against my pallor and platinum blonde hair. I was channelling Stephen King's Carrie. Dark roots were just beginning to peak through, it had been six weeks since I'd had them done and they enhanced my rock chick look.

I packed away Ben's necklace back in the gift box and slid it into my drawer. I didn't want to risk it getting damaged or having to explain its meaning. I repacked my bag twice, considering each item and double-checking everything. All my planning and training had been for tonight, but I still didn't feel ready.

I had another gin, reciting the telephone number I needed repeatedly. I couldn't forget it. It might just save my life later. Time was slipping away, and I had to leave soon if I didn't want to be late to meet Ian. I'm sure he wouldn't appreciate being kept waiting. I didn't really care but I didn't want to start the evening on the wrong foot. I wanted him onside for as long as possible.

The flat was empty when I left. I'd made sure everything was tidy and in its place. All my affairs in order. My footsteps weighed heavy on the walk into town. It was dark, cold, but dry at least. The streets were buzzing. Groups of people lined the pavements ready to hit the pubs. It was Saturday night after all, payday weekend for some. For the first time, I felt at ease walking alone. Too preoccupied with plans for later to worry about feeling vulnerable.

After tonight I would be able to close the door on this and start over. Get another job, try and find something I wanted to do. I wanted to fall in love, settle down. I was halfway there already. I hoped to be able to look back and be proud of what I'd achieved, not dwell on how I'd fucked everything up. After tonight I'd be something, a hero and a villain combined, but already I was out of my depth. Hadn't it been play acting until now? When push came to shove, could I really do it?

Ian stood outside Mangos waiting for me. He looked sharp in jeans, shirt and a blazer, raising his eyebrows as I approached.

'Wow, you look...' He was lost for words.

'Scary?' I asked, stifling a laugh. Perhaps my eyeliner was more goth than rock chick. I smoothed down my hair.

'No. I was thinking sexy, but not sure whether it was a bit creepy to say it?' We were way beyond creepy by that point. He bent to kiss me, and I assumed he was going for my cheek. Instead he pulled me into a full embrace, right outside Mangos. It was too public for me and I eased away, which seemed to amuse rather than irritate him. 'What are you drinking?' he shouted above the music as we made our way to the bar.

'Gin and tonic for me please,' I shouted back. I'd already had a shot but had become quite tolerant of gin in the past few weeks. Perhaps I was more like my mother than I thought?. However, I had to keep my wits about me so would be keeping an eye on my alcohol consumption.

Ian ordered our drinks and we retreated to the same table we'd sat at on our first date. I slipped off my leather jacket and watched Ian's eyes widen. I'd never normally show this much skin, although it seemed to be having the desired effect. Ian's gaze lingered on my neck a touch longer than was necessary and my shoulders stiffened. He launched into the tale of his team winning their rugby game that morning. His mate had dislocated his knee towards the end and they'd spent most of the afternoon in A&E. I tried to focus on his words, looking at his mouth to avoid his eyes. Paranoid he would know what I was thinking, or worse, what I was planning? I couldn't stop fidgeting.

'Are you okay? You seem nervous.'

What the hell, I might as well be honest. 'I am, a bit,' I said, my cheeks glowing pink.

'Why would you be nervous?' he said, leaning back in his chair. I knew he found me amusing, quirky even. He was cool and collected and I was this bumbling naive girl. He was in control and he liked it.

'I haven't, you know, seen anyone in a long time,' I said. Trying my best to appear shy rather than apprehensive of what was to come.

'Come here.' Grabbing the seat of my stool, he pulled it across the wooden floor towards him with ease. Resting his hand on my back, goosebumps appeared beneath his palm. It was good that fear and excitement could have the same physical effects on the body. I had that in my favour. Ian assumed I was putty in his hands. His arrogance gave it away. I wasn't sure if I was being courted or groomed? He stroked my back, his thumb rubbing the feather tattoo that Ben's lips had been on last night. It made me squirm. 'I'm not going to hurt you,' he said, kissing the side of my head. Little did he know, he already had. But I would be getting my own back later.

We sat side by side with Ian's fingers caressing my skin until we finished our drinks and he suggested we move on to the restaurant. I climbed down from the stool and Ian held out my jacket to slip on. Mangos was full of revellers; I hadn't notice it get so crowded. As Ian led me toward the door, he reached back and caught my hand, entwining his fingers in mine so as not to lose me. Or maybe he thought he owned me already? Outside, the temperature had dropped and I kept my head down as we hurried along, into the wind.

'Eve?'

I lifted my head. Ben stood in front of us, blocking the pavement, a quizzical expression on his face. He caught sight of our interlocked hands. My fingers slackened, but Ian held my fingers in a vice-like grip. He wasn't letting go.

* * *

Sunday 28 January 2018 – DC Becker

I grab a coffee from the machine and ring the childminder to see if Lily is still being clingy; but no, of course not, today she is fine. She's an angel with anyone who isn't me. Sometimes it feels like a vendetta, but that's the sleep deprivation talking. It's impossible to grasp that someone who relies on you so much, someone you adore, can be so awful. Steve is concerned its post-natal depression, but I'm sure it's not. Motherhood is just hard, right? For everyone?

Back at my desk, I pick up the map and shake my head to refocus. So, Eve isn't all she seems. I hate that Hicks gets these hunches, this sixth sense, that bypasses me. Is it his years of experience, he's been in the force since he was eighteen, or is being a copper not what I was destined for? Too late for a change of career now, almost ten years in.

Was Ian Eve's attacker last year? I have to give it to her, if it's true, she's smart. If I wanted to track someone down, I'd go back to the scene of the crime and wait for them to show up. People's habits are what get them caught. We all have a pattern of behaviour that's inherently hard to deviate from. Things we say and do, the places we frequent. But, if that's the case, how did he not recognise her?

I read the original report again and sift through the mess of my desk until I find the newspaper Guy gave me earlier. Eve has long mousy brown hair in the photo they've printed, a stark contrast to the platinum blonde she is today. I find it hard to believe that changing her hair would make her unrecognisable to him, although on reverting back to the notes, most of the sexual assault took place from behind, the initial jump and the act itself.

Does this prove Ian's death was premeditated? The closest

CCTV in the area is from the gym; the one where Ian and Eve apparently met. It yielded no results before, but I message Guy to see if he can get more recent footage and give him the dates. He's been running around all over the place for me today. I must remember to say thank you. He's done so much of the groundwork and with Hicks retiring we'll need another permanent member of the team.

When Guy responds, I ask to see the days Eve was camped out in the area, according to the mobile phone triangulation, up until the day she became a member at the gym. I tell him the beers are on me on Friday night.

Within twenty minutes, a message is in my inbox. I'm going to have to recommend his transfer is made permanent. He's too handy to let go. Hicks has been away from his desk for a while, most probably trying to find another way to prove Eve's intentions. Time is running out.

I take my hair out of the bun, releasing the painful hairgrips and give my scalp a rub. I can't help but enjoy the sensation of knowing something he doesn't. The camera at the door of the gym covers around ten feet and is motion-activated; picking up all the customers who enter or exit. It's easy to whiz through images of a twenty-four-hour period and watch the comings and goings. I spot Ian early on. His visits are regular, same times on the same days, but I can't find anyone that looks like Eve.

I check the day she registered, then I find her. She arrives at the gym late in the afternoon. Ian had been in earlier that day too and I scroll back to see him entering at around quarter past ten. I rewind it back to watch again, but my finger slips on the mouse and pushes the timer further back. I catch a glimpse of a figure on the periphery of the screen. She looks up towards the camera before swiftly turning away out of shot. On the screen for maybe two seconds at most. The back of my neck prickles and the fluttering develops into giant swoops in my stomach. I slow the video down, holding my breath. Twenty or so seconds after Ian enters the gym, I freeze the video and it stutters. Eve's grey image nods at me in agreement, eyes wide and lips parted. She doesn't look vengeful. She looks terrified.

I hear footsteps come down the corridor and close the video down, rushing to the toilets to be alone. I lean over the sink, staring at my reflection, inhaling deeply. The blood has drained from my face. The initial elation of my findings dissipated as the stretch of skin on my inner thigh burns incandescent. The memory of a cigarette end pushed into my flesh all those years ago. A reminder of why it is hard to see women like Eve dragged through the system. Victims whose assailants are never caught. Did she take matters into her own hands? Would I? If I could go back?

55

SATURDAY 27 JANUARY 2018

'Ben! It's been years, how are you, mate?' Ian stuck out his free hand towards Ben, who looked shell-shocked; still trying to connect the dots. I was pleased I could blame the cold wind for the colour of my face. How on earth did Ian know Ben? They couldn't be more different if they tried. My stomach knotted.

'I'm good, thanks, I hope you're treating my flatmate well?' Ben said. I saw his body stiffen, but he shook Ian's hand, glaring at me with a 'what the fuck' expression.

'Of course, you know me. I didn't know you two lived together?'

'It's a small world,' I chipped in, adding, 'I thought you were at a wedding?'

'Amy was sick, so we left after the service.'

'How do you two know each other?' I asked.

Ben continued to frown at me.

'We used to do door work together. Good times, good times.' Ian chuckled nostalgically before glancing at his watch. 'Anyway, we've got a reservation. I'm sure I'll see you around, Ben.'

'I'm sure. You'll have to come for beers,' Ben replied in a blokey tone that was out of character. Was he being sarcastic? If he was, Ian didn't seem to notice. He pulled me away, his hand still clenched around mine and swept me along the street to La Casa. My stomach was in knots, the furthest thing from my mind was food. I wanted to break free of Ian and run back towards Ben; to explain what was going on. But I didn't dare look back.

Before I knew it, Ian had led me inside the restaurant, the warm air a welcome relief. The décor was modern but dimly lit, giving the illusion of privacy even though you were feet away from another table. I couldn't get the image of Ben's face out of my mind. He looked horrified. I had to get my head back in the game. I couldn't focus on that now. Ian gave his name to the hostess and she seated us near the back of the restaurant. I slipped off my jacket and our waitress came over to give us menus.

'Can I get you anything to drink?' She beamed at us, her shift must have just started.

'Can we have a bottle of the Catena Alta Malbec please?' Ian asked. 'Do you drink red wine?' The question directed at me was an afterthought.

'I'll give it a go,' I said, smiling at the waitress. 'Could we have some water too, please?'

She nodded and stepped away, returning in less than a minute with a jug and two small glasses.

'Sorry, I should have got you a gin, I wasn't thinking. It's been a long week and I fancied a bottle of red wine.' He leant across the table and took my hand. I still couldn't get used to him touching me. He did it a lot. I'm sure he thought I was a bit stiff, or maybe a prude. Perhaps he enjoyed a challenge and wanted to warm me up?

'Trouble at work?' I asked as the waitress returned and uncorked the bottle, leaving it on the table to breathe. I knew almost nothing about red wine. Every time I'd been offered a glass, it tasted like vinegar to me. Tonight was all about Ian and getting him into the right frame of mind so I was happy to go with the flow. I'd noticed, when we were seated, there was a large pot plant to my left which would come in handy later.

'You know, trouble with clients again. One of the ad execs double-booked space we'd secured in a glossy magazine. Another client lost the plot as there was a typo in their advert that no one picked up on.'

'Sounds stressful.'

'It can be. I just have to find ways to relax.' He stroked my fingers and my flesh crawled as though insects were running beneath my skin. I smiled sweetly though, this was going in the right direction.

'How do you do that?' I purred. Although I already knew the answer. He went out, stalked and attacked women for his own perverse pleasure.

'I may show you later.' He looked like he wanted to have me for dinner. I bit my lip.

'You haven't got a dungeon hidden away in that apartment of yours?' I asked, trying to lighten the mood.

'AKA Christian Grey, you mean?' He raised one eyebrow and for a moment he looked charming.

'That's the one.'

He chuckled but didn't answer. The waitress returned, but I hadn't even looked at the menu. I opened it to make my choice, but Ian got there first.

'We'll have the steak please, both medium rare with peppercorn sauce on the side.' He snapped his menu shut and I handed mine over to the waitress. We exchanged a quick look. I could tell we were thinking the same thing. Why was I having dinner with such a pompous prick? No woman likes having her choice made for her. It's not romantic; it's controlling, but she didn't know I was just playing along. For now anyway.

'What would you like with it, chips, jacket potato or salad? Any other sides?'

'Chips I think, Eve?' Now he wanted my opinion?

'Yes, chips please.'

The waitress nodded and left. What was it with men and steak anyway? Why come to an Italian restaurant and order steak? I wanted the spaghetti carbonara, the thought of creamy sauce and pancetta with a dough ball starter made my mouth water. I should have intervened; it could be my last meal. Counting to ten in my head, and then on to fifteen, I took a sip of the wine Ian had deemed ready to pour. Surprised at how smooth it was, I had not tasted red wine like this. It must be expensive.

'Good, isn't it,' he said with a wink.

'It is.' I would have to pace myself, but the more pliable Ian was the better.

'Have you heard about the attacks?' he said. My glass was half raised to my mouth, suspended in mid-air. Ian took my pause as interest. 'I was reading in the paper. Women, walking on their own, getting jumped in broad daylight.'

Out of the corner of my eye, I saw my glass wobble in my hand. I took a large mouthful and lowered it carefully to the table. Was he fucking with me?

'Robbed?' I asked, playing the game.

'Assaulted. Sexually assaulted.' The look on his face and the pitying shake of his head made my stomach burn.

I sat on my hands to stop myself throwing the wine at him. Although I couldn't control my mouth.

'What sad pathetic man does that to a woman?' I asked.

Ian coughed, choking on his wine and stifling a laugh. 'One that can't get a woman any other way I should imagine,' he said.

I took a large gulp of my drink and jumped up, catching the table as I went. Struggling to keep it together. 'Excuse me, I'm going to use the ladies.'

I marched through the door and up the stairs two at a time. Shit. What the fuck was that? Was he goading me? I balled my hands into fists and paced in front of the sinks. Had I got it wrong? Had I made a massive mistake? My mind raced, and I locked myself in a cubicle. I was so furious, I'd forgotten to take my bag. It was on the floor by my chair. Would he go through it? There was nothing of interest in it to him, but I was annoyed I'd left my phone and couldn't text Ben. The look he'd given me was cutting. What must he think of me?

I sat on the toilet, blinking back tears of rage, my blood bubbling beneath the surface. Ian deserved everything he was going to get. I didn't care if he knew who I was. I didn't care if he was fucking with me. I was going to enjoy every minute of this.

56

SUNDAY 28 JANUARY 2018 – DC BECKER

I exit the toilets; using my wet hands to cool the back of my neck as I make my way down the corridor. Guy is coming from the opposite direction, striding briskly, and I feign a weak smile.

'Transport is around half an hour away,' he says as he whisks past. I'm glad he doesn't stop. The headache I was trying hard to keep at bay has broken through the surface and feels like a relentless woodpecker at my temple.

'Thanks, Guy, you've been great today. I'm going to recommend you join the team permanently,' I call over my shoulder.

Hicks is back at his desk, waiting for me to return and jiggling his leg up and down like an impatient child. 'You okay?' he asks.

I nod and take a seat, steeling myself to reveal the new information that could prove Eve's actions were premeditated.

Hicks whistles and runs his palm across his stubble. His frustration evident, but before I can speak he jumps out of his seat. 'Did Guy catch you? She's getting picked up shortly,' he begins pacing, 'and I don't know what else I can throw at her.' I've never seen him so agitated.

'Maybe, you've just got to let it go, Hicks,' I offer, searching his eyes for a sliver of understanding or empathy.

'I can't let her win.' He slams his hand down onto the desk making me jump.

'It isn't about winning. She's lost too. Eve Harding is going to prison; isn't that enough?'

Hicks narrows his eyes at me, indignant because I don't understand why he's so upset. He's right, I don't. Is it because she's got one over on him? Compounded by the fact she's female? What does it matter? It isn't a game. Eve's been shafted by the system that was supposed to protect her. If Ian was her attacker, and Alice's too, there may be countless others we haven't connected him to yet. Maybe he got what he deserved?

Hicks huffs and turns back to his computer, hammering his mouse loudly and he thunders through the online file.

'There must be something,' he mutters.

I grit my teeth and turn back to my screen. My mouse hovers over the delete button, my brain whirring. What would a jury do? I can imagine how a prosecutor would tear her apart on the stand. She'd be sent to prison for the rest of her life. Maybe it's time for a change of career after all? I delete the email from James and the CCTV from Guy, then empty the deleted folder.

'Our time's up on this one. She's practically out of the door. It's in the hands of the CPS now. All we can do is build the case to secure a conviction.'

'She'll be out in four years, or roll over on a suspended sentence,' Hicks snaps without bothering to turn round.

I smile and breathe a sigh of relief. I'm counting on it.

* * *

Saturday 27 January 2018

When I returned to the table, composed and focus intact, my steak was waiting. Ian was measuring the cleanliness of his fork. I could see he didn't like to be kept waiting and enjoyed the flicker of irritation in his eyes as I took my seat. He was trying hard to control it.

'I'm sorry, there was a queue,' I said, rolling my eyes for effect.

He smiled, lips pressed tightly together and picked up his knife and fork. He could have started without me, but good manners, the gentleman in him, didn't permit it. The different sides to Ian were extreme. It was odd. I'd read somewhere that most sexual assaults were more about power than carnal desire. He fitted that theory; he was an obvious control freak.

'What are you thinking?' he asked.

I was holding my knife and fork mid-air but hadn't attempted to cut my steak yet.

'Oh nothing. How's your steak?' I cut a slice and popped it into my mouth. It wasn't a spaghetti carbonara, but it was melt in the mouth tender. My taste buds kicked into gear and hunger pangs niggled my sides.

'Fantastic, don't you think?'

I nodded, my mouth full. The plate had been delivered with the sauce on the side as requested and chunky chips. I forgot myself for a second and dived in, as he watched on in amusement.

'How long have you lived with Ben?'

Hearing his name made my steak hard to swallow. I sipped my wine to help it go down.

'Not long, a few months. I don't know him that well. He works nights, so I don't see him much.' I was babbling, trying to remove Ben as far as I could from the situation.

'The best kind of lodger then.' Ian seemed content with my response.

'What about you? I know you said your dad lives in Oxford, but do you have any other family nearby?' I poured more wine into Ian's near empty glass and topped mine up. He was on his third glass already.

'No, my mother passed away when I was six.' He took another mouthful of wine and I momentarily felt sorry for him. Until I remembered what he'd done to me and the other women whose lives he'd destroyed.

'I'm so sorry, Ian.'

'It was a long time ago and I'm an only child, like you, so no family here.' He forked the last slice of steak into his mouth. 'Would you excuse me?' he said a minute later, standing and placing his napkin on his plate. He disappeared through the door to use the bathroom upstairs.

Glancing around at the surrounding tables: one couple were deep in conversation and the second were feeding each other dessert. There was a man sat alone, at the table closest to us, eyes down as he scrolled on his mobile phone. Confident I wouldn't be seen, I causally tipped my wine into the plant pot. The rest of the bottle, I poured into Ian's glass. The waitress who was passing stopped to ask if I would like another? Hesitating, I didn't know what to do. Yes, I wanted another bottle. I wanted Ian well lubricated for when we got back to his. Would it upset him if I ordered another one without asking him first? To hell with it. What was he going to do, punish me? I agreed and before Ian had returned a full bottle sat on our table and I was still trying to finish my steak.

'You eat like a bird,' he mused when he came back.

Knowing he was watching made finishing my meal even harder. I managed three quarters of the steak and half the chips, which were cold by then, and was full. My stomach churned with the combination of food and nerves. It would be a miracle if I kept anything down tonight.

'Do you fancy dessert?' he asked, as the waitress cleared our plates away, returning with a menu. What was the right answer? I didn't want anything, but would he be annoyed? Would our meal be cut short? I didn't want to go back to his any sooner than I had to. Although I was only postponing the inevitable.

'I don't think so,' I said, perusing the dessert menu. Out of the corner of my eye, I saw him lift the bottle, frowning at the weight, and pour us both another glass of wine.

'I ordered another, I hope you don't mind?' I stretched my hand across the table and laid it on top of his. The feel of his skin made me squirm.

'Of course not,' he replied, gifting me an easy smile.

The waitress returned but I declined dessert. Ian chose a cheese board and I was pleased I'd had a reprieve in the restaurant for a bit longer.

I was eager to text Ben. He'd been playing on my mind, I had to try and explain. I didn't know when I'd get to see him again after tonight.

'Would you mind if I went for a cigarette?' I wasn't sure why I was asking, I was going regardless of what he said. The role of subdued Eve was becoming a bit of a habit and I didn't like her one bit.

Ian raised his eyebrows, the corners of his mouth twitching. 'You never said you smoked?'

I was expecting a lecture, but it never came.

'Only socially. When I have a drink.'

'I'll join you.' My heart sank, texting Ben would have to wait.

Ian popped to the front of the restaurant to advise the hostess we were leaving the table to go for a cigarette. I used the seconds he had his back turned to pour my half-full glass of wine into the plant pot. As he returned, I raised the glass to my lips to sip the drops that remained. I slipped my phone back into my bag, no point in taking it with me.

'They've got a balcony out the back, upstairs.' He held the door open for me and as we reached the door to the balcony I cursed not taking my jacket. It was freezing and the thin material of my camisole clung to my body. Ian had left his blazer downstairs too. He gasped as we emerged into the icy air and we huddled in the corner to light our cigarettes. 'You look beautiful tonight,' he said, lacing his finger through the spaghetti strap of my top. It made me shiver, though it was masked by the cold. I swallowed the lump that had formed in my throat.

'I'm not the sort of girl you would normally take out, am I?'

'What makes you say that?'

'I don't know. I get the impression I'm not really your type.'

Ian stared at me, his chin jutting upwards. Cupping my cheek, he guided my face towards his. Penetrating me with his stare. I wanted to shrink back, to run. I avoided looking in those eyes for fear he would see who I really was. Forget the hair and the contacts, I was sure he would see straight through me and the damage he'd left behind. 'You are perfect,' he whispered.

Before I could react, his mouth was on mine. He tasted of red wine and smoke. His hand found the curve of my behind, pulling me towards him. I knew he was excited as he leant in to kiss my neck. My head whirled, his words echoing in my mind. I couldn't move. Bare shoulders pressed against the brickwork took me straight back to that morning. He pulled away. Looking me up and down as I leaned against the wall for support, catching my breath, he began to laugh.

57

SUNDAY 28 JANUARY 2018

I didn't have long to wait, and I'm surprised to feel relieved when the door finally opens. No point trying to put off the inevitable. The floor of the cell seems to shrink by the hour. The walls close in on me. The acidic smell of my vomit has settled in my nose and I can barely breathe in here. A man in uniform that I haven't seen before stands in the doorway. He's stocky with a shaven head and looks like he can handle himself. He won't have any fight from me.

'Eve Harding?' he asks flatly, and I nod as he checks his list and ticks me off. 'You'll now be taken to HMP Downview where you'll be remanded in custody. You'll have the opportunity to speak with your solicitor again when you arrive. You're in luck, it's only fifteen minutes in the van, so it won't take us long.'

My stomach gurgles and I feel the urge to go to the toilet. I can't hide my terror. I've been so naive. How did I not see this would happen?

I am handcuffed before we leave. It's such a strange sensation to be shackled. Metal cuffs drown my tiny wrists. They are heavy, pulling on my arms which hang limp in front of me.

Once the paperwork is completed at the desk, I'm led onto the van. I snatch a glimpse of grey sky and suck in a lungful of air before it is gone. The freshest I may have for a while. Inside the van, I'm locked in a small cubicle which feels like an upright coffin. It's claustrophobic. The inside like a public toilet, with a seat instead of a pan, but much more confined. There's barely enough room to move. No gaps beneath the doors either. The familiar smell of urine comforts me like an old friend.

I gaze out of the small tinted window as the engine starts and we bump along the road. Driving past places I recognise. It's surreal. My jaw aches from grinding my teeth. It's been constant since my arrest and I have little control over the compulsion. I start again, wringing my hands, unsure what is ahead of me. How will I cope? I've heard stories of beatings and abuse in prisons and the unknown makes me feel sick. Tubes constricting, sharp shooting pains in my chest hindering the ability to breathe. I tell myself it's just another panic attack, but there is no room in my cubicle to lower my head to my knees. I close my eyes to ride it out. My body sways with the motion of the van. The fight has left me. I've lost.

* * *

Saturday 27 January 2018

'I'm sorry, I got carried away,' he said, licking his lips and taking another cigarette out of the packet I was holding. We'd dropped the first ones and they had burnt out at our feet.

We smoked in silence for a minute.

'Do you want to come back to mine? We can have a drink there?' he said, his bottom lip jutting out ever so slightly.

'Sure,' I replied. Relieved that the invitation had been extended and I wouldn't have to suggest it myself. It came with a plummeting feeling down to my ankles that I had signed my own death warrant.

Back at the table, Ian's cheese board had arrived, and he took pleasure in feeding me different types as I sipped the Malbec. I was a bit light-headed since we'd returned into the warm. Ian was on his fifth glass and was beginning to slur slightly.

I tried to go halves when Ian asked for the bill, but he would not hear of it.

'Thank you, it was lovely.' I leant across the table to give him a quick peck on the lips.

He slid his foot up my calf under the table and winked at me, leaving me cold.

'You're welcome.'

I wobbled as I stood from the table, Ian wrapped an arm around my waist to steady me.

'Ready to stumble home?'

I nodded, happy to let my nerves be confused with inebriation. We exited the restaurant onto the street. The bitter air a shock after being indoors.

'You know what I fancy?' I said, and Ian smirked.

'Do tell.'

'A gin and tonic,' I replied. I didn't want one in the slightest, but it was all part of the plan.

'I have gin.'

'Ah, but do you have lemons?'

He grimaced and pushed me towards the door of Tesco Express. 'If the lady wants lemons, lemons she will have.'

A few minutes later we continued our journey, a shopping bag swinging from Ian's hand. I couldn't believe the time, noticing as we left the store that it was almost eleven. Where had the evening gone? It seemed to have flown by. My legs were heavy. Dread weighed in the pit of my stomach like a bowling ball. I was sinking in it. Turning into his road, I had to fight the urge to run. Thankfully Ian was mid-conversation, airing his annoyance that people parked on grass verges. He hadn't noticed me slowing my pace. I could do this. I would do this. Now was the time to focus.

We'd barely made it inside the door when Ian pushed me against the wall in a passionate embrace. I hadn't expected it to happen so fast and my knees buckled underneath my weight.

'I've been dying to get you here all night.' Did his tone sound sinister or had I imagined it?

I squeaked and wriggled out of his grasp. He stepped back, lip curled. Did he think I was being a tease?

'Gin,' I slurred, pushing him towards the kitchen and slipping out of my boots. Alcohol would be my excuse.

As soon as he was out of the room, I dived for the camera, still hidden in the bookcase. A thin layer of dust coated the top and I was satisfied it hadn't been found. I unplugged the small device and slipped it into my handbag. The lead I discarded on the floor, hidden behind the plant pot.

I took off my jacket and joined Ian in the kitchen, leaning on the door frame. I watched him stumble around, it was like he was in slow motion.

'I think we may have had too much wine,' he said, reading

my mind and pausing to grin at me. He took a tray out of a cupboard and placed two glass tumblers on it.

Whilst he was occupied, I returned to the front room. Underneath the low coffee table was the metal box still there from my last visit and I knelt to pick it up. All the time straining my ears to listen, sounds of the fridge opening and shutting carried from the kitchen.

'Fuck,' Ian yelled, and I jumped, banging my wrist on the table.

'You okay?' I called, praying I wasn't about to be discovered.

'Yep, cut my finger that's all.' I heard him mutter. 'Fucking lemons.'

I lifted the lid of the box and froze. The balaclava stared out at me accusingly, eyes slashed. I tried to move, but I was rigid, unable to take my eyes off the black woollen mask. If I wanted proof that Ian was a monster, here it was. I tried to stand, to run, but my joints locked. I was paralysed.

'Eve,' Ian called.

My heart was in my mouth. I moved my lips to speak but nothing came out. I didn't have enough time. Any second now he would poke his head around the door and I would be found knee deep in his box of tricks. Game over.

'Eve!' Ian shouted.

Forcing my legs to work, I clambered up, tipping the contents of the box into my handbag and slipping it back under the table. In the kitchen, Ian was by the sink, holding his thumb under the tap. The water diluted the blood that dripped onto the steel below.

'Shit, I didn't realise it was so bad.'

'It's not, but can you grab me some kitchen towel? There's plasters in the drawer, I think.'

I ripped a few sheets off the roll and held them out to Ian. Saving a sheet for myself to open the drawer. It was a mess, a mixture of phone chargers, batteries, measuring tape, tealights and matches. The plasters were at the back. I grabbed one, peeling the film off as he held his hand out to me. Blood was still oozing from his finger. I cringed for a second but successfully wrapped two plasters around his thumb. Hoping that would stop the bleeding. Then I rinsed the knife and placed it back on the tray.

'Thanks,' he said, leaning in for a kiss. My throat constricted.

I can't do this. I really can't do this. Faced with the reality I couldn't believe I ever thought I could. I needed to get some air. My chest was wound tight like a spring.

'Let me carry this in.' I picked up the tray and carried it to the coffee table. Before slicing his finger, Ian had filled the tray with almost everything we needed to mix our gin and tonics.

'I'll get the ice,' he called from the kitchen.

'I'm just going to use the bathroom,' I called back. He wouldn't check the box, would he? There was nothing I could do. I scooped my bag from where I'd left it and locked the door behind me. Sitting on the toilet, my chest felt like it was in a vice, slowly compressing. I tried to concentrate but my head swam. I needed to get out of here. No, I had to stick to the plan. I put my head between my knees, gasping for air. I couldn't breathe.

'Eve, are you all right in there?' Ian was the other side of the door.

'I'm okay, I just feel a bit sick. I'll be out in a minute. I think it was the blood,' I added, listening for sounds as the room spun. I grabbed the towel rail to steady myself.

'Do you want to get some air?'

Yes, air was exactly what I needed. The outside. Where I could run.

The balaclava had made it real. This was not a game. I was in serious danger.

'Good idea. Just a second.' The panic attack passed as air forced its way into my lungs and blood returned to my head. I needed to get rid of what was in my bag. I turned on the tap, hoping the noise would cover me. Pins and needles in my fingers hindered me as I put the contents of Ian's box in the black carrier bag I'd brought with me. I moved as fast as I could. It was a complete rape kit. As well as the balaclava, there were cable ties, duct tape, a rag, and a small vial of liquid. The label read gamma hydroxybutrate. It meant nothing to me, but I had an idea of what it was. Perhaps I could use it. Tucking it into my back pocket, I tied the bag, trying to be as quiet as possible. Ian's bathroom window squeaked as the metal bar lifted out of its resting place. I winced and froze, listening for sounds from the other side of the door. Nothing. I couldn't hear Ian at all.

Beneath the window, at the base of the building grew dense bushes. I leant out and dropped the bag into the darkness. The wind carried it left, where it disappeared from view. I crushed the camera under my boot, the plastic casing splintering into pieces. The tap had already been running for too long, so I turned it off. Wrapping the shards in tissue, I flushed them down the toilet along with the tiny memory card.

I had to get rid of anything that tied me to Ian. Or rather, anything that gave me a motive to harm him. If they realised he was behind my rape in September, I'd no longer be a credible victim. Not one without a motive anyway. If it went badly,

I'd have evidence to give to the police. I'd concoct a story that I'd found it and got out of there, fearing for my life.

I wiped where I'd touched the window, ledge and sink with toilet wipes and spent a few seconds checking my reflection in the mirror. My face was pale, like porcelain, emphasised by the black eyeliner which didn't look as crisp as it did earlier. Steeling myself, I relaxed my shoulders, stretching my neck from side to side. I had a job to do.

58

MONDAY 29 JANUARY 2018

This is the longest night of my life. The wing is so quiet, you can hear a pin drop. I feel totally alone. I have no nails left, having bitten them down to the quick. Sleep will not come. It's dark, probably around three or four in the morning by now. My limbs ache and my eyelids are heavy but I'm too scared to close them.

On arriving at HMP Downview there was more paperwork to go through, so I could be processed. Followed by a short interview to determine whether I am suicidal. *Not quite.* Then I had to sit in a special chair which by some magic indicated whether I had anything hidden in a bodily cavity. As I sat, waiting to be examined, the officer snapped on some blue gloves and told me I wouldn't believe what people managed to shove inside them. It was gross and humiliating and that was even after the strip search.

I've been given an identity card with my own prisoner number and a breakfast pack. Apparently, I'm 'lucky', as I have my own cell. For the time being anyway. Right now, I wouldn't mind someone to talk to. Anything to stop my mind whirring.

I perch on the thin mattress that's stretched across my bunk, it smells musty and I don't want to touch it, let alone sleep on it. I'm terrified to move or make a sound. Every prison drama I've ever seen flashes before me. All the violence I've heard goes on. How safe am I in here? I've never felt so vulnerable. I'm going to be easy pickings. Or maybe not? When they find out what I'm charged with.

I can do this. One day at a time, small steps. I'll cope, I must. What choice do I have? This might not be it for me. Terry might be able to get me out. It's so hard knowing your fate is in another's hands. It's just a waiting game now. I'll talk to him later, see what my options are.

I know I did the right thing. Ian got everything he deserved. The streets of Sutton are a safer place and the world could do with one less misogynist. If I could go back, I'd do it again, in a heartbeat. My only regret is getting caught.

59

SATURDAY 27 JANUARY 2018

'There you are,' Ian said, patting the sofa next to him. Had I been too long? Was he suspicious?

I put my bag down and sat next to him. He looked drunk, his eyes were glazed, and he was leering at me. The drinks were already mixed, and I took a sip of mine. It was refreshing after the intensity of the red wine.

'Are you feeling okay?' he asked.

'A little light-headed. Can we get some air?' I said, standing and grabbing my handbag.

He looked first at me, then at the bag. 'You won't need that.'

'Cigarettes.' I shook the bag by way of explanation. Ian ignored me. I reached inside to pull out the pack. No matter, I could leave everything here. I could just run? Because I wasn't sure that, when push came to shove, even with how much I hated him, I'd be able to do it. Bravado aside, could I really kill a man?

'Where are you going?' he asked as I headed towards the front door.

I turned back to face him, frowning.

The corners of his mouth were turned up into a smirk.

'I've got a balcony.'

My heart plummeted. I wasn't getting out of here.

On the balcony, the wind whipped around us. The space was empty except for a pitiful solitary pot plant. Ian leaned over the railing to look below, his head disappearing from view.

I shuffled forward and reached out my hand. I could just about touch him. His shirt flapped in the wind, tickling my fingertips. Could I push him over the wrought-iron bars? I stared out into the blackness, watching the twinkling lights of the surrounding houses. A train chugged past, slowing down for the station. Ian pulled himself upright, turning to take the cigarette I'd lit for him. Unfortunately, he didn't live high enough for a fall to do any serious damage.

'Better?' he asked, pulling me close and nuzzling my neck. He smelt of red wine, smoke and a hint of citrus. The scent rooted me to the spot. I'd recognise it anywhere.

'Yes. Tired. I feel wiped out.' I'd made such a stupid mistake. I blinked back tears, grateful for the darkness. My insides squirmed.

'The night is still young,' he said matter-of-factly and steered me back inside. I wasn't going anywhere. Not until he got what he wanted. I knew that now. What had I got myself into? I was out of my depth.

Ian turned the television on, flicking through the films on offer until he chose an old thriller, *Donnie Brasco*. I'd not seen it for years.

'I'm sure I know you from somewhere,' he said suddenly, leaning forward to kiss me.

'No. I don't think so.' I managed a giggle but inside I was squirming.

His lips moved around to my neck and his hand to my breast. A voice whispered; *play the part, Eve, pretend it's Ben. You need him this close.*

I closed my eyes to shut in the tears and reached for Ian's face. Pulling it towards mine until our lips met. We shuffled down on the sofa, which creaked under our weight. His body, pinning me down, pushing his groin into mine. It was a mistake. I couldn't do it. I couldn't give myself to him. Not willingly, I just couldn't. He'd have to kill me first.

'Hold that thought,' he said, jumping up and heading to a door off the lounge. His bedroom. Did I have time to escape?

I sat up, my mind raced. No, I wasn't going to run. If I did then he wouldn't get what he deserved. I wrestled the small vial of liquid out of my back pocket and put the tiniest drop into my drink. Wiping the bottle with my camisole to remove my prints, I pushed it under the sofa. I stirred my drink and took a mouthful. Hopeful it would be enough to hit my bloodstream but not so much that I passed out.

Ian was taking a while and I stood, ready for his return.

He strolled back into the lounge. I worried he was going to be carrying handcuffs, but he was empty handed. What had he gone out for?

'Making a run for it?' he laughed, but it was more like a sneer.

I sank back into the sofa. The way he was acting chilled me to the bone. Alarm bells sounded in my head like Big Ben at midnight. I had no time to act, a second later we were in the same position as before. He ran his hands over me and I squeezed my lids shut, pretending to be into it as I ran through what I needed to do. My body trembled, legs quivering uncontrollably.

'Cold?' he asked. The beginnings of a smile on his lips.

I nodded and closed my eyes. A tug at my waistband made them fly open. He was staring right at me, an odd expression on his face as he unbuttoned my jeans.

'I think I've seen you out running, or maybe walking.'

I didn't like where the conversation was going. Was he trying to provoke me?

'I would remember you,' I said, lifting my backside as he roughly pulled my jeans from under me. There was no turning back now. Exposed on his sofa in my camisole and underwear, I considered whether the bedroom would be better. No, we had to stay here. Near the front door. Close to my escape route.

I watched as he moved to his shirt, unbuttoning and sliding it off. Dread washing over me at what was to come. How far would I have to go before the perfect moment presented itself? His chest was hard and smooth, a vein in his neck bulging. In other circumstances he may have been attractive, but all I wanted to do was end his reign of terror. I tried to speak, but I couldn't make any sound come out. Fear had me frozen.

'You do,' he whispered in my ear, opening his fly and sliding his hand inside my knickers, pulling on the hair there.

My forehead wrinkled as I tried to connect his words. To understand what they meant.

His lip curled back into a sneer.

'You do remember me,' he said. Cold, flat eyes flashed to life like a shark mid-kill, and a hand gripped my neck.

I made to scream, a choking noise erupting from my lips. In an instant he reached into his back pocket and stuffed a sock in my open mouth. His hand squeezed my throat, and I struggled to breathe. I clawed at his fingers and he jeered, enjoying the power he held over me. My vision began to blur, eyes rolling in their sockets. Choking on the wet fabric of his sock in my mouth, I thrashed underneath him. Seeing I was losing consciousness, he loosened his grip, eyes alive with excitement, face twisted in pleasure. This was a game to him. I coughed, precious air flooding into my lungs bringing me round.

'I remember you too,' he whispered in my ear. He'd had me from the start. Always knowing who I was. I'd been played.

Hot tears ran down my cheeks. I tried to struggle, but he held me fast. I gave up trying to weaken his grip on my throat and lashed out at his face. If I could get to his eyes. If I could hurt him; I might stand a chance. My plan seemed ridiculous now, like a child's. How could I have even thought I could do it? He must have seen me coming a mile off.

'Oh, I forgot to tell you... my father says hello,' he grinned, baring his teeth.

I bucked underneath him, and we slid, legs entwined, onto the floor with a thud. I could see he was enjoying the fight I was putting up. Laughing at my flailing arms, until I caught his eye and he snarled; a speck of blood appeared. His arm swung back, and my eye socket exploded. Searing pain ripped through my cheek and a metallic taste pooled on my lips. I turned my face to the side and spat out the bloody sock. He wasn't done. A cracking sound stung my ears as my head bounced off the floor. For a second there was nothing but darkness until I was choking again. His hands enveloped me, thrusting me back into consciousness.

He was going to kill me. I had no doubt in my mind. I was

going to die. To think I'd orchestrated this; that I hoped he'd invite me back. I should have known.

He loomed above me, wild eyes sparkling, and lips pulled back, revealing his gums, teeth clenched tightly together. I clawed at his fingers to loosen his grip.

'Ian, please,' I gasped.

'I've been waiting for this.' He leaned forward and took in a long breath, drinking me in. Releasing my throat, he pinned my wrists to the floor with one hand, whilst trying to push down his jeans and boxers with the other. He was going to rape me again.

Air flooded into my lungs, bringing my senses back to life. I wrenched an arm out of his grasp, whirling it madly and knocking the tray from the table, covering us in gin. Ian snarled and tried to catch my hand. I dragged it across the floor, searching for the knife, or glass, something, anything I could use as a weapon. There, something, a blade. The lemon knife! Thoughts ran through my head at speed as I wrapped my fingers around the handle. *You have to do it. He'll rape you again if you don't. Then he's going to kill you. You're not going to walk out of this.*

'I'm not finished with you yet,' he snarled.

Closing my eyes, I drove the knife upwards into Ian's armpit. Twisting once as far I could get it and thrusting it forward. Just like I'd read online. His grip on my wrist went limp and blood showered from above, dousing me before he collapsed. The cream rug turning crimson beneath him. He lay on his side, trying to stem the blood flow streaming through his fingers. A deep guttural sound came from him. I rolled over, panting and coughing. I didn't want to miss this. My throat burned and waves of exhaustion washed over me, but I had to remain conscious. I was no longer afraid. We faced each other as though we were lovers in bed. Basking in the afterglow. My eye already swelling and pain radiating through my body. I couldn't tell where it was coming from. Everything hurt. But I was alive. I'd won.

I leant forward, my face inches from him. His pale face glistened damp with sweat. He was fading, but his stare remained hard.

'You *will* remember me,' I whispered.

His hand reached for me, searching, clutching nothing but air. I pushed it away. Using the last bit of energy I had left; I rolled onto my knees. Dragging myself up the sofa to my feet. Vaguely aware I was naked from the waist down, I pulled on my jeans, not bothering to do them up, and staggered to the door. I waited, catching my breath as I watched his pallor turn a greyish-white and his body became still. Leaving everything behind, my bag, my shoes and all my hatred for Ian Shaw, I made my way down the stairs and out onto the street. I didn't look back.

* * *

Tuesday 30 January 2018

The bright sunlight makes me squint as the guard draws back the heavy metal door. It groans as it's dragged through the gravel, as though it isn't opened often. I shield my eyes with the palm of my hand, gazing up at the morning sky and drinking it in. I've only been incarcerated for around sixty hours, but I will never again take for granted the sun on my skin or a breeze through my hair.

'You look like shit!' A voice comes from my left and Ben

stands grinning, illuminated in the light. A halo surrounds him.

'Thanks,' I say, smiling up at him. There's a moment of awkward silence where neither of us knows what to do or say next. In the end, Ben steps forward with open arms and hooks them around my waist.

'Come here.'

I throw my arms around his shoulders. It feels so good to hold him, I'm reluctant to let go. In return, he squeezes me tight, face buried in my neck even though I am less than fragrant.

'So, they've dropped the charges?' he asks, finally pulling away from me.

My hair catches on his stubble. I nod, letting out a sigh I feel like I've been holding for a long time. It doesn't feel real. Am I really free?

'Terry, my solicitor, thinks the CPS were pressured to drop the case. Not in the public interest to proceed, apparently.' It seems he wasn't only good at Candy Crush after all.

'I'm not surprised. You won't believe what's been going on. There's been loads of press coverage. Jane's been amazing. She launched a campaign on Facebook, Twitter, and in the newspapers. Everyone was outraged they were going to prosecute. She got a few local MPs on board too. I think you were even mentioned in the House of Commons yesterday!'

'Fuck!' I say, eyes wide, trying to take it all in. I can't begin to tell Ben, and Jane, how grateful I am. 'Did she not go travelling?'

'No, she's at home waiting for you, your mum's there too.'

My eyes widen.

'Can we walk?' I ask, desperate to stretch my legs and

move away from the high walls and razor wire. There's so much to digest. Walking away from prison feels like shedding my skin, even though I am still wearing the grey issue sweatshirt and tracksuit bottoms. The locals will think I've escaped. 'How's Amy?' I ask tentatively, bracing myself for the answer.

Ben pauses and gives me a sideways glance.

'She's going to put in for a transfer.'

I nod, trying to conceal my relief.

'How did Jane know I was arrested? Did you tell her?'

'No, she saw it on the news first. I've got no idea how the press got hold of it.'

I didn't want to tell Ben that I was the one who leaked it to the press. My one phone call wasn't to my mother or a solicitor. It had been to the national tip line to report a miscarriage of justice. A woman going to prison for killing her attacker in self-defence. A nice juicy story on what I'd hoped would be a slow news day. I'd lucked out. Ben doesn't need to know. He doesn't need to know any of it.

We walk for half a mile or so, Ben updating me on what I've missed in the days I've been away. He shows me the articles written about me on his phone and the Twitter followers he and Jane amassed overnight. I blink back tears as a warm glow spreads throughout my body. I feel my shoulders ease down; I can finally relax.

'Why were you at the station?' I ask.

'They wanted a statement but made me come in to give it. I was only there half an hour. It was a complete waste of time.' Ben clenches his jaw for a second and reaches down to take my hand in his, our fingers interlock, and we walk along in comfortable silence. 'I want to be honest with you,' Ben starts, his voice shaky. What am I about to hear?

We stop walking and turn to face each other. I wrap my

arms around myself. We're standing outside a greasy spoon café, the smell of bacon reminding me of hungover breakfasts past.

'I followed you. When I saw you with him, I couldn't put it all together. It just didn't feel right.'

'I didn't know you knew him,' I reply.

'Pacino? He was a violent prick back then. I didn't want you anywhere near him. It wasn't until I was waiting outside his apartment, wondering what to do and I saw you. Well, I assumed it was you. I saw you throw something out of the window, then I connected the dots.'

I shiver, the memory still as fresh as some of my bruises. The bag was always going to be a risk. I knew the police might search the area and, if they found it, possibly connect DNA to Sophie, Alice or the others. I had to absolve myself of any motive, any history Ian and I shared.

Ben shoves his hands into his pockets. 'I hid the bag. Once I'd had a look through it of course. I hid it under the railway bridge, in some of the broken brickwork.'

I have no words. I'm exhausted. All I want to do is go home and have a long bath. Followed by a bottle of wine, and to sleep for a week, cuddled up beside my flatmate.

Ben pulls me towards him in bear hug. 'I've missed you,' he says, his voice breaking, and I sink into him. I can't hold back the tears any longer.

Placing my hand back in his, I whisper, 'Let's go home.'

EPILOGUE

ONE YEAR LATER

I sit clutching the latte, warming my hands. The heat and aroma of freshly ground coffee is a comfort. Like a hug in a mug. My dad used to say that, first thing in the morning, with a roll-up dangling from his lips. I've been drinking more coffee lately, but it's hardly surprising. The lack of sleep is a killer, but everyone says it won't last forever.

Susie slides into the booth opposite me, an enormous grin on her face. 'When can you start then?'

'Whenever you want. Will afternoon shifts be okay? I've got to work around Ben's nights.'

'Of course. I'm so pleased to have you on board. I love your tea shop idea. I've been shopping for gingham fabric already. Anyway, we'll have plenty of time to brainstorm on expanding.'

'I'm looking forward to it to. I owe you one,' I lean forward and whisper, nodding towards the three remaining computers at the back of the shop. A gap on the left where the fourth used to be. My computer.

'Don't be silly, pet. I just should have been more careful

where I put my bucket. Soaked everything. The hard drive was ruined.' She winks and pats my hand.

I have to stop myself from throwing my arms around her. Instead I bite my lip and swallow the lump that has formed in my throat.

I gave it my best at the boxing club and stuck it out for as long as I could, almost nine months to be exact, but after a heart-to-heart with Jason I resigned. As it happened, Louise stepped in to take on my role and she's working out fine. It's keeping her out of trouble and Jason is smitten. I'm there most mornings for an hour or so, it keeps me sane. I'd missed sparring and dancing around the punchbag and I was never going to set foot inside Pulse again.

I decided to invest some of the money from the sale of Mum's house into Baristas and give Susie a hand with the business. After the boxing club, I didn't want to go back to working in an office and was happy to lend my marketing skills to ensure the coffee shop kept thriving. I'll be more behind the scenes than customer facing, starting with the rebranding Susie suggested last year. We won't be going with the name 'Roasted' though. I wasn't expecting her to make me a partner, but she did. We signed on the dotted line yesterday. Now we're stuck with each other whether we like it or not.

'It'll be your legacy one day, won't it, sweetie,' she says in a sing-song voice, brushing her hand over my daughter's cheek. Phoebe gurgles and manages a half-smile before dribbling down her chin. I gently bump her up and down on my knee as she grips Susie's finger. 'She is gorgeous.'

'She's got Ben's eyes,' I reply. Susie fell in love as soon as she saw Phoebe and was ecstatic when I asked her to be her joint godmother with Jane.

She's somewhere in Indonesia currently, due to come home next month and meet her goddaughter. I've missed her terribly. She put off travelling for a couple of months and in the end Doctor Lush took a sabbatical and went with her. She's head over heels and it wouldn't surprise me if there's another wedding on the cards.

With Mum's help and the rest of the proceeds of the house, Ben and I moved out of the flat and bought a three bedroom terrace with a garden. We both attended her wedding, which I'm happy to report was a sober affair. Patrick, who turned out to be one of the nicest men I've ever met, got her enrolled onto a treatment programme and after a couple of blips, she hasn't had a drink for over seven months.

I am adjusting to motherhood now. The apprehension I had all the way through my pregnancy disappeared the moment I looked into Phoebe's eyes. They were dark and angry. Furious at being pulled from her nice warm cocoon out into the world. I wasn't sure whether I could do it alone, but I didn't put pressure on Ben to stand by me. I felt responsible, having taken advantage of him when he came home drunk that night. But Phoebe melted him as soon as she arrived and my heart burst with love and pride for the family I never knew I wanted.

'Right, my turn for a cuddle. You drink your latte,' Susie says before whisking Phoebe away to play peekaboo at her reflection in the window.

I sip my coffee, rubbing my fingertips over the semi-colon pendant. I haven't taken it off this past year.

I bumped into Detective Becker last week at the doctor's surgery of all places. She was with her daughter, Lily, and I was taking Phoebe for her first set of jabs. We made polite conversation and she commented on my necklace, saying how pretty it was. She smiled, but her eyes carried a sadness. Lily's name was called first but before she stood, Becker pulled back the sleeve of her coat to reveal a tiny semi-colon tattoo on the inside of her wrist, inked over a jagged scar. It seemed we had more in common than I first thought.

I still have nightmares. I wake up beside Ben screaming and choking, although the periods between them are increasing. Occasionally I'll see someone that resembles Ian. The first time was in the supermarket, at the checkout. I left my trolley mid-aisle and bolted out of the door. Doctor Almara is helping me through it, one session at a time. One day, I'll be able to put the trauma behind me. I'll look back without any guilt, happy in the knowledge that the world is that little bit safer. For me. For Phoebe.

ACKNOWLEDGMENTS

Huge thanks to the fabulous team at Boldwood Books. Their enthusiasm for Stalker as well as their support and advice throughout has been amazing. Special thanks as well to my copy editor, Jade Craddock, for her superb skills, waving a magic wand over my debut.

Massive thanks to my readers Kathrine Stewart and Denise Miller, who gave up their time, and encouraged me with their feedback to make the book the best it could be.

I'll be forever be grateful to Mark Zivilik and Sophie Comport who schooled me in all things police and human resources. Answering all my questions, on top of their day jobs, without complaint.

Thanks to my champion, Alison, who always believed I could and made me believe it too. Lastly but by no means least, thank you to my husband, Dean, who has never complained while I shut myself away, and looked after our daughters single-handedly, while I got on with my 'Janet & John'. I couldn't have done it without you.

MORE FROM GEMMA ROGERS

We hope you enjoyed reading *Stalker*. If you did, please leave a review.

If you'd like to gift a copy, this book is also available as a ebook, digital audio download and audiobook CD.

Sign up to Gemma Rogers's mailing list for news, competitions and updates on future books.

http://bit.ly/GemmaRogersNewsletter

ABOUT THE AUTHOR

Gemma Rogers was inspired to write gritty thrillers by a traumatic event in her own life nearly twenty years ago. *Stalker* is her debut novel and marks the beginning of a new writing career. Gemma lives in West Sussex with her husband, two daughters and bulldog Buster.

Visit Gemma's website: www.gemmarogersauthor.co.uk

Follow Gemma on social media:

facebook.com/GemmaRogersAuthor

twitter.com/GemmaRogers79

ABOUT BOLDWOOD BOOKS

Boldwood Books is a fiction publishing company seeking out the best stories from around the world.

Find out more at www.boldwoodbooks.com

Sign up to the Book and Tonic newsletter for news, offers and competitions from Boldwood Books!

http://www.bit.ly/bookandtonic

We'd love to hear from you, follow us on social media:

facebook.com/BookandTonic

twitter.com/BoldwoodBooks

instagram.com/BookandTonic

CPSIA information can be obtained
at www.ICGtesting.com
Printed in the USA
LVHW050331070220
646095LV00017B/397